Joan Jonker was born and bred in Liverpool. Her childhood was a time of love and laughter with her two sisters, a brother, a caring but gambling father and an indomitable mother who was always getting them out of scrapes. Then came the Second World War – a period that Joan remembers so well – when she met and fell in love with her late husband, Tony, while out with friends at Liverpool's St George's Hotel in Lime Street.

For twenty-three years, Joan campaigned tirelessly on behalf of victims of violence, and her first book, *Victims of Violence*, is an account of those years. She has recently retired from charity work in order to concentrate on her fiction writing. Joan has two sons and two grandsons and she lives in Southport, where she is busy working on her next bestselling saga. Her previous novels of life in Liverpool's backstreets have won her legions of fans throughout the world:

'You've done it again! Molly and Nellie are so funny, I love the bones of them. More please' Jean Breward, Norfolk

'Your books are fantastic' Jill Gibas, Slough

'Your latest saga had me laughing and crying. Keep them coming, I can't wait for the next' Norma Kemp, Bolton

'Once again your book had me laughing, crying and falling deep into the story' Joanne Ryder, London

'Absolutely wonderful' Jean Bowers, Canada

'Being an ex-Scouser, I find your books thoroughly enjoyable' Norma Holborow, Western Australia

'Your sense of humour and knowledge of the old Liverpool is unsurpassed by any other writer' Judy Down, New Zealand

Also by Joan Jonker

Victims of Violence

When One Door Closes
Man Of The House
Home Is Where The Heart Is
Stay In Your Own Back Yard
Last Tram To Lime Street
Sweet Rosie O'Grady
The Pride of Polly Perkins
Sadie Was A Lady
Walking My Baby Back Home
Try A Little Tenderness
Stay As Sweet As You Are
Down Our Street
Dream A Little Dream
Many A Tear Has To Fall
After The Dance Is Over
Taking A Chance On Love
The Sunshine Of Your Smile

Strolling With
The One I Love

Joan Jonker

First published in 2002
by HEADLINE BOOK PUBLISHING

First published in paperback in 2002
by HEADLINE BOOK PUBLISHING

10 9 8 7 6 5 4 3 2 1

ISBN 0 7472 6798 7

Typeset in Times by Avon Dataset Ltd, Bidford-on-Avon, Warks

Printed and bound in Great Britain by
Clays Ltd, St Ives plc, Bungay, Suffolk

HEADLINE BOOK PUBLISHING
A division of Hodder Headline
338 Euston Road
London NW1 3BH

www.headline.co.uk
www.hodderheadline.com

To my family – Philip, Paul and Marie, Mark and Rachel, David and Heather, and my new great-granddaughter Olivia – I dedicate this book with love.

Hello readers

We have a lovely young heroine in this book who I am sure you will take to your hearts, along with her friends, family and neighbours. There's a little sadness along the way but plenty of humour too. A half-box of tissues required, I think!

Take care.

Love

Joan

Chapter One

Kate Spencer lowered the gas under the pan of potatoes then turned over the sausages sizzling away in the large iron frying pan. She sniffed up in appreciation of the mouth-watering smell given out by the sliced onion she'd just added to the sausages, and speaking aloud in the tiny kitchen, said, 'Only another five minutes, thank goodness, 'cos me tummy's rumbling.'

Wiping her hands down the sides of her pinny, Kate made her way through the living room to the front door. The first sight that met her eyes was of two young boys kneeling in the gutter playing ollies. One of them was her ten-year-old son, Billy. 'In the name of God, Billy, will yer get up out of there! Yer'll be as black as the hobs of hell, and yer dad' s due home any minute.'

A face smudged with dirt looked up at her in horror. 'Ah, ay, Mam, I'm beating Pete by two flicks! If I stop now he'll say I haven't won and take his bobby dazzler home. I've been after this ollie for two weeks now, it's a beauty!'

His mate, who had more dirt on him than Billy, grunted, 'We can finish the game after we've had our tea. Me mam's probably looking for me anyway so I'd better go.'

This didn't go down well with Billy, who was nearer to winning the bobby dazzler than he'd ever been. For weeks now he'd lain in bed dreaming of making the multi-coloured marble his and walking around with his chest sticking out, the envy of every lad in the street and at school. But he could see by his mam's face that she meant business, so settled for saying, 'As long as yer remember where we're up to, and I've got two goes when we start again.'

The boys picked up their ollies and stuffed them in their

1

pockets as they stood up. 'Holy suffering ducks,' Kate said, rolling her eyes towards the sky, 'will yer just look at the state of the pair of yer! Yer'll need a scrubbing brush to get that dirt off yer knees, it's an inch thick. And if yer've ruined those trousers, Billy Spencer, so help me, I'll clock yer one.'

Pete thought it was time to make himself scarce. 'I'll see yer later, Billy.'

'I wouldn't count on that, Pete Reynolds,' Kate said, ''cos your mam will have a fit when she sees the state of yer.' The look of dejection on their dirty faces made her smile. 'Our coalman's been today, and he wasn't as black as you two.'

'I'd better go in the back way,' Pete said, 'and with a bit of luck I can wash meself before me mam sees me.' With that the boy took to his heels and disappeared down the side entry.

Billy glared at his mother. 'Just two more goes and I'd have won that ollie. Yer should see it, Mam, it's a beauty. Every lad in the street is after it and none of them's got as near as I got just now. Me luck was in, and now it's been spoilt.'

'I'll tell yer what, son, there's more for yer to worry about than a ruddy ollie. If yer've torn those kecks then yer luck will most definitely not be in 'cos I'll give yer a thick ear.'

'I haven't torn them, I've been careful.' The boy shook his head in disgust. How could she think about trousers when he'd come so close to winning the pride of the neighbourhood? 'I can't get over being so close to winning, and then you have to come out!' The boy scratched his head as a woebegone expression crossed his face. 'Another two minutes and it would have been mine.'

'If yer don't get in this house right away, yer'll really have something to moan about. Yer'll be getting burnt sausages for yer dinner.' As her son passed her, Kate patted his head. 'Right to the sink and wash some of that dirt off yer hands and face while I rescue the sausages. And then yer can go and fetch yer sister, wherever she is.'

'She's in next door with Dolly, playing some daft girls' game.' The boy watched his mother pour hot water into a bowl for him then picked up a block of carbolic soap. 'Ay, those sausages don't half smell nice, Mam, how many am I getting?'

'Ye're getting two, as usual, and I don't want to hear any moans from yer. There's plenty of starving people who would gladly swap places with yer.' Kate had an urge to kiss the boy's dirty face, 'cos she loved the bones of him and his sister, but decided she'd wait until he'd washed. 'Put a move on, I don't want yer dad seeing yer like that or he'll think I don't look after yer properly. I'll knock next door for Nancy.' She got to the middle of the living room and turned back. 'I know how many sausages there are, son, and if yer pinch one then watch out, 'cos I'll be giving yer a thick lip to go with the thick ear I promised yer.'

Left alone, the boy grinned as he washed his hands and face. His mam was always threatening to give him a thick ear and lip, but he knew it would never happen. The most he got if he'd been really naughty was a smack across the back of his legs. And that didn't hurt a bit, although he pretended it did. Not like getting the cane off the headmaster. Now that was something dreaded by even the toughest boys in his class. Four strokes off Mr Sykes and you couldn't sit down for a few days. A picture of the headmaster flashed through his mind, and even that was enough to make Billy shiver. Mr Sykes was a very tall man, very well-made and very bad-tempered. He could reduce a boy to a mass of quivering jelly just by glaring at him. The best course with him was to behave yourself, keep your nose clean and try not to blot your copy book. Billy made sure he watched his behaviour at school which was why he'd only been caned once in all the time he'd been in the junior.

Kate knocked a second time on the front door of the house next door, then shouted through the letter box, 'Are yer all deaf or something? Me dinner will be ruined at this rate.'

The door was finally opened by a woman who looked as impatient as her neighbour. 'In the name of God, Kate, what's yer hurry?' Monica Parry's mousy-coloured hair was standing on end as though she'd just run her fingers through it. 'Yer nearly knocked the ruddy door down, and I thought the rent man had sent the bleedin' bailiffs in!'

She was a nice-looking woman was Monica, with a slim figure and a face that was never far from a smile. But her looks couldn't be compared with her neighbour's. Kate Spencer had been blessed with an abundance of rich dark auburn hair which framed a face of real beauty. With her high cheekbones, clear, faultless complexion, a set of strong, even white teeth, perfectly arched black eyebrows and long curling eyelashes, she was the envy of every woman in the street and of interest to quite a few of the men.

'If our Nancy's here, Monica, will yer tell her to come home pronto while the dinner is still fit to eat?' Kate saw a familiar figure walking up the street and groaned. 'Oh, here's John now, I'd better scarper. Be a pal and chase our Nancy home, will yer?'

'Of course I will, girl. Are yer coming in later for a cuppa and a natter? I get fed up looking at four walls when my feller goes to the pub.'

'I'll see how the land lies, Monica,' Kate shouted over her shoulder. 'I'll give a knock on the wall if I can get away.'

'Do yer best, girl, or I'll end up talking to meself, and I've already told meself all I know. I mean, I can only laugh so many times at me own jokes.' Monica saw her friend disappear into the house next door then waved to the man who was coming closer. 'All right, John? How's the world treating yer, lad?'

'Fair to middling, Monica, I can't complain.'

'I was going to say yer can complain if yer want to, John, but everyone's got their own bleedin' troubles and wouldn't listen to yer. Anyway, I've got to chase yer daughter home or Kate will

4

have me guts for garters. So leave the door open, save her knocking.'

Billy was sitting at the table when Kate got in, wriggling about in anticipation of the meal about to be put before him. 'Hurry up, Mam, I'm starving.'

If he hadn't spoken his mother would have gone straight through to the kitchen without giving him a glance. As it was she took one look at his neck before putting her hands to her mouth. 'Oh, my God! Don't yer ever look at yerself in the mirror when yer get washed? Yer've got a bigger tidemark than Seaforth Sands.'

Billy heard his dad coming in and tried to pull up his shirt collar to cover the dirt. But John had heard his wife's words. Trying to keep back a smile, he put a hand on his son's head and pushed it sideways, all the better to see the unmissable tidemark. 'Oh, dear, oh, dear, oh, dear! What have we here?'

Kate could see the twinkle in her husband's eyes and laughed to herself as she carried on to the kitchen. Like father, like son. Her husband and Billy were as alike as two peas in a pod, with their dark blond hair and hazel eyes. Their natures were alike, too, Kate thought as she stood listening to them talk instead of draining the potatoes, and their keen sense of humour.

'It's a tidemark, Dad,' Billy said, stating the obvious. 'But I'll have a good wash when I've had me dinner.'

'A tidemark! Yer call this a tidemark? I'd have been ashamed of meself at your age if that was the best I could come up with. Why, my tidemarks would have knocked yours into a cocked hat!'

Billy cheered up. 'And did your mam tell yer off, and make yer use a scrubbing brush to get rid of the dirt?'

Kate was back in the living room like a shot, wagging a stiffened finger. 'Don't you be making a joke of it, John, 'cos it's not funny. You side with him and he'll never wash his neck again.' She tapped Billy on his nose. 'It's the tin bath in front of the fire for you later, me laddo. Yer dad can carry it in from the yard after we've had our dinner.'

'Ah, ay, Mam! I'm too big to be getting in that thing with all of yer watching! I'll give meself a good wash in the kitchen, I promise.'

'Yer don't have to worry about me watching yer,' the young girl standing in the doorway said, 'I don't want to give meself nightmares.'

Kate grinned across at her twelve-year-old daughter. Nancy had inherited her mother's features and colouring, but her beauty had yet to blossom. 'You and me will make ourselves scarce, eh, sunshine? We'll nip next door for an hour, so Billy can have some privacy.'

Nancy grinned. 'I beat yer to it, Mam, 'cos I've already told Dolly I'll have a game of Snakes and Ladders with her.'

'That's settled then. Now perhaps I can get the dinner out. It's a wonder the sausages haven't got fed up waiting and walked out of the frying pan on their own.'

John slipped his work coat off and hung it on a hook in the narrow hall. 'I'm ready for a plate of sausage and mash, I'm starving.' He winked at his son to let him know that what he was about to say was only teasing. 'And it'll give me the strength to stand the sight of me son in his nakedness without fainting with shock.'

'Ay, don't yer be making fun of my kid brother,' Nancy said, giving Billy a hug as she passed his chair. 'When he gets older he'll be as big and strong as Tarzan. And to make sure he gets plenty to eat, I'm going to give me mam a hand with the dinner. Sit yerself down, Dad, and I'll wait on yer.'

'I'll have to wash me hands first, pet, otherwise I'll get a go-along off yer mam for sitting at the table with dirty hands.'

Billy's shoulders shook with laughter. 'She'll make yer get in the tin bath after I've been in. Wouldn't that be funny?'

Kate came in carrying a plate in each hand. 'It would be more than funny to see yer dad getting in that tin bath, son, it would be hilarious.' She put the two plates down and chuckled at the look on her husband's face. 'In fact, I could sell tickets to the neighbours and make meself a few coppers.'

'Yer'd make more than a few coppers!' John rose to his full height and pushed his face close to his wife's. 'There's women in this street would pay at least a tanner to see my fine physique. And they'd queue up a second time.'

'If they did, it would only be because they didn't believe what they saw the first time. Yer've got legs like knots in cotton, sunshine, and there's no getting away from it.' Kate gave him a playful push. 'Get those hands under the tap, love, and then perhaps we can sit down to eat in peace.'

'Ay, Mam,' Billy said. 'These sausages are talking to me and they're not in a very good temper, either!'

'Neither would you be, son, if you'd been frying away for an hour in hot fat. Even sausages have feelings, yer know.'

'One of these is dead bad-tempered, it's just spat at me.'

'Well, yer know what to do.' Nancy put her plate down on the table and pulled out the chair next to her brother's. 'Stick yer fork in it and that will shut it up.'

Alone in the kitchen with his wife, John put his arms around her waist. 'How about a nice, long passionate kiss?'

'Let me go, yer daft nit, or the kids will hear yer.' Kate had a plate in her hand and she held it aloft. 'This is your dinner, and yer'll get it on yer head if yer don't behave yerself.' She looked over her shoulder and smiled at him. 'There's a place for long passionate kisses and it's not a kitchen smelling of fat.'

'I don't know why ye're whispering, Mam,' Nancy called. 'Me and our Billy can hear every word ye're saying. He's just asked me what the difference is between a kiss like yer give us, and a passionate kiss?'

Kate slipped from her husband's arms and carried the plate through. 'Well, son, ye're ten years of age now, I reckon it'll be seven or eight more before yer know the difference. Yer see, it's not something yer can put into words, yer have to experience it for yerself.'

The boy gave a grunt of disgust. 'Ugh! I bet it's sloppy, and sloppy things make me want to be sick.'

'Just eat yer dinner for now, then, sunshine, and leave the sloppy things for the next seven or eight years.' Kate speared a piece of sausage ready to put in her mouth. 'I can't wait until yer get your first girlfriend, that should be very interesting. At least it will be for me, I can't speak for the poor girl. It might be a case of one kiss and she'll take off and yer'll never see her again.'

Then with all the experience of his ten years, Billy curled his top lip and said, 'Well, let her take off, it won't worry me.'

Nancy couldn't resist joining in. 'Let who take off, Billy?'

'The girl me mam said would take off and I'd never see her again.'

John decided to add his twopennyworth. 'Which girl was this, son?'

Now Billy didn't like girls, nor did he like sloppy things. But he did like a good laugh. 'I don't know, Dad, I didn't even have time to get a proper look at her. She gave me a kiss and then was off before I could even ask her name!'

Next door, Monica jerked her head towards the wall. 'Can yer hear them laughing? Kate's coming in later, I'll have to ask her what the joke was.'

'Oh, Nancy's coming in as well,' said Dolly, her daughter and only child. 'We're going to play Snakes and Ladders.'

'I think I'll poppy off to the pub then,' said Tom, the man of the house. 'I'll get out from under yer feet.'

'What are you talking about?' Monica rested her knife and fork. 'Anyone would think yer were being chased out of yer own house, when the truth is yer go to the ruddy pub every night! In fact, I'm of the firm opinion that if yer missed going one night, the bleeding landlord would come knocking for yer!'

'Now come on, my love,' Tom laughed. 'Aren't yer exaggerating a bit? I don't go every night, so don't be giving me a bad name.'

'Apart from the odd times yer take me to the pictures, and that's under protest, yer go to the pub every single night without fail.'

Tom shook his head. 'No, love, I do not, and I can prove it. Have yer forgotten that none of the pubs is open on Christmas Day?'

Next door, Kate said, 'Listen to Monica laughing. She's got a real belly laugh and it always makes me chuckle. It sounds as though she's got something funny to tell me when I go in. I hope so, I just feel like a good laugh.' She raised her eyebrows at her husband. 'I don't know why yer don't go for a pint with Tom, he's good company. Yer used to go out with him, but yer haven't been for ages.'

John shook his head. 'No, I'd rather put me sixpence on a horse. At least yer stand a chance of winning a bit back, but with a pint of beer yer money's gone and yer've got nothing to show for it.'

'Oh, ye're not gambling, are yer, love? I thought yer had more sense than that. It's a mug's game, with the bookie the only winner. And another thing, yer know it's not legal and yer could get into trouble with the police.'

'I wouldn't get into trouble, love, it would be the bookie. But I don't even see him 'cos one of the blokes in work puts the bets on for all the lads.' John could see this wasn't making his wife feel any better, so he added, 'It's only a tanner, love, and yer never know, I might win a few bob and then yer can buy something new for you and the kids.'

'Aye, and pigs might fly!' Kate wasn't a bit happy about it as her own father had been a compulsive gambler, and there were times when he was keeping so much back out of his wages to pay the bookie that her mother was left without enough money to pay the rent man. Memories of her crying were still fresh in Kate's mind, even though she'd been young at the time. But she couldn't imagine John being as reckless as her father, he wouldn't do anything to hurt her or the children. 'Just don't ever come to me and tell me ye're in debt, sunshine, 'cos I couldn't stand it.'

Kate could feel the children's eyes on her and was sorry she hadn't kept quiet until she and her husband were alone. It wasn't fair on the kids, they were too young to understand. So she put a smile on her face. 'Anyway, if yer do win any money, I could do with a new sideboard. That one's seen better days and is falling to bits.'

John's smile came with a sigh of relief. 'Okay, a sideboard it is, sweetheart. Your every wish is my command.'

As Billy listened to this, he was worried at first because his mam appeared to be upset. But she was smiling now, so he felt it was all right to say what was on his mind. 'Mam, have yer forgotten about me game of ollies? It'll be dark by the time you and our Nancy go out and I have that blinking bath. Too dark to play ollies.'

'Yer don't imagine for one moment that I'd let yer go out and get yerself filthy again, just after yer've had a bath? Not on yer life, sunshine! Pete can hold on to his bobby dazzler until tomorrow, nothing's going to happen to it before then.'

'That's what you think!' Billy looked glum. 'Half the lads in the street are after that ollie, and they'll be knocking on his door right now and asking for a game.'

'But Pete is yer best mate. He won't break his promise to let yer carry on where yer left off.'

'Being his mate doesn't mean a thing, Mam! If some lad offers him ten marbles for that bobby dazzler, he'll take them, friend or no friend.'

Nancy leaned forward to look her brother in the face. 'Is that what you'd do, Billy? Break a promise to yer best friend?'

Now he was in a quandary. This was definitely a no-win situation. That is it was a no-win situation until out of nowhere came a flash of brilliance. 'It's not me we're talking about, it's Pete. And it's not any old ollie, either! If that bobby dazzler was mine, I wouldn't even play with it, never mind letting anyone win it off me. I'd keep it wrapped in a hankie in me pocket, and show off with it.'

'Then why do yer think Pete should let you win it?' John asked. 'When yer wouldn't even let him play for it if it was yours? Not very sporting that, is it, son?'

Billy wasn't a bit put out. He didn't worry whether he was sporting or not. 'Dad, haven't yer ever heard them say that all's fair in love and war?'

John couldn't keep the chuckle back. 'I have heard that, son, of course I have. But I don't think it applies in this case. Yer see, ye're not in love and there is no war!'

Billy's face split into a wide grin. 'I've got yer there, Dad, 'cos I am in love. I love me mam, you, our Nancy, and that blinking marble what's coming between me and me sleep.'

'There's one good thing,' his sister said. 'At least he put us all before the marble.'

Monica pushed the couch nearer to the fire. 'We may as well make ourselves comfortable and warm. The girls are all right at the table, we won't be in each other's way.'

Dolly pushed her counter across the board to the bottom of one of the ladders. 'As long as yer don't keep gabbing and putting us off our game.'

'Ah, well, wouldn't that be just too bad?' Monica pulled a face. 'It's not us what make the noise, it's you two. Yer should hear yerselves screaming when the throw of a dice takes yer to the top of a ladder. Anyone would think yer'd won the pools. And when yer lose and have to come down again, well, the groans are unmerciful.'

Nancy giggled. 'We'll try to groan quietly, then, Auntie Monica.'

'You do that, girl, while me and yer mam have a natter. I'll make us a cuppa a bit later on, 'cos it's not long since we had one after our dinner.'

The two mothers watched their daughters playing for a few minutes, smiling indulgently as expressions changed at the toss of a dice. Then they settled one at either end of the couch with their feet tucked under them. After a quick glance to make sure the girls were intent on the game, Monica said softly, 'Ay, have yer heard about Betty Blackmore? You know, her what lives at the back with number twenty-eight painted in white on the entry door?'

'Of course I know Betty, she's the one who knocked on the door the day we moved in to ask if we'd like her to make us a pot of tea. I've never forgotten that 'cos I thought it was really nice of her.' Kate raised her eyebrows. 'Why d'yer ask, is she not well or something?'

'Out of her mind, more like it.' Again Monica cast a quick glance over to the girls at the table. This was definitely not something for young ears. 'Her daughter Margaret is expecting a baby.'

'Go 'way, I didn't think she was married! She's only about seventeen, isn't she?'

'Right on both counts, girl! She is only seventeen, and no, she isn't married. Betty is out of her mind with worry.'

Kate gasped. 'She must be, the poor woman! But the girl must have a boyfriend, so why couldn't they just get married without any fuss? It would stop the wagging tongues and sly glances.'

'There's a bit of a problem there, girl, I'm afraid. Yer see, the girl hasn't got a boyfriend. I was talking to Betty in the entry before, and the poor woman is so ashamed she can hardly look yer in the face. Apparently the boy who put her daughter in the family way lives a few streets away, and Margaret had only been out with him twice. Betty went around to see his parents as soon as she knew, but the lad denied everything, said he'd never laid a finger on her. And when Mr Blackmore went around to have it out with the lad's father, I believe it came to blows. The parents chased him off and told him not to be spreading rumours about their son.'

Kate let out a deep sigh. 'What a mess! How old is this boy?'

'He's nineteen, and according to what his mother told Betty, he's never had a proper girlfriend. He admits to going to the pictures twice with Margaret, even said he'd kissed her, but nothing more than that.'

'And d'yer think he might be telling the truth?' Kate asked. 'Perhaps Margaret has been with another bloke but is too frightened to say. It wouldn't be the first time a lad got the blame for something he hadn't done.'

'Oh, I don't think that's likely, 'cos she's very shy, is Margaret, she wouldn't say boo to a goose.'

Kate pulled a face. 'She can't be that shy if she's got herself pregnant. But whichever way it goes it's the parents that'll be left to shoulder the shame of the daughter, and the responsibility of bringing up the child. It's not a position I'd like to find meself in.'

'Me neither! But she's well liked is Betty, and the neighbours will rally round. They'll not turn their back on her.'

'I should think not! After all, it could happen to anyone. Yer know the old saying, "There but for the grace of God go I"? Well, it's certainly true in this case.'

Monica leaned closer. 'I'd kill our Dolly if she brought that kind of trouble to me door. I'd never be able to lift me head up in the street.'

'I hope it never does happen to yer, sunshine, but if it did, yer'd just have to get on with it. Like Betty's going to have to do. As yer say, her friends won't desert her, and those that do were never true friends in the first place and not worth losing any sleep over. Anyway, like everything else, it'll be a nine days' wonder and then something else will come along to take people's minds off it.' Kate cupped her chin in her hand. 'If I was in Betty's shoes I'd do me damnedest to find out who the father is, though. I couldn't go through life not knowing. Whoever he is, good or bad, he's the child's father and should come forward so the poor mite isn't born illegitimate. That's a terrible stigma for an innocent child to have to shoulder all through his life.'

'I know, it's lousy for the poor kid.' Monica's serious expression didn't sit well on a face which was usually creased in a smile. 'I feel sorry for the baby already.'

'Who d'yer feel sorry for, Mam?' Dolly asked, causing the women to sit up straight and wonder how much the girls had heard. 'Is someone's baby sick?'

'What are yer on about?' Monica was racking her brains for an answer. 'Yer must be hearing things 'cos I never mentioned no baby, did I, Kate?'

Kate shook her head and crossed two fingers. She didn't like telling lies but right now there was no alternative. 'Yer mam said lady, sunshine, not baby. We were just talking about a woman we meet at the shops who hasn't been well lately.'

'Well, what about the cup of tea yer promised us an hour ago, Mam?' Dolly kept half an eye on Nancy to make sure she didn't cheat. 'The woman won't get any better by you not giving us a cuppa. Besides, me throat is parched.'

'I'm not surprised,' Monica said, uncurling her legs. 'Yer've shouted yerself hoarse, and it's a wonder next door haven't knocked to complain about the noise.'

Dolly pointed to the far wall. 'The neighbours that way have gone to the pictures and the house is empty. And these two aren't likely to complain, are they?' Her grin widened. 'Especially when they get a cup of tea and a gingersnap.'

Monica tutted as she passed her daughter's chair. 'Cheeky article! I don't know what sort of a mother yer've got, girl, but she wants to try teaching yer a few manners.'

Chapter Two

Kate stood on the front step watching Billy ambling up the street with his mate Pete. At the rate they were going, they'd never make the school gates before the bell rang. And it was her son's fault because his head was nodding and his mouth was working fifteen to the dozen. She'd bet any money he was giving his mate a hard time about that ruddy ollie, he seemed to be obsessed with the thing.

Folding her arms, Kate leaned back against the door jamb. It was a performance every morning trying to get her son out of the house on time, and she thanked her lucky stars she didn't have the same difficulty with Nancy. Her daughter was no trouble at all in the mornings, getting herself washed and dressed before having her breakfast. And there was no need to check her neck for tidemarks, or make sure her shoes weren't covered in scuff marks.

Kate waited until the boys had turned the corner, then looked up at the sky. It was clear blue, not a dark cloud in sight. 'It's a good day for getting clothes washed and dried,' she muttered aloud as she stepped into the hall. 'I can have them blowing on the line before Monica calls to go to the shops.'

The kitchen of the two-up-two-down was so small Kate barely needed to move her feet. Her movements quick and efficient from long practice, she filled a large black iron pan with water and set it on the gas stove next to the kettle. 'Now, where did I put the ruddy matches?' She spied them on the shelf and soon had the two gas rings lit. Then she pulled the dolly tub into the centre of the floor and attached one end of a piece of hose to the cold-water tap, and let the other end hang over the dolly tub.

15

'Now, while I'm waiting for the water to boil, I may as well make the beds and gather up any clothes that need washing.' Kate thought nothing of talking to herself, she did it all the time. She said it made her feel she wasn't alone, that there was someone in the house with her. Someone who didn't answer back.

Halfway up the shallow stairs, Kate suddenly came to a halt and slapped an open palm to her forehead. 'You stupid bugger, yer've got no soap powder in!' She quickly made her way back down to the kitchen. 'I'll nip to the corner shop and be back before the water boils. And I'll go the back way so no one sees me in me muck.' She took her purse from a drawer in the sideboard, opened it to make sure she had enough money, then slipped it into the pocket of her pinny.

The shop was run by a husband and wife, Les and Violet Riley, and their fifteen-year-old daughter Doreen helped out when they were busy. Right now Kate was glad to see there was only one other customer, and she was already being served by Les. 'Come on, Vi, let's be having yer.' Kate smiled at the shopkeeper who was very popular with everyone. Violet Riley had a bonny figure, a round face with rosy red cheeks, black hair, brown eyes and a very hearty laugh. 'I was full of good intentions, Vi. In me mind I had me washing blowing merrily on the line. That is until I remembered I didn't have no washing powder. So could I have a small packet, please?'

'Yer certainly can, sweetheart! In fact, I'll let yer have a large one if yer'd like to take my washing home and put it in with yours? I mean, yer wouldn't even notice an extra six shirts, three white coats and two pair of long johns. So how d'yer fancy that?'

Kate pulled a face. 'Sod off, Vi, I've got enough on me plate washing for me own family. Particularly our Billy, he's a holy terror. And by holy I don't mean religious holy, I mean he doesn't possess a thing that doesn't have a hole in. And he's a dirty beggar, I'm sure he rolls in the dirt for spite.'

Vi's laugh came from deep within her. 'Well, yer will have boys, won't yer? That's why I put me foot down after our Doreen was born. I wasn't going to be lumbered with another boy, thanks very much.'

Kate's face showed surprise. 'But you never had a boy. Yer've only got Doreen.'

'Are yer forgetting him over there?' Violet nodded to where her husband was handing over change to a customer. 'He still thinks he's a boy. Talks like one and acts like one. He's forgotten to grow up.'

Les walked along the counter towards them. 'I know my dear wife has been talking about me, I can see it in her face. What's she been saying, Kate?'

'She's been paying yer compliments, Les. Telling me how ye're still young at heart.'

'Then she's after something.' Les Riley was tall and slim, with fine sandy hair, hazel eyes and a pleasant disposition. 'The only time my one ever says nice things about me is when she's after something.' There was affection in the gaze he turned on his wife. 'I wouldn't care if she was only after a slab of chocolate like, but she doesn't believe in skimping it, she likes to push the boat out. For instance, last week it was a new three-piece she was after. But I had to put me foot down with a firm hand, 'cos if I started giving in to her, we'd be skint.'

'Go 'way, ye're rolling in it, Les Riley,' Kate said. 'I bet yer've got a few long stockings hidden under the floorboards upstairs.'

Les feigned annoyance as he shook a fist at his wife. 'I thought I told yer not to tell anyone about those floorboards! Honest, yer can't be trusted to keep anything to yerself. In fact, no women can, they're all gossip-mongers and janglers.'

Kate's eyes narrowed and her nostrils flared as she leaned across the counter. 'I came here for a packet of soap powder, not to be insulted.' She straightened up and took on a haughty pose. 'Violet, would you kindly serve me, please? I prefer to be served by a woman as I find men can be so supercilious.'

Vi's mouth gaped. 'Men can be what? My God, girl, how did yer get yer tongue around that, and what the blazes does it mean?'

'I bet she doesn't know,' Les said, grinning. 'She's just made it up.'

'Of course I know what it means! I wasn't dragged up like you common as muck people, I was brought up proper. And for your information, Les Riley, supercilious means looking down yer nose at someone. Which is what men do, 'cos they think they're the superior race.'

'But we *are* the superior race, everyone knows that! At least all men do.' Les was beginning to enjoy himself and was hoping no other customers would come in for a while. 'But we don't keep bragging about it 'cos it would be just the excuse you women need to start one of yer crying matches.'

Violet stared at him straight-faced for a few seconds, then she moved towards him and put a closed fist on his chest. Pushing him backwards, she curled her lip and snarled, 'Oh, so ye're superior to me, are yer? I'm as thick as two short planks, eh? Well, at least now I know where we stand.'

Every time Les opened his mouth, he was pushed further backwards. Both he and his wife were acting a part and thoroughly enjoying themselves. And it was such a funny scene, Kate was doubled up with laughter. She was wiping tears of mirth from her eyes with the back of a hand when she remembered the water she'd left to heat.

'Oh, my God!' she cried.

Violet and Les looked startled. 'What's up, girl? Yer look as though yer've seen a ghost.'

'I've just remembered I left two pans on the stove. The backsides will be burned out of them by now! I only intended to be out for a few minutes.' Kate's hand fluttered nervously to her throat. 'Vi, throw us a packet of soap powder, I'll have to dash. I'll pay yer later, save time now.' She got to the door of the shop and called, 'If me house is burned to the ground, or flooded, I'm going to blame you two for keeping me talking.'

With that parting shot she took to her heels and ran like the wind. She was expecting the pan and kettle to be boiled dry, but to her surprise the water in the large pan hadn't even come to the boil, and the kettle was just beginning to whistle. So she'd panicked for nothing. She'd better tell Les and Vi all was well when she called in to pay for the powder.

'Until then, I'd better pull me socks up and get this tub filled. I won't have time now to get the clothes washed and on the line before Monica comes, but I'll give them a good go with the dolly peg to get the dirt out, and then leave them to steep until I come back from the shops.'

Running upstairs to gather the dirty clothes, Kate puffed, 'So much for me grand ideas. I was going to break eggs with a big stick but end up doing sweet Fanny Adams. Me mam was always telling me it was unlucky to make plans, and she was right, as usual.'

Monica's eyes popped when Kate opened the door to her. 'I thought yer'd be waiting for me, but ye're not even ready!' After a closer inspection of her mate, she said, 'Yer look all hot and bothered, girl, what's wrong?'

'It's a long story, sunshine, so yer'd better come in and listen to it in comfort.' Kate ran the back of one hand across her forehead. 'The sweat is pouring off me with plunging that dolly peg up and down.'

'But what are yer washing today for?' Monica asked. 'Yer don't usually do a big wash on a Wednesday with it being half-day closing at the shops. And just look at the state of yer! Ye're sweating cobs, yer hair's a mess and yer've no stockings on.' She pulled a chair out from under the table. 'Ye're not a bit organized today, girl, what's got into yer?'

Kate sat on a chair facing her. 'Well, if yer must know, it all started with the weather. When I was seeing our Billy off to school, I happened to look up and saw this beautiful blue sky. I told meself it was a perfect day for a line full of washing.' She sighed. 'But it hasn't turned out that way.'

Monica undid the buttons on her coat and crossed her shapely legs. 'Okay, girl, let's have it. What have yer been up to?'

Ten minutes later, having embellished events a little to make the tale more interesting, Kate was chuckling as she neared the end. 'There was me, leaning on the shop counter, really enjoying meself watching Vi and Les acting daft, and not giving a thought to the time. Then, when I did, I imagined I'd been there ages and panicked. The trouble is, Vi and Les will be wondering if me house is still standing. I'll have to call in on our way past and let them know all is well. And pay them for the packet of soap powder.'

'Ye're not fit to be on yer own, yer know that, don't yer?' Monica clicked her tongue on the roof of her mouth. 'You get yerself ready while I work up a sweat on the flaming dolly peg. And when we come back from the shops, providing we ever get there, well, I'll give yer a hand to rinse the clothes out and put them through the mangle. They'll dry in no time in this weather.'

Kate jumped to her feet and planted a kiss on her friend's cheek. 'What are yer? Only the best mate in the world.'

'Don't push yer luck, girl, this is only a one off 'cos I'm feeling in a good mood. Just don't make a habit of it.' Monica slipped off her coat and threw it over the back of the chair. 'Move yerself or the shops will have sold out.'

Kate stopped at the bottom of the stairs with her hand on the banister. 'Ay, yer good moods don't last long, do they, sunshine? Two minutes and ye're back to being yer normal self . . . bossy and bad-tempered.' Laughing, she took the stairs two at a time when she saw her mate coming towards her with hands curled in a circle, warning that if there was any more cheek she'd strangle her, best friend or not.

As Kate was getting ready upstairs, Monica was plunging the dolly peg up and down on the clothes in the tub. And she was talking to them. 'I know it's not nice to have someone banging hell out of yer, but there's no need to moan. Yer'll be on the line before yer know it, wafting in the nice soft breeze.'

'Are yer calling in the corner shop first or leaving it until we come back?' Monica sounded matter-of-fact but she was hatching a plot in her mind. 'What d'yer think?'

'We'll call in first, in case I spend all me money.'

'Then will yer let me pull their legs a bit?' Monica asked, devilment dancing in her eyes. 'I could just do with a laugh.'

'Oh, aye, and what have yer got in mind?' Kate was apprehensive. Her neighbour was always playing tricks on people, and not everyone appreciated it. 'Ye're not going to make fools of them or me, are yer?'

'What d'yer take me for? I'm just going to have a bit of fun, and I promise it'll be a ruddy good laugh. I know Vi and Les will see the joke, but I'm not so sure about you, yer don't always see the funny side.' Monica squeezed her friend's arm to show she was only kidding. 'All you have to do is agree with everything I say, or else stand there like a lemon and say nowt.'

'All right, I'll stand still and say nowt. But if I think ye're going too far and taking the mickey out of them, I'll stick me oar in.'

The corner shop did a brisk trade, particularly in the early mornings between half-five and half-seven when the men were going to work and needed cigarettes and matches. But business was always steady as they stocked everything under the sun and were handy for when people ran short of anything. There were four customers in the shop when Kate and Monica arrived, and both women thought they were in for a wait. But as soon as

Violet set eyes on Kate she said to her elderly customer, 'Will yer excuse me a minute, Maggie? I just want to have a word with Mrs Spencer.'

Maggie didn't mind at all, it was one way of passing the time. There was many a bit of juicy gossip to be heard standing in this little shop, and as the old lady lived on her own it was the goings-on of other people that kept her mind active. So, thinking she wasn't being observed, she inched further along the counter.

'Was everything all right when yer got home, Kate?'

Monica jumped in before an answer could form on Kate's lips. 'Ye're joking, aren't yer, Vi? When I called for Tilly Mint here, I had to wade through a foot of water! She said she'd been talking to you and Les and forgot the time. We've had a hell of a job brushing out and mopping up.' She looked down at her feet. 'Me shoes are still sodden.'

Violet screwed up her eyes. 'How could that be? She said she had two pans of water on the stove and was frightened of them drying up and burning! No matter what happened to them, they couldn't have flooded the place like you're saying.'

By this time Les and the four customers were all ears. And there was nothing Monica liked better than an appreciative audience. Her face and voice were set for high drama. 'Oh, yeah, but she'd forgot she put the hose pipe on the tap and turned it on to fill up the tub. All over the house was flooded, kitchen, living room and hall. Everywhere was sopping wet.'

One customer thought she was being helpful by suggesting, 'Yer should leave the front and back doors open, queen, to dry the place through.'

Another one thought that was a good idea. 'That's right girl, yer'll get a draught through if yer leave yer front and back doors open.'

'That's terrible, that is,' Violet said. 'I'm sorry for yer, Kate.'

Kate was giving the floor her full attention while hoping Vi, her husband, and the customers who were clicking their tongues in sympathy, had a good sense of humour. 'It's just one of those things, Vi, can't be helped.'

Les was beginning to smell a rat. Why was Kate standing there saying very little, and leaving all the talking to Monica? 'Have yer got the place sorted out now, then?'

Once again it was Monica who answered. 'The worst thing was getting rid of all the soapsuds, they were everywhere. Flying through the air getting up our noses, and landing on the mantelpiece, chair legs, even the aspidistra plant on the little table by the window. That looked as though it was covered in snow.'

Les was dying to laugh, but composed his face before saying, 'Must be good soap powder to make all those suds. We'll have to put the price of it up, Vi, if it's good enough to make suds from here down to Kate's house.'

'What are you on about, yer stupid nit?' Violet asked. 'Honest, yer haven't got a sympathetic bone in yer body.'

'Oh, I don't know, love, I'm quite impressed, really. I mean, Kate didn't have any soap powder in the house, that's why she came here for some. So soapsuds appearing in water from a cold tap, well, that's a miracle.'

His wife looked at him for several seconds as though he was mad. Then the penny dropped and she shook her fist in Monica's face. 'This is your doing, missus! What a conniving cow yer are.' Then she let go with her hearty laugh. With her two hands holding on to her generous tummy, she chortled, 'Yer really had me going then. I could almost see those soapsuds flying through the air.'

Maggie's lined face was creased in laughter. 'It was the aspidistra I could see, all covered in white and looking like a Christmas tree.' She nodded her head. 'That's really cheered me up, that has.'

The other three customers, who were friends, thought it was hilarious. 'We were even thinking of offering to come to your house and give yer a hand to mop out! Oh, dear, we've been well and truly had.'

'Serves us right,' another woman said, 'for listening to other people's conversations.'

'No wonder you were so quiet, Kate,' Violet said. 'Yer looked as though yer didn't know where to put yerself, and I thought it was because yer'd had a fright.'

'I didn't know where to put meself,' she admitted. 'Yer never know what Monica's going to come up with next. Many's the time I've prayed for the floor to open up so I could disappear. But having said that, she's got her good points. She got stuck in right away and helped with the clothes in the tub while I made meself respectable.' She grinned sheepishly. 'Everything was fine when I got home, the water wasn't even boiled.'

'Well, it broke the monotony if nothing else,' Les said, walking back to his customers. 'At least we had a laugh and it'll make the day seem shorter.'

Kate put a threepenny piece on the counter. 'I think that's right, Vi, it was only a small packet, wasn't it?'

'Yeah, that's just right. Yer didn't have to go out of yer way to bring it, yer could have paid at the weekend.'

'Out of debt, out of danger, Vi! Anyway, it wasn't out of our way, we had to pass to go to the shops to get something in for the dinner.'

'What are yer thinking of having?' Violet asked as she leaned her elbows on the counter. She hadn't forgotten that Maggie still hadn't been served, but knew the old dear lived alone and didn't get about much. She'd be doing her a favour by letting her listen in to the conversation. 'Tell me it's something tasty so me mouth can water.'

'We're going to ask the butcher to chop a sheet of ribs in half for me and Monica. That's always a firm favourite in our house.'

'With a cabbage cooked in the water?' Maggie couldn't keep the words back. 'That's a real treat. It used to be me husband's favourite meal. He'd enjoy sucking the bones to get all the meat off.'

Kate smiled at her. 'That's what we're going to do. My husband says the meat on the bones is the sweetest.'

'Yer want to see my feller when he's eating them,' Monica said. 'He doesn't care that his fingers are greasy because he says that's what we were given hands for.'

'Yer've got me mouth watering now. Would yer do us a favour, Kate?' Monica asked. 'See if the butcher's got a spare sheet. If Bob serves yer, tell him who it's for and he'll make sure I get a nice lean meaty one.'

Monica chuckled. 'Which me and Kate will promptly swap for the one he gives us. How soft we'd be to give yer the best one.'

'Take no notice of her, Vi, she's having yer on.' Kate was remembering all the favours the family in the corner shop had done for her, so she wasn't going to cheat them. 'I'll tell Bob to put your name on the paper so I don't get them mixed up.' Then a grin appeared. 'Mind you, if he gives yer a leaner one than he gives us, he'll get a piece of me mind. Me and Monica are good customers, and I'll remind him of the fact.'

'Yer can do that by all means, girl, if we ever get to the ruddy shops!' Monica pulled on her friend's arm. 'Ye're standing there as though we've got all day.' She waved to everyone in the shop, and there was hearty laughter when Kate was pulled through the door behind her with some force.

'Let go of me before I lose me balance.' When she felt her feet firmly on the ground, Kate smoothed down the front of her coat before turning accusing eyes on her neighbour. 'Well, clever clogs, I hope yer've got enough money on yer to pay for Vi's sheet of ribs? I would have asked her for it, only I was dragged out of the shop before I had a chance.'

'I haven't got no money on me,' Monica said. 'Only enough for meself, like. So Bob will have to put what Vi owes on the slate. She can pay at the weekend.'

'She's not going to like that! I know she gives customers tick in her shop, but that's only to help them out when they're skint. She doesn't need to get tick herself.'

'How lucky she is then, eh? I've had quite a few things on tick in me life, and it never did me no harm. So it won't hurt her for once.'

'I'm not going back in that shop with a sheet of ribs and telling her she got it on tick.' Kate's mouth was set firm in determination. 'We'll pool our money when we get down the street and out of sight. Perhaps between us we can manage to pay for it.'

Monica shook her head slowly. 'Kate Spencer, yer can be a stubborn bugger when yer feel like it. If we can't afford to buy it between us, and yer feel so strongly about it, then I'll get my own ruddy ribs on tick. They'll probably choke me, but anything's better than seeing you with a sour face. Anyone would think yer were sucking a lemon.'

That calmed Kate down somewhat, and she linked her friend's arm. 'I'd like to sort something out, sunshine, 'cos Vi and Les have been good to me in the past when I haven't had two ha'pennies to rub together. I'd like to think I could do them a small favour in return.' She glanced sideways. 'I'm not the only one they've helped, either! There's a lot of women around here who've got good reason to be grateful to the Rileys. They'd have been in Queer Street sometimes without that corner shop. And that includes you, Monica Parry, so just you think on it.'

'Okay, girl, there's no need for a lecture. We'll get that sheet of ribs come hell or high water.' Monica saw a figure coming towards them and groaned. 'Oh, no, that's all I need, here comes Winnie Cartwright. Now don't stop and talk or she'll keep us for ages, passing on all the gossip and pulling everyone to pieces.'

The woman approaching them lived three doors down from Kate, and was in her early sixties. She had snow white hair that was always untidy, was small in stature, as thin as a rake, and always on the go. Every one of her movements was quick and jerky, making her look like a puppet worked by strings. She had never had any children so when her husband had died two years ago she was left alone in the world. This was enough for Kate to have time and sympathy for the woman. 'Go 'way, she's not that bad! She's no worse for jangling than we are. I know she talks a lot, but you and me can beat her on that score.'

'Hello Kate, Monica, are yer off to the shops, then?' Winnie didn't have a tooth in her mouth. What she did have were two rows of false teeth which at that moment were in a glass of water at the side of her bed. She hated the things and only wore them on high days and holidays. 'I got out early and have done enough shopping to last a few days.'

'We're late, 'cos we got held back,' Monica said before hinting, 'so it's going to be a rush now getting to the shops before they close.'

There were daggers in the look Kate gave her friend. There was no need to be so curt with the woman. 'A couple of minutes aren't going to hurt, so stop fussing. Anyhow, how are yer keeping, Winnie?'

'I'm fine, queen, can't complain. Everyone has their own bleedin' problems, no one wants to hear mine. And as long as I wake up each morning to find I haven't died in me sleep, then that suits me.'

Although Monica's smile was reluctant, she couldn't stop it putting in an appearance. 'I think yer'd have a job, girl, to wake up and find yer had died in the night.'

Winnie's two sets of gums were exposed. 'Ye're right there, queen, it would be a bleedin' miracle! I might even end up on the front page of the *News of the World*! I've always wanted to be famous.'

'A fat lot of good it would do yer if yer were dead,' Kate said. 'Anyway, can't we find something more pleasant to talk about than death?'

'Yes, queen, we can talk about how nice it'll be when the summer comes. It won't be long now, and I'll be able to go out and show off me figure.'

'What figure's that, girl?' Monica asked. 'There's not a pick on yer.' She dropped her head back and roared with laughter at what she was thinking. 'Me and Kate are going for a sheet of ribs which will have more meat on than you've got.'

'There's good stuff in little parcels, queen, like my husband used to tell me. And while your sheet of ribs will be history by eight o'clock tonight, I'll still be here.'

Kate decided they'd better move on. 'We're going to have to make tracks now, Winnie, but I hope yer wake up every morning to find yer haven't died in yer sleep.'

'Yeah,' Monica said. 'Especially with the summer nearly here, we wouldn't want yer to miss that.' She put a hand on Kate's arm and jerked her head. 'Betty Blackmore has just come out of the side entry, shall we wait for her?'

'We can do, keep her company.' Kate had been thinking a lot about Betty, knowing how hurt and upset she must be about her daughter expecting a baby. 'We can walk to the shops with her.'

Winnie glanced at the woman who was walking down the opposite side of the street. 'Someone should tell her to keep an eye on that daughter of hers before she gets herself into trouble.'

'What makes yer say that, sunshine?' Kate asked with surprise. 'Why would Betty's daughter get herself into trouble?'

'I'm not saying any more, queen, perhaps I shouldn't have said what I did. I should mind me own business and let others get on with theirs. I'll see yer again, ta-ra.' With that, Winnie left the two friends standing staring at each other in amazement.

'I wonder what made her say that?' Kate said. 'I thought no one knew about Margaret yet?'

'They don't, and neither does Winnie. She said the girl would be getting into trouble, not that she was in trouble. Anyway let's talk about it later, here's Betty.'

Chapter Three

The two friends walked either side of Betty and each laid a hand on her arm to slow her down. 'Take it easy, girl, we can't keep up with yer!' Monica said. 'What's the hurry, anyway?'

'It's me nerves, Monica, I've been like this for nearly two weeks now – darting down entries 'cos I'm afraid of bumping into anyone I know. I feel so ashamed I can't look anyone in the face.'

'I thought yer hadn't told anyone yet?'

'I haven't, only a couple of me best friends. So God knows what I'll be like when our Margaret starts showing, I'll be frightened to cross me front door step then.'

'Don't be silly, Betty, there's no need for yer to sneak around like a thief in the night, yer've done nothing wrong.' Kate was very sympathetic when she saw how upset the woman was. After all, the poor soul was being made to suffer for something over which she had no control. 'Hold yer head high, sunshine, and let people see ye're not going to let it affect yer. I know ye're going to stand by yer daughter, and that's something yer can be proud of.'

'I wouldn't mind so much if we knew who the father of the baby is. I mean, it would still be bad, but not as bad as the child being born illegitimate. Our Margaret insists it can only be Greg Corbett, 'cos he's the only boy she's been out with. And I've never known her to tell lies, so I believe her. Not that it does much good when the lad flatly denies all knowledge of it. We've tried to get her to see him, face to face, thinking he might admit it if she's standing in front of him. But she's too afraid. I don't think she's had a wink of sleep for weeks, worrying about when she starts to show and the girls she works with find out.'

They came to a halt outside the butcher's shop. 'This is where we part company, Betty, but any time yer feel like talking to someone, yer can always come to my house,' Monica told her. 'And for heaven's sake, stop worrying because it won't do yer any good. It certainly won't get yer anywhere.'

'It'll get me and Jack to an early grave, girl, 'cos we're both out of our minds. We never thought we'd come to this.'

'Listen, sunshine, your Margaret isn't the only one this has happened to and she won't be the last.' Kate wished she had a magic wand to waft away this woman's heartache. 'I bet any money that all this will be forgotten once the baby arrives. Yer'll love it, and yer'll make the best grandparents in the neighbourhood.'

There was a catch in Betty's voice when she said, 'Thanks, girl, I'll keep that in me mind. It might make life a bit easier.'

'Yer can keep this in mind, too,' Monica told her. 'Me and Kate will start knitting matinee coats and other little things, and we'll be proud to be aunties to the new arrival.'

Betty waved them away, but there was a faint smile on her face. 'Go on, the pair of yer, yer'll have me bawling me eyes out.'

'Ta-ra then, Betty, but you look after yerself.' And as the woman walked away, Monica called after her, 'Don't forget, me front door is always open.'

Bob the butcher was wearing a cheeky grin. 'Is that invitation open to everyone, Monica?'

There was a blank look on her face. 'What invitation?'

'That yer front door is always open! But could yer tell me if I'd need to buy a ticket?'

'Sod off, Bob Grisedale!' Monica placed her basket on the counter. 'For your information the invitation is for ladies only.'

'What about you, Kate?' The butcher was thinking that if her front door was always open, with those good looks there'd be a queue outside all day and every day. 'Is your door always open?'

'The only door in my house which is always on the latch is the door of the lavvy at the bottom of the yard. But ye're quite welcome to use it.' Kate didn't like being looked up and down, it made her feel uncomfortable. 'And I only charge a penny if yer bring yer own paper.'

Monica chortled. 'That's put you in yer place, me laddo. The trouble with you, Bob, is ye're too fond of the ladies and think ye're God's gift to women. And now, if yer can tear yer eyes away from me mate's legs and put them back in their sockets, we'd like two sheets of ribs. And they have to be exactly the same weight otherwise there'll be holy murder.' She took her purse out of the basket. 'Come on, girl, let's see how much we've got between us. Don't forget we have to buy bread as well as cabbage.'

Bob held his hands up, a sheet of ribs in each. 'There yer are, ladies, there's no difference in the weight of these, and they're both lean. In fact, they could be twins.'

'How much for the two?' Monica asked bluntly. 'We're counting our coppers.'

The butcher put both sheets on the scale. 'They should be three and ninepence, but seeing they're for you, yer can have them for three and a tanner.'

'We'll take them,' Kate said. 'And will yer chop both sheets in two, like yer always do?' She glanced at her friend. 'We might just about make it, but if not I'll come back later for whatever we're short of. I'll have the money from Vi by then. Is that okay with you?'

'All right, girl, yer've no need to bawl me blinking head off! I don't know why ye're looking at me like that, I haven't said anything to get yer knickers in a twist.'

The cheeky smile was back on the butcher's face. 'Ah, are yer knickers in a twist, Kate? Can I be of any assistance?'

She looked at his eager face and burst out laughing. 'Ye're all talk, Bob Grisedale! If I said I'd be grateful for your assistance, yer'd faint.'

'Not until I've got the money for the ribs I wouldn't, Kate. I might fancy yer like mad but I've got a wife and three children to think of. They like to eat, yer see, and I need the lolly to feed them.'

Monica handed over the right money. 'Me heart bleeds for yer, Bob. The thought of your wife and kids starving will come between me and me sleep.'

Bob made sure his assistant was coping with the other customers passing in and out before saying, 'Blimey, yer mustn't half live a very dull life! If you're laying in bed next to your feller, and all yer can think of is my wife and kids, then yer can tell Tom from me that there's something he's not doing right.'

Monica wasn't going to have that. 'Ay, my feller doesn't need lessons from you, mate! In fact, I bet he could teach yer a thing or two.'

'Excuse me for interrupting,' Kate said, 'but can we go now, sunshine, before the conversation gets any more personal?'

'Ooh, ay, look, she's blushing!' Bob threw his head back and roared. 'It's not often yer see a woman blush.'

The assistant and the customer he was serving turned their eyes on Kate. They were both used to Bob's bawdy humour, as were most people who came in the shop, and thought nothing of it. But this customer came out on Kate's side. 'That's because this woman is also a lady.'

'Oh, thank you!' Kate did a curtsy. 'That's very kind of you.'

'Yer should be used to me by now, Kate,' Bob said, looking a little bit sheepish. 'I didn't mean no harm.'

'I know yer didn't, sunshine. If I thought yer did, I'd have clocked yer one.' Kate picked up her basket and linked arms with her mate. 'Come on, sunshine, we're running late. See yer again, Bob, ta-ra.'

The two friends were still laughing as they made their way home. 'Just fancy, all we've got between us is three-ha'pence,' Kate said. 'Talk about being poverty-stricken isn't in it.'

'I think we did very well.' Monica nodded for emphasis. 'We got everything we wanted and we'll have a couple of coppers in our purse when Vi pays us for the ribs. Not a bad day's work, eh, girl?'

Kate was in full agreement. 'Excellent is the word, I think.'

'Well now, perhaps not excellent. That would mean it had been perfect, and the morning was anything but perfect, thanks to you. In fact, yer made a right pig's ear of it and I was stuck in the middle. So I think yer owe me, missus. And a good way of paying me back is to invite me into yours for a well-deserved cuppa.'

'Yeah, okay, that's fine by me. So if you'll call into the corner shop and see Vi, I'll go home and put the kettle on. And I'll put the ribs in steep while I'm at it. Then I'll have to see to me washing before it gets too late to put it out.'

'Don't worry about that, girl, it won't take us long. Once I've had a cuppa and a biscuit to dunk, I'll be full of the joys of spring. I'll be fighting fit and as fresh as a daisy.'

'Yer'll be all those things after one gingersnap? Ay, if I give yer two, will yer do cartwheels down the street?'

The two women came to a halt, bent over with laughter. 'Only if yer promise to get Bob the butcher to come and see me.' Monica rocked to and fro. 'And charge him, 'cos I'll have me best fleecy drawers on.'

'Ha-ha,' Kate chortled. 'In that case I think yer'd have to pay him to look, never mind you charging him. I don't think fleecy drawers are his cup of tea, even if they are yer best ones.'

Monica straightened up and wiped the back of a hand across her eyes. 'Ooh, I enjoyed that laugh. As good as a dose of Carter's Little Liver Pills any day. But time is marching on and we've work to do. So I'll nip into the corner shop while you go home and put the kettle on.'

There was a smile on Kate's face as she walked down the

street. It was still there when Monica came in fifteen minutes later. 'I didn't expect yer to be so long, the tea's been made for a while now. But I've had the cosy over it, so it should still be hot.'

'Vi kept me talking. But it was worth it 'cos she gave me a packet of custard creams to share between the two of us. She said she usually gives a kid a ha'penny for going on a message for her, but she thought we were a bit old for that.' Monica pulled out a chair and sat down with a sigh of relief. 'Ooh, isn't it good to take the weight off yer feet?'

Kate held out her hand. 'Pass the biscuits over and we can have a couple now with our tea. Any left we'll divide between us.'

A minute later the friends faced each other across the table, cups of tea to hand. Kate was looking very thoughtful, as though her mind was miles away.

'What are yer thinking about, girl? Whatever it is, let's in on it, yer know we don't have secrets from each other.'

'Well, if yer must know, I was thinking about Winnie and what she said about Betty's daughter. I mean, yer must admit it wasn't something anyone would say if they didn't have a reason. I wonder if she knows anything?'

'She can't do, if she doesn't even know Margaret's in the family way. Perhaps she doesn't like Betty, and just said the first thing that came into her head,' Monica replied. 'I know yer don't agree with me, but I think Winnie Cartwright likes to cause trouble.'

'I don't know why yer think that about her, there's nothing wrong with the woman! She'd rather do yer a good turn than a bad one any day. And yer've no reason to say she's a trouble-maker 'cos I bet there's not one instance yer can tell me where she caused trouble.'

'She spends her life jangling!' Monica wasn't going to be convinced otherwise. 'And it can only be gossip, 'cos she never goes anywhere and I don't think she's got many friends.'

'That's where ye're wrong, sunshine, 'cos she's got me and our Nancy. And most of the neighbours speak well of her.'

'Your Nancy!' Monica's voice rose in disbelief. 'Your Nancy's only a child, she's too young to be able to suss people out. And why would she like an old lady anyway?'

'Because, unlike you, she can see the goodness in Winnie. You've made up yer mind yer don't like her, for some reason known only to yerself, and yer won't even look for her good points.' Kate tutted. 'Anyway, that's up to you, I'm not going to fall out with yer over it. But I'm still curious about what she said about Betty's daughter. In fact, I'm so intrigued I think I'll nip down there after I've got our dinner over, and ask her.'

'Huh! She'll tell yer to mind yer own business.' Monica wasn't going to give way on her view of Winnie Cartwright. 'Ten to one yer'll get nothing out of her because she doesn't know anything. She was just being nasty perhaps because she doesn't like Betty.'

But Kate had other ideas which she wasn't inclined to share with her friend right now. 'Ye're on, Monica, I'll take yer up on that bet. Ten to one I'll get something out of her. If I don't, I'll give yer tenpence. But if I do, yer'll have to stand by the deal and fork out tenpence to me.'

'I'll agree in words, girl, but as we're both strapped for cash there's no point in agreeing to part with tenpence. So we'd better settle for a tuppenny slab of Cadbury's.'

Kate pushed herself to her feet and reached for the cups and saucers. 'If I don't get cracking, that washing will still be in the tub when John gets home from work. And yer can't move out there with the ruddy tub taking up all the room. So are yer going to help me put the clothes through the mangle then I can get them on the line?'

'Ye're a slave driver, Kate Spencer, but a promise is a promise and I'll not go back on it or yer'll call me all the names under the sun. So it's all hands to the pump for the next half-hour. Then I'll get back to me own house, 'cos I've got work to do as well, yer know, missus!'

Kate waited until the dinner was over and all the dishes washed. Then she said, 'I'm just slipping down to see Winnie Cartwright, I shouldn't be long.'

'I'll come with yer, Mam,' Nancy said, her face brightening. 'I like Mrs Cartwright, she always makes me laugh.'

'No, not this time, sunshine, 'cos she's not expecting me and I don't think she'd appreciate two of us landing on her. Another time, perhaps.'

Billy didn't care who went where 'cos in his pocket, wrapped in a piece of cloth, was the prized marble. Pete said his father wouldn't let him play with it for real again in case someone won it off him. His dad said he'd never get another one like it and should hang on to it. So Pete, being Billy's best mate, had told him he would lend it to him for a few days. Since he'd got home from school he'd washed it under the tap three times and polished it with a cloth so there wasn't a mark on it. 'I'll be going out to play, Mam, but I'll only be in the street if yer want me.'

'Before yer go, love, could yer lend me sixpence until I get paid?' John's mouth was dry with nerves. He hated himself for having to tell his wife a lie, but he'd lost his tram fare on the horses. The bloke in work who collected the bets had said he'd been given a tip on a horse that was a dead cert to win. Like a fool, John had put a whole shilling on it and the flaming horse hadn't come anywhere! In fact, it was probably still running. He'd never do it again, he promised himself, he was finished with the gee-gees. 'I must have lost a tanner somewhere, or else there's a hole in the lining of me coat pocket.'

'I haven't got one to spare,' Kate told him. 'I'll barely manage until Saturday as it is. If I lend you any money the family will go short on food.'

'If yer could lend me tuppence for the tram to get me there

and back, that would help me out. I could borrow a few coppers off one of me workmates to keep me going until Saturday.'

'Don't yer start borrowing from yer workmates, they'll think ye're a scrounger. I'd rather borrow it off one of my mates instead.' Kate undid her pinny and began to fold it. 'I'll have a look at yer coat when I come back, see if yer've got a hole in the pocket.'

'I had a look, love, but couldn't see one. I might have pulled the tanner out with me hankie or something.' John could feel his colour rising and hung his head in shame. 'I'll give it yer back on Saturday, love.'

'Yer better had, 'cos it's a struggle every week as it is. I'm not moaning, I know yer work hard, sunshine, and yer keep very little back from yer wages, but we can't afford for you to be losing sixpence very often.' He looked so unhappy, Kate's heart went out to him. 'Cheer up, it can't be helped, we'll get over it.'

'I'm thirteen in June, Mam, then I'll only have one more year at school before I start work,' Nancy said. 'Yer won't know ye're born when I start bringing a wage in.'

'I'm looking forward to it, sunshine. And when our Billy leaves school we'll be rolling in dough. No more being skint, or robbing Peter to pay Paul. I might even be able to buy meself a fur coat.' Kate laughed. 'Can yer imagine me, or anyone else for that matter, walking down this street in a fur coat?' She put a hand on her hip and walked across the room with a very exaggerated swagger. 'I'd be a laughing stock.'

'No, yer wouldn't, Mam,' Billy said, while thinking he'd thump anyone who laughed at his mother. 'Yer'd look like a film star.'

'Oh, yeah, I don't think!' Kate ruffled his hair as she passed. 'Anyway, I'm off to see Winnie, I'll not be long.'

To say that Winifred Cartwright was surprised to see her when she opened the door would be an understatement. She received so few visitors it was a treat to say, 'Come in, queen, this is a lovely surprise.'

'I'm not stopping yer from doing something, I hope? I can always come back if it's not a convenient time?'

'I've got all the time in the world, queen, so don't be worrying. Sit yerself down and make yerself at home.'

Kate looked around the room which was spotless, not a thing out of place, and the hearth and all the furniture polished so you could see your face in them. 'Yer keep yer house nice, Winnie, I must say. Mine looks a tip compared to this.'

'Ah, yes, queen, but there's no one to make mine untidy. I'm on me own here, and I'm inclined to be a fuss-pot, as my dear husband used to say. I'm up and down like a yo-yo, don't give a spot of dust time to settle. Sometimes I get on me own nerves.' Winnie suddenly covered her mouth with a hand. 'I've just thought on, I haven't got me teeth in.'

'I'm so used to seeing yer without them, sunshine, I wouldn't have even noticed.' Kate was telling herself to get on with it. 'I hope yer won't be annoyed with me over what I'm going to ask yer, and if yer don't want to tell me I won't mind. Just tell me to get lost.'

'Until I know what it is, queen, then I can't say. But I can't see meself ever telling you to get lost, so get it off yer chest.'

'It was what yer said about Betty's daughter. I wondered if yer had any reason for saying what yer did?'

'Forget it, queen, I should have kept me big mouth shut. I felt like kicking meself all the way home for letting me tongue run away with me. I didn't mean nothing by it, so yer'd best forget it, Kate.'

'There is a reason for me asking this, Winnie, a really important reason. I'll tell you about it later, perhaps, if what yer tell me has any bearing on it. In any case, I promise that whatever yer tell me won't be repeated if yer don't want it to be.'

The little woman let out a deep sigh. 'I'm probably old-fashioned but I don't like to see youngsters messing around with each other in a dark entry. That's why I said someone should tell the girl's mother what she's up to. Yer see, queen, I nip down to the corner pub every night just before closing time for a pint of milk stout. I use the entry and wrap me knitted shawl around me so no one will see the jug I'm carrying. Anyway, one night, oh, it must be a few weeks ago now, I'd let meself out of the yard door when I heard voices. I could see a couple against the wall, and from the lamp at the top of the entry I could see who they were. I was so disgusted, I turned back up the yard and went out of the front door.'

'Were the couple doing something they shouldn't have been, sunshine?'

Winnie's eyes went to the floor. 'They were, queen, and it fair upset me. I asked meself what the world was coming to.'

'I'll tell yer what I know now, Winnie, and then I'm going to ask yer one more question.' Kate leaned forward, her elbows resting on her knees. 'Margaret Blackmore is expecting a baby, and her family are out of their minds. The boy Margaret said is the father is denying all knowledge of it and his family won't even listen. Betty and Jack Blackmore are worried sick with the shame of it. I feel heartily sorry for them.'

'And yer want to know the name of the lad I saw her with in the entry? Is that it, queen?'

'I don't want yer to get involved with anything yer don't want to be involved in, sunshine, so it's up to you. Margaret says she's only been out with one boy, on two occasions, and her family believe her 'cos she's never lied to them before and is actually a very shy girl. But now she's ruined her own life and her family's. And of course the baby's. It won't have a father's name on its birth certificate.'

'They're a good family, queen, I've known them twenty years. And I'm sorry about what yer've told me 'cos Betty Blackmore doesn't deserve that kind of worry. Will yer tell me the name of the boy Margaret says is responsible?'

'Greg Corbett.'

'That's him, queen. That's the lad I saw her with, no doubt about it. He lives three streets away and I know his mother from seeing her at the shops. I've had many a chat with her and she's not a bad person. Her name's Maude, and the husband is Albert.'

'But are yer sure they were up to no good when yer saw them in the entry?' Kate asked. 'I'd hate to point the finger of blame at the wrong lad, 'cos his life could be ruined. He says he kissed her, but that's all.'

'They were doing more than kissing when I saw them, queen. The girl's clothes had been pulled up and I could see the tops of her legs. There's nothing wrong with my eyesight. I didn't hear her saying anything, it was the boy doing all the talking, telling her there was nothing to worry about, it would be all right. That's all I heard, queen. I couldn't get away quick enough, I was that disgusted.'

Kate sighed. 'I think Betty should be told this, it would be a crime not to. But how to go about it I have no idea. I don't want to drag you into it.'

'Couldn't yer say someone had seen them in the entry but yer didn't want to give their name unless the boy denied it? Then I would come forward, queen, because he shouldn't be allowed to get off scot-free, leaving the girl with all the worry and shame.' Winnie shook her head. 'I couldn't have that on me conscience, I'd never live with meself.'

'I'll have to give it a lot of thought before I do anything, sunshine, in case I blunder in where I'm not wanted. It's a delicate subject and needs to be handled with care, or it could cause holy murder.'

'You do what yer think best, queen, and I'll go along with yer. I know whatever yer do will be the best for all concerned.' The little woman seemed to spring off the chair, her movement was so quick. 'And now, seeing as ye're a guest in my house, I'll offer yer a nice cup of tea.'

Kate grinned up at her. 'And I'll accept, thank you! I take one sugar and just a spot of milk, please, if yer don't mind.'

'Coming up, queen, coming up.'

Kate wrapped her arms around herself as she hurried up the entry. It had been a lovely day but now there was a definite chill in the air. There was a chill in her heart, too, because of the knowledge she now had. What on earth could she do that wouldn't cause hurt and shame to two families? Then, as she lifted the latch on the back door, she told herself firmly that it wouldn't be a case of bringing hurt and shame to two families, more like those families sharing the hurt and shame brought about by the actions of their children.

John heard the kitchen door close and glanced at the clock. 'I thought yer said yer wouldn't be long!'

'I know, but Winnie made me a cup of tea and I didn't like rushing out. She doesn't get many visitors, she was glad of the company.'

'What did yer want to see her about? I didn't think yer were that friendly with her?'

'Good grief, John, anyone would think I'd been gone all day! And what I wanted to see Winnie about was women's talk, yer wouldn't be interested. For your information, while we don't live in each other's pockets, I've been friendly with Winnie for years.' Kate studied her husband through narrowed eyes. 'What's got into yer, anyway? Yer sound like a bear with a ruddy sore head! Don't tell me yer've missed me, 'cos yer usually sit with yer head stuck in the *Echo* and don't even notice whether I'm here or not.'

'I didn't get an *Echo* tonight, I couldn't afford one.' John forced a smile although his heart was heavy. 'And I'm not like a bear with a sore head. More like a man who was missing his wife and wanting her home.'

'We'll have less of yer flattery if yer don't mind, I'm getting a bit too old for that. And it's coming to something if yer can't even afford a penny to buy a paper, isn't it?'

'I told yer I'd lost sixpence and it's left me skint. I'll be all right when I get paid on Saturday, I can straighten meself up.'

'Don't forget I'll sort yer out with yer tram fare, I'll cadge it off Monica. So don't borrow off any of yer workmates, it's belittling.'

'Don't be soft, love, all the lads borrow off each other. There's no harm in it.'

'I'm asking yer not to, so don't do it, even if it's only to pacify me.' Kate looked at the clock. 'It's time our Billy was in. I'll give him a shout before I make yer a drink.'

Kate couldn't concentrate on anything that night because her mind was full of what she'd been told by Winnie. She couldn't sit back and say nothing, even though that was what she'd like to do. The situation was too serious for that. She could imagine what it would be like in the Blackmore house right now: worry, tears and tension. If she could only find the right way to do it, she could relieve some of that worry and tension. It meant making another family unhappy, but so be it. It took two people to make a baby, and those two, plus their parents, would have to do what was right.

Kate tossed and turned in bed, sleep eluding her because her brain was racing. In the end she decided she couldn't manage this on her own, she had to confide in someone. And the one person she knew who would tell her straight what she thought should be done was her best mate Monica. She was the one person to be trusted not to repeat anything she heard.

'Yes, that's what I'll do,' Kate muttered softly, the sheet over her mouth muffling her words so as not to waken her husband. Once that decision had been reached, a weight seemed to be lifted from her shoulders. Kate felt herself drifting off to sleep with John's arm across her body as though protecting her.

Chapter Four

Kate got herself into a real flap the next morning, wanting badly to open her heart to Monica so she wasn't carrying the burden alone. But she was being kept back by slow-coach Billy, who dawdled over everything. Nancy was no bother, she got herself washed, dressed and had her breakfast without any fuss at all. After she'd kissed her mother before leaving for school, she would knock next door for her best friend Dolly. They always gave themselves plenty of time so they wouldn't be rushing at the last minute to get to the school gates before they closed. Their school reports always gave them good marks for punctuality.

But Billy was a different kettle of fish. He would dilly-dally over every task, getting washed, dressed, and chewing his toast as though he had all the time in the world. And because Kate was eager for him to leave that particular morning, he seemed to be doing everything in slow motion. 'Billy, if yer don't get a move on I'm going to get really annoyed with yer. It's the same every morning, yer've got me nerves wrecked.'

'I always get to school on time!' He thought his mother was making a big fuss over nothing. 'Me and Pete run like whippets all the way.'

'That's as maybe, but yer keep me behind with me work.' Kate was pushing him towards the door as he was putting his coat on. 'I've got a message to go on this morning and I don't want to be late.'

This turned out to be the wrong thing to say because curiosity stopped the lad in his tracks. 'Where are yer going?'

'Never you mind, it would be of no interest to yer.' Kate

cupped his face and gave him a kiss. 'Run along, and remember, I love the bones of yer.'

Billy grinned. 'I love the bones of you, too, Mam, but I love the rest of yer as well.'

'Away with yer.' Kate gave him a playful clip over his ear. 'Pete will be waiting.'

Sure enough he was, showing his impatience by passing the time kicking the front doorstep. 'Yer'll have no toes left in those shoes, Pete,' Kate said, eyeing the scuff marks on the toe-cap. 'Yer mam would have yer life if she saw yer.'

'Nah! I'll cover them over with black shoe polish,' Pete said, as though he'd just solved one of life's problems. 'She won't notice.'

Kate made herself wait until they'd reached the top of the street and turned to wave. Then she flew back inside the house and set to with a vengeance. The grate didn't take long because the fire was only lit for a couple of hours yesterday to warm the place up, so there weren't many ashes to take out to the bin set in the entry wall. The table was cleared in no time, and the dishes washed. And never had the furniture been dusted so quickly. As she moved the duster over the sideboard, Kate told it, 'It's only a cat's lick and a promise today, but I'll give yer a good going over tomorrow.'

By the time she was finished making the beds, she was puffing and blowing. So she made herself sit down until her heart stopped beating like mad. 'I'd have been better off keeping me nose out of it,' she told the empty room. 'I've given meself worries I could do without.' She sat for a few minutes until her breathing was back to normal, then she got to her feet. 'I'll see what Monica has to say. If she thinks I should stay out of it, then that's what I'll do.' But even as she spoke, Kate knew she wouldn't walk away from this particular problem because too many people were being hurt and their lives ruined.

It was a nice sunny morning so she didn't bother with a coat.

She knocked on the wall dividing the two houses to let her friend know she was coming, then went out the back way, leaving the kitchen door on the latch.

'In the name of God, yer must have been up with the lark!' Monica's nose was itchy, and when pulling faces didn't help matters, she wiped the bottom of her nose with a soot-covered hand. 'I hope ye're not ready for the shops, girl, 'cos I'm not halfway through me work yet! And don't tell me yer've done your house from top to bottom, 'cos I know bleeding well that yer can't have done.'

Kate ran a hand down her pinny. 'Do I look as though I'm ready for the shops? And all me house has had, for your information, is a quick flick of the duster. I've got more important things on me mind than housework, and I think yer'll be very interested in what I've got to tell yer. It kept me awake half the night, tossing and turning.'

Monica looked from her dirty hands to the hearth, which needed wiping down with a wet cloth. 'Whatever it was what kept yer awake, was it exciting? I mean, shall I put the kettle on so I can sit down with a well-earned cuppa and be all ears?'

'That's a good idea, sunshine, I could just do with a cup of tea.' Kate followed her neighbour into the kitchen. 'I haven't had a proper drink all morning, I just managed a few sips while I was making the kids' toast.'

'You get the cups down while I rinse me hands.' Monica picked up the scrap of carbolic soap which was all that was left. 'Remind me to get some soap when we go to the shops, and a packet of Rinso. I've got a pile of clothes to put in steep tonight.' She turned the tap off and reached for the piece of towel that was hanging on a hook behind the door. 'If this bit of news of yours doesn't fill me full of excitement, or thrill me to pieces, then I'll strangle yer for stopping me getting on with me work.'

'Oh, I think what I've got to tell yer will be enough excitement to last yer a couple of weeks.' Kate nodded. 'Yes, I think I can safely say the surprise will knock yer off yer chair.'

'Tell me while I'm leaning against the sink, girl, and I won't fall.'

'The kettle's coming to the boil now so yer can wait.' Kate put a spoon on one of the saucers and poured a drop of milk into each of the cups. 'Five minutes isn't going to kill yer.'

When they were sat facing each other, their cups in front of them, Kate started by saying, 'By the way, yer owe me tenpence.'

'Tenpence! What for?'

'Come on now, Monica Parry, don't be coming the little innocent with me. It was you what said yer'd bet me ten to one I wouldn't get anything out of Winnie Cartwright. So don't be trying to wriggle out of it.'

'That was if yer got anything off her, but yer didn't, did yer?'

'Only the name of the lad who fathered Margaret Blackmore's baby.'

Monica nearly choked on the mouthful of tea she'd just sipped. She swallowed before saying, 'That's not something to make a joke about, girl.'

'You don't really believe I'd joke about anything so serious, do yer, sunshine? No, it's the God's honest truth.' Kate related the whole story, leaving nothing out, while her friend stared at her with amazement and bewilderment. 'That is the whole story, word for word,' she finished.

'Greg Corbett, eh?' Monica was still trying to come to terms with what she'd been told. 'His mam and dad are in for a shock, aren't they?'

'That's if we tell them. I want to hear what you think would be the right thing to do?'

'The right thing would be to go round to Betty's right now and put her in the picture. It won't solve all her worries, but it'll sure help to relieve them.'

'Yes, that is what I thought at first,' Kate told her. 'Then when I'd had time to think it through, I wondered if it would do more harm than good. I mean, I can just picture what would happen if Betty was told. Her first reaction would be to go round to the boy's house and create merry hell. And that wouldn't make for good relations between the two families, would it? Also, it would mean dragging Winnie into it which is what I didn't want to do. She had the guts to tell me what she saw, and I don't think she should be put through it again.'

'I agree with yer there, girl. I was very wrong about her, she's certainly come up trumps.' After being silent for a short while, Monica said, 'I also think what yer said about Betty going round to the Corbetts' house is right, too. If she went in there with all guns blazing, it wouldn't help. But there is one thing that springs to mind that won't involve anyone but Margaret and the boy. If it was handled right, it could solve everything.'

'What have yer got in mind, sunshine? It would be marvellous if, after all the hurt and heartache, there could be a happy ending.'

'I couldn't promise a happy ending, girl, though it would be better to aim for that than spoil everything by going about it in the wrong way. But it's your shout because you were the one who was clever enough to pick up on what Winnie said. I wouldn't have given it another thought, she was just a gossip-monger to me.' Monica realized how wrong she'd been to criticize the woman she really knew little about. 'I can be a clever bugger sometimes, can't I, girl? I certainly got me facts wrong with regard to Winnie.'

'Yer can make it up to her by asking her round for a cup of tea one day. When yer get to know her, yer'll find out she's a lovely little lady.' Kate leaned her elbows on the table and cupped her face in her hands. 'Yer still haven't said what yer had in mind?'

'It could be a load of rubbish, girl, just me talking out of the top of me hat. But listen, and see what yer make of it.' Monica drained her cup before carrying on. 'I think it would be worth trying to get through to the boy, Greg. He's probably terrified of his parents being upset, and that's why he's telling lies. If he's confronted by someone telling him he's been seen in the entry with Margaret, it might make all the difference. But whoever it was that told him would have to be diplomatic and not frighten the life out of him. After all, he could still deny it, even if he knows he's been seen. No one can make him marry the girl if he doesn't want to. So it needs to be handled with kid gloves.'

'That lets me out, then, 'cos I wouldn't know what to say to the lad. I'd be so embarrassed, I wouldn't be able to look him in the face.' Kate's brown eyes rolled. 'After all, it's not a subject I'm well up in!'

Monica chortled. 'Yer know more on the subject than the lad does. Yer should do, anyway, after being married for fifteen years and having two children of yer own.'

Kate suddenly sat up straight. 'Ay, I've just had an idea. What about talking to Margaret and seeing if she'll tell the boy? What d'yer think?'

Monica pursed her lips and shook her head. 'She'd run a mile if anyone mentioned it to her. She's frightened of her own shadow, that's why I find it so surprising she's pregnant!' Once again she shook her head. 'Yer can forget about her, she'd take to her heels before yer could get a word out.'

'Well, I don't know what we're going to do,' Kate said. 'Everything we come up with, we find a reason for not doing it! At this rate, we'll be too late, Margaret will be showing soon.'

'It's far better to take a little longer and get things right, than to go at it like a bull in a china shop and end up with a disaster. You've come up with something of importance which could help at least one young girl and her family. So yer've got to make good use of it. How it should be done, well, we've got to give that some very serious thought.'

'I know that, sunshine!' Kate was beginning to despair. 'But we could think about it until the cows come home and still not have an answer.'

'I'll mull it over in me head while I'm getting meself ready for the shops. I've got a glimmer of an idea, but I want to give it more thought before I tell yer. And with no offence to you, girl, I can think better when I'm on me own.' Monica scraped her chair away from the table. 'You go and get yerself ready, but give me at least half an hour to finish this room and tidy meself up.'

'Yeah, okay.' Kate made for the kitchen. 'I'll go the back way 'cos I've left the door on the latch.' She stepped down on to the cobbled yard, then looked up at her neighbour. 'Two heads are better than one, sunshine. I'm glad ye're me mate. When we're walking down to the shops, the fresh air might clear our brains and we'll come up with an inspiration.'

Monica's laugh was loud and hearty. 'I've never come up with an inspiration in me whole life!' Then she held up a hand. 'No, I tell a lie. When I first saw my feller, it was at a tuppenny hop and I didn't know me left foot from me right. Anyway, he caught me eye, and I didn't half like what I saw. But he was such a good dancer, all the girls were excusing him. He didn't even notice me until two months later after I'd made it me business to learn to dance as good as anyone. I excused him in a waltz one night, and we've been together ever since. So Tom was my first inspiration, if yer see what I mean.'

'Ah, that's not half romantic,' Kate said, her pretty head tilted. 'Did he ever find out that yer'd set yer cap at him?'

'Not bloody likely! After that first dance, he did all the running and I lapped it up. We didn't go to many dances after that, we preferred the back row of the pictures or the couch in his mam's front parlour.'

'Ooh, did Tom's mam live in a parlour house?'

'Yes, she did, girl, but if I start to tell yer about that we'll never get the other business cleared up. So scram, poppy off, and I'll see yer in half an hour.'

* * *

Later, on their way to the shops, Monica said, 'I've made up me mind that you and me have got to be positive. Otherwise we'll dither for so long, nothing will get done. So what I was thinking is that if we can find out where Greg works, we could meet him one night and confront him.'

Kate missed a step and gave a little skip to get back in line. 'Ooh, er, d'yer think that's wise? We could end up with the whole of his family on our backs.'

'That's if he tells them, which I very much doubt. Admitting to being the father of the baby is one thing, but to have to tell his parents he was seen in the entry performing the very act that made Margaret pregnant, well, that's a different ball game. If we can persuade him at least to see the girl that would be a start and wouldn't involve you and me in anything to do with the families.'

'That would be wonderful, sunshine, but how will we find out where he works?'

'Leave that to me. I'll call at Betty's later, just to see how they are. In the course of the conversation I might get the opportunity to ask where he works.'

But Kate had spied someone ahead of them. 'Yer might not have to call to Betty's, I'm sure that's her walking up the road. Can yer see her, she's by the Post Office?'

'Yeah, that's her, we're in luck. Let's catch up with her, we can worry about our shopping later.'

Betty Blackmore turned when she heard her name being called. Both Kate and Monica were shocked at how bad she looked. Lines were etched deep into her face. Her eyes were dull and she seemed weary, as though she was carrying the woes of the whole world on her shoulders. 'Hello, ladies, I was miles away. I hope yer weren't shouting me for long?'

'No, we were just strolling along window gazing,' Monica lied, 'when we saw yer in the distance. Where are yer off to?'

'Great Homer Street Market. Everything is a lot cheaper there.

Anyway, I thought the walk and fresh air would do me good. I'm not sleeping too well.'

'We'll walk that far with yer, it'll do us good to stretch our legs. We can just as easy do our shopping there as along Stanley Road, and as yer say, it's cheaper.'

The two friends automatically walked on either side of the tormented woman, and linked her arms. 'How are yer getting on, sunshine?' Kate asked, her heart filled with pity. She wanted to blurt out what they knew. But Monica was right, that would solve nothing. 'Are you and yer husband feeling any better?'

There was a deep sigh. 'Worse if anything. Our Margaret comes home from work and goes straight up to her bedroom. She won't have anything to eat, and we can hear her crying her heart out, night after night.'

'No word from Greg Corbett or his family then?' Monica asked. 'They haven't been in touch?'

'No, lass, and I'm too weary to go fighting it out with anybody. Jack said he thinks we should move out of the area before anyone knows about the baby, but it would break my heart! We moved into that house as newly weds, and I don't want to live anywhere else. Why should I when I haven't done nothing wrong?'

'I should jolly well think not!' Monica's voice rose. 'Why the hell should you? As yer say, you haven't committed a crime. You just stay put and to hell with everyone else.'

'I would do, lass, if it weren't for the fact that we live so near the Corbetts, and Margaret would continually be coming face to face with the boy. Well, he's not a boy, he's a man. He's nineteen now. I think he told Margaret, before this trouble came up, that he'll be twenty in July.'

Monica asked casually, 'Has he got a decent job, or don't yer know where he works?'

'Yeah, he works for Jenkins and Howett in Seaforth. It's a place that makes railings and iron gates, that sort of thing. And she did say something about machinery which was made to be sent abroad. When he's out of his time he'll be on a decent wage.' Another deep sigh. 'Our Margaret really likes him, that's the hardest part. She only went out with him twice on proper dates, but she used to dance with him a lot at Blair Hall and if they met in the street they'd always stop for a chat. She's spoken to him a few times since he . . . er . . . since, well, yer know what I'm getting at. But when she missed her period, she avoided him like the plague. I didn't know this, of course, because at that time the poor girl was terrified to say anything. I always thought of him as being a nice, quiet lad.'

'Perhaps he is, Betty, and what happened wasn't something yer'd expect of him in the usual way of things,' Kate said, thinking the time might come when the lad would have to face this woman. 'He might have got carried away and not thought of the consequences.'

'Well, it's too bloody late to be thinking of the consequences now, 'cos yer can't turn the clock back.' There was bitterness in Betty's voice. 'I hate him for what he's done. He's ruined our Margaret's life and put the whole family through hell. I just wish he could have a taste of what we're going through, see how he'd like it.'

Monica put her arm across Betty's shoulder and pulled her close. 'He'll get paid back, girl. Some way or another, he'll get paid back. And God is good, He'll look after Margaret and the baby. But let's not talk about it any more, 'cos ye're only getting yerself upset. Let's put our minds to what we're giving our families for their dinner.'

'I'm doing liver and onions for my lot,' Kate said, her voice light even though she felt quite upset. 'With potatoes mashed with a knob of margarine. That usually goes down well with all of them.'

'Thanks, girl!' Monica leaned forward to look at her mate. With a conspiratorial wink, she said, 'Yer've saved me racking me brains. We'll have the same as you. What about you, Betty?'

'I might as well join the club. Liver and onions sounds good to me. I'll get a pig's trotter while I'm in the butcher's for my feller's dinner tomorrow. He says yer can't beat a pig's trotter for getting yer teeth into, but no one else in the house will eat them.'

'Me neither!' Kate shivered at the thought. 'Just the look of them puts me off.'

'I'm not keen,' Monica agreed. 'But I've got to say they do make a good pan of scouse. With carrots and turnip, onions and barley, left to simmer for a few hours, they're delicious. And cheap, so I have them when I'm hard up.'

'Shut up, ye're making me mouth water!' Betty said, licking her lips. 'I could just go a bowl of it now.' For a short while she forgot her heartache. This cheered Kate and Monica, who made sure she didn't have any further chance to dwell on her worries until they left her at her front door two hours later.

'We can't both go, we'd frighten the life out of the lad.' Monica was in Kate's house and they were facing each other across the table. 'If we both turned up, it would look as though we'd come to make trouble. Whereas if he found himself being stopped by one woman, especially someone as good-looking as you, he wouldn't run off before yer could get a word out.'

'Me? On me own!' Kate was horrified. 'Oh, no, yer don't, I'm not doing that on me own. How soft you are, Monica Parry, palming all the dirty work on to me!'

'In case yer've forgotten, girl, it was you being a detective what started this off. Yer were full of righteousness then, wanting to help a family in trouble. Now ye're getting cold feet and don't want anything to do with it.'

'But I'd be hopeless. You'd be a much better choice, sunshine. Yer have no trouble talking to anyone . . . even complete strangers!'

'Yes, I am more talkative than you, girl, I admit. But sometimes I speak before I think. And I lose me rag and flare up, which is something you never do.' Monica leaned across and patted her hand. 'Besides, one look at your face and figure, Kate, and no man with red blood in his veins would walk away from yer. My money would be on you to pull it off.'

'Well you'd have to come with me 'cos I can't stop every man coming out of the factory and ask him if he's Greg Corbett, I'd look ridiculous. That's if I could find the ruddy factory! I haven't a clue where it is.'

'God, yer can be a right pain sometimes, girl! If I hadn't lived next door to yer for fifteen years, and been yer mate, I'd say yer were frightened of yer own shadow. But I know better, don't I? I know yer can be as stubborn as a bloody mule and yer'll get yer own way even if it kills yer.'

'Ay, I'm not stubborn! No more than you, anyway! And I don't always want me own way, yer make me sound like a spoilt brat.' Kate stuck her chin out, a sign she meant business. 'Ye're a fine one to talk about anyone getting their own way. I don't think Tom stands an earthly with yer. The poor man is henpecked!'

Monica's shoulders began to shake with laughter. 'Don't let him hear yer say that or he might start sticking up for himself, and we can't have that.'

'Ye're awful, you are! Yer don't know how lucky yer are, having Tom for a husband.' Kate couldn't keep back a chuckle when Monica started to contort her face. She had the ability to touch her nose with her tongue while squinting with both eyes. This always reduced Kate to hysterics. 'Will yer stop it, yer daft nit! We'll never get anywhere at this rate. Now put yer tongue back where it belongs and put yer eyes straight. Yer'll be stuck cock-eyed one of these days and it'll serve yer right.'

Monica pouted like a child. 'Will yer still be me mate if I go cross-eyed?'

Kate tutted while shaking her head. 'We're not going to get

anywhere the way we're going on. Will yer be serious for a few minutes until we get the problem sorted? I'll agree to go and see the lad if you'll come with me. I'll approach him on me own and even agree to tell him what he needs to know without rubbing him up the wrong way. But I'll only agree to that if you're around in case I need yer. Yer can stand on a corner somewhere and just keep an eye out to make sure he doesn't take off on me. I'm not a coward, but I'm no ruddy hero either.'

'I'll come with yer, girl, there's no way I'd let yer go on yer own. But we do have a problem, in that when Greg's coming out of work, so will our husbands be. How do we get over that little obstacle?'

'That had crossed me mind, sunshine. I've decided I'm going to have to tell John the truth. I can't just say I'm going somewhere with you and not say where or he'll think it's fishy. It'll be quite safe to let him in on it 'cos he wouldn't tell anyone.'

'I'll tell Tom as well or he'll wonder what's going on. But what about their dinners, and what about the kids? I wouldn't trust our Dolly not to say anything, she'd broadcast it all over the street and then it would be round the neighbourhood in no time.' A glimmer of a smile came to Monica's face. 'The women in the wash-houses would have a field day. A bit of juicy gossip like that would keep them going for weeks.'

'Couldn't we say we're going to see yer sister Beryl? We could always tell them she wasn't well and that we were going to do some shopping and housework for her.'

'Oh, our Beryl would love that, girl! Us saying she wasn't well would be inviting trouble, and she wouldn't thank us for it. Besides, the least thing after that and I'd get the blame. Every headache or twinge would be put down to me, and there's nothing our Beryl loves more than being a wounded soldier. It's the only thing she's good at, come to think of it.'

'How would she find out? She lives the other side of the city and yer only see her every blue moon.'

'Okay, we'll use our Beryl as an excuse. But if she does find out by some strange chance, I'll be pointing me finger at you. She's got a temper has my dear sister. She's definitely not as sweet-natured as I am.'

'One thing yer are good at, sunshine, is blowing yer own ruddy trumpet! There's nowt bashful about you! It's no wonder there's not a mirror in the house that's in one piece, your vanity was too much for them.'

Monica gave her friend full marks for that joke. 'Nice one, girl, I couldn't have thought of a better one meself. And for being so bleeding clever, I'm going to solve all our problems so yer don't have to worry yer pretty little head about them.' She sat up straight, laced her fingers and placed her two hands on her tummy. 'We'll tell our husbands the truth, use our Beryl as an excuse for the children, and make them wait for their dinner until we get back with a parcel of chips and scallops in our hands.'

'I agree with everything except the last bit,' Kate said. 'I'm on me uppers, I can't afford to go to a chippy for chips and scallops. But I can make them a pan of chips when I get home. It won't take me long, and it's cheaper.'

'Yer won't feel like standing in the kitchen when we get back, so it's the chippy whether yer like it or not. I owe yer tenpence for that bet, yer'll have plenty of money.'

'I'm not taking that off yer, the bet was only made as a joke!'

'I was the clever bugger who made it, 'cos I thought yer didn't know what yer were talking about. I told meself yer were talking through yer hat. So ye're not going to hurt my feelings by refusing to take the money, are you? If the positions were reversed, d'yer think I wouldn't take it off you? Too bloody right I would!'

Thinking of the extra coppers she needed for John to pay his tram fare, Kate didn't argue. But she'd find a way to make it up to her mate in some way, she'd make sure of that. 'All we need now is to find out what time Greg finishes work, what he looks like, and where the factory is.'

'I'll do that, girl, don't worry. When I see yer in the morning it'll be in hand. All you need to do is get yer little speech ready for when yer approach him. Not that he'll hear what ye're saying, he'll be too busy thinking his luck must be in with a beautiful woman accosting him.'

Chapter Five

'Can I go out now, Mam?' Billy asked as he pushed his empty plate away. 'I told Pete I'd get out right after me dinner so we can walk to the park and have a game of rounders with some of the lads from our class. The Watson brothers are bringing their bat and ball.'

'Yeah, go on, sunshine, it's too nice to stay indoors. But watch where ye're hitting the ball, otherwise yer'll have the parkie after yer and yer'll get into trouble.'

'I'll help yer clear away and wash the dishes before I go out,' Nancy said, reaching for her father's plate. 'Then I'm going next door to play with Dolly. We're fed up with Snakes and Ladders, so we're playing schools. Dolly's the teacher tonight, 'cos she said that's only right with it being her house.'

Kate grinned. How innocent children were. 'Is she better at sums than you are?'

Nancy pulled a face. 'No, not really, but I can't tell her that.'

Billy punched his sister's arm. 'Yer'll be all right, then, 'cos she won't know whether yer've got them right or wrong.'

Nancy glared at him. 'I will get them right 'cos I'm good at adding up and subtracting.'

'That's enough now,' John said, 'we don't want any squabbling. Yer can both go out and I'll give yer mam a hand with clearing away.'

Kate was glad to see the back of the children because she needed to explain to her husband what was happening. But she managed to contain herself until everywhere was tidy and the dishes washed and put away. Then she sat down facing him. 'I've got something to tell yer, sunshine. I couldn't talk in front of the children because I don't want them to know, for reasons yer'll understand when I bring yer up to date.'

'It sounds very cloak and dagger, love, what have yer been up to? Don't tell me yer've found yerself a rich sugar daddy, or yer've robbed a bank?'

'There's nothing funny about what I'm going to tell yer, as yer'll soon find out for yerself.' Kate wasted no time in getting it all off her chest. She was nervous and agitated, worrying how John would take it. She could tell by his face he was having difficulty believing it. But she didn't stop to explain her reasons or make excuses for what she had been party to. She knew what she was planning was the right thing. Even if John disagreed, it wouldn't put her off. 'So now yer know why I didn't want the kids to hear. I'll tell them I'm going with Monica to her sister's 'cos she's not well, and yer'll have to wait for yer dinners until I get in. I shouldn't be much after you, and I'll bring chips in with me.'

John struck a match and lit his Woodbine. 'Isn't it amazing the things that go on around yer and yer don't know anything about them? I feel sorry for the girl, and I do think the boy should shoulder some of the responsibility, but I don't know whether I like the idea of you getting mixed up in something that's really got nothing to do with yer! What will yer do if the lad tells yer to go to hell and mind yer own business?'

'Is that what yer'd tell our Billy to do if he got a girl into trouble when he grows up? I wouldn't think much of yer if yer did. And I wouldn't think much of meself if I didn't tell this boy there was a witness in the entry that night who recognized him. If he tells me to go to hell after that, I certainly won't take his advice. What I will do is tell both sets of parents.' There was determination in Kate's voice and in the set of her chin. 'And I don't care whether yer like it or not, John, my conscience wouldn't allow me just to walk away from what I see as an injustice.'

He was taken aback by his wife's firm stance. She was usually so easy-going, just taking things as they came and never really losing her temper. He'd never known her feel so strongly about anything in all the time they'd been married. 'All right, love, don't bite me head off! It's just I feel a bit concerned about yer facing this lad on yer own. Yer never know, he might lash out at yer.'

'I'm not going on me own, love, I'm going with Monica. She'll be there to jump in if things turn nasty. I don't think they will, though, 'cos I'm not going to have a go at the lad, I'll not be raising me voice or calling him bad names.'

John leaned forward and rested his elbows on his knees. 'If he so much as laid a finger on yer, love, he'd have me to answer to. And that is not an idle threat either. See how he liked facing a man.' He grunted in disgust. 'Mind you, from what yer tell me, he's not a man, he's a coward.'

'D'yer know what I think, sunshine? I think he's a young lad who got carried away, and now he's worried sick. Frightened of what he's done and frightened of telling his parents the truth because he doesn't want to hurt them. Let's give him the benefit of the doubt until it's proved otherwise. After all, he isn't the first young lad to get a girl into trouble, and he won't be the last. But if there's a slim chance of him standing by her, then I'm going to make sure he knows what that chance means, to his future and to Margaret's. Plus the two sets of parents and an unborn baby. I think that's worth sticking me neck out for. Don't yer agree with me, love?'

'I do think ye're doing right, love, and I admire yer for it. The only reason I said that about yer getting mixed up with something that doesn't concern yer was because I was afraid of how the lad would take it, and if he'd turn nasty with yer.'

'Well, this time tomorrow we'll know how much of a man he is. But don't forget, ye're not to breathe a word to the children. And when I come in, don't ask me how I got on unless the kids are out playing.' Kate stifled a yawn. 'I feel dead tired. It must be because me head's been going around and around. I'm not cut out for an exciting life, I much prefer to plod along, looking after me family, with just enough money to put food on the table and have a laugh.' A picture of her friend flashed before her eyes and she grinned. 'There's never a dull moment with Monica, yer couldn't be miserable if yer wanted to. I was trying to get her to be serious this morning, and in the middle of it she pulls one of those faces, with her tongue touching her nose and her eyes crossed. Honest, yer can't help laughing at her even when ye're not in the mood.'

John chuckled. 'I've seen her do that and she is funny. But she's been a good mate to yer over the years, hasn't she?'

'I couldn't have had a better one. We've never had a falling out in all those years. We can go at each other hammer and tongs, but we always end up laughing.'

'I hope ye're laughing when yer come in tomorrow night,' John said. 'If yer've got a smile on yer face, I'll know all has gone as yer hoped.'

'Keep yer fingers crossed for me, sunshine, 'cos what comes out of this meeting with Greg Corbett will affect a lot of people.' Kate reached down and picked up her sewing box from the side of her chair. 'Our Billy's only got two pairs of socks, and they've both got ruddy big holes in. I'll see if I can get one of the pairs darned tonight. Oh, and by the way, he always has a jam butty when he comes in from school, to keep him going until his dinner's ready. Will yer make sure he doesn't scoff the whole loaf or there'll be none for yer carry-out or our breakfast.'

'You'd better warn him about it tonight, love, because he's got two hours to go before I come home from work. In that time he could eat us out of house and home.'

'I'll tell him, but it'll be in one ear and out the other. I'll ask Nancy to keep an eye on him.' Kate broke off a length of darning wool and licked the end of it so it would go through the eye of the needle easier. 'While I'm doing this, sunshine, make us a nice cup of tea, eh? Me mouth is dry with all the talking I've been doing. But go easy on the milk, there's barely enough to last until the milkman calls in the morning.'

'I'll make yer a cuppa if I get a kiss in return.'

Kate smiled and lifted her face. 'A price I will gladly pay, my lord and master. I insist on giving you one kiss in advance and another when you have completed the task to my satisfaction.'

'Could I swap the kisses for one early night in bed? Surely as your lord and master I can make this an order if you refuse to comply.'

'I've got a feeling I'm going to have a headache tonight, sunshine, there's too much on me mind. But I'd say yer were in with a good chance if all goes well for me tomorrow.'

John shook his head. 'I think I'll pinch a kiss now, and take me chances on what tomorrow holds in store for me.'

'I don't know much about the gee-gees, love, but I think the bookies would say that was an each-way bet.' Kate tapped a finger on her temple, as though she was thinking something through. 'Or, should I say, yer were hedging yer bet?'

John bent down and claimed her lips for a second. Then, as he pulled away, he sighed. 'Are yer sure ye're going to have a headache tonight? Couldn't yer put it off until another night?'

'No, I couldn't, so don't be trying to get around me. And how long am I going to have to wait for this cup of tea? Me throat's as dry as a bone. If I don't have a headache tonight, I'll definitely have a sore throat.'

'All right, love, I've got the message. One cup of tea coming up, but no early night.'

The two women stepped down from the tram platform and linked arms. 'I'm shaking like a leaf, Monica,' Kate said. 'I can't stop meself, I'm so nervous.'

'Yer don't have to tell me, girl, I can feel yer!' Monica looked both ways before leading her friend across the road. 'If yer like, I'll swap places with yer. I'll meet Greg while you be the look-out.'

'No, I've got to do it, otherwise it'll haunt me for the rest of me life if I chicken out now.' Kate's lips were quivering, like the rest of her body. 'I'm determined to see it through to the bitter end.'

'And make yerself sick into the bargain! Don't be so bleeding stubborn, girl, and give in. The state of yer, yer wouldn't get yer words out proper, yer'd be stammering and stuttering. I'll do the necessary and you keep watch in case I need yer.'

Kate's voice sounded stronger when she said, 'I'm not giving in! Once I start talking to the lad I'll be all right. If I think there's any danger of me not being able to go through with it at the last minute, I'll give yer the wire and we'll swap places. But I really don't think that's going to happen. All I need to strengthen my resolve is to remember Betty's face and the despair in her eyes.'

'Oh, well, we're nearly there now, those are the factory gates over there. We're about ten minutes early, but it's better than being late and missing the lad.' Monica pulled her friend to a halt at the corner of a street facing the factory gates. 'We've got a good view from here, and I've been given a very clear description of what he looks like. Not that Betty knew she was giving me a description or she might have twigged. I just asked a few questions casually, as though they were of no importance. Anyway, he's nearly six foot, well-built, with light blond hair and blue eyes. From that he sounds like a nice-looking bloke.'

'Let's hope his nature is as good as his looks then, eh, sunshine? I lay in bed last night and willed meself to believe he'll think we're doing him a favour. That he really does love Margaret and wants to marry her. That it's his parents who are the wicked ones.'

It didn't seem to be ten minutes before they heard the sound of a hooter coming from the factory. 'This is it, girl,' Monica said. 'All the workers will be laying their tools down and taking off their overalls. In a few minutes they'll be coming through those gates. We'll have to keep our eyes peeled so we don't miss him.'

'When yer spot him, sunshine, give me a good push 'cos me feet will be stuck to the ground with fright. Don't give me time to think.'

And Monica did as she was told. There weren't many blokes coming through the gates with blond hair, not six-foot well-built ones anyway, so Greg Corbett was easy to pick out. 'That's him, girl!' The push nearly sent Kate flying. 'Make it quick before he gets too far away and we lose him.'

Kate couldn't feel her feet, but she knew she was crossing the road quickly. The young man she approached had his back to her, calling to a workmate who was going in the opposite direction, 'See yer tomorrow, Mike!'

She touched his arm. 'Excuse me, are you Greg Corbett?'

He looked down at her in surprise. He was struck by her beauty, but she was a complete stranger to him. 'Yes, that's me.'

Kate licked her dry lips. 'Could I have a word with yer? I won't keep yer long.'

Greg moved to the side of the gates, out of the way of the other workers coming through. This woman didn't look like a gypsy, but you never knew. 'I don't know who yer are, but if ye're trying to sell something yer've come to the wrong person, I'm skint.'

'I'm not selling anything, sunshine, and although we've never met before we don't live far from each other. I haven't come to cause trouble. In fact, just the opposite, I'm trying to help. I know something I think you should be made aware of, and after I've told yer it's up to you what yer do with the information.'

Greg was now looking at her with suspicion. 'I don't know what ye're talking about! I don't even know yer!'

Afraid he might walk away before she had a chance to explain,

Kate said, 'No, yer don't know me, but I think yer know Margaret Blackmore, don't yer?' She saw his face drain of colour and felt a pang of pity for him. But she'd got this far and had to carry on. 'Please don't think I've come looking for trouble or to lay blame. I'd just like yer to know what I've been told, then the rest is up to you. So will yer hear me out, please? Yer'll find it a lot easier coming from me than anyone else.'

'Did Margaret ask yer to come and talk to me?'

Kate shook her head. 'No, she knows nothing of this. In fact, I have never spoken to Margaret. But she and her parents will be told what I am about to tell you unless yer do what yer should have done when Margaret first told you she was expecting a baby.'

When Greg spoke there was no conviction in his voice. It was as though he was saying what he thought he should say, but his heart wasn't in it. 'Margaret says the baby is mine but it's not, it could be anybody's.'

'I don't know Margaret but I do know her family, and I doubt very much that she's the type of girl who goes with every Tom, Dick or Harry. By all accounts she's a very shy and reserved girl.' Out of the corner of her eye, Kate could see Monica standing on the corner of the street opposite, shifting impatiently from one foot to the other. 'Do you think Margaret is a good-time girl?'

He was shaking his head as he lowered his eyes to the ground. 'No, she's a nice, quiet girl. I would talk to her but me parents have forbidden me to go near her. If I did, and they found out, I'd get a dog's life.'

'I'm afraid they're not going to be allowed to bury their heads in the sand for much longer, Greg, because yer see a woman saw yer in the entry with Margaret, and she saw what was happening.' For a moment Kate thought he was going to faint. His face ashen, he stepped back as though he didn't want to hear what she was saying. 'Look, I'm not very happy about giving yer this news, and neither Margaret nor her parents have been told, but the woman who saw yer thinks it right they should know. I asked her not to speak out until I'd had a word with you. I thought perhaps now you'd admit you are the father of the baby, and tell your parents. If yer don't, they're in for two shocks. First that the baby is yours, and second that yer were seen in the entry by a neighbour. Yer might like to save them from the shame of that.'

'Yer wouldn't tell me mam, would yer?' He was obviously afraid of hurting his parents. 'It would break her heart.'

'I told yer I hadn't come to cause trouble and I haven't. Neither am I threatening yer. But what I have told yer is the truth. Wouldn't it be better for you to tell yer parents that you are the father of the baby Margaret is carrying than leave them open to gossip? Not to mention what the Blackmore family will have to go through when it becomes obvious Margaret is expecting. At the moment nobody knows anything except meself and a friend, and I can promise yer it won't go any further.' Kate could see Monica waving to catch her attention. 'I'll have to leave yer now because I need to get home and see to my family. It's up to you what yer do, it's your life. But don't forget, yer'll have to live with the consequences.'

When he saw Kate turn to walk away, Greg seemed to come to life. There were lots of questions running through his head and this woman was the only one he could ask. 'Will yer not tell me what yer name is?'

Kate smiled, her heart lighter now she'd actually done what she'd set out to do. But she still felt sorry for this lad whose world had probably just turned upside down. 'Me name is Kate Spencer, sunshine, and if there's anything else yer'd like to know, I'll help yer if I can. But yer'll have to be quick, my husband will be worrying.'

Greg had a feeling he could trust her so he asked, 'What d'yer think I should do? I don't want anyone to get hurt because of me. I was stupid, I never should have done what I did. And worse still, I should never have lied to me mam and dad and Margaret's parents.'

'Do yer like Margaret, sunshine?'

'Yeah, she's a smashing girl and we got on great. We'd still be friends if it hadn't been for my stupidity. I must have been mad! It was all my fault, but I left Margaret to carry the can. Doesn't say much for me, does it?'

'Then why don't yer see her and have a good talk to her? I'm sure yer'd find some way of meeting her. Yer know where she goes dancing and where she works. It's for the pair of yer to sort out what yer want to do, then tell both sets of parents. That's the advice I'd give yer if yer were my son. I'd be hurt, like your mam will be, but I'd try and give my son as much help as I could, for the sake of the child.' Kate touched his arm. 'After all, this baby didn't ask to be born.' She was stepping down from the pavement when a thought struck her and she quickly drew back her foot. 'By the way, nobody knows about this woman who saw yer in the entry, only me and a friend, and I'm hoping nobody need ever find out. I wouldn't mention it to Margaret if I were you, she's got enough on her plate without thinking the whole neighbourhood is talking about her. Anyway, the best of luck, sunshine! Ta-ra!'

Kate hurried across the wide road. As she neared the pavement, she heard Monica hiss, 'Carry on walking down the street, girl, 'cos he's still watching yer.' So Kate carried on, hearing her friend's footsteps behind her.

'It's okay now, kid, we're out of sight.' Monica linked arms with her. 'This street will take us to Marsh Lane, and we'll walk up there to Stanley Road where we can get a tram.' She could barely contain her curiosity. 'Well, don't keep me in suspense, how did yer get on? And what was your impression of him?'

'If yer'd slow down a bit, I might be able to tell yer! Yer walking me so fast I'm out of breath.' When their pace slowed,

Kate gave a sigh of relief. 'That's better, me heart isn't going hell for leather now. Anyway, I thought he was a nice lad. A bit confused, which is only natural, with his head telling him one thing and his mother telling him another.'

'Take me through everything that was said, girl, and how he responded. Don't leave anything out, 'cos I deserve to be included after standing like a lemon on the other side of the road trying to lip-read.'

As they walked up the two streets that would take them to Stanley Road and the tram to carry them home to their families, Kate repeated everything. 'So there yer have it, sunshine, yer know as much as me now.'

Monica was very impressed. 'Ay, yer did very well, I'm real proud of yer. What d'yer think he'll do now he knows about Winnie?'

'I never mentioned her by name, so for heaven's sake, Monica, don't you either! She'd go mad if she thought I was broadcasting it everywhere. She will tell Betty if nothing comes of this meeting with Greg, but I've got a feeling she won't have to. I don't know what makes me think so, but a little voice in me head is saying that some good will come of our journey to Seaforth. That our time wasn't wasted.' Kate pulled her friend to a halt and said, 'If I tell yer what I'm hoping will happen, yer won't repeat it or tell me it's wishful thinking on my part, will yer? Promise?'

Monica made a sign across her chest. 'Cross my heart and hope to die, if this day I tell a lie. Go on, girl, yer've done well so far, I'm not going to disagree with anything yer say.'

'Well, as yer know, I suggested he try and see Margaret so they could sort things out between them. I'm praying he takes me up on that, and in the end does the right thing by her. Then the story would have a happy ending for everyone.'

'I hope we find out if anything comes of it.'

'That's your part of the operation, sunshine. You keep in touch with Betty. She's bound to tell yer if Greg puts in an appearance.'

Monica tugged on her arm. 'Here's our tram, girl, don't let's miss it or my feller will lock me out.'

Greg stood watching the woman walk down the street away from him. She'd said her name was Kate Spencer and she lived near him, but he'd never seen her before. She was nice, though, and didn't treat him like the rotter he felt. It was because she didn't condemn him that he stopped to think seriously about what she'd told him. Had she approached him in a bullying manner, he would have bluffed his way out of it and sent her packing. He knew only too well how badly he'd behaved, and wasn't proud of himself, but he didn't need a stranger lecturing him about it.

'Are yer waiting for someone, Greg?' The man coming through the gates worked on the same furnace as him. 'Let yer down, has she?'

'No, I'm not waiting for anyone, Ted, I was just taking advantage of the fresh air after being in that stifling foundry all day.'

'Come on, I'll walk with yer to the tram stop.' Ted jerked his head.

'I think I'll walk part of the way home, Ted, get some clean air in me lungs. I'll walk with yer to the stop, but I won't get on the tram. It's shanks's pony for me.'

'It's easy to see you haven't got a wife waiting for yer.' Ted was a man in his fifties, old enough to be Greg's father. 'If I'm five minutes late, the wife's at the door with a face on her that would stop the clock. Frightening it is.'

'I bet she wouldn't like to hear yer saying that.' Greg tried to sound interested, but really his mind was miles away. 'She'd take the poker to yer.'

Ted heard a tram rumbling behind them and took to his heels. 'I'll see yer tomorrow, mate, if I can dodge the poker.'

Left alone, Greg walked slowly, deep in thought. There was a niggle at the back of his mind, telling him his mother would go mad if he was late getting home and his dinner ruined. But for once he decided to banish all thoughts of her and concentrate on what he would like to do with his life. He thought of Margaret, and how he'd used her then left her to shoulder all the blame. She must really hate him now. He had wanted to go round to her house and talk to her only his mam and dad wouldn't hear of it. But like that Mrs Spencer had said, it was up to him and Margaret to sort out what they wanted, then tell their parents. And he should be man enough to do that. He'd be twenty very soon, old enough to think for himself. And Mrs Spencer had given him plenty to think about.

Forgetting the time and his ruined dinner, Greg asked himself if he had the nerve to seek out Margaret? And if he did, would she even talk to him after what he'd done to her? He'd called her a liar by saying the baby she was carrying wasn't his. Could he ever expect her to forgive him for that? He could soon find out by asking her, but was he man enough to try?

Billy was playing in the street when Kate and Monica turned the corner. The boy raced towards his mother. 'Where've yer been, Mam? We're all starving! I've only had a round of bread, our Nancy wouldn't let me have any more.' The smell from the parcel his mother was holding close to her chest wafted up his nostrils and the frown on his young face turned to a wide grin. 'I'll let yer off this once, seeing as yer've come bearing food.'

'If any of the neighbours heard you, they'd think I starved yer! This is the very first time in yer life that I haven't been in when yer've come home from school, so don't pretend ye're badly done to.' She passed him the steaming parcel. 'Run on with these, sunshine, and ask yer dad to put the kettle on.'

When they got to Kate's front door, Monica said, 'Well, it's been a good day, girl, thanks to you. A day of accomplishments, wouldn't yer say?'

'More a day of hope, I think. Only time will tell, though. Anyway, I'll see yer tomorrow, all being well. Ta-ra!'

John was in the kitchen setting the plates out, and Kate grinned when she heard him growl, 'Keep yer dirty fingers off the chips, Billy, or yer'll poison the lot of us.'

'I only pinched one, Dad! I haven't mauled the whole lot!'

Nancy was setting the knives and forks out. 'He's a holy terror when you're not here, Mam. Yer should have heard him 'cos I'd only let him have one slice of bread. I told him it's not a tummy he's got, it's a bottomless pit.'

'Ah, well, we've got to make allowances for him 'cos he's a growing lad.' Kate walked to the kitchen door. 'Am I going to get waited on tonight?'

John was happy to see her smiling face. It meant she hadn't had a hard time with the lad she'd gone to meet. 'You are, my love, if this son of ours will move out of the way. He's actually counting the chips I'm putting on each plate! And yer'd better tell me how many scallops are in the other parcel before he bursts a blood vessel.'

'There's two scallops each, so don't be moaning, Billy,' Kate said, ''cos I'm dead tired and me feet are killing me.'

'How did yer find Monica's sister?' This was one way of finding out quickly if things had gone well, instead of having to wait until the kids were either out playing or in bed. 'Does she need looking after?'

Kate crossed her fingers before telling the lie. 'She's just been a bit under the weather, that's all. But I'm sure she'll be fine in a day or two. There's no need for me and Monica to go again, thank goodness.'

John had to be content with that until the children went out to play for the last hour before dusk. Then he stretched his long legs, made himself comfortable and lit a Woodbine. 'Well, let's have it, love.'

So for the second time in an hour, Kate had to go over the

whole episode again. When she'd finished she sighed. 'So now we've just got to wait and see.'

'I didn't think yer'd have the nerve to go through with it,' John admitted. 'But I'm really proud of yer, love.'

'I'm pretty proud of meself, even though I shouldn't say so. And I feel certain some good will come of it.' She tilted her head and smiled across the room at him. 'There's another thing I'm certain of, which I believe will be of more interest to you.'

'Oh, aye, love, and what's that?'

'That this is one night I will not be having a headache.'

John's smile was full of mischief. 'I think I'll put the clock forward half an hour. The kids won't notice.'

'Don't you dare! You're terrible, you are!' Kate tried to look as though she disapproved of his suggestion, but she couldn't keep a smile back. 'Make it fifteen minutes forward and I'll go along with yer.'

Chapter Six

Greg took a key from his jacket pocket as he neared his home. He was three-quarters of an hour later than his usual time for getting in from work, and knew his mother would be in a state. He could see it in his mind's eye now. She would take off on him as soon as he put his foot over the door, mad at him because his dinner was ruined, and also because she'd been worried sick in case anything had happened to him. She liked everything to be just right, did his mam. Meals on time, and everywhere in the house immaculate. She was very houseproud and kept their small two-up-two-down like a palace. If you dropped a crumb while you were eating, you could bet your life it would not have time to reach the floor before his mother caught it and threw it in the grate. She was so fussy, she sometimes got on his nerves, and his dad's, but they both loved her dearly, no matter what.

Greg felt so sad and guilty that he was about to hurt her more than she'd ever been hurt in her life. He would give anything not to have to do it, but on the long walk home he'd considered every aspect of the situation, and all the people who were suffering because of his actions. He had committed a terrible wrong. The only way forward, for all concerned, was for him to put things right.

'Where the blazes have yer been?' Maude Corbett had the front door open before her son had a chance to put his key in the lock. 'I've been backward and forward to the ruddy window for the last half-hour, sick with worry in case yer'd had an accident.' As he passed her, she added, 'And yer bleeding dinner has dried up, it's not fit to eat now!'

His father, Albert, lifted his eyebrows in sympathy for what he knew his son was in for. He'd had to listen to his wife's ravings for nearly half an hour, and his head was aching. 'Let the lad get in before yer take off on him! Yer've got yerself in such a state, when there's probably a perfectly good reason for him being late. I did try to tell yer that, but would yer listen? Would yer hell! Yer had the lad in hospital after being run over by a car or tram. Yer always think the worst, you do, woman!'

Maude took a deep breath and tried to steady her nerves before asking, 'What kept yer so late, love? Yer know I worry about yer.' Greg was her only child and she'd always watched over him like a mother hen. 'Tell us, then I'll do yer some chips and an egg.'

Greg swallowed hard. He couldn't sit and eat a meal, it would choke him. He had to unburden himself now, and suffer the consequences, as he knew they too would suffer. 'Sit down, Mam, there's something I've got to tell you both.'

'Leave it until yer've had something to eat, son,' she said. 'Yer've usually had yer dinner by this time, yer must be starving.'

'No, I want to tell yer now, while I've still got the courage.' He waited until his mother was seated, then took a chair opposite. He clasped his hands and laid them on the table, bowing his head. When he looked up, it was to see a worried frown on her face, and for a split second he thought he couldn't go through with it. But if he chose the easy way out now, he'd have to live with it until the day he died.

'I've been a coward, Mam. I lied to you and me dad about Margaret. I am the one who got her into trouble, but I didn't have the guts to admit it.' He heard her gasp, and also his father's sharp intake of breath. 'I've got to put things right, Mam, I can't leave her to shoulder all the responsibility when it was more my fault than hers.' He lifted a hand. 'No, let me finish, Mam, please. I know this is breaking yer heart, but it's not easy for me, either. And just think what Margaret and her parents have been going through, particularly when I said the baby had nothing to do with me. How could I do that to her?' His head dropped. 'It was all my fault. I persuaded her to go down an entry for a kiss, she really didn't want to, yet she's been left with all the shame and the worry.' Suddenly it all became too much for Greg. His shoulders shook with the sobs he'd tried to hold back. 'What sort of a man does that make me? A liar and a coward.'

Maude wiped away her tears with the back of her hand as she rounded the table to hold her son in her arms. Seeing him crying, and calling himself a liar and a coward, helped her to forget for a while the devastating news she'd been told. He was now her main concern. 'Don't cry, son, 'cos yer'll have me at it. I won't say that me and yer dad aren't shocked, it's the last thing we expected. But what's been done can't be undone, and what's been said can't be taken back. Both me and yer dad said some pretty nasty things to Margaret's parents when they came around, but it's never too late to say ye're sorry or ask forgiveness. We'll do anything to help, and it's not the end of the world. There's still time to put things right with the girl but I wouldn't want yer to rush into asking her to marry yer if yer don't love her, because that would mean two people imprisoned in a lifetime of unhappiness.'

Maude felt she couldn't say any more right at that moment. Shock was beginning to set in, and the implications of his confession were making her feel sick. 'Look, I'll put the kettle on while you have a good talk to yer dad, man to man, like. Yer might find it easier talking to him.' Maude made her way through to the kitchen where she leaned against the sink and softly cried her heart out.

'I've got to say it's bad news, Greg, I would never have thought that of yer.' Albert wasn't going to smooth it over, the lad had to be made to realize exactly what trouble he'd brought to their door, not forgetting the heartache of the young lass and her family. God, how they must be suffering! 'What on earth possessed yer to do this to a young girl? It could ruin her life because no decent man would take her on, knowing she's got an illegitimate child.' His voice softened when he saw the despair in his son's eyes. 'Yer said yer were going to see her. Well, it's the least yer can do. Although saying ye're sorry yer lied and left her in the lurch isn't much use to her.'

Greg nodded in agreement. 'I haven't the guts to call to her house, but I'll wait for her coming out of work. She might refuse to talk to me after all the lies I've told, but that's a chance I'll have to take. I'll clock off half an hour early tomorrow so I can be outside the factory where she works before she gets out.'

'And what do yer intend to say to her, son?'

'I don't know, Dad, I can't even think straight at the moment. All I know is, I've got to do something. And I wouldn't blame her father if he came round and belted me, 'cos that is what I deserve.'

'I'm not going to say yer don't deserve it, son, because if I was in his position that's precisely what I would do. It wouldn't help but as a father I'd feel it my duty to punish the man who had sullied my daughter's name.' Albert sighed. What an absolute mess his son had made of his life. His reputation would be in the gutter. No decent girl would touch him with a barge pole after this. 'Me and yer mam have only met this girl once, we really know nothing about her. Did she give her consent to what happened? In other words, did she go down the entry willingly?'

'To be honest, she wasn't very happy about it in case we were seen. But when she did, it was because she thought it was only for a kiss. She's a nice girl, Dad, decent like the rest of her family. But I've certainly messed that up for her. When the neighbours find out, she'll be called a cheap slut and people will be looking down on her. She doesn't deserve that, Dad, honest she doesn't.'

'Then go and see her. At least she'll know there's someone standing by her. And when yer've done that, me and yer mam will call on her parents and let them know we're all in this together.' There was something else on Albert's mind. He searched for the right words in which to put a question to which he needed to know the answer. 'Son, I want yer to tell me the truth. Have yer ever done this with any other girl?'

'No, Dad, I swear! I'm shy around girls. That's why I always danced with Margaret, 'cos she's on the shy side as well. I've walked her home from the dance dozens of times, and we'd never even kissed before – er – before that night.'

'Okay, son, I believe yer. But don't say a word to anyone until yer've met up with the lass herself. And yer must tell her, honestly, the way yer feel, how sorry yer are, and what help yer'll give her. See what her response is, then me and yer mam will take it from there.' Albert jerked his head towards the kitchen, and in a low voice, murmured, 'I think yer need to mend some fences now, son, and yer should start by giving yer mam a big hug. I've a feeling she's badly in need of comfort.'

Greg pushed back his chair. 'Thanks, Dad, for taking it the way yer have. I really thought there'd be fists flying, and I'd be sent packing and told never to darken yer door again.' He put a hand on his father's shoulder. 'I'll go and give me mam a big hug and kiss, though that's not going to take the pain away, is it? But I swear I'll make it up to both of yer, and one day yer'll have reason to be proud of me.'

Albert wasn't a man given to tears but he could feel a lump forming in his throat when he told his son, 'Greg, me and yer mam have been proud of yer since the day yer were born.'

As soon as John walked through the front door on Saturday, Kate was waiting for him with hand outstretched. 'I haven't a thing in for our dinner, sunshine, so yer'll have to wait until I come back from the shops. Talk about Mother Hubbard having a bare cupboard! I'm in the same boat. Cupboards and purse empty.'

'Yer might at least have let me sit down before holding

yer hand out.' John passed his wage packet over and smiled. 'I dunno, I've slaved all week and I'm not even allowed to hold the money.'

'I won't have it in my hand for long, sunshine, by the time I put me rent money aside, and coal and gas money.' Kate slit open the small, square buff-coloured envelope with her finger, and emptied the contents on to the table. 'I'll take the ten-bob note for now, it'll get me everything I need for the weekend.' She picked up the basket which was placed ready near the door. 'The kids are out playing so make yerself a drink. I'll be back as quick as I can to make us something to eat.'

As he watched his wife walk through the door, John felt so guilty he wanted to call her back. The trouble was, while he was delighted with his good fortune, Kate might not appreciate it. A bloke he worked with, Bill, had a bet on the horses every day. He could afford it, though, 'cos he had three children working. And he was a lucky bloke, winning more in a week than he lost. On Thursday he'd told John he had a dead cert in the two o'clock race, and was putting a shilling on to win. He'd tried to coax his workmate to have a tanner on but John told him he was skint. He could have kicked himself yesterday when Bill had come in all smiles to say the nag had romped home at ten to one, giving him winnings of ten shillings. The bookie's runner had given him another sure thing for that day, and Bill was gambling half-a-crown on the horse his informant told him couldn't lose.

John dropped into his favourite chair and let his mind wander back to yesterday, and the conversation on the factory floor. 'Have a tanner on, mate, it yer can't afford any more,' Bill had said. 'I got this tip straight from the horse's mouth, and yer'll be bloody sorry if yer miss out.'

'Bill, I haven't a penny to spare, never mind sixpence. Perhaps next week I'll be a bit better off and I'll have a flutter.'

'I mightn't have any good tips next week,' Bill said. 'Yer've got to strike while the iron's hot, and I'm having a lucky streak.

Tell yer what, I'll put a tanner on for yer, and yer can pay me back when yer get yer wages. Or next week some time, I'm in no hurry.'

And that was how it happened. John had had no idea the horse had won until this morning when Bill came swaggering in like a toff and handed him six shillings. 'Wouldn't yer be a sorry man now if I hadn't talked yer into having a bet? She romped home first, at twelve to one.'

John was over the moon. 'How come yer always bet on a horse that's almost an outsider? Yer never put money on the favourite.'

'It's not worth backing a favourite, mate, unless yer've got more money than sense and can put a couple of hundred quid on. If I backed a favourite, I'd only get me money back, and perhaps an extra shilling. With an outsider, yer taking a chance but it's worth it in the end.'

And that was how it came about that John had six shillings burning a hole in his pocket. He would willingly give Kate five and be delighted to see a smile light up her face. But he was afraid she wouldn't take kindly to his having won the money by gambling.

Kate pressed Monica's elbow to speed up her pace. 'I don't want to be too long at the shops 'cos my lot haven't had anything to eat yet. I'll buy bacon and eggs, they're about the quickest to get ready.'

'Yeah, that's an idea. And we could ask Sid in the green-grocer's if he's got any over-ripe tomatoes. There's nothing I like better than bacon and eggs with mushy tomatoes. Ooh, me mouth's watering at the thought of rubbing me bread in the dip. We'll get a bag between us, and he'll only charge us a penny or two. He'll be glad to get rid of them because they'll be past selling by Monday.' Monica didn't see an uneven flag-stone and tripped. If she hadn't been linking Kate, she'd have fallen face forward. 'Blimey! I nearly came a cropper there. If I hadn't been holding on to your arm, I'd have gone flat on me face.'

Kate grinned at the thought. 'So what do I get in return for saving yer front teeth?'

'Ay, don't be getting greedy, girl, I've already done one favour for yer this morning.'

'Done me a favour? I didn't ask yer to do me no favour.'

'There yer are, yer see! You never think of me, but I'm always thinking of ways to help you. So this morning I nipped down to Betty's, just to see how she was, like, but hoping she'd give me some news of Greg Corbett. But not a word, so I can only think he's chickened out.'

Kate shook her head and her rich auburn hair bounced with the movement. 'Give the lad a chance! It's not even one full day since I saw him, I'm not giving up hope yet.'

The women turned into Irwin's grocery store where they bought their bacon, eggs, and other groceries to last them over the weekend. The next stop was the butcher's where the pair argued with Bob until he found them a breast of lamb each which wasn't too fatty. Then on to the greengrocer's where they bought their potatoes, a cabbage and a pound of squashed tomatoes for a penny.

'Let's make a dash for it now, sunshine, John and the kids must be starving.' Kate broke into a hop, skip and a jump type of walk as she was hindered by the heavy basket. 'But I'll give yer a knock this afternoon, and if the weather stays fine, we could walk to the park for some fresh air.'

'Good thinking, girl, it'll get us out of the house for an hour. Give a knock on the wall when ye're ready. Are yer getting changed?'

'Yeah!' Kate looked down at herself. 'I'm not going for a walk like this, I'd never get a click.'

'With your face, girl, yer'd get a click even if yer were wearing a bleeding sack. So count yer blessings and shut up.'

* * *

The children were still out playing when Kate got home, and John thought he'd never have a better opportunity. As he was helping his wife take the groceries out of the basket, he took his chance. 'Listen, love, I've got something to tell yer, and I want yer to promise yer won't fly off the handle until yer've heard me out?'

'Oh, lord, what have yer been up to now? If it's anything serious then of course I'll fly off the handle! What d'yer expect?'

'It's not that serious, for heaven's sake! Anyone would think I'd robbed a bank! Just stand there and listen, before the kids come in.'

Kate leaned back against the sink and listened as John told her word for word what had happened, and how he came to have six shillings in his pocket.

She looked sceptical at first, her brows furrowed. 'Is that the whole truth, or just what yer think I want to hear?'

'If yer don't believe me, yer can go and ask Bill. Of course it's the truth! I could keep the money for meself and say nothing, and yer'd be none the wiser. But I wanted to give yer a nice surprise, 'cos it's not often I can give yer anything.'

Kate was immediately contrite. Her husband must have been expecting her to be over the moon, as he probably had been. Instead, she'd practically called him a liar. Flinging her arms around his neck, she kissed him soundly. 'I'm a miserable so-and-so, aren't I? I shouldn't have doubted yer. And I'm made up that yer can have a few bob in yer pocket, and I'll have the same to help with the housekeeping.'

'I'll just keep a shilling for meself, love, and you can have the other five. I get me tram fare and me ciggie money, so a shilling extra is enough for me.'

'No, we'll split it.' Kate thought that was fair. After all, as he said, he could have kept the money for himself and said nothing. 'Then we'll both be well off.'

'I want yer to have the five shillings,' John insisted. 'Yer can put it towards something for yerself or the kids.' He waved a hand when she went to argue. 'No, me mind's made up. It's not often I've been in a position to give yer a bit extra, so take the money and make me a happy man.'

Kate put her arms around his waist and squeezed him tight. 'It won't be just put towards something, sunshine, yer can get quite a lot from Paddy's Market for five bob. I bet I can buy presents for the kids and meself for that money. But don't tell them, let it be a surprise.' She squeezed him again before letting go. 'Thank you, love, that's wonderful and has really cheered me up.'

They heard footsteps on the lino in the living room and moved apart. 'This sounds like Billy,' Kate whispered. 'Don't forget, not a word or he'll be giving me a list as long as yer arm of the things he wants me to buy for him.'

'Oh, ye're home, are yer?' Billy, as usual, was sporting a dirt-streaked face and knees. 'Me tummy thinks me throat's cut! How long am I going to have to wait for something to eat, Mam? Me stomach's rumbling.'

'Ye're not the only one in the house, son,' John told him. 'We're all hungry, but yer mam can't perform miracles. If she's got no money, she can't buy food. So be like the rest of us and show a little patience.'

'Aye, okay, but can I at least know what we're having so I can picture it in me mind? That should keep me tummy quiet for a while.'

Standing on tip-toe, Kate reached for the frying pan from the top shelf. 'We're having bacon, egg and tomato. It'll only take me ten minutes, so go and find our Nancy and tell her. And don't think ye're sitting down at the table with the dirt yer've got on yer. It's enough to put anyone off their food. Find Nancy, then come back and get a good scrub.'

Billy's face held an expression of disgust. What was it about grown-ups that they always wanted you to be spotlessly clean? When he went out to play again after his dinner, he'd be black in no time. Pete's mam wasn't so bad, it didn't seem to bother her. She'd once said that a bit of dirt never did no one no harm. 'Do I have to?'

'Yes, do as ye're told,' John said, trying to look severe while all the time he was thinking the boy wouldn't be normal if he never got dirty. 'Go and find yer sister.'

'I don't need to go and find her 'cos she's only next door with that daft Dolly Parry. I'll knock on the wall for her.'

'Yer will not!' Kate said, as she laid slices of streaky bacon in the hot fat. 'Go and knock on the front door, and don't be so ruddy lazy. And less of the "daft Dolly Parry", 'cos if her mam hears yer, she wouldn't think twice about boxing yer ears.'

'I'm not only picking on Dolly,' the boy growled as he walked away, 'I think all girls have got a screw loose.'

When he was out of earshot, John said, 'I don't want yer to spend all the money on the kids, I want yer to buy something for yerself as well.'

'Don't worry, I will!' Kate stepped back, out of range of the spitting fat. 'Yer'd be amazed what yer can get from the market for five bob. I might come home this afternoon looking like Lady Muck in all me finery.' She turned the bacon over and placed the three eggs close to hand, ready to crack into the frying pan when the bacon was done. 'Yer like yer egg runny, don't yer, so yer can make a butty with it?'

'I'm so hungry, love, I don't care how it comes. I'll slice some rounds of bread while I'm standing here.'

'Don't cut it too thick, 'cos I'll make us a piece of fried bread each. The kids love that, and it'll make up for them having to wait so long.'

It was half-past two by the time Kate got the dinner over, and John saw her casting an anxious eye at the clock. 'You get yerself ready, love, I'll see to everything here. Otherwise it'll be time to come back before yer get there.'

Kate didn't have to think twice. 'Ye're a pal, sunshine.' And because Nancy and Billy were still at the table, she added, 'Yer never know, I might bring yer a lollipop back.'

The idea of his dad sucking a lollipop brought chuckles from Billy. 'I don't think they make them that big, Mam. But I'll tell yer what, I'll give me dad a hand with clearing away and yer can bring *me* a lollipop. I wouldn't look as daft as me dad.'

'Ye're certainly not daft!' Nancy pulled a face at her brother. 'Yer only want to help if yer get something for it! If me mam's going to buy yer anything, it should be a gobstopper, to shut yer up.'

Kate looked at John. 'You can sort them out while I change into something decent.' She touched the skirt she was wearing. 'This is as old as the hills and makes me look like Orphan Annie.'

Monica was ready when Kate knocked. 'I thought yer were never coming! Have yer seen the blinking time?'

'Never mind the time, d'yer feel like coming to Paddy's Market instead?'

'What have yer changed yer mind for? Yer were full of going for a walk in the park.'

'That's before my feller gave me five bob to do what I like with. He had a tanner bet on a horse that came in at twelve to one. So I thought I'd get meself a blouse and something for the kids.'

Monica turned back into the house. 'Just hang on a second.' She stood in front of her husband's chair and pulled down the paper he was reading so she could see his face. 'Have yer got two bob to spare, Tom?'

His eyebrows shot up. 'No, I haven't got two bob to spare! Where the hell d'yer think I'd get that from? I've only got enough to see me through the week.'

'Oh, I know what yer've got, love, yer don't have to tell me. Yer've got enough for yer ciggies every day, and the paper, and we mustn't forget yer beer money either! Yer won't let yerself go short of anything, will yer?' Monica's face was set. 'Well, it's about time yer thought of somebody else. That somebody being me. The woman who cooks and cleans for yer, washes yer clothes, does the ironing, and everything else a skivvy does. But let me tell yer, unless yer cough up with two bob, this skivvy is going on strike. I'll look after me and our Dolly, you can see to yerself. And don't for one moment think I won't carry the threat out, 'cos I ruddy well will.'

Tom folded the paper over while he lifted the left side of his bottom from the chair to reach into his trouser pocket. He pulled out a silver coin and held it up. 'Half-a-crown, will that keep yer quiet?'

'As a mouse.' Monica's hips did a little wriggle. 'Like I tell anyone that'll listen to me, I've got a husband in a million.'

'Don't push yer luck,' Tom said, while his eyes told her he loved the bones of her. 'If there's any change, I'd like it back.'

Monica was on her way out when she answered, 'Oh, I think I can safely say there won't be any change, lad, not even a ha'penny.'

Kate was shaking her head in wonder when her friend stepped into the street. 'Yer'd get away with murder, you would. And although I know yer were being sarcastic to Tom, yer do have a husband in a million, but yer don't appreciate him! It would be no use me asking John for two bob any time, 'cos he wouldn't have it. The poor bloke works all week and doesn't see much for it at the end.'

They began to walk up the street to the main road. 'I'm fed up telling yer that we're a bit better off than you 'cos we've only got one child!' Monica was wearing a cotton floral dress with a scooped neck, and looked nice and cool. 'I mean, your Billy can eat nearly as much as a man, and look at the trousers he goes through! One extra in the house can make a hell of a lot of difference.'

Kate, also in a cotton floral dress, gave her friend a slight dig in the ribs. 'Ah, but I'll see the difference when my two are working. I'll have the laugh on you then.'

Although they saw each other every day, the two mates always found something to talk about and the conversation never stopped until they stepped off the tram near the market. 'My God, have yer seen the crowds!' Kate's mouth gaped. 'We'll get trampled to death!'

'The nice weather brings them all out,' Monica said knowingly. 'It's better than looking through yer window on to a yard. Anyway, let's push our way through until we see a stall selling ladies' clothes. I fancy a nice blouse in a blue or lilac.' And Monica didn't let anyone stand in her path. If she wanted a blouse, a blouse she would have, come hell or high water.

Kate got behind her and held on to her waist. 'Go on, sunshine, I'm right behind yer.' Being at the back of her mate, she didn't see the angry glares directed their way from people who hadn't come to buy but to meander at will. Fresh air was what they were after, not to be pushed aside by a woman who was hell-bent on reaching a stall.

'Here yer are, girl, dresses and blouses galore.' Monica pulled her friend round to the side of her. 'Feast yer eyes on them and take yer pick.'

'I'll find out the prices before I get me hopes up.' Kate spotted a pile of boys' summer shirts. 'Can yer see how much it says on that card by the boys' shirts?'

'One and three, girl. Now that's not at all bad, is it?' The woman standing next to Monica wouldn't have any difficulty remembering how she got her bruises when she got undressed that night. Whether her husband would believe her was a different matter. 'Ay, and they're a decent cotton, too!'

Kate was starting to get her hopes up. 'Can yer catch the attention of the man and ask how much those blouses are? You've got more cheek than I have.'

The woman next to Monica stepped in then. Rather than get a dig in the ribs, or an elbow in her eye, she volunteered the information. 'Girls' blouses are elevenpence ha'penny, and women's one and six. And they're good quality for the money.'

'Thank you, sunshine.' Kate smiled at the woman before tugging on Monica's dress. 'Get us a white shirt for Billy, a lilac blouse for Nancy and a pale green one for me.' She opened her purse which was clutched tight in her hand so she wouldn't lose it, and took out two florins. 'You get them, sunshine, yer've got a louder voice than me. There's four bob, and I get it to three shillings and ninepence so I want threepence change. I'll stand at the back of the crowd now to give someone else a chance.'

Kate stood and watched the hustle and bustle. She loved the atmosphere of the market, except today it was a bit too crowded and she felt sticky with the heat.

'Here yer are, girl!' Monica pushed her way through the heaving mass and handed a paper bag to her. 'I think we did very well on the money we had. And we've both got some over to play with.'

'D'yer know what I was thinking?' Kate put the threepenny bit in her purse. 'There's second-hand stalls here where yer can get dresses and skirts for coppers. Some of them are rags, only fit for dusters, but now and again yer come across something that would come up all right after a good wash. I wouldn't mind having a look for something for me and Nancy. If I saw a dress that took me eye, I could unpick it and make it into a skirt for one of us.'

'That's a good idea, girl! I'm pretty good with me fingers, and I could do with some summer skirts too. Let's look for a stall.'

Later, as they walked towards the tram stop, they were carrying an old torn paper bag, which was all the stallholder had had to hold the three dresses and two skirts they'd got for two bob. It was a happy twosome that boarded the tram. 'We'll have to sort the money out when we get home and see what condition the clothes are in,' Kate said. 'I'd like two of the dresses and one of the skirts, so there won't be much in it, 'cos I paid one and threepence, and you paid ninepence.'

'We'll call it quits, girl. As long as we've got the tram fare home, I'm happy. And I think we've done very well. Although our Dolly won't be happy with me, I've got nothing for her unless I can unpick the skirt and cut it to fit her. That's an idea, isn't it? If not, Tom will have to fork out again next week. But all I want now is to put me feet up, 'cos they're practically talking to me.'

Chapter Seven

'I've nothing in for the tea, sunshine, so I'll stop at the corner shop and get some corned beef for sandwiches. Are yer coming in with me?'

Monica nodded. 'Yeah, I'll get some meself for quickness.' She pulled a face. 'Now we're nearer home, I'm starting to feel guilty about our Dolly. She's not going to be too happy when she sees Nancy with a new blouse.'

'Yer can nip down to the market on Monday and get her one.' Then Kate remembered herself as a young girl, how easy it was to have your heart broken over a little thing which in later life you would take in your stride. 'I'll tell yer what, sunshine, I'll show our Nancy her blouse but I won't let her wear it until Dolly has one. Does that make yer feel any better?'

'It makes me feel better, but I don't know about our Dolly. She'll go mad being left out, especially as they're best mates. And it's not really fair on Nancy, expecting her to wait until next week. A new dress or blouse is a big thing for a young girl.'

'I'd offer to keep Nancy's back until yer had one for Dolly, but John would be disappointed. It's the first time he's ever had any money to spare and he'll be dying to see their faces.' Kate put on her thinking cap. 'Our Nancy is very understanding, I'm sure she won't mind keeping quiet about the blouse for a few days. She wouldn't want to upset Dolly.'

'Tell her I asked if she'd do it as a special favour.' Monica stood aside to let Kate go through the door of the corner shop first. 'In fact, I've got a spare penny in me pocket, I'll get some Mint Imperials and they can divide them between them.'

Les Riley was busy serving at the far end of the counter while

Violet was leaning her elbows on it, eating a sticky bun. She grinned when she saw the two friends. 'Don't tell me yer've come in for a quarter of Mint Imperials split into two bags! Me and my feller will never get rich at that rate.'

'Keep yer hair on, Mrs Woman!' Monica winked at Kate before saying, 'No, it's not all we've come in for, smart arse, so there! We want two separate quarters of corned beef, if yer can be bothered putting that bun down and moving yerself.'

Vi popped the last mouthful of the bun into her mouth before dusting her hands together. 'I've been on me feet since six this morning, queen. Surely yer don't begrudge me a five-minute break?' Her round chubby face creased into a wide smile and she nodded to the bags the women were carrying. 'Been out spending all yer money, have yer? Did yer get anything nice, then?'

Kate nodded. 'Yeah, we got ourselves a blouse each. They're only from the market, but I think they're nice.'

The shopkeeper put a block of corned beef on the slicing machine and began to turn the handle. 'D'yer want it cut thick or thin, ladies?'

'Middling, if yer don't mind.' Monica eyed the slice that was dropping on to a piece of white greaseproof paper. 'That's about it, girl, just nice.' She looked to the other end of the counter where Les was deep in conversation with the young woman he'd just finished serving. 'Ay, Vi, I'd keep me eye on this feller if I were you. I've heard it said that the bit of stuff he's talking to is very free with her favours.'

Vi's hearty laugh was just a shade louder than the customer's. 'Is that why she can afford half a pound of boiled ham, queen, while you can only afford a quarter of corned beef?'

Kate could feel herself blushing and lowered her head. You never knew what Monica was going to come out with. And the next words out of her friend's mouth turned the pink of her cheeks into the deep red of beetroot. 'Ay, I'll have to come out with yer one night, Vera,' Monica roared. 'My feller wouldn't mind me going out with yer, 'cos he's very partial to a bit of boiled ham.'

Vera bit on her bottom lip to keep her face straight. 'Friday night down Lime Street is the best, girl! Yer could make enough money to give your feller boiled ham for his carry-out every day.'

'Oh, that's the gear, I'll be made up to have a few bob in me purse.' Then, winking broadly, Monica added, 'Shall I bring Kate with me? With her looks she'd attract every feller that went past. We wouldn't be standing around all night, waiting for customers.'

Kate's eyes and mouth were wide open. 'Ay, you just leave my name out of it, Monica Parry! You may see the funny side to this talk, but I'm blowed if I can.'

Monica shook her head sadly. 'It's a shame, isn't it, folks? God saw fit to give her beauty, but He forgot to give her a sense of humour.'

Violet shrugged her shoulders. 'It's like the toss of a dice, queen, pot luck. Or standing in a queue. When it's your turn, yer get what's left. God had given all the beauty out by the time it was my turn, so I got the sense of humour instead.'

'I'd say He wasn't generous with that, either!' Les decided to add his twopennyworth. 'Anyone seeing yer getting out of bed in the mornings, sitting on the side of the bed moaning about yer lot in life, with yer hair in rags and yer face all screwed up, well, they'd never believe yer had any sense of humour.'

'Yeah, ye're right there, lad, I hold me hand up on that. My first smile of the day is when money is being handed over the counter, and I think of how rich we're going to be some day. That's when me sense of humour comes to life.'

'At least ye're honest about it, sunshine,' Kate said, wishing they'd all stop nattering and she could get home to her husband. 'And while the conversation has been very pleasant, I'd be grateful if yer'd serve me and then I'll be on me way. Me throat is parched, and crying out for a cuppa.'

'We aim to please, queen, that's our motto. So here's your quarter of corned beef, and will yer pass the other over to yer mate? That'll be fourpence each, plus a penny if yer still want the Mint Imperials.'

Monica took the penny from her pocket and passed it over. 'That's for the sweets. Now I'll have to check me purse to see if I've enough left for the meat. If not, yer'll have to put it on the slate.'

Kate glanced at her friend to see if she was in earnest because neither of them got anything on tick unless they were desperate. They'd found out early in their married lives that if you couldn't afford to pay one week, then you certainly couldn't make it up the next. All you did was dig yourself deeper into debt. But it was easy to see now, by the mischievous glint in Monica's eyes, that she was only pulling the shopkeeper's leg. 'Am I good for credit, Mrs Riley? Or do I have to go home and tell my husband and child that they'll have to go hungry because of the wicked witch in the corner shop?'

'Wicked witch? Why, you cheeky bugger! I've a good mind to take the flaming corned beef back off yer!' Violet appealed to her husband. 'Did yer hear what she called me, Les?'

'Oh, I'm sorry, my beloved, I'm afraid I didn't. Yer see, I was trying to count how many jelly babies there are in that jar and me mind was occupied.' Les scratched his head and tutted. 'Yer've made me lose count now, I don't know where I was up to! It was either a hundred and six, or a hundred and twenty-six. See what yer've made me go and do now! I'll have to start counting all over again.'

'No, yer won't, Les, 'cos I was counting with yer.' Kate showed she hadn't been left out altogether on humour. 'It's a hundred and twenty-six.'

Monica chuckled. 'There speaks the voice of wisdom. And

the same voice is telling me to shut me gob so she can get home to her family.' A silver sixpence was laid on the counter next to where Kate had put four pennies. 'I'll take two of these pennies, Vi, and that will make us quits. And after thanking you for the service and the pleasant conversation, my friend and I will take our leave of yer.'

'Ye're a sarcastic beggar,' Vi said with a smile. 'I bet as soon as yer get out of the door yer'll be calling us fit to burn.'

'No, she won't, sunshine,' Kate said. 'I can guarantee that, 'cos I'll be running her all the way and she'll be too puffed to talk.' With that she walked across to open the shop door, and then came back to drag her friend through it. 'We'll be seeing yer. Ta-ra!'

'Let go of me,' Monica cried, 'ye're going to pull me over!'

'It was the only way to get yer out of there. My feller will be thinking I've left home. Besides, I'm dying for a sit down and a cup of tea.' As she turned her head Kate saw her son in a side entry with his mate Pete. They were taking turns kicking a football against a yard wall. 'Hey, Billy, I'll have yer tea ready in ten minutes so I want yer home by then. D'yer know where our Nancy is?'

'Last time I saw her she was sitting on next-door's step with ... er ... with Dolly.' Just in time Billy remembered his mam's friend was the mother of the girl he called daft. Not that he meant anything by it, 'cos his sister was just as daft. 'They were reading a book between them.'

'Yes, I can see them,' Monica said. 'At least I can see their legs.'

'If she asks what's in the bags I'll put her off so Dolly won't be any the wiser,' Kate promised. As they neared the Parrys' house, and saw the bodies attached to the legs, Kate gave her daughter the same instructions she'd given Billy. 'Tea in ten minutes, sunshine, and don't be late. Don't have me coming out for yer 'cos me feet are dropping off.'

'Okay, Mam, I'll be there.' Nancy eyed the bags. 'What have yer been buying?'

'Nothing you'd be interested in, love, but yer'll find out later.'

Kate was putting the key in her front door when she heard Dolly asking, 'Have yer got anything in there for me, Mam?'

'Not really, sweetheart, but I'm going to get yer something nice next week.'

'Is that a promise, Mam? Cross yer heart and hope to die?'

When Kate stepped into the hall she was smiling. Kids were so innocent.

John Spencer sat back in his favourite fireside chair, a happy, smiling, contented man. His heart was overjoyed because he was the one who had brought the sound of laughter to this room, and made his children's faces light up with pleasure. And Kate, his beautiful wife, looked the picture of happiness to see her children's contentment. John was only sorry that he hadn't been able to treat them more often, but it was impossible on the poor wages he earned.

The loudest laugh came when Kate was holding Billy's shirt out. The lad had looked horrified. 'I'm not touching that until I've washed me hands.' It was the first time he'd ever washed himself without being told.

Nancy was delighted with her present. Holding the blouse against herself, she sighed, 'Oh, it's lovely, Mam! Thank you a million times.'

'It's yer dad yer have to thank, sunshine, not me. He gave me the money to buy it.' Kate held her own blouse up to her shoulders, the pale green a perfect foil to her auburn hair. 'I think we owe him a big hug and kiss.'

Happy as he was, this was going too far for Billy. 'Boys don't kiss men! That's soppy, that is! Don't yer think so, Dad? Yer don't want me to kiss yer, do yer?'

John chuckled. 'It would be worth it to see your face, son. But no, I wouldn't expect yer to kiss me. We'll shake hands, eh, man to man?'

Billy's chest expanded so much Kate thought she'd have to take the shirt back and ask for a bigger size.

'What else have yer got there, Mam?' Nancy asked, eyeing the bag she could see wasn't empty. 'Anything exciting?'

'No, sunshine, just a couple of things I bought from a second-hand stall. They're nothing to write home about now, but by the time I've washed and altered them to fit, I think they'll come up a treat.'

'What colour blouse did Auntie Monica get for Dolly? I hope it's not the same colour as mine or we'll look daft.'

'Ah, well, thereby hangs a tale. Yer see, Monica didn't have enough money on her to buy Dolly a blouse. Don't forget I had extra off yer dad. But Monica will get Dolly a blouse sometime in the next few days. So, until then, I want yer to hang yours up in my wardrobe and don't say a word to yer mate.' She saw her daughter's face fall. 'Yer wouldn't want to upset Dolly, would yer? And yer must admit it would look as though yer were swanking and showing off. She would be really upset, sunshine, and after all, she is yer best mate. Is it worth falling out with her for the sake of a few days?'

Nancy was disappointed but put a brave smile on her face. 'Ye're right, Mam, it would be mean of me 'cos she is me very best mate. So I'll hang it up, like yer said, and I'll not say a word about it.'

Out of the corner of her eye, Kate had seen Billy's eyes going back and forth from her to his sister. 'Billy, I hope you understand you mustn't let the cat out of the bag by repeating anything yer've heard just now.' She put a finger to her lips. 'Keep these closed, son, and be a good boy.'

He jerked his head back. 'I don't know, women and girls don't half have some queer ideas.' He appealed to his father.

'Don't yer think, Dad, that life would be much easier if there were only men in the world?'

John had great difficulty keeping the laughter back. 'I'm afraid that is something you and me disagree on, son. Yer see, without women, there wouldn't be a world!'

Billy looked puzzled. 'How d'yer make that out?'

John asked himself how he could get out of that poser. 'Erm, I'll tell yer when ye're a bit older, son. Yer see, it's complicated.'

Time to change the subject, Kate thought. 'That's enough now. Just remember what yer've been told and put yer new shirt away. I'll have some sandwiches ready for our tea in a few minutes.'

She poured the boiling water into the teapot, then refilled the kettle. After they'd had their tea, she'd pull the dolly tub out and put the dresses and skirt she'd got from the market in steep. There was no need to fill the tub just for those few things, so it wouldn't take long. Then she remembered it was Sunday the next day, and no one washed or put their clothes out on a Sunday unless they wanted the whole neighbourhood to say they were heathens.

She stood with her chin in her hand. If she put the clothes in steep now, and gave them a good bashing with the dolly peg to make sure all the dirt was out, then after tea, she'd have time to rinse them, wring as much water out of them as she could, then get them on the line. In this weather they'd be dry by the time she was going to bed. Then she could spend time on them tomorrow, cutting and sewing.

Happy that she'd sorted herself out in her mind, Kate carried the teapot through and put it on the stand in the middle of the table. 'Sandwiches are on their way.'

John Spencer wasn't a church-goer, and no amount of coaxing or arguing on Kate's part would make him change. He lived a decent life, he said, doing a bit of good when someone needed help, and he never harmed a soul. Better than some of the men in the street who went to church every Sunday and came home to treat their wives and kids like slaves. No, going to church didn't make you good, it was what you did in life. So every Sunday he had a nice lie-in while his wife and children went to ten o'clock Mass, and he would have a cup of tea ready for them when they got home.

This Sunday morning, Kate ran her eyes over Billy to make sure the people sitting in the pew behind them couldn't see a tidemark, and that his socks were neatly pulled up to his knees and not around his ankles like a concertina. Then she went to the bottom of the stairs and called, 'We're off, John! I hope ye're up by the time we get back.'

'I will be, love,' a sleepy voice answered. 'I'm giving the matter some very serious consideration right now.'

'Well, don't spend too long considering, or yer'll wear yerself out and go back to sleep again.' Kate winked at the two children. 'If ye're still in bed when we come back from church, and there's no pot of tea on the hob, I'll be up these stairs with the rolling pin in me hand.' Without waiting for a reply, she ushered the children through the front door.

'Yer wouldn't really hit me dad with the rolling pin, would yer, Mam?' Billy had noted her wink earlier and took it to mean she was kidding. But it was best to make sure, because hitting someone with a rolling pin sounded a bit drastic. 'He wouldn't be able to go to work tomorrow if yer did, 'cos he'd have a lump on his head the size of a football.'

Kate grinned. 'He'd have to keep his cap on all day then, wouldn't he, to hide it?' She heard a door closing nearby and turned her head to see Monica and Dolly on the pavement. 'Your feller still in bed as well, is he?'

Monica nodded. 'The only thing that would get Tom out of bed on a Sunday morning would be if I told him the laws had been changed and the pubs were open.'

'Married to heathens we are, the two of us.' Kate gestured to the girls to walk on. 'When the time comes to climb up that stairway to heaven, I hope Saint Peter doesn't add their sins to our slate or we'll be sent right back down the staircase with our heads bowed in shame.'

Walking behind the two women, young Billy rolled his eyes. What were they on about now? Why did they suddenly start talking about stairways to heaven, sins and slates? They were barmy, the pair of them. Mind you, as he'd tried to tell his dad, all the female sex were the same. Barmy.

Kate turned her head. 'Pete's in front with his mam, sunshine, d'yer want to catch him up?'

Billy didn't need to be asked twice. Mrs Reynolds, Pete's mam, was on her own, no other woman to natter to about stupid things. 'I'll see yer in church, Mam.' Then you couldn't see his heels for dust.

'Listen,' Kate kept her voice low, 'have yer heard anything from Betty?'

'Not a dickie bird,' Monica said. 'I don't think we will, either, 'cos I've got a feeling that Greg's a mummy's boy, and he's been told to keep well away. He's probably more afraid of her than he is of Margaret and her family.'

'Well, I'm not giving up hope yet.' Kate was resolute. 'I'm going to light a candle and say a couple of prayers. It's all very well for us to stroll along discussing whether we think he will or he won't, but what about Margaret and her mam and dad? Life must be hell for them right now, with their lives ruined. It'll be on their minds night and day. I know how I'd feel if I was in their shoes.' Kate could feel herself getting very emotional, and it was obvious in her voice. 'Don't forget, we've got daughters and, God forbid, could very well have to go through the same nightmare. So it wouldn't hurt yer to say a prayer, Monica Parry, instead of being full of doom and gloom.'

'Oh, dear! Oh, dear! Oh, dear! That's me put firmly in me

place, isn't it?' Monica linked her friend's arm and squeezed. 'Taking off on me isn't going to help, girl, but if I thought it would, I'd let yer kick me the length of the street. However, if yer think a prayer will help, then I'll say a prayer. And I'll light a candle if it makes yer feel better. But if that Greg doesn't come up trumps after all that, I'll go round to his house and box his ears for him.'

Kate could imagine it too! Her mate would think nothing of giving someone a hiding if she thought they deserved it. 'Perhaps if my little effort didn't do the trick, yours just might. Anyway, let's put a move on or we'll be too late to get a pew to ourselves.'

The church was full, and the friends and their daughters were lucky to find space in a pew at the very back. 'We left the house in bags of time, but still manage to be late,' Monica said softly. 'The trouble is, we talk too much.'

'Ay, you speak for yerself, sunshine,' Kate said, kneeling down with the rest of the congregation. At least those that were able. The elderly and infirm remained seated.

It was when they rose to sing a hymn that Monica whispered, 'I've just spotted Betty at the front, with Margaret. We'll be out first, so we'll wait and have a word with them.'

'We will not! Imagine how embarrassed the poor girl would be if she thought all the neighbours knew about her.' Kate's eyes went down to the hymn book and she raised her voice in song to stop her friend carrying on the conversation. Church was hardly the place to gossip, and several people had already turned around and tutted.

At the end of the mass, Kate looked for her son, but there was no sign. He'd probably go with Pete now, and come home when he thought dinner would be ready. That meant poor Mrs Reynolds would have him under her feet while she was trying to get the Sunday roast on. Unless of course her husband liked peace and quiet on the Sabbath, and sent Billy packing.

There were small groups of people waiting outside the church. Monica clung tightly to Kate's arm. 'Just hang on for a few minutes, it won't kill yer. And I'm sure ye're as nosy as I am to find out whether there's been any development.' She smiled at their two daughters who always looked neat and tidy on a Sunday. 'You run along home, girls, and make sure the kettle's on. Dolly, tell yer dad I'll only be ten minutes.'

The girl pulled a face. 'He won't believe that! We all know your ten minutes can turn into a couple of hours.'

'Just do as ye're told, girl, and I promise I'll be home in plenty of time to get the dinner on. But, just in case, make yer dad a cup of tea to be going on with.'

'I'll go on and tell me dad the same thing, Mam,' Nancy said. 'But if he asks me what's keeping yer, what shall I tell him?'

'Yer don't need to tell him anything, sunshine, 'cos I'm a big girl now. I don't have to ask permission to stop and talk to friends.'

'I know that, Mam! But yer did say if he didn't have a pot of tea made when we got home, yer'd be after him with the rolling pin. So I want yer to tell me what to do if I'm faced with two choices. Say me dad's still in bed, then do I have to take the rolling pin to him? And if he does have the tea ready, and you're not there to drink it, what excuse do I have to give for you not coming home with me?'

'Blame yer Auntie Monica, sunshine, that's what I'm going to do. Tell him she forced me to stay behind because she wanted to talk to a friend.'

'Oh, aye, and what friend would that be, Mam?' Monica's daughter was eyeing her with suspicion. 'In case me dad asks, like?'

'Never you mind what friend it is, just tell him yer don't know.' Monica spied Betty and her daughter coming through the church doors. 'Now, get yer skates on, or there'll be two lots of tea getting thrown out. And go straight home, don't stand around talking.'

'Well, I like that!' Dolly said. 'You and Auntie Kate are going to stand around talking, but we're not allowed to!'

Monica thought of a way to stop this. 'Did I, or did I not, promise to buy yer a new blouse this week, if yer were a good girl?'

Kate quickly took Dolly's side. 'That's blackmail, that is!'

Monica just as quickly agreed. 'I know it is, girl, but can you think of any other way of getting rid of them? Our Dolly is like a dog with a bone. Once she gets something between her teeth, she won't let go.'

'Come on, Dolly,' Nancy said. 'We can tell when we're not wanted.'

Betty Blackmore had seen the two friends and said to her daughter, 'I want a word with Monica. You stay here, I won't be a minute.'

'No, I'm coming with yer.' Margaret clung to her mother's coat. 'If I stand here like a lemon, they'll think I'm too frightened to talk to them. I've got to get used to looking people in the face, I can't spend the rest of my life staring down at the ground.'

Betty sighed to think of her daughter being forced to do either. 'Come on, then, we won't be long.' Walking around the groups of people standing inside the gates of the church, talking to friends they only met on Sunday, Margaret's mother was trying to think of an excuse that would sound plausible to see Monica again later. 'Good morning, Monica, and you, Kate. It's a beautiful morning, isn't it?'

'It certainly is!' Kate smiled at Betty's daughter who was trying to look as though she didn't have a care in the world. 'All right, Margaret?'

'I'm fine, thanks. It was warm in church, though, I couldn't breathe.'

'We were lucky, we were at the back near the door. There was a nice breeze blowing through.'

The two friends noticed a difference in Betty today though what it was exactly was difficult to say, and they didn't like asking. At least, Monica would have loved to ask, but she knew Kate would have her guts for garters for embarrassing her. Margaret's mother seemed to be working on a spring, her every movement jerky. Her eyes didn't look so tired, though, which was a good sign.

'Monica, I was wondering if yer'd found that knitting pattern yer were telling me about? If yer have, I'd like to borrow it to make a start.'

'I think I know where it is, girl, although I couldn't walk in and put me hand on it. I will find it, though, and bring it round to yours this afternoon.' Monica didn't have a clue which pattern the woman was talking about. Was it for a baby's matinee coat or a man's pullover? Or was it just an excuse? 'I've got a couple of patterns somewhere, I promise I'll find them and bring them round to yer.'

'No, I'll come for them.' Betty was trying to send a message with her eyes. 'If I come about two, would yer dinner be over by then?'

'It's no trouble to bring them, yer know. I don't mind.'

But Betty stayed firm. 'No, I'll come to yours about two. Yer see, we're having visitors at four o'clock, and I want the place just right.'

'I'm sure your house is never anything else but just right,' Kate said. 'I know ye're very houseproud.'

'Oh, she is!' Margaret said, surprising them all. 'Yer never see me mam without a duster or a brush in her hands.'

'Better that than living in a pig sty, sunshine.' Kate was thinking she'd never realized before how pretty the girl was. Mind you, she'd only spoken to her a few times. 'I used to think my mam was too fussy, until I went home with a girl from work one day and her house was a disgrace. Absolutely filthy – and smelly. So after that I never complained again about me mam being fussy.'

103

'We'll get fussy if we don't get home,' Monica said. 'My feller will think I've left him. So I'll see yer about two, Betty, and I'll root those patterns out before yer come.'

They parted company then, and the two friends walked on for a few minutes until they were sure they couldn't be overheard. Then Monica asked, 'Well, what d'yer think, girl?'

'I'd say there's something in the air, but what I don't know. What I do know, though, sunshine, is that I'll have to put a move on if I want to get the dinner over and be at your house for two o'clock. And you'd better send Dolly in to ours, out of the way.'

'And what d'yer suggest I do with my feller?'

'Send him down the yard to the lavvy with the *News of the World*.' Kate chuckled. 'That should keep him occupied for at least an hour.'

Chapter Eight

Kate used a thick cloth to cover her hands to save them from the heat of the oven as she slid the roasting tin on to the top shelf. Then, after closing the oven door, she ran the back of her hand across her forehead to wipe away the beads of sweat. What with the heat from the oven and the gas ring, it was sweltering in the tiny kitchen. 'I'll baste them in half an hour, so they'll come out nice and crispy brown.'

'Are you talking to yerself?' John's voice floated through from the living room. 'They can lock yer up for that, yer know.'

'I've been talking to meself for years now, sunshine, and I haven't been locked up yet.' Kate lifted the lid of the pan on the stove to make sure the carrots were still simmering before making her way out of the kitchen. 'Anyway, you're a fine one to talk! Ye're always jabbering away to yerself, even in yer sleep. Many's the night I've had to turn yer over on yer side 'cos in between yer talking, ye're snoring like no one's business.'

She stood for a few seconds with her hand on the doorknob, watching the concentration on the faces of her two children who were playing Ludo. Sitting opposite each other at the table, Nancy and Billy kept their eyes peeled to make sure there was no cheating. After all, the winner got the pick of the roast potatoes. On a weekday, if their mother could afford it, the prize would be a ha'penny, but Kate wouldn't allow gambling in the house on a Sunday.

With the kids occupied, she seized the opportunity to have a word with John about why she would be nipping next door at two o'clock. What with getting the dinner on, she hadn't had a chance to get him on his own since she came back from church.

'Will yer give us a hand in the kitchen, love? I want yer to push the mangle back to the wall so I've got enough space to breathe. It won't take yer a minute,' she said to him.

John shoved his Sunday paper down the side of his chair before raising himself up. 'Yer can have as much of my time as yer like, love, yer know that.' He chuckled as he followed her into the kitchen. 'It just so happens that I don't have any important business to deal with today, so my butler can attend to anything that crops up.'

Kate put a finger to her lips and spoke softly. 'Keep yer voice down 'cos I don't want the kids to hear any of this. The mangle doesn't need shifting, it was only an excuse to get you out here.'

John drew her close. 'Ooh, I hope yer intend to have yer wicked way with me. But wouldn't it have made more sense if yer'd asked me to help yer move the bed instead of the mangle? It would have been much more comfortable.'

Kate gave him a quick peck on the cheek before pulling away. 'There's a time and place for everything, sunshine, but right now I don't have the time. And I'm dead sure the kitchen isn't the place.'

'Wishful thinking on my part again.' John put on a woeful expression. 'I hope yer realize it's bad for a man to have his passion repressed? They say it stunts his growth.'

'Tell me about it in bed tonight when I've not got so much on me mind.' After popping her head around the door to make sure the children weren't listening, Kate explained all about the meeting with Betty and her daughter outside the church. 'She's coming to Monica at two o'clock, so don't start asking awkward questions when I say I'm going next door for half an hour.'

'Do Betty and her daughter know about your involvement in all this?' John asked. 'I mean, do they know yer went to meet this bloke?'

'No, of course not! And I don't want them to either. If the lad has been to see Margaret, and I've got a feeling that's what Betty wants to tell us, then I'd rather they believed he'd done it off his own bat and wasn't pushed into it. I'm keeping me fingers crossed that everything turns out fine for the Blackmores, so they can smile again and plan for a happy future. No more worrying about neighbours talking behind their backs.'

'Ay, love, don't be building yer hopes up. Even if the lad has been to see Margaret, it doesn't mean he wants to marry her. And there isn't a law in the land that would make any bloke marry a girl if he doesn't want to. I know the law is one-sided and unfair, but that's the way things are and we can't change them.'

Kate clicked her tongue on the roof of her mouth. 'You men have an easy life, yer've got everything going for yer. Yer get away with flaming murder, and that's a fact. Get a girl in the family way, then just walk away and leave her stranded. There's no shame attached to the man, only the poor girl.'

'It takes two to make a baby, love,' John reminded her. 'Yer can't put all the blame on the bloke. A girl can always say "no", and chase him.'

'Aye, I know,' Kate sighed. 'I remember someone saying to me once that only good girls have babies, the bad ones don't get caught 'cos they're too wise. And it's right, 'cos Margaret isn't wise at all. She's a quiet girl, on the shy side, and I'll lay odds that Greg Corbett is the first boy ever to kiss her or touch her where he shouldn't. And I don't think I'm far off in saying the boy has never been with another girl. I could be completely wrong, of course, but I'm a pretty good judge of character, and that's the impression I got. Just a case of two young people losing their heads for a short time without realising what the consequences could be.'

'It does happen, love, and people do get over the gossip and learn to cope. After all, it's not the end of the world.'

'It's all very well for you to stand there saying that, John, 'cos this doesn't affect you. But if yer were in Jack Blackmore's shoes, yer'd be feeling just as bad as he does.' Kate tilted her head. 'Would yer be so easy-going about it if it was our Nancy? No, yer'd be singing a very different tune then, because yer'd be weighed down with worry and grief.'

'I think ye're getting ahead of yerself, saying that, love. The chances of it happening are very remote, and there's no point in worrying over something that's not going to happen.'

Kate put her hands on his chest and smiled up at him. 'Ye're right, sunshine, I'm being a real misery. It was Betty that got to me, seeing the sadness in her eyes. But my carrying on about it isn't going to help her, so I'll keep me feelings to meself and not upset you.' She made a quick movement with her hands and was tickling his ribs before he knew what was happening. He was very ticklish and in between roars of laughter begged her to have mercy and stop.

'Give me a break, will yer?'

The children kept their eyes on each other even though they wanted to run to the kitchen and join in the fun. But as the laughter and begging continued, Billy couldn't stand it any longer. 'Let's both stand up at the same time, so there's no cheating,' he suggested.

Nancy would much prefer to have fun than a potato, even if it was big and golden and crispy. She pushed her chair back, telling him, 'Yer can cheat if yer want to, Billy, I'm going to see what me mam's doing to me dad.'

Billy stayed just long enough to pick up the dice. His had been the last throw and the dice had come down on a two. So now he quickly turned it over so the six was on top, before following Nancy to join their mother in reducing their father to a helpless, laughing, curled-up figure on the kitchen floor.

There was nothing John liked better than the whole family having fun together. So he rolled from side to side, supposedly convulsed with laughter. Then he opened one eye and fixed it on his son. 'Ay, I thought we men were supposed to stick together? Ye're not allowed to join the opposition!'

Billy thought about this for a second then nodded his head. 'Yeah, ye're right, Dad, we men must stick together.' With that, he turned on Nancy and soon had her rolling on the floor with her legs kicking wildly, letting out loud shrieks of laughter.

'I'll get you, our Billy! Stop it, will yer, I've got a pain in me side now.'

Kate pushed herself to her feet. 'We can all stop now before somebody pulls the hot pan over or bangs their head on the oven. Come on, kids, I think yer dad's had enough and it's time for me to see to the dinner.'

'That was good, that was, Mam,' Billy said. 'Now I know what to do to get me own way with our Nancy. Just tickle her ribs.'

'Yer caught me when my guard was down,' Nancy told him. 'Yer won't find it so easy to catch me next time.'

'Go in and finish yer game,' Kate said. 'Let me have the kitchen to meself.'

'Yeah, come on, our kid.' Billy was practically rubbing his hands in glee. The biggest roast potato was as good as on his plate. 'We'll have the game finished by the time me mam has the dinner ready.'

'I'm not playing with you, ye're a cheat, Billy Spencer.'

His eyes flew open in pretend surprise. 'I haven't cheated! How could I when we've been together the whole time? Tell her, Dad, that she's got to finish the game. Trust her to be a spoilsport 'cos she knows I'm a better player than her.'

'If that's the case, why did yer have to change the dice?' Nancy was looking down her nose at him. 'Anyway, cheats never prosper.'

'I'm not a cheat.' The biggest golden-brown crispy potato seemed to be getting further away and Billy was determined not to let that happen. 'Come and finish the game, and don't be a blinking cry baby.'

'I know yer cheated, I saw yer through the crack in the door!' Nancy would never knowingly get her brother into trouble, so she thought she'd meet him halfway. 'I'll tell yer what, if that dice is on a two, I'll play with yer. If it's not, then yer can finish the game all by yerself.'

Neither of the children noticed their father leaving the kitchen. But they heard him call, 'I don't know what difference it makes, but for what it's worth the dice is showing two.'

The children looked at each other and grinned, knowing their father had solved the argument and saved the situation. Nancy was aware her brother had cheated, he always did. And when he got a bit older, she'd not let him get away with it because she didn't want her brother to be known as someone you couldn't trust. As for Billy, he took it for granted that everyone cheated. All his mates did, otherwise they'd never win a game of marbles, footie or rounders. They'd never get all their sums right at school, either, if they didn't copy off the boy next to them.

Billy winked at his mother before following Nancy out of the kitchen. His philosophy of life, at ten years of age, was that if girls didn't cheat then that was their look out, and just went to prove they were as daft as he'd always said they were. There'd be no excitement in any game if you didn't cheat.

'Dolly, you go next door and have a game of something with Nancy so me and me mates can have a chin-wag in peace.'

'Ah, ay, Mam! There's a play on the wireless this afternoon that I want to listen to.' Dolly rolled her eyes. 'Anyway, Auntie Kate won't want me there on a Sunday, yer know that.'

'That's where ye're wrong, young lady.' Monica was standing with her hands on her hips. 'I've told yer Auntie Kate is coming here, and seeing as she can't be in two places at once, she won't care whether ye're in her house or not. And Nancy's been told ye're going so she'll be disappointed if yer let her down.'

Dolly knew all her mother's mannerisms, and the hands on

the hips were a sure sign she meant business this time and no amount of coaxing would make her change her mind. The only thing to do was save your breath and give in gracefully. 'I hope they're going to listen to the play on the wireless, 'cos it's a murder mystery and I'll go mad if I miss it.'

Tom raised his head from the *News of the World*. 'Yer'll be all right there, sweetheart, 'cos yer Uncle John loves a good thriller so he's bound to be listening.'

'Same as you,' Monica told him, trying to keep her face straight. 'Kate said she'll leave a pot of tea ready for yer.'

Tom lowered his paper. 'What are yer on about, woman! Yer know I spend every Sunday afternoon reading the paper from front to back page. I certainly won't be listening to the ruddy wireless.'

'I'm afraid you and I aren't going to see eye to eye over this, love, but a little understanding on your part wouldn't go amiss.' Monica went to stand in front of his chair and looked down into his puzzled face. 'Every night except Sunday, without fail, you're off to the pub. I never complain that yer leave me here like a grass widow, do I? No, because I believe that after working all day, yer deserve a pint, or two. But I'm not allowed to go off gadding every night, am I? And I work just as bleeding hard as you do, even though I know nothing on God's earth will get that through that thick head of yours. As far as you're concerned, after I've given the place a quick flick with a duster, I'm free for the rest of the day to stand having a good gossip to all the neighbours, with me arms crossed and leaning back against the wall. That's until half an hour before ye're due in from work when I dash in to throw something on the stove for yer dinner. Oh, yeah, it's a real easy life I've got. No worries over work or money, eh? Wouldn't yer just like to swap places with me?'

Tom folded the newspaper slowly and neatly before looking up with laughter in his eyes. 'What time did yer say the play started? And did Kate say there'd be a gingersnap biscuit with the cup of tea?'

Monica cupped his face and kissed him soundly on the lips. 'Haven't I always told everyone that I've got the best husband in the world, bar none?'

'Okay, okay! I give in! What time are they expecting me and Dolly? Oh, and how long are we to stay out?'

Monica glanced at the clock on the mantelpiece. 'Yer were expected there five minutes ago. And I think it's safe to say yer'll be allowed back in an hour's time. I'll give a knock on the wall to tell yer when the coast is clear.'

'Bloody marvellous, getting chucked out of me own home on the only day I have off.' Tom put his arm across his daughter's shoulder and walked her to the front door. 'Kicked out by a wicked, cold-hearted woman, sweetheart. She doesn't care that there's thick snow on the ground and neither of us has soles to our shoes. Heartless, that's what she is.'

Dolly giggled. 'Yeah, I'm going to tell me teacher on her on Monday. And I'll tell her I get beaten every day and never get anything to eat.'

'And don't forget to tell her about how yer old dad gets treated, either.' Tom stepped out into the sunshine. 'Orphans of the storm, that's what we are.'

'Ah, yer poor buggers, me heart bleeds for yer,' Monica called after them before closing the door and dashing to make herself presentable for visitors. Her pinny was folded and put in a drawer, and she'd just run a comb through her hair when there was a knock on the back door. 'Ooh, that was good timing.' She mentally gave herself a pat on the back. 'I wonder who it is?' She opened the door to find both Kate and Betty looking up at her. 'Come in, ladies.' She stepped aside to let them pass. 'I'll stick the kettle on.'

Betty's eyes went to the living-room door and she mouthed, 'Is yer husband in?'

112

'Nobody in but me, girl, I'm all on me lonesome.' Monica closed the door behind them. 'I've sent Tom next door to keep Kate's husband company. If he can have his pint or two every night with his boozing pals, then I've told him I can entertain my friends for a couple of hours every now and again. So go through to the living room and make yerselves at home. Yer can put yer feet on the mantelpiece, if yer like, Betty.'

The woman smiled. 'I think I'll keep them firmly on the floor, lass, I wouldn't want yer to see everything I've got.'

'Yer've got nothing we haven't got, sunshine, but I think yer'd be more comfortable on a chair.' Kate, who felt as much at home in her mate's house as she did in her own, led Betty through to the living room. 'Sit down, sunshine, while Monica makes the tea.'

Her friend's voice came floating through to them. 'No talking until I'm sitting with yer, d'yer hear, Kate Spencer? I don't want to miss a word.'

Kate rolled her eyes to the ceiling before calling back, 'Is it all right if we talk about the weather, and the price of fish?'

'As long as yer speak up and I can hear what ye're saying. I know you, yer can be a sly one when it suits yer.'

In a loud voice, Kate said, 'It's a lovely day, isn't it, Betty? I think we're in for a scorching summer, don't you?'

Monica popped her head around the door. 'Not so flaming loud, please, or next door will think we're having a row.' The neighbour next door was the street gossip, who spent most of her life finding out how her neighbours lived. Her name was Thelma Robson, married but childless, just her and her long-suffering husband Arthur in the house – the only man in the street who couldn't get out to work quick enough every morning to escape his wife's never-ceasing whining. He'd told Tom one day, as they walked down the street on their way to the tram stop, that he'd even work Sunday if he could. Without pay!

Monica came to stand in the centre of the room, and nodded to the wall separating the two houses. 'I can just see her now, ear pressed to the wall, telling her husband in that whingeing voice of hers that we must be the lowest of the low to be rowing on a Sunday. This will be her.' Monica was marvellous at impersonating her neighbour. She seemed to shrink in size, her lips became a thin line, there was a deep frown on her forehead and her eyes were like slits. 'Just listen to them, on a Sunday as well! I don't know what the world's coming to. They've got the cheek to go to church then come home and start swearing like troopers. I bet the air is blue in there.' Monica tutted and pulled a comical face. 'And they call themselves ladies! My mother would turn in her grave if she heard carry-on like that on the Sabbath. But, of course, my mother was a real lady.'

Kate and Betty were in stitches as Monica had every one of the nosy woman's actions off to perfection. 'Yer missed yer vocation, Monica,' Betty said, wiping away her tears of laughter. 'If I'd closed me eyes, I'd have sworn it was the woman herself.'

'I'd hate to be her,' Kate said, 'she leads a miserable life. Not one friend in the whole neighbourhood, but she seems to thrive on gossip. I bet she knows more about us than we know ourselves. No matter what time of day yer pass her house, yer can see her peering through the net curtains. I think she's sad, doesn't know what it is to enjoy herself. In all the years we've been here, I've never once heard her laugh.'

'Have yer ever noticed,' Betty chuckled, 'how quickly a shop empties when she walks through the door? I was in the Maypole one day, and when the queer one walked in all the girls behind the counter fled in different directions. And I heard the manager groan as though he had a bad pain.'

'It's her husband I feel sorry for, the poor bugger must have a dog's life.' Monica shivered as though to rid herself of an unpleasant thought. 'Anyway, there's the kettle whistling away so yer'll have a cup of tea in yer hands in a few minutes.'

'I can't stay very long, yer know, lass,' Betty told her, ''cos we've got visitors coming.'

Kate watched her mate hurry to the kitchen, and laughed. 'If you can talk quickly, Betty, we can listen just as quick. Especially if it's good news, which we're hoping it is.'

There was a loud rattling of crockery then Monica's head appeared. 'I'm warning both of yer, one more word and I'll have yer guts for garters.'

Kate was the first to put a hand over her mouth, followed quickly by Betty. Their action brought a nod of approval from Monica. 'That's better. Now I can pour the tea without spilling it and making a mess everywhere.'

The cups of tea were carried in on a tray and Monica handed them out before sitting down with her own. 'That's better. Now, we're all ears, Betty. We know the knitting pattern was only an excuse, so bring us up to date with the news.'

Betty took a mouthful of tea before resting the saucer in her lap. 'Yer'll never guess what's happened. Greg Corbett met our Margaret outside work yesterday, and they had a good talk. It ended up with her bringing him home, and I got such a shock I nearly fainted. I wasn't the only one, either, 'cos the lad looked green around the gills. Me and Jack were polite with him. I mean, it took some nerve to walk into our house after him denying he was the father of the baby. But he told us that everything Margaret had said was true, and he was really sorry he'd lied to us.' She sat back in her chair, remembering just in time to right her cup and saucer which almost toppled over. 'So what d'yer think of that?'

'I think it's marvellous news,' Monica told her. 'And I can see by yer face that it's taken some of the load from yer shoulders.'

'I'm glad the boy came round, sunshine, and I admire him for it.' Kate meant it sincerely, and it raised her hopes of this story having a happy ending. 'What's going to happen now, have they said?'

'Well, I've got another little surprise for yer.' It was a long time since Betty had felt so light-hearted. 'The visitors I'm expecting at four o'clock are Greg's mam and dad.'

Both listeners leaned forward, eyes wide with surprise. And as though it had been rehearsed, they spoke as one: 'Go 'way!'

Monica fell back in her chair. 'Well, I never! That certainly is a surprise. It's the last thing I expected after the way they carried on.'

'I can't hold that against them,' Betty said. 'They were only protecting their son because he'd lied to them and told them he hadn't been with Margaret. They thought we were trying to blame him for something he didn't do, and there's not a parent breathing who wouldn't want to protect their child. But he's told them the truth now, and he's bringing them around so we can sit down together and clear the air.'

'I'm so pleased for yer, sunshine, I really am. And for Margaret, of course, because the last few weeks must have been hell for her.' Kate was afraid it might sound nosy, but because of her involvement it was something she desperately wanted to know. 'Has Greg said anything about marriage?'

'That I couldn't tell yer, lass. It's what me and my Jack would like, but Margaret is being very tight-lipped about it. I might be wrong, but I've got a feeling they've discussed it between themselves and don't want to say anything until both families are together.' Betty drained her cup. 'To tell the truth, I've said so many prayers, I'm hoping God has heard them and takes pity on me. No, that sounds selfish, as though I'm the only one going through the mill. I should have said, I hope God takes pity on all of us.'

'Wouldn't it be lovely if they did get married, though?' Kate could feel herself getting emotional, and not for the first time in her life wished she had more control over her feelings, like Monica did. But she couldn't change the way she was made. 'Just think, you and Jack would have a grandchild and a son-in-law. And the baby would have a real mam and dad.'

Monica tutted as she shook her head. But there was affection in her eyes when she said, 'Just listen to this one, Betty, she's got it all worked out so everyone is happy. She's me very best mate, and I love the bones of her, but she's not half soppy.'

'Well, if all her wishes are granted, me and Jack will be the happiest couple in Liverpool.' Betty's sigh was wistful. 'But we haven't got a magic wand to wave, or a fairy godmother to make all our wishes come true, so we'll have to wait and see what this meeting with Greg's parents brings. They may be in favour of them getting wed or they may be dead against it.'

A picture of Greg flashed through Kate's mind and she said, without thinking really, 'I believe it's up to the young couple themselves. Greg must think something of Margaret to have come back on the scene and admitted he lied. And if they both want to get married, then I don't think the parents can stop them.'

'Margaret would need our permission, being only seventeen, and the lad's not yet twenty-one, so he needs his parents' permission too.' Betty wriggled to the edge of her chair. 'I'd better be making tracks, I've to make sure the place is like a new pin. First impressions are very important, and I don't want the Corbetts to think we're as common as muck. I won't be satisfied until everything in the room is shining.'

'Even your feller's bald head?' Monica asked with a cheeky grin.

'Ay, you, I'll have yer know my Jack's got a fine head of hair. There's a couple of grey ones here and there, but not as many as I've got. Mind you, I'm surprised I haven't gone pure white with the worry of the last few weeks.'

'Keep yer pecker up, sunshine, and a smile on yer face.' Kate nodded to emphasize the importance of her words. 'If the Corbetts see that ye're not worried, then they'll feel better about it. A smiling face can work wonders. And who knows? In a couple of hours all yer worries could be behind yer.'

'I've certainly been glad to have you two to talk to. It takes some of the weight off yer mind when yer can confide in friends.'

Betty couldn't push herself off the chair with the first attempt, but managed on the second. 'As soon as I know anything definite, yer'll be the first ones to know.'

'Come up in the morning about ten,' Monica suggested. 'Me and Kate usually have our morning cuppa around that time. We'll be on pins, wondering what's going on.'

Betty nodded. 'I'll let yer know, I promise. But yer can throw me out now or my feller will be having a heart attack, thinking he's going to be left to greet the Corbetts on his own.'

Monica walked to the kitchen door with her. 'Betty, me and Kate wish yer all the luck in the world. And I hope at ten tomorrow morning yer'll be skipping up this yard with a huge grin on yer face.'

Now the meeting with the Corbetts was getting closer, Betty's nerves were playing her up. But she managed a shaky smile. 'Thanks for listening to me troubles. I'll see yer tomorrow. Ta-ra for now.'

When Monica walked back into the living room, Kate leaned forward, her lovely face full of expectancy. 'I think everything is going to turn out fine for her. Greg wouldn't have plucked up the courage to do what he's done if he didn't care for Margaret.' She clasped her hands together. 'I think I'll pray to Saint Anthony tonight, to ask if he'll put a word in.'

'Don't build yerself up for a let-down, girl! Try and put it out of yer mind until tomorrow, 'cos all the worry in the world won't change things. I'll put the kettle on for a fresh cup of tea for us, but I don't want to hear a word about the Blackmores or the Corbetts. We'll sit quietly with a nice cuppa, and pull everyone in the street to pieces. Now that should cheer us up, eh?'

Chapter Nine

Betty Blackmore was expecting a knock on the door at any minute, but she still jumped when it came. Her nerves were as taut as a violin string, and she had to struggle to stop her teeth from chattering. 'I'll go.' Her eyes swept the room for the umpteenth time to make sure everywhere was neat, tidy and shining. 'You can put the kettle on, Margaret.'

Her husband Jack was concerned for her because she'd looked awful for the last few weeks. 'Betty, love, stop worrying, they can't eat yer.'

'I'm doing me best, Jack, I can't do any more.' She shook her head as she walked into the tiny hall. Her husband was good, but like all men didn't understand the things women worried about.

When Betty opened the door it was plain to see that while Greg managed a smile and a greeting, his parents weren't sure what kind of a reception they'd get or how they should act. 'Come in, won't yer?' Her smile was stiff because her cheeks refused to move. It was understandable, really, because the last time she'd seen Greg's parents there was shouting and screaming, and fists were flying. 'Margaret's putting the kettle on, she won't be long.'

'I'll give her a hand,' Greg said, leaving his parents standing in the middle of the living room watching his retreating back with surprise written all over their faces. Hadn't they agreed that they'd see what the Blackmores had to say before getting too friendly?

Jack Blackmore jumped to his feet. Someone had to make an effort to lighten the tension so he held out his hand to Greg's father who was looking very ill at ease. 'It was good of you and yer wife to come, Albert. Here, let me take yer jacket and hang it up.'

Bert Corbett slipped his arms out of his short jacket and passed it over. 'I don't know why I had to wear the blessed thing anyway in this weather! But Maude insists she doesn't like to see men in their shirt sleeves, and I learned a long time ago that it was pointless to argue with a woman.'

Maude herself wasn't wearing a coat, but looked very smart in a white cardigan over a cotton dress. In seconds her eyes had taken stock of the neat, comfortable room with its highly polished furniture. And while they'd been waiting for the front door to be opened, she hadn't missed the shining windows and white as snow net curtains. The step and windowsill too had been scrubbed so clean you could eat your dinner from them.

'Sit down, Mrs Corbett, please.' Betty waved a hand towards the couch. 'I'm sure Margaret won't be long with the tea.'

Albert bent his knees slightly, straightened the creases in his trousers, then stretched to his full six feet. 'Her name's Maude, and I like to be called Bert. There's no need to stand on ceremony.'

'That's how it should be,' Jack agreed. 'There's no sense in us being at daggers drawn, it won't solve anything.'

Maude nodded as she sat gingerly on the edge of the couch with her knees pressed tightly together and her dress pulled down to cover them. Her handbag stood on her lap like a sentry on duty, and her two hands rested on top. She looked for all the world like a woman who was ready to make a quick getaway if the need arose. 'Yer shouldn't bother going to any trouble on our behalf, Mrs Blackmore, we've not long had a big dinner.'

'It's first-name terms from now on, Maude, so call me Betty. And we haven't gone to a lot of trouble.' She glanced anxiously towards the kitchen. What on earth were the youngsters doing out there? It didn't look good on Margaret's part, for Greg's parents could be forgiven for thinking she was shunning them.

'Just a few sandwiches and a cup of tea.'

The words had hardly left her lips when Margaret came through carrying a wooden tray set out very nicely with matching cups and saucers, all with handles and no cracks, arranged on a hand-embroidered cloth with a pattern of flowers in the corners. She placed it carefully on the table before facing Greg's parents. 'Hello, Mrs Corbett, Mr Corbett.'

Bert Corbett smiled back at her and said, 'Hello, lass.' But his wife merely inclined her head. That was until her son came through the kitchen door when her eyes widened in surprise. He was carrying a plate of thinly cut sandwiches in one hand, and a plate of iced fairy cakes in the other. And the cakes looked really inviting, sitting on a very fancy white doily.

'Well,' said Maude, 'that's something yer've never done at home. Waited on hand and foot yer've been, all yer life.'

'Yer've never let me!' Greg's white face showed he was under strain, but he was doing his best to be friendly, hoping his parents would follow his lead. 'Every time I go in the kitchen yer chase me out!'

'The kitchen's no place for a man, that's why.' Things weren't going as Maude had anticipated. She'd had it all planned out in her head. Half an hour's discussion of the coming baby, then home. But it wasn't working out that way. She'd have something to say to her husband when they got home. He was sitting comfortably, with a smile on his face, looking as though he'd been friends with the Blackmores for years. She might have known she'd get no help from him. Typical man, he always looked for the easy way out.

'Shall I pour the tea, mam?' Margaret asked.

'If yer would, love, and I'll pass the sandwiches round.'

Before Betty could pick one of the plates up, Greg beat her to it. 'You sit down, Mrs Blackmore, I'll do that. I may as well make meself useful.'

Maude looked at her son and mentally shook her head. He

seemed to be quite at home here, even though he could only have been over the threshold a couple of times. They'd probably fawned over him, making a fuss to get on his right side. Well, she'd make sure her beloved son wasn't coerced into something he didn't want. She wasn't going to let him ruin his life because of one stupid mistake.

'These sandwiches are very tasty, Betty,' Bert said, ignoring the daggers his wife was sending his way. She wouldn't accept that it was her son who had brought all this about. As far as she was concerned, the girl was the one who egged him on. 'A touch of mustard makes all the difference to brawn, gives it more taste.'

Maude was glaring at her husband as her hand went out to take one of the sandwiches offered by her son. Anyone would think they'd been invited for a social visit, instead of something which was going to affect all their lives. But after two bites she had to admit that the sandwiches were indeed very tasty, and didn't hesitate to take a second when offered. Nor did she refuse another cup of tea, or two of the fairy cakes which were much lighter than the ones she made. These just melted in your mouth. Not that she was about to say aloud what she was thinking, she hadn't come here to pay compliments.

Bert was sitting in a fireside chair, facing Jack across the hearth, while Betty was seated on the couch next to Maude, who was keeping a close eye on her son. He was sitting at the dining-room table next to Margaret, their chairs too close together in his mother's opinion. And they seemed happy to be in each other's company, too, which didn't please her. So she decided to broach the reason why they were here, and ask what the Blackmores had in mind. 'We can talk while we're eating and drinking, otherwise it'll be time to go home before we've done what we set out to do. And that is to tell Margaret, and her mam and dad of course, that we'll help her in any way we can. Greg knows his responsibilities, and he'll not shirk them.' There was a squaring of Maude's shoulders and a slight shake of the head which practically told those watching that the Corbetts knew their duty. 'He'll continue to pay as much as he can afford each week while the child is growing up.'

Betty's heart sank. She knew her husband and daughter would feel the same. There was to be no wedding then, no making an honest woman of Margaret, and no father's name on the baby's birth certificate. But Betty wasn't going to lower herself by saying that if Greg was as good as his mother was making out, he would marry the girl he'd got into trouble. Oh, there was a lot that could be said, but to what purpose? And why embarrass Margaret? The poor girl was feeling bad enough. No, her mother wasn't going to see her belittled. 'It's good of yer to think of helping out, but we wouldn't dream of letting you. Me and Jack can give Margaret and the baby everything they need. They'll want for nothing as long as we're alive.'

Sensing victory, Maude was in a mood to be generous. 'Oh, no, yer must let us help out. Never let it be said that we didn't do our duty. And we can afford to help, having two wages coming in every week, can't we, Bert?'

Her husband's face was like thunder. Wait until they got home! He'd have something to say about the way his wife was talking down to the Blackmores, as though they came from a lower class. In fact, it almost sounded as though she was saying they'd got themselves into this mess but her son was generously offering to help with a few bob a week. 'I've nothing to say. Not yet, anyhow.'

Maude was taken aback by her husband's answer and began to flounder. 'But yer said yer agreed we should help out?'

'There's no need for all this, Mam,' Greg said softly. 'Yer see, me and Margaret want to get married. And as soon as possible.'

Maude looked as though she'd been dealt a body blow, but Betty had to force herself not to jump up and punch the air with happiness, while the two men, Jack and Bert, sat quietly with smiles on their faces. Even when Maude took off on her husband, he stayed calm and collected. 'Have yer got nothing to say for yerself?' she asked. 'Don't sit there leaving it all to me. Tell yer son he's being crazy, that he's not to get married, I forbid it.'

'I'll do no such thing, love! It's only right and proper that he marries the girl after getting her in the family way. It's his responsibility and I'm glad to see he's man enough to admit it. But I would like to ask them both if it's what they really want. How about it, Margaret?'

'I'd like to get married, Mr Corbett, and not only because of the baby.'

'What about you, son?' Bert looked him in the eye. 'There's no going back once yer've taken the vows, yer know. Marriage is not a game, it means spending a lifetime with someone and raising a family. Yer can't come running home to yer mam if yer don't like it.'

'I know that, Dad. Me and Margaret have had a long talk and gone through all the good things and the snags. Neither of us is stupid, we know exactly what we'd be letting ourselves in for. And we know it will be a struggle for a few years, until we get on our feet and can afford to have a home of our own around us. But it's what we both want, and we're looking forward to the baby and will give it the best start we can in life.'

'It's ridiculous,' Maude cried. 'Yer can't get married at your age, ye're too young! Anyway, yer need yer parents' consent, and I certainly won't give it because I don't think yer've thought it through properly.'

Bert banged a clenched fist on the wooden arm of his chair. 'For God's sake, woman, yer son is the one to blame for all this trouble, and if he's man enough to try and right a wrong then yer should be supporting him, not treating him as though he's weak in the head and can't think for himself!' He turned to Greg who was now holding the hand of a very tearful Margaret. 'If yer need a parent's permission to get wed, son, then yer've got mine.'

'Thanks, Dad, I appreciate that 'cos we want to get married as soon as possible.' Greg squeezed Margaret's hand. 'Before the gossip starts.'

'Have yer all lost the run of yer senses?' Maude was sitting forward now, her face set. 'Where are they going to live, and how will they manage for money? I don't suppose anyone has thought about the practical side of things, have they?'

'They can live here,' Betty said quietly. 'Margaret has a furnished bedroom and it'll suit them nicely. So they won't need to worry about where they'll live, or about furniture, 'cos they can make this their home until such time as they can afford their own. There's room for the baby's cot as well, and my grandchild will be very welcome in this house. Margaret is only seventeen, but she's a kind and caring girl who'll make a wonderful mother.' Maude Corbett's face turned dark as thunder as she realized things weren't going her way. Who the hell did she think she was? When Betty next spoke, it was in a strong voice. 'I would like to see her married for the sake of the child, but we'd get along perfectly well if she didn't. Me and Jack will always be here for her, and for our grandchild.'

Maude sensed the battle was lost, but how could she redeem herself without looking foolish? The word 'grandchild' had suddenly brought her down to earth. She hadn't really given the baby any thought, she'd been too busy trying to protect her son. The prospect of a child hadn't meant anything to her as yet, except for the trouble it had caused. Now she was thinking of it in a different light. It was her son's flesh and blood, and that meant it was part of her and Bert as well. The enormity of how much she could be throwing away came like a second body blow. If she didn't watch it, she'd be excluded from her own grandchild's life, and for that she'd never forgive herself. And she'd have Bert to reckon with because it was obvious he'd thought everything through while she was busy shouting her mouth off.

Bert could almost see the way his wife's mind was working. She'd got herself into a corner and was wondering how to get out of it without losing her dignity. And although he didn't see eye to eye with her over this, it didn't mean he didn't love her dearly. 'Oh, I think me and the wife can see that Greg is quite certain of what he wants to do, and we'll go along with it, won't we, love?'

Maude swallowed hard. 'Yes, of course we will. I just wanted to make sure they both know what they're doing. They're very young and have a lot to learn.' Then came what was the nearest to an apology they were likely to get. 'I only want what's best for my son.'

'That's understandable,' Betty told her, not wanting to cause friction when things seemed to be going well. 'That's exactly what I want for my daughter. So if you and your husband are agreeable to Margaret and Greg getting married, perhaps we can get our heads together now and see if we can agree on when and how?'

'It can't be done as quickly as they seem to want,' Maude said. 'They haven't put the banns up yet, that's going to take at least a month.'

'We weren't thinking of a church wedding, Mam,' Greg told her. 'We've decided that under the circumstances a register office would be better.' He saw dissent written on his mother's face and quickly added, 'Father Kelly would lecture us something rotten, and he probably wouldn't marry us at the altar anyway.'

Bert waved his hand as though to brush aside what had been said. 'What difference does it make where yer get married, as long as it's legal and binding? It could be done in a week at Brougham Terrace, and that would cut out the expense of a reception and new clothes.'

'Although it goes against everything I believe in, and I don't know how I'll face the priest, I have to agree with Bert,' Betty said. 'A short ceremony at Brougham Terrace and then back here for a drink and a bite to eat. I've two friends I'd like to invite, if that's all right, but that's it. What about you, Maude? Anyone you'd like to invite?'

She shook her head. 'No, I'll tell the neighbours about Greg getting married, but the less they know the better. And we'll help with the food and a bottle of port.' Her eyes narrowed with suspicion. 'Who are the two friends ye're going to ask?'

'You wouldn't know them, they live at the back of us. I told them about Margaret because they're not janglers and I know they won't spread it around.' Betty caught her daughter and Greg smiling shyly at each other. She'd bet her last penny that this marriage would be a good one. The path leading up to it may have been rough, but they were over the worst now. 'Have you anything yer'd like to say, Greg? Or you, Margaret?'

'No, Mam, except I'd like it to be a nice wedding, even if it is in a register office. I don't need to buy a dress, I've got a couple in me wardrobe to choose from. But I would like a posy of flowers, and a few photographs to remember the day by. I could borrow a camera off one of the girls in work.'

'There's no need to do that, love,' Greg said, feeling more confident now his mother had come around to the idea of his getting married. 'I've got a decent camera, and me dad's pretty good at taking snaps. At least he doesn't chop people's heads off.'

'It's no use you taking a day off work to go to Brougham Terrace for details of what yer have to do, Margaret, 'cos yer need all the money yer can get,' Betty said, beginning to feel quite excited at the prospect of a wedding. 'I'll slip down tomorrow for yer and get all the information.'

Interest was stirring in Maude's breast too, and she wasn't going to be left out of anything now. 'I'll come with yer, Betty. And I'll buy some wool while we're out, to start knitting for the baby. I think it's best to stick to white to be on the safe side, don't yer agree?'

Betty nodded. 'I've already knitted two matinee coats, they

127

only take a couple of hours. Yer can borrow the pattern, if yer like, 'cos I won't be using it for a while. I'm going to make some pillowcases for the cot next, and sheets and blankets.'

'Ooh, that's an idea! I've got an old sheet I could cut up for pillowcases and sheets. But I'll borrow the knitting pattern off yer, Bet, so I can get me hand in. It's years since I knitted anything so I'll be slow at first.'

'Yer'll soon pick it up. It's like riding a bike, once yer learn yer never forget.' Betty was feeling light-headed with relief. All her worries seemed to be slipping away from her, and it was like having a weight lifted from her shoulders. 'What time shall I meet yer tomorrow?'

'Make it early,' Maude said. 'How about ten o'clock?'

'Could we say ten-thirty, 'cos I've got to go on a message at ten?'

Greg's mother nodded. 'I'll meet yer at the tram stop at ten-thirty. It's a date.'

The two fathers sat back in their chairs, laced their hands across their stomachs, lifted their bushy brows and smiled the smiles of men who believe they've done a good job and are satisfied. In fact, they were more than satisfied, they were very happy – Jack in particular that he hadn't had to get too involved, even though there were a couple of times when he had to bite his tongue to stop him from telling Maude, in no uncertain terms, to get off her high horse. He was glad he'd kept his temper because things had worked out fine. He was happy for his wife and daughter, and was experiencing a strange feeling of well-being. Just think, before very long he'd be a grandfather. And a proud one, at that.

On the opposite side of the hearth, Bert's feelings weren't very different. For a while he'd thought Maude would put her foot in it altogether and they'd be politely asked to leave. But it hadn't happened, and looking at her now, smiling and animated, he silently thanked Betty and Jack for their indulgence. Because if the joy of becoming a grandfather had been taken away from him, he didn't think he could ever have forgiven his wife. Granda and Grandma, eh? My, but it did sound wonderful. Definitely something good to look forward to.

Greg leaned sideways and whispered in Margaret's ear. 'See, I told yer everything would be all right, didn't I? How d'yer fancy being Mrs Corbett, and me coming to live here?'

Her eyes bright, Margaret said, 'I can't believe it's happening. I never thought yer mam would come round the way she has. I'm so happy, Greg, I really am. And when we're married and yer move in here, I'll think I'm in heaven.'

Kate waved goodbye to Nancy and Dolly, then turned to hurry back into the house. Billy was being a holy terror this morning, taking his time over everything. She couldn't get him to put a move on, and if he wasn't careful he'd be late getting to school, and then he'd be in for it. He played her up every morning without fail, but on a Monday he was hopeless and had her a bag of nerves.

She found her son standing by the dining table with a pained expression on his face and one hand clutching his throat. 'I haven't half got a sore throat, Mam, it really hurts. And me head is whizzing around as well. I think I must be in for something.'

Kate didn't believe a word of it. Her son had tried every trick in the book to have days off school. Nevertheless she felt his forehead, just in case he wasn't pulling her leg. 'Yer haven't got a temperature, sunshine, so open yer mouth and I'll see if I think it's inflamed.' The inside of Billy's mouth, and what she could see of his throat, looked particularly healthy so she had no qualms about telling him, 'There's nothing wrong with yer, son. Get yer satchel and off to school with yer. And if I were you, I'd be smart about it.'

'But I feel sick, Mam, honest!' With that, Billy let out a groan and clutched at his tummy as he doubled up. 'I'm in agony.'

'Billy, how many times have we gone through this performance? Yer've cried wolf once too often, sunshine. Get it through yer head that ye're going to school this morning if I have to drag yer there. And I mean it!'

The boy knew he was beaten, but he wasn't going to give in graciously. 'If I'm not better by dinnertime, I'll ask teacher to let me come home.'

This was one of his stock answers to what he saw as Kate's hard-heartedness. She merely nodded. 'Okay, but put yer blazer on now and start running.'

Billy's sigh was from the heart. A stranger listening would think the boy was really suffering, and Kate had a heart of stone. With his satchel over his shoulder and his head bent, he went out of the door, his mother behind him. His mate Pete was standing outside waiting for him, and Kate thought he looked near to tears. But she quickly dismissed the thought and told herself the two pals had obviously planned to play sick so they could both have a day off school.

'Hurry up, for heaven's sake,' she called as they appeared reluctant to put one foot in front of the other. 'Yer'll be getting the cane if ye're not careful.' But still the boys dawdled, as though they had plenty of time. Tutting, she watched until they were near the top of the street, then turned and put her foot on the bottom step. If they got into trouble it would serve them right, they were asking for it.

She was about to step inside, her mind now on the washing that was waiting for her in the dolly tub. She'd never know what made her turn her head for one last look at her son and his mate, but what she saw then horrified her and sent her running towards them. For three lads, a few years older and much bigger, had appeared out of the entry and were attacking the two friends. Billy and Pete had their arms up to shield themselves from the blows which were raining down on them from all directions. As she ran, Kate called for the bullies to stop, but they were intent on giving the smaller boys a hiding and didn't hear. But her neighbour did, and the urgency in Kate's voice had Monica flying out of her house and hot-footing it after her mate.

'What the hell d'yer think ye're doing?' Kate pulled at one of the bigger boys' arm, but he shook her off. The clout she gave him around the ear stopped him, though, and he grimaced as he rubbed his ear. He had his hand out to push her away so he could go back to beating the cowering boys, but changed his mind when he saw Monica swinging one of his mates around by the arm in the middle of the street, and the language she was using told him he'd do well to make his own getaway. He ran off without a backward glance. When Kate saw Monica had the second boy in a tight grasp, she shouted for her friend to hang on to him while she grabbed the third. He would have pulled away, because he was a big lad and she was no match for him, but Billy felt safe now. He put his arms around the boy's waist and hung on for dear life.

'Now, will someone tell me what this is all about?' Kate was blazing. 'Yer should be ashamed of yerselves, picking on kids younger than yerself.'

'We didn't pick on them, missus, they went for us for no reason at all.' This came from the one Kate was holding. He was a nice-looking boy with fair hair who looked as though butter wouldn't melt in his mouth. Looking across at his friend who was being firmly held by Monica, he said, 'Didn't they come at us, Andy, and start punching and kicking?'

'You flaming liar!' Kate's face was red with anger. Putting two and two together, she realized this was why her son had been more reluctant than ever to go to school today. 'I saw yer coming out of the entry, I'm not ruddy well blind! Nor am I stupid. Yer'd been laying in wait for them, hadn't yer? Well, unfortunately for you, I was watching and saw the whole thing.' She glanced from Billy to Pete. 'You both knew about it, didn't yer?'

Her son nodded. 'They want Pete's marble, the big whopper,

and they said they'd flay us alive if he didn't give it to them.'

'Me dad would kill me if I gave it away,' Pete said, not far from tears. 'Anyway, I wouldn't have given it to them 'cos they're bullies. They pick on all the kids, especially the small ones.'

'Oh, is that so? Cowards, eh?' Monica gave her prisoner a sharp slap across the face. 'That's for all the little kids who can't hit back.' She glanced across at Kate. 'What are we going to do with them, girl?'

'Let them go. I'll comb me hair and make meself presentable, then I'll take Billy and Pete to school. We'll see what the headmaster has to say about three big brave boys who like to pick on little children. I know they go to the same school because I've seen them.'

'They're in the seniors, Mam,' Billy said. 'They leave school at Christmas.'

'It wasn't our idea,' one of the lads said, 'it was Alex who started it. Wasn't it, Paul?'

'Don't be trying to wheedle your way out of it,' Kate said. 'Anything yer've got to say, say it to the headmaster. But don't forget, me and my neighbour saw exactly what happened and I intend to make sure that ye're punished for it. Now, off yer go. I'll see yer later in the headmaster's office. I might even stay for the caning.'

The remaining two boys slunk away, looking anything but happy and blaming each other. 'Yer shouldn't have let Alex talk us into it, I told yer not to.'

'I didn't twist yer arm, so stop yer whingeing. But I'll get Alex for this, I'm not letting him get away with it. And if we do get the cane, I'll batter him.'

Kate jerked her head as the boys rounded the corner. 'Just listen to them. They were going at it hell for leather when I got here, now each one's blaming the other. That's typical of cowards.' She put an arm across Billy's shoulders while Monica hugged a very pale Pete.

'I'll make us all a nice cup of tea and then yer'll feel better. I'll walk yer to school later. And for once yer don't have to worry about getting the cane.'

'Don't forget, Betty's coming at ten o'clock,' Monica reminded her. 'Will yer be back in time?'

'I doubt it, sunshine, 'cos I'll have to wait until after assembly to see the headmaster. I'm not going to let those boys get away with it, me conscience won't let me. Unless someone stops them in their tracks they'll grow up to be real bullies, always picking on those who can't fight back. If I'm not home in time for Betty, tell her what happened and she'll understand. And you can get all the news off her, anyway, and tell me over our morning cuppa.' Kate sighed. 'God knows what time I'll get me washing on the line, but it can't be helped. I'll have to move a bit quicker this afternoon, that's all.'

'I'll give yer a hand, girl, don't worry. We'll have yer washing out in no time.'

Kate squeezed her son's shoulder. 'See, that's what being a good friend means. Always there to help each other.' She bent down to look into Pete's face. 'Are yer feeling all right, Pete? Yer look a bit pale.'

'I'll be fine, Mrs Spencer. I'd been worried about those boys all night, 'cos they said they'd get me and beat me up. Me and Billy said we'd pretend to be sick so we wouldn't have to go to school, only you didn't believe him and my mam didn't believe me. But Billy didn't have to stay with me when they were beating us, 'cos it was me they were after, not him. He could have run away and left me but he didn't, he stayed, and that's like you said. A good friend is always there to help yer. That means Billy's a good friend, doesn't it?'

'It certainly does, sunshine! He's a good lad is my Billy. But it takes two to make a friendship, and I've seen for meself that over the years you've always been there for him as well. So that really makes yer true friends, like me and Mrs Parry. We've been mates now for over fifteen years, let's see if yer can beat that record.'

Billy liked the sound of that. After a little mental arithmetic, he said, 'We'd be twenty-five then, grown men. But I bet yer we beat your record with Auntie Monica, Mam. Me and Pete will still be friends when we're really old – about forty. That'll beat yours any day.'

Kate grinned across at her best mate. Neither of them wanted to shatter his illusions by telling him that when he was forty, they'd have been true friends for nigh on forty-five years, so he'd lose his bet. At least they hoped, please God, that they'd still be around at that time. Neither of them had plans to go anywhere.

Chapter Ten

When Kate arrived at the school with the two boys, the gates were closed but not locked. Although she felt as apprehensive as her son and his mate, she wasn't going to let it show, even though Billy had warned her that the headmaster was the devil in a suit. She opened the big heavy gates, let the boys and herself through, then closed the gates behind them. 'Ye're going to have to show me where Mr Sykes's office is because it's many years since I was in here.'

'Yer turn left when we get through the doors,' Pete told her as they crossed the playground. 'Then it's down a long corridor.'

'Well, there's no need to look so frightened, yer won't be in trouble.' Kate walked behind them up the two wide steps to the school entrance. And with her own heart hammering fifteen to the dozen, and her mouth dry with nerves, she told them, 'I'll make sure of that.'

But her words didn't help Billy at all. He was a very unhappy boy. 'You don't know what Mr Sykes is like,' he growled, 'he's dead mean and has a terrible temper.'

The corridor was long and wide, and there wasn't a soul in sight. The only sound came from the classrooms they passed. Kate could see pupils at their desks listening intently to what their teachers were telling them. In one classroom, the teacher was writing on the blackboard with a piece of chalk. They could hear him say, 'Take good notice of what I'm writing, because you'll be getting asked questions about it later.'

'This is Mr Sykes's office, Mam,' Billy said, wishing he was a million miles away. 'He won't be in, though, 'cos the door's open.'

'Then we'll just have to wait.' Kate kept her hands on the

boys' shoulders, thinking it would give them a little comfort. 'Although I hope he won't be too long, I've got stacks of washing to go back to.'

'Here he is now.' Billy's teeth were chattering. 'Be nice to him, Mam, or he'll take it out on us when yer've gone.'

Kate studied the man walking towards them. He was very tall and broad, and walked with his back held ramrod straight. His complexion was healthy, his mousy hair greying at the temples. He was obviously a man used to giving orders and being obeyed. And the stern expression on his face now was enough to put fear into any pupil.

'What have we here?' he barked. 'Overslept, did you, Spencer, and you, Reynolds? Well, speak up, boys, I'm waiting!'

He completely ignored Kate, taking away some of her fear and replacing it with anger. He's treating me as though I'm not here, she told herself. Well, that's ignorant, and I'm not going to stand for it! 'I've come to speak for the boys, Mr Sykes. My name is Kate Spencer and I'm Billy's mother.'

For the first time, the headmaster turned his eyes to her. For several seconds he didn't speak, he was so taken aback by the woman facing him with anger in her eyes, for hers was a face of great beauty, absolute perfection, such as he'd never seen before. He realized he was staring and quickly recovered. 'I'm so sorry, Mrs Spencer, please forgive me, I've been very rude.'

'I've come to explain why the boys weren't in school on time. I was afraid yer wouldn't believe them if they told yer what happened, and I didn't want them to be punished for something that was not their fault. But that is only one reason, I have another more serious reason for being here.'

Henry Sykes waved a hand towards the open door. 'Please go in, Mrs Spencer, and sit down. I think the boys should go to their classroom.'

'I would rather they didn't, Mr Sykes, because I believe they will learn a lesson here, now, that is far more important than any they'd learn in the classroom. So please let them stay.'

'By all means, if that is what you wish. But I'm afraid there aren't enough chairs. Reynolds, bring a chair from the staff room, please. If there's a member of staff there, explain that I have sent you.'

The last thing in the whole world the two boys had expected was to be sitting on chairs in the headmaster's office. The only time they went there usually was for punishment. So it was with wide-eyed amazement that they watched this turn of events. Oh, and with bated breath, because they still couldn't see Mr Sykes letting them off for being late. If he did, it would go down in the history books as a first.

'I'll start from the beginning, Mr Sykes, and you can question the boys afterwards to see if they agree that my version of events is correct.' Kate started with Billy's reluctance to go to school that morning, through to her seeing him and his friend being attacked by three bigger boys. Her face grew red as she told of running up the street, asking the other boys to stop, and being pushed aside. Then she described the intervention of her neighbour, who'd helped hold one of the boys until they found out their names. 'I don't usually tell tales, Mr Sykes, but these three were much older and bigger than Billy and Pete, and they could really have hurt them. They are bullies, and should not be allowed to get away with it. And that is why I wanted the boys to stay in your office, so they could see justice done. If those three aren't punished, I'm afraid that Billy and Pete might think, well, if they get away with it, why shouldn't we have a go at being bullies? That isn't something I want for my son, and I feel sure Mrs Reynolds would say the same about Peter.'

The headmaster sat back in his chair, his fingers laced across his stomach. 'This is a very serious matter and I will deal with it immediately. I will not have pupils from this school behaving like ruffians. Is it true, Spencer, that even very young children are picked on by these three pupils?'

137

Billy swallowed before answering. He just hoped the headmaster punished the bullies so much they'd never hit anyone, or steal from anyone, ever again. Because otherwise, he and Pete would be in real trouble. 'Yes, Mr Sykes. I can give yer some names and yer can ask for yerself. They probably wouldn't tell yer, though, they'd be too frightened.'

'You can give me the names of these three boys?'

It was Kate who answered. 'Only the first names. They are Alex, Paul and Andy.'

Mr Sykes left his chair and strode across the room. 'Excuse me, Mrs Spencer, I shan't be more than a minute.'

Billy groaned. 'Have we got to stay here, Mam? That Alex and the other two will batter us when they get hold of us.'

'Don't worry, sunshine, 'cos if they even look sideways at yer, I'll be round to see their parents. And I'll take yer dad with me.'

'Mrs Spencer, would yer have time to go round to see me mam and tell her what's happened?' Pete wasn't sure his mother would believe him. 'Otherwise I might end up getting a hiding.'

'I'll tell her, sunshine, so stop worrying. You and Billy have been very brave today, and she'll be proud of yer. There'll be no more kids frightened of coming to school or being threatened with a hiding if they don't do as the thugs want. No, I've got a feeling Mr Sykes is going to teach them a lesson they'll never forget. It might even make men of them.'

'Hush, Mam,' Billy said. 'Here they come.'

The door was flung open and they heard the headmaster's voice. 'Inside, the three of you.' The boys walked in with their heads bowed. No cockiness now, and too ashamed even to face Kate and the boys. The positions were reversed from this morning when they'd thought they were the big cheeses and everyone was afraid of them. Now they were going to get a taste of their own medicine, and it was they who were afraid.

Henry Sykes stormed round the desk to sit on his swivel

chair. 'Hudson, Wright and Fleming, I want to hear your account of what happened this morning. Why you attacked these two young boys who would not have been able to protect themselves if Mrs Spencer and her neighbour had not intervened. But before going any further, I would like each of you to give me your account of exactly what took place.'

'We were only playing around, sir,' said the leader, Alex Hudson. 'We didn't mean no harm, we were just acting daft.'

'That's right, Mr Sykes,' Paul Wright said, wringing his hands. 'Then these two women came up and started to hit us for nothing.'

When the third boy remained silent, the headmaster asked, 'Well, Fleming, what have you got to say for yourself?'

'We were hitting the boys, sir, because Alex wanted a marble off Pete and had threatened to give him a hiding if he didn't hand it over this morning.' Andy Fleming was really ashamed of himself, and regretted he'd ever let himself be talked into it by Alex. 'I'm really sorry, sir, and apologize for my part in the incident.'

Henry Sykes laid his hands flat on the desk. He didn't think he'd ever been so angry in all his years at the school. 'A marble?' he bellowed. 'You would beat boys younger and smaller than yourselves for the sake of a marble! Never, ever, have I heard of such thuggery from a pupil at this school.' Almost breathing fire, he said, 'There are three of you, and I have in mind three punishments for each of you which you richly deserve. First will be six strokes of the cane, a punishment I will mete out myself. Then your parents will be sent a letter, and the incident should be recorded on your school leaving report. The latter I would be reluctant to do, though, because it would affect your chance of gaining worthwhile employment. So, if you can prove to me in the short time you have left at this school, that you have really changed for the better, I might reconsider. But the other two punishments still stand and will be carried out today. Come back to this office at twelve o'clock sharp.'

As the boys turned to leave, their faces drained of colour, the headmaster asked in a stern voice, 'Have you no manners? Don't you think you should apologize to Mrs Spencer and the boys for your disgraceful behaviour? That at least would show you acknowledge the need to change your whole attitude and manner.'

The apologies from Alex Hudson and Paul Wright were grudging, given only because the headmaster was glowering at them. Andy Fleming was the only one who sounded sincere and showed true remorse.

After the door was closed on their backs, Kate asked, 'Can Billy and Pete go back to their lessons now, Mr Sykes? It's been quite a morning for them and the normality of the classroom would help them calm down.'

'Certainly, Mrs Spencer.' He looked from Billy to Pete. 'I'm sorry you've had to endure such an ordeal, but I assure you it will never happen again. Now join your class and tell Mr Wharton I'll be along presently to explain the reason for your being late.'

After a hug from Kate, which they could have done without because they felt really embarrassed in front of the headmaster, the boys left the room. This gave her the chance to say what was on her mind. 'If those three boys have a bad report when they leave school it will go against them getting a job, and I wouldn't want that on me conscience. They were very wrong to do what they did, and I'm glad they are being punished. But I would appreciate it if yer would think again about noting their behaviour in their end of school report.' Kate rose from the chair and faced Mr Sykes across the desk. 'Thank you for giving me your time and listening to me, I really do appreciate it. And now I'll leave you to get on with your work. I realize you must be a very busy man. Running a school with so many pupils in your charge can't be easy.' She held out her hand. 'Goodbye, Mr Sykes, and thank you once again.'

He rushed to open the door for her. 'Thank you for bringing such a serious matter to my attention. I shall be speaking to all the senior classes this afternoon, and the pupils will receive a warning. Although I have to admit the majority of them are polite, well-behaved and will never be in trouble.'

As Kate walked through the door, he said, 'If you ever have any queries regarding your son, I'm always here to listen.'

She nodded and smiled. 'Thank you.'

Henry Sykes watched her walk down the corridor, thinking what a lucky man Mr Spencer was to have such a beautiful wife. And it wasn't only her looks he admired. He believed she would be a generous person, kind and warm. The perfect wife, in fact.

'I'd just about given yer up,' Monica said when she opened her door. 'Yer've been gone ages, girl, I was beginning to think yer'd been run over.'

'I've been sitting in the headmaster's office, haven't I? With Billy and Pete, and chairs provided for all of us.'

'Go 'way! Well, I never!' Monica closed the door and followed her friend into the living room. 'Ye're not pulling me leg, are yer?'

'I am not! If yer make us a cup of tea, I'll tell yer all about it.'

'I'll have it on the table in the blink of an eye, girl, 'cos the kettle's been on the boil for the last half-hour.' Monica was true to her word, and was soon carrying two steaming cups through. 'To tell yer the truth, I was nearly going out to look for yer. I had no idea yer'd be that long, I half expected yer back for ten o'clock.'

Kate sipped on the tea and sighed blissfully. 'Oh, that tastes good. Me nerves were so bad when I got to the school, me mouth felt like sandpaper. And I can still see our Billy's and Pete's faces – they were a picture no artist could paint. I bet I won't be able to shut Billy up tonight, he'll never stop talking about sitting in his headmaster's room. As he said, the only time kids go there usually is to be punished.'

'I hope ye're not going to tell me this in dribs and drabs, girl, I'd far rather yer started at the very beginning. Right from the time when yer walked through the school gates, when, knowing what ye're like, I imagine yer were a bundle of nerves.'

'That's putting it mildly, sunshine, it would be nearer the truth to say I was terrified. And when I saw the headmaster striding down the corridor looking so stern, I knew just how the boys feel when they're waiting to get the cane for being naughty. But he was very nice really, and everything went well. Still, seeing as yer want me to start at the beginning, I'll take another sip of me tea then start.'

By the time Kate had finished the tale, Monica was nodding her head. 'I should think so, too! I'm glad those louts got their comeuppance. Perhaps they'll think twice in future before picking on kids smaller than themselves who can't fight back. If they had to face a proper man, they'd run a mile.'

'Oh, I think they'll be feeling very sorry for themselves right now.' Kate glanced at the clock. 'In an hour's time they've to report to Mr Sykes for six strokes of the cane. Not a pleasant prospect, I imagine. Then they'll get it in the neck from their parents when they read the letter from the headmaster.' Kate drained her cup and put it back on the saucer. 'One of the boys, I think his name was Andy Fleming, wasn't as brazen as the other two. He sounded ashamed of himself, and genuinely sorry.'

'Well, yer seem to have had an exciting morning, girl, but ye're not the only one. Betty came with some very good news.'

Kate raised her brows. 'Margaret and Greg are getting married.'

Monica gaped. 'How did yer know? Here's me waiting on pins for yer to come home so I could break the news to yer, and yer already know!'

'I didn't know, sunshine, it was just a guess. But it's something I hoped would happen for the sake of everyone concerned.'

'Ye're wasting yer time, yer know, girl, yer should get yerself a job as a clairvoyant in the fair at New Brighton. Ye're as good as Gypsy Rose Lee any day.'

'I'm not that good, sunshine, or I wouldn't have to ask yer what else Betty had to say. So, out with it, and from the very beginning.'

'Wait until I pour some more water into the pot, we may as well have another cuppa. And when I've finished telling yer Betty's news, we've got that washing of yours to put on the line before we go to the shops.'

The added water made the tea very weak, but Kate was glad to have it to sip on while Monica brought her up to date with the Blackmores' news. 'Yer mean, she wants us to go to the house for a drink after the wedding?'

'Yeah! They're not having a big spread, just the two families and us. And Betty said there's no need for us to go to the register office 'cos it's not a long ceremony. Just a few words and they'll be in and out.'

'Ah, it's sad if Margaret doesn't have anyone there to see her married.' Kate's tender heart came to the fore. 'You make it sound like a business deal, not a bit romantic.'

'They can't afford a big wedding, and with the girl being pregnant, well, it wouldn't be right anyway.'

'I'd still like to go to the register office,' Kate said firmly. 'We can at least throw a bit of confetti over them.'

'And what would yer suggest we wear, eh? I haven't got anything decent enough for a wedding.' Then Monica pursed her lips. 'Mind you, Betty said neither she nor Margaret is buying anything new, 'cos they need the money for other things.'

'Our summer dresses will be fine,' Kate said. 'No one will ever guess we got them from a second-hand stall at the market. All we need is a flower each, and we'll look as good as anyone.'

'I think ye're forgetting something, girl. What happens when yer meet Greg? He won't know whether to say he's met yer before or not!'

'I'm way ahead of yer, sunshine,' Kate giggled. 'That was the first thing I thought of. So, what I'll do, I'll see him before the wedding. I could wait for him outside his works one night, but that's too inconvenient for the family's dinner. So I'll have to try and find out what time he gets off the tram at night, and be waiting there for him. One way or another, I'll sort something out.'

'I've been wondering whether we should buy them a wedding present?' Monica sighed. 'Trouble is, I'm going to be strapped for cash. It's Dolly's birthday at the weekend, and your Nancy's two days later. And we can't let that pass without buying them a present.'

'Funny you mentioning their birthdays, 'cos I was looking in the window of the chemist's as I passed on me way home and saw something I thought would be ideal as one of their presents. They've got small bottles of toilet water for threepence. There's sweet-pea, rose or violet. As soon as I saw them I thought our Nancy would be delighted with one as a present. She wouldn't half feel grown-up.'

'So would our Dolly, she'd stink the ruddy house down,' Monica gurgled. 'I bet the bottle would be empty that very same day.'

'If it was, sunshine, yer could hardly shout at her, seeing as it was a birthday present.' Kate rapped her fingers on the table. 'Listen to this idea and see what yer think. For the girls, a bottle of scented water each, plus a fancy lace hankie for them to dab it on. That would cost us sixpence each, which we're going to have to afford because we can't let their birthdays go without a pressie. And as a present for Margaret on her wedding day, we could both knit a matinee coat, matching bonnet, gloves and socks. The wool wouldn't cost much, and they'd make a nice present. How about it?'

'Sounds good to me, kiddo! We could get an ounce of wool while we're at the shops today, and make a start.'

'Right, that's sorted out.' Then Kate frowned. 'Yer didn't say anything about Greg's mam! Was she all right about them getting married?'

'Must have been. Betty didn't say much about that, but then she wouldn't, she's not one for talking behind people's backs. But what I forgot to tell yer was that when Greg's parents left, he stayed behind and the two youngsters sat on the couch, close together. He seemed to unwind, with the wedding and everything sorted, and told Betty and Jack that Margaret was the only girl he'd ever wanted to go out with. He'd been wanting to ask her for a date for ages, but was too shy. And Margaret said she'd never wanted any other boy but Greg.' Monica took one look at Kate's face, rolled her eyes and groaned. 'Oh, God, yer've got that soppy look on yer face again. Ye're not half a sucker for sentiment. Romance, kisses, a love story, and ye're in yer element. Always want the happy ending, don't yer, girl?'

'There's nothing wrong with that, sunshine, it's better than having a heart of stone. Aren't yer pleased Margaret's getting married?'

'Are yer by any chance trying to tell me, in a roundabout way, that I haven't got a heart? And before yer answer that, I'd advise yer to remember who's going to give yer a hand to get that washing on the line.'

'Ooh, I'd forgotten about that for the minute, yer crafty beggar. But isn't it true that if yer don't get yer washing done first thing on a Monday morning, the whole day goes topsy-turvy? Anyway, to answer yer question, and with me dolly tub full of washing in mind, I do know yer've got a heart as big as a week.'

'Yer'd talk yerself out of anything, you would.' Monica picked up the cups. 'And where d'yer get this topsy-turvy from? Don't yer mean arse end up?'

'Yer know I hate that word, I think it's really crude.' A thought flashed through Kate's mind. 'Eh, sunshine, I wasn't half posh with the headmaster. D'yer know what I said to him when I asked if the boys could go back to their classroom? I said it had been quite a morning for them, and the normality of the classroom would help calm them down.'

Monica's chin dropped. 'In the name of God, girl, where did yer find a word like that? I've never heard it in me life! And even if I had, I wouldn't know where to use it.'

'It's the first time in me life I've used it, sunshine, and it'll probably be the last. But listening to how nicely Mr Sykes speaks, I wished I could talk like that. Not to show off, or try to be something I'm not, but because it's the way English should be spoken.'

'There's a lot of things that should be but aren't. Like men who slog their guts out every day and don't even earn a decent enough wage to keep a family on.' Monica was on her high horse now. 'Just take the men in this street . . . those that are lucky enough to have a job. They can't afford luxuries or to live in posh houses. They're lucky if their kids have got shoes on their feet, even if the soles are falling off.' She put the cups back on the table so she could wave her hands around for emphasis. 'But the men who own the factories, they don't go short of anything. They live in posh houses, have maids to wait on them hand and foot, and live on the very best food that money can buy. Only the best quality clothes for them – they probably don't even know Paddy's Market exists. And, of course, the best la-di-da schools for their toffee-nosed children. And where do they get their money from? From your John, my Tom, and all the other poor sods who slave six days a week for a bleeding pittance. Honest, it makes me blood boil.'

'Oh, dear.' Kate sucked in her breath. 'I've really started something, haven't I? I didn't think my saying I'd like to speak nice would have got yer so worked up. I mean, it's not going to happen, is it?'

'Not bloody likely it's not, not if yer want to stay my friend.' Monica was slowly calming down. 'I don't mind people having

146

more money than me, but some of them are so rich they won't be able to spend all their wealth in their lifetime so it's handed down to toffee-nosed kids so they can live a life of luxury without doing a hand's turn.' She clenched her fists and rested them on the table. 'I don't think I've ever told yer this but me mam's sister went into service when she was only thirteen. Mind you, this is going back many years, but I remember it well even though I was only about ten when she died. Her name was Auntie Florrie, and she used to visit us sometimes on her half-day a week off. From six in the morning until ten at night she worked, every day, except for the half-day off. She was nothing more than a skivvy, treated like a slave. And for that she received the princely sum of two shillings a month. Thirty years she was with the same family, and she was so loyal to them, she never took time off even when she was sick.'

Monica stopped and looked at Kate, who was sitting wide-eyed. 'I'll finish this tale if it kills me, 'cos it'll tell yer why I have such strong views. But knowing what ye're like, yer'll probably be crying yer eyes out by the time I've finished. So shall I carry on, or don't yer feel like a bleeding good cry?'

'At the moment, there's two things I'm sure of. First, I don't feel like a good cry, not when I've got that washing to do. But secondly, I really do want to know about yer Auntie Florrie, 'cos I'll never sleep tonight if yer don't tell me.'

Monica pulled a chair out and plonked herself down. 'If yer start bawling I'll crack yer one, 'cos yer'll probably start me off too. It takes a lot to make me cry, but I remember crying for days over me Auntie Florrie. Me mam and the whole family were really grief-stricken when they found out what had happened. Yer see, me auntie had taken very ill, and instead of her employers looking after her, as they should have done for all the years she'd slaved for them, they told her she wasn't fit to work any longer so she would have to leave. And instead of contacting us they had the chauffeur take her to the poorhouse on Belmont Road.

The only way me mam found out was because she was worried that her sister hadn't been for a while, so she went up one day to see if she was all right. Me mam was kept standing at the door of this big house while a maid told her what had happened. As yer can imagine, me mam was heartbroken and angry, so she demanded to see the mistress of the house. But there was no chance. A manservant was called to escort her down the path and told her not to come back. The poor man said he felt terrible about the way the family had treated me auntie, but he was only a servant and had to keep his views to himself or he'd have got the sack.'

Kate was sniffing up hard now. 'Ooh, that is so sad! What horrible people they must have been to treat someone like that when she'd been so good to them.'

'I knew what I'd like to do to them, but at the time I was still in junior school. Anyway, let me finish the tale or the men will be in from work and we'll still be sitting here.' Monica took a deep breath and continued, 'Me mam went straight to Belmont Road poorhouse, or workhouse as most people call them, and said she'd never seen anything like it in her life. The smell and the state of the place made her want to vomit. And when she asked to see her sister, a woman took her to a room where there was a worse smell than outside! It was the smell of death. And Auntie Florrie was lying on a makeshift wooden bed. The only thing covering her was her coat. Me mam said she looked so thin, and so sad, but she still wouldn't let me mam criticize the people she'd worked for. Anyway the only good thing was that me mam got there an hour before Florrie died, so at least there was a member of her family there to hold her.

'And d'yer know what sticks out in me mind, girl? Even after all this time? Me auntie had skivvied for thirty odd years, and all she had in the battered purse, which she gave to me mam, was a half-crown. Not much to show for thirty years' work and loyalty, is it? She died in a place which was so damp you could smell it.

There were bugs crawling up the walls and rats running over the floors. And my mother had to live with that scene in her mind until the day she died. She wasn't to know Auntie Florrie was ill, no one told her. But still she blamed herself for her younger sister having to end her days in a place like that.'

Childhood memories were flooding back for Monica, and tears came to the eyes of a woman who seldom cried. Although the image of her auntie was vague, blonde hair, light complexion, very small and slim, the memory of her had never faded. And the tears she was shedding for her Auntie Florrie were mixed with tears for her own mam who had died three years ago, just weeks before her sixtieth birthday. 'I don't know why I bothered telling yer all that, 'cos I've made meself all upset now.'

'I think what happened to yer auntie was terrible. How could anyone be so heartless? Yer'd think they'd have grown fond of her, living in the same house all those years. She should have been treated like one of the family.'

'Huh! She was never well treated, although she'd never say a word against the people. And the sad part is, she was a lovely-looking girl. Could easily have found herself a good husband and had her own home and family. But no, she wouldn't leave the Ashcroft-Palmers, she thought the world of them. And in the end, that's how they treated her. So, yer know now, girl, why I've got very strong views on the injustices in our country. There's too big a difference between the rich and the poor, some living off the fat of the land while others are starving. That can't be right, and surely to God one day someone will try and even things up a bit. Share the wealth out, like. I don't mind the rich having more than me, but I'd like a little more meself so you and me could go to the pictures in the afternoon occasionally, or down to Blackler's to buy ourselves something nice without worrying about being skint the next day. And the kids could have new clothes on their backs instead of second-hand ones. I don't think that's asking too much, there's enough to go round.'

Monica nearly knocked the chair flying when she jumped to her feet. 'That's today's lesson over, girl, it's time to see what's in yer dolly tub.'

Chapter Eleven

Kate took two pegs from her mouth to hang a pair of Billy's trousers on the washing line, then wiped her hands down her pinny. 'That didn't take long, sunshine, thanks to you.'

Monica was standing on the kitchen step, watching the line of washing begin to flutter in the soft summer breeze. 'They'll be dry by the time we get back from the shops and yer'll be able to bring them in and fold them ready for ironing in the morning.'

'I might do a bit tonight, if me legs are not too tired.' Kate put the wooden prop under the clothes line and lifted it higher. 'I hate to come downstairs in the morning and be welcomed by a high pile of clothes and bedding waiting for me. It's much easier if it's done in two lots.' She lifted her face to the warm sun. 'Doesn't a day like this make yer feel glad to be alive?'

Monica moved back into the kitchen to let her friend in. 'It's far too nice for a hot meal, but my Tom says he's starving an hour after he's had a salad. Still, yer get fed up wondering what to get every day.'

'I was thinking of getting some mince-meat and onions, and making a shepherd's pie. It's quick, easy, and all the family like it.'

'I'll be a copy-cat and have the same as you, girl. Save me racking me brains.' Monica picked up her basket which she'd left by the front door. 'Come on, slowcoach, the shops close for dinner in half an hour.'

'We'll split up,' Kate said, banging the door behind them. 'I'll get the onions and potatoes, and you get the mince. We can settle up with the money after. I need bread and carry-out, but I can get them later from the corner shop. Or I can send our Nancy for them while I slip down to see Winnie.'

Monica linked arms as they walked at a steady pace towards the main road. 'What d'yer want to see Winnie for?'

'To tell her about Margaret and Greg getting married!'

'It's got nothing to do with her! She'll only blab it all over the place and Betty will go mad.'

Kate brought them to an abrupt halt. 'I think she has every right to know because, like meself in a roundabout way, she had a hand in bringing this about. If she hadn't told me what she saw in the entry, and I hadn't made it me business to see Greg, everything might have turned out very different. I'm not saying it would, just that it might.'

'Can we have this argument on the way home from the shops, girl? Because the way we're going on, they'll be closed before we get there. And I know what ye're like when yer get in a paddy, there's no stopping yer.'

The couple carried on walking, their pace quicker now. But Kate couldn't keep things bottled up for long. She had to say what she wanted, when she wanted. 'I think Winnie has every right to know, and I bet she'll be over the moon that they're getting married. And as I've told yer before, she's not a gossip and doesn't repeat anything she's told. She keeps herself to herself.'

'Ah, come off it, girl, she talks to everyone she meets!'

'Yes, she does! And d'yer know why she talks to everyone she meets? Because once she shuts her front door, she's got no one to talk to but the four walls. It's a lonely life living on yer own as yer might find out for yerself one of these days. None of us knows what's going to happen to us when we get older, and it's a good job we don't.'

'All right, girl, keep yer bleeding hair on! I wouldn't have opened me mouth if I'd known I was letting meself in for a lecture. It doesn't take much to get you rattled, does it?'

'That's because yer sound really hard-hearted sometimes. I

don't know why yer do it, 'cos I know ye're really as soft-hearted as I am.'

'Oh, I wouldn't go that far! Not by any stretch of the imagination can yer say I'm soft-hearted. Compared to you I'm as hard as nails.'

They came to the butcher's and Kate pulled her arm free. 'I'll go for the spuds and onions, and meet yer down at the green-grocer's. We'll continue our conversation then. In the meanwhile I don't want yer thinking ye're as hard as nails, 'cos ye're not. If yer were, yer wouldn't be me best mate in all the world.' She waved through the window to the butcher. 'Tell Bob I want nice lean mince, not a load of fat.'

'Go on, yer hard-faced article, giving me the dirty work to do.' Monica watched her friend walk away, and stood for a few seconds asking herself why Kate had the power to make her feel so lacking in compassion? Compared to her neighbour she was, of course, but she wasn't going to admit it out loud. But she could be truthful with herself and admit that, unlike Kate, she would never have given two thoughts to Winnie Cartwright's being lonely. Or the other women in their street who lived alone.

Monica gave a quick shake of her head to clear her mind. Now wasn't the time to be having these thoughts, not when the butcher was watching her through the window, wondering if she was coming or going.

The two friends stood outside Kate's house later sorting their money out. 'The potatoes and onions came to threepence each,' Kate said, her purse open in her hand. 'And you say the mince came to one and six altogether?' She screwed her eyes up as she mentally added and subtracted. 'I owe yer a tanner, and then we're quits.'

'Leave it and pay me later,' Monica told her. 'I'm in no hurry and I know ye're not going to run away.'

'Out of debt, out of danger, sunshine.' Kate counted out a threepenny bit and three pennies and handed them over. 'I'll know where I'm working now. Once I've got the spuds peeled, and the mince and onions simmering, I'll nip to the corner shop for a loaf and something for the carry-out. Save worrying about it later.'

Too embarrassed to meet her friend's eyes, Monica looked down at the ground as she casually asked, 'What time are yer thinking of going to Winnie's?'

'It'll be after seven by the time I get the dinner over and the dishes washed. I'll sit with her for half an hour, then come home and start on some ironing. It'll be cooler then, I won't be sweating cobs over a hot iron.'

'I'll come to Winnie's with yer, if yer like? It would get me out of the house for a bit of fresh air, and I'll be company for yer.'

Kate's eyebrows nearly touched her hairline. 'And what would yer want to be coming to Winnie's for after all yer've said about her?'

'Well, I just think she'd rather have two people to talk to instead of the four walls. I mean, there's not much pleasure in holding a conversation with four bleeding walls. She wouldn't get many laughs out of them.'

Kate knew her friend was trying to make amends, and wasn't finding it easy. So she thought she'd help her out. 'I don't know so much! I've had many a conversation with my walls, and I always get the best of the argument.' She chuckled. 'Except for the back wall in the kitchen, now that's a real trouble-maker. Many's the time I've had to speak sharply to it and remind it who's the boss.'

'Yer don't have to tell me, I've heard yer.' Monica grinned. 'I only wish yer would swear now and again, though, girl, 'cos ye're never going to win an argument by being ladylike.'

'Oh, I have me moments, and can swear when I think it's necessary. But I don't agree that yer have a better chance of winning an argument by swearing like a trooper. Yer only lower yerself to the other person's level.' Kate stifled a yawn. 'It's been quite a day and I'm tired. I could just put me head down and drop off.'

'Then put yer dinner on, go to the corner shop, and come back and stretch out on the couch for half an hour. It'll do yer the world of good.'

'I think I'll take yer up on that, sunshine, 'cos I can't stop yawning. But I'll give yer a knock tonight when I'm going to Winnie's. Any time between seven and half-past. Ta-ra.'

'Ta-ra, girl, and you do what I said. Have forty winks before the kids come in, it'll perk yer up.'

Kate was turning the key in the lock when she heard her friend shout, 'Eh, girl, we've only gone and forgotten to buy the blinking baby wool! Shall I run down to the wool shop later and get a skein for each of us?'

'If yer would, sunshine, but only one skein, I can't afford any more.' Kate opened the door and stepped into the hall. 'And definitely in white, Monica, even if they have a half-price sale on of yellow or blue. It must be white.'

Monica couldn't see her mate, but she called back, 'Okay, I get the message. Ta-ra.'

It was a noisy hectic meal in the Spencer household that night with everyone talking at once. Billy's was the loudest voice, but Nancy was trying to get a word in because her mam, brother and Pete Reynolds had been the talk of the playground. There was great excitement as each girl gave their own version of why Mrs Spencer and Billy and Pete had been in the headmaster's office for ages and ages.

The boys' and girls' schools were housed in one building, but completely separate. The huge playground had high iron railings running down its centre, and it was by the pressing of faces between these railings that information was given and received.

No one knew exactly what had taken place so the various accounts were all guesswork and down to the imagination of the individual. Billy and Pete were the centre of attention and really enjoying their moment of fame, but nothing would have prised the truth from them. They wouldn't tell Nancy, or their best mates, in case Alex Hudson and his sidekicks decided they wouldn't start amending their ways until the next day, after they'd taught the lads a lesson they'd never forget.

Finally John banged on the table with the handle of his knife. 'Can we have one talking at a time, please, because I'm not clever enough to listen to three people at the same time.'

'Yer'd better let our Billy go first,' Nancy said, 'otherwise he'll burst a blood vessel.'

Her brother glared. 'Well, it was me being kicked and thumped by those lads, not you! So how can yer tell me dad what happened?'

Kate could see this was going to her son's head, and tried to bring him down to earth. 'What about Pete? Or have yer forgotten about yer best mate being there, in the thick of it?'

Billy was getting agitated. Why didn't they just keep quiet while he told his dad the tale? 'It was Alex Hudson wanting Pete's marble that started it all! So I couldn't forget he was there, could I? Not when I was trying to help him.' Then, in a defiant tone, he added, 'After all, I could have run away and left him.'

'Of course yer could, sunshine,' Kate said. 'Yer were very brave and I'm really proud of yer.'

Nancy was feeling contrite. She shouldn't have been so nasty with her brother, 'cos he had been brave to stay with Pete and take a battering. Most boys would have run away. 'Yes, I think it was really good of yer to stay with Pete. Ye're a hero, our Billy.'

Now that was more like it, the boy thought as he squared his shoulders. His sister had called him a hero, and he felt if he stood up he'd be ten feet tall. 'Aw, it was nothing. They didn't hurt us anyway.'

'Now ye're being modest,' Kate told him, affection in her voice. 'Yer've got an ugly bruise on yer arm, and another on yer leg.'

'Nah, they're nothing.' Not for the world would Billy say that the kick he'd received on his shin bone was giving him gyp, and his arm was sore. He was nearly eleven years of age and would be going into the seniors after the summer holiday. And senior boys should be able to take it, they weren't cissies. 'I can't even feel them.'

Eventually, John got Billy's version of events, then Kate's, and thought they both came out of it with dignity. 'Like mother, like son, eh? Well, I think yer both did very well, and I know where to come if I ever need help.' He pushed away his empty dinner plate and leaned his elbows on the table. 'But, as man of the house and Billy's father, don't yer think I should go round to see the ringleader of these bullies and his parents, to give them a piece of my mind? I know yer said the headmaster was going to write to them, but a face-to-face confrontation might have more effect than words on a piece of paper.'

Kate shook her head with some vigour. 'No, sunshine, leave things as they stand. I know how yer must feel, being Billy's father, but that Alex lad was a real arrogant bully and his parents might be the same. He may even have got it from them. So don't start anything, please, sunshine, 'cos I've had enough excitement for one day. I firmly believe Mr Sykes will sort this out in his own way. A few words from him will mean more than a hundred from us, believe me.'

'I suppose ye're right, love, but I believe in an eye for an eye. You punch me, then yer deserve a punch back.'

'Yeah, but you punching a fourteen-year-old boy, well, that's hardly fair play, is it?'

Billy took umbrage at those words. 'What about those lads battering me and Pete? They're years older than us, and bigger.'

'I know that, sunshine, but two wrongs don't make a right. So

157

let's not talk about it any more unless there's further news.'

'Can I tell me friends in school what really happened?' Nancy asked. 'There were all sorts of stories going around, and they're bound to ask me what really went on.'

'I'd far rather the truth stayed between us and Mr Sykes. But I know yer can't pretend I only went to see the headmaster to have tea with him so just say that a couple of lads were fighting with Billy and Pete, and that's why I was there.' She looked to her son. 'And I would like you to stick to the same story, Billy, d'yer hear?'

'Okay, Mam, if that's what yer want.'

'Good boy!' Kate's eyes slid to the clock on the mantelpiece. 'Look, I want yer all to do me a favour. I promised to call for Monica around seven, we're going to see Winnie Cartwright for half an hour. I haven't seen her around for a few days and I like to keep in touch with her 'cos I'm quite fond of her. So who's going to offer to help with clearing the table and washing up? I want it done by the time I get back so I can start on that mound of ironing that needs to be done.'

'I'll clear the table, Mam.' Billy sounded willing. Which he was, because he reckoned he owed his mam a big favour. If she hadn't turned up this morning things might have turned very nasty, and him and Pete would never have gone to the headmaster to tell on the boys so they'd have got off with it. 'And I'll shake the cloth in the yard and fold it away in the sideboard.'

'Me and Nancy will wash the dishes,' John told his wife, thinking she looked a bit tired tonight. Mind you, she'd had a very busy day. 'I volunteer to wash and Nancy can dry. Does that suit you, pet?'

'Yeah, I don't mind.' Everyone told Nancy she looked like her mother, and she hoped so because her mam was really pretty. 'You get ready to go out, Mam, me and me dad will clean up and have everywhere tidy for yer to come back to.'

'I'm only swilling me hands and face, I'm not getting changed. What's the point of me dolling meself up to go four doors away?' Kate's mouth opened wide in a yawn. 'I put me feet up for half an hour before yer came in, but for all the good it did me I might as well not have bothered 'cos I'm still yawning me head off.' She pushed herself away from the table. 'I might feel better after I've swilled me face.'

Kate held her cupped hands under the tap and filled them with cold water. Several times she did this, splashing the cold water on to her face. And it did the trick, she felt a lot more awake after it. 'I won't be out long, love,' she told her husband, 'it's just to keep her company for a while. And Monica said she'd come with me tonight, for a change.' She kissed his cheek. 'You behave yerself now, and don't do anything I wouldn't do.'

He glanced away quickly to make sure the children weren't listening, then winked up at her. 'I can't do anything when you're not here, so don't stay out too long. Yer should have an early night in bed 'cos yer look worn out.'

She chucked him under the chin. 'One-track-minded John, that's my husband. But I can't help meself, I do love him.'

Billy was coming through the door after shaking the tablecloth in the yard, and he heard. 'Ye're sloppy, you two. I'll never be like that 'cos I've made up me mind I'm never going to get married. I think I'll be a sailor and go away to sea.'

'Well, that's a lot different to getting married, son,' John said with a twinkle in his eyes. 'I personally don't think it's as exciting, but then everyone has different tastes.'

Billy shook his head in disgust. 'How can being married be more exciting than going to sea? Just think of the ship tossing in the waves during a storm, and of landing in different places all over the world.'

'What about the pirates?' John kept his face straight. 'They jump on board the ships, waving their cutlasses in the air. They'd

159

slice yer throat if yer didn't give them all the treasures yer were carrying. Oh, yes, son, if it's that kind of excitement yer want, a life on the ocean wave will give yer that.'

Kate smiled at the doubt on her son's face. 'I'll leave you to yer pirates and cut-throats, but ye're not to sign on before I come home, Billy, d'yer hear? I don't want yer going without giving me a farewell kiss. After all, I might not see yer for years.'

He chortled. 'I won't do nothing till yer get back, Mam, I promise.'

'Yer mean except helping yer dad and Nancy tidy up, don't yer?' Kate gave one quick glance in the mirror to make sure her hair wasn't all over the place, then made for the door. 'I'll see yer later.'

When she opened the front door it was to find Monica waiting for her. 'Yer can hear everything through the walls, girl, yer know that. I knew yer were coming out so there was no point in waiting for yer to call for me.' They fell into step and Monica said, 'So, yer son is going to be a sailor, is he?'

'Over my dead body! I'm not raising a son to go off to sea so I'll only see him once every blue moon. No, I'll talk him out of that. Or get a pretty girl to do it.'

They came to Winnie's house and Kate rapped with the knocker. There was no sound so after several seconds she knocked again. But still no answer. 'That's funny, she doesn't usually go out at night until she nips down to the pub at ten o'clock for her jug of stout.'

'Shout through the letter box,' Monica suggested. 'She may be in the kitchen with the tap running.'

Kate dropped down so that her mouth was near the letter box and lifted the flap. 'Winnie, it's Kate, can yer come to the door?' Her eyes narrowed and she looked puzzled. 'I can't hear a voice, but I'm sure I heard some sound. You have a listen, sunshine.'

They changed places, and Monica held her ear to the letter box. 'I dunno, but has Winnie got a cat?'

'Not that I know of, I've never seen one. Why?'

'I can hear something, but it's very faint. Look through the window, girl, see if yer can see anything.'

'I can't look through her window, what would the neighbours say if they saw me? They'd think I was being nosy.'

'Mrs Hastings lives next door, she wouldn't mind yer knocking to ask if she knows where Winnie is. After all, she may have only gone to the corner shop.'

'I'll give Peggy a knock, then, but I'm not looking through anyone's window. That's an invasion of their privacy. What if she's having a bath in the living room?'

Monica looked up at the sky. 'God give me the patience not to get all het up about me mate. She's just too bleeding good to be true, and she's getting on me nerves.'

'And you're too impatient, that's your trouble,' Kate told her with a nod of her head for emphasis. 'Yer'd think nothing of booting the door in, would yer?'

'Well, I certainly wouldn't hang around like you, that's for sure. Now give Peggy a knock and see if she can tell us anything.'

But Peggy Hastings couldn't help. 'To tell yer the truth, Kate, now as I come to think of it, I haven't seen Winnie for a few days.' Her forehead creased. 'And d'yer know, I don't think I've heard a sound from there, either! She's not a noisy person by any means, but I can usually hear her pottering around.'

Kate turned her head to look up and down the street. 'I don't know what to do. For all we know she may have gone for a walk and we're worrying for nothing.'

'Look through her window, like I told yer.' Monica could tell by the expression on her friend's face that she was going refuse, so she said, 'All right, I'll do it. I don't give a bugger whether the neighbours think I'm nosy or not.' She walked to Winnie's window, and with one hand shading her eyes from the sun, peered through the glass. Within seconds she was back to where Kate and Peggy were watching closely. 'She's on the couch. There's something not quite right, 'cos she seemed to have her eyes on me but didn't make any move at all.'

'Oh, dear, what can we do?' Kate was wringing her hands. 'I'm not a ha'porth of good in a situation like this, I go to pieces.'

'I'll go and get my feller,' Monica said. 'He can climb over the back wall and with a bit of luck the kitchen door won't be locked.'

'There's no need for that,' Peggy told her. 'I've got a front-door key. Winnie locked herself out one day, oh, it was years ago now, and asked if I'd mind her spare key in case she did it again. Hang on a minute, I'll get it for yer.'

'You go in first, please, sunshine,' Kate pleaded when the key was handed over. 'I'll probably pass out on yer.'

'You just dare and I'll clock yer one.' The two women were in the narrow hall now, and Monica pressed her friend's hand away. 'Don't be hanging on to me dress, ye're nearly strangling me!' She pushed the living-room door open and said softly, 'It's only Kate and Monica, Winnie, there's no need to be frightened.'

She tip-toed into the room, Kate right behind her. And they both gasped when they saw the plight of the little woman. She was stretched out on the couch, one arm hanging loosely over the side, and for a woman who was always spotlessly clean, she looked dreadful. Her dress was covered in what could only be vomit because the room reeked of it, and although her mouth was moving there was no sound. But what affected the two friends the most was the look in her eyes, as though she was saying she was sorry they were seeing her like this.

Kate dropped to her knees and gently lifted the arm that was hanging over the side of the couch. She placed it across Winnie's waist, and held it in place with hands she was trying to keep still because she was shaking all over with fear. 'Oh, sunshine, what's wrong with yer? How long have yer been like this?'

Winnie's tongue came out to lick her dry lips, and she tried to speak but no sound would come. 'I'll put the kettle on,' Monica said. 'What she needs is a drink.' She moved quickly to the kitchen and filled the kettle. There was a box of matches handy on the draining board and she lit one of the gas rings. Then she had a peep in the larder where she could see tea and sugar but no milk.

'Kate, I'm slipping home to get some milk. I'll be as quick as I can.' Monica popped her head around the door. 'There's water on for tea, and to wash Winnie. Try and get that dress off her if yer can, girl, 'cos she must be really uncomfortable.'

Kate opened her mouth to call her friend back, thinking she couldn't handle Winnie on her own. But just in time she asked herself how the older woman would feel if she thought she was being a burden, and forced a smile on to her face. 'Winnie, have yer got a set of clean clothes upstairs?' There came a slight nod of the head, and again the lips moved. This time there was a faint sound. Not a word, more of a grunt, but it gave Kate some hope. 'I'll go up and get the clothes ready for when Monica comes back. After we've got these off, washed yer down and put all nice clean clothes on, yer'll feel much better. And when yer've had a drink, yer might be able to talk a bit and yer can tell us how yer got yerself into this state.'

Kate was upstairs, going through the tallboy drawers gathering the clothes and nightdress Winnie would need, when she heard Monica come in by the front door which had been left open. 'I'm upstairs, sunshine, seeing to some clean clothes. I'll be down in a tick.'

Monica, a small jug of milk in her hand, smiled down at Winnie. 'I think a cup of sweet tea will do yer the world of good. God knows how long yer've gone without a drink.'

When Kate came down with the clothes on her arm, Monica said, 'Give us a hand to sit her up, girl, and we can give her this.' Between them they managed to sit her up with pillows behind her, and Kate held the cup while Winnie sipped from it. Monica had put plenty of milk in so the tea wasn't too hot. As she sipped, the older woman was nodding her head as though telling them it was what she badly needed. And she gave a sigh as gentle as a leaf being blown along the ground.

'We'll get these stinking clothes off yer now, girl,' Monica said. 'And when we've given yer a wash down, put nice clean clothes on yer and made yer comfortable, then yer can have another cup of tea.'

There came a knock on the door and Kate saw Winnie's eyes fly open in distress. 'I'll see who it is.' She hastened to the door to find Peggy Hastings standing on the pavement.

'I'm not being nosy, Kate, but is Winnie all right? We've been neighbours for years, and I'd hate to think she wasn't well and didn't give me a shout.'

Kate was flummoxed for a second. What should she do? But she knew Winnie wouldn't welcome any more visitors, not the way she was. 'She's been a bit off colour, Peggy, that's all. Some sort of bug going around which makes yer feel sick and upsets yer tummy. She hasn't been eating properly, but she seems to be brightening up now.'

'She an independent so-and-so,' Peggy said. 'I'm fed up telling her that if she ever needs anything, day or night, all she has to do is knock on the wall and me or my feller will be in like a shot.'

'I'll remind her when I go in. We've just made her a cup of tea and we'll try and get her to eat something. But thanks, Peggy, it was nice of yer to come. We'll keep her key until tomorrow, if yer don't mind, 'cos I'll nip down early in the morning to make sure everything's okay, and I don't want to be annoying you too early.'

'Yer wouldn't be annoying me, Kate, I'd be only too glad to help.'

'Thanks, Peggy, I'll tell Winnie what yer said. It's good she's got a neighbour like you.'

When Kate got back in the room it was to find Monica had managed to get the dress over Winnie's head. 'Did yer bring a clean vest down with yer, girl, 'cos she's badly in need of one.'

Kate nodded. 'Nightdress, knickers, vest and brassiere. And her tallboy drawers are a damn' sight neater than mine are. She puts me to shame.'

A large towel was put around the older woman to preserve her modesty while Monica washed her top half with scented soap on a nice warm flannel. Then, while she carried the bowl back out, Kate slipped the clean vest over a body that was so thin, there wasn't a pick on her. A nice floral cotton nightdress came next, and Kate managed to raise Winnie off the couch so it could be pulled down over her knees. 'Now I'm going to take yer knickers down, and put clean ones on. So don't be going all red and embarrassed, it'll be over in a couple of seconds.'

'Ask her if she wants to go down the yard to the lavvy?' Monica was rinsing the bowl under the tap, and the sound of running water had made her wonder how the older woman had managed. 'I noticed there was a pair of slippers by the hearth. Put them on her feet if she wants to go down the yard.'

But Winnie's legs gave way when Kate stood her up, and there was no way she was going to attempt the task on her own. 'Yer'll have to give me a hand, sunshine, it needs two of us. Otherwise Winnie's going to end up on the ground, with me on top of her.'

Between them they managed to get the woman down the yard, each holding her up by an elbow. Monica threw open the lavatory door, and said, 'Let me lift yer clothes. We'll sit yer down then wait outside until ye're ready. Will yer be all right?'

Winnie nodded, and when the door was closed she gave a sigh of relief. This was the first time she'd been to the lavatory since yesterday, and then she'd been so weak she'd never have made it if she hadn't steadied herself on the wall. She didn't know what was wrong with her but it had started three days ago.

Everything she ate came back, she couldn't keep it down, that was why she felt so weak. And today she hadn't had the strength to do anything but lie on the couch. Nothing to eat or drink, and afraid of knocking for her neighbour in case they thought she was a nuisance.

Kate opened the door a little and peeped in. 'Are yer ready to go back in now, sunshine? Monica put the kettle on for a pot of tea before she slipped to the corner shop for some bread and milk.' She held out an arm. 'Get hold of that and I'll pull yer to yer feet, then I can put me other arm around yer waist and see if we can make it up the yard. If not, we'll just have to wait for me mate.'

It was a slow process, but they finally made it, and when Monica came back from the shop Winnie was on the couch, surrounded by pillows and looking much better. 'I'm making bread and milk for yer, girl, it'll take the wind off yer tummy and it should stay down.'

When Kate went to feed her the bread and milk, Winnie shook her head and uttered her first word. 'Me.'

Monica chuckled. 'Yer sound like Johnny Weissmuller! "Me Tarzan, you Jane".'

Winnie ate quickly, showing the two watching women that she must be starving. When she'd finished, Kate took the plate from her, saying, 'That should keep yer going until tomorrow, sunshine, but yer need to drink a lot to make up for what yer've missed. So would yer like me to stay here with yer for tonight, just in case?'

Winnie's lips were cracked and dry. When she spoke her voice too was cracked, and faltering. 'No, thank you. Stay down here.' She closed her eyes as though talking was painful. 'Couldn't climb stairs. Now you go home to yer families, I'll be fine.'

'I'll give yer a drink, girl, to wet yer whistle.' As she reached the kitchen door, Monica turned and looked at Kate. 'Oh, I forgot to tell yer, I gave your feller a knock to tell him yer'd be later than yer expected.'

Winnie reached out a hand. 'You go home, queen, I'll be all right now.'

'There's no hurry, sunshine, John's perfectly capable of looking after himself. I'm waiting until yer feel up to telling us how yer got in this state.'

Winnie's head fell back on the pillows. She felt better than she had now she had clean clothes on and knew she didn't have to be as frightened of dying on her own as she had been. But all she wanted to do was sleep, she felt so weary. In a faltering voice she told them she'd bought a piece of cod from the fishmonger three days ago and had thought it tasted a bit off but foolishly she'd eaten it. Within an hour she was running to the lavvy and vomiting.

Talking was taking its toll. She could barely keep her eyes open so Monica gave Kate a nudge. 'Come on, let's get her ready for the night before she goes to sleep on us.' She moved quickly, Kate keeping up with her, and in a quarter of an hour Winnie was settled for the night, a chair set in front of the couch within easy reach with a cup and a jug of water standing on it. 'That should see yer through the night, girl.'

But Winnie was already asleep, and didn't hear Kate say she'd be down at half-seven in the morning. Nor did she feel the kiss dropped on her forehead, or the closing of the front door behind them.

Chapter Twelve

Kate rapped on the knocker before inserting the key in the lock. She didn't want to walk in on Winnie and frighten the life out of her. 'It's only me, sunshine, are yer decent?'

She strained her ears as a faint voice called, 'Come in, queen.'

Kate popped her head in, hoping to see an improvement in her neighbour. When she saw Winnie certainly looked better than she had yesterday, Kate closed the front door behind her. 'I've got John off to work, and the kids are getting themselves washed and dressed. They all send their love and hope yer'll be soon better.' She was carrying a small bowl with a saucer over it acting as a cover. When she placed it on the table, she said, 'I've brought yer a bowl of porridge to put a lining back on yer tummy.'

'You and Monica have been very kind, queen, I don't know what I'd have done yesterday without yer.' A faint smile crossed Winnie's pale face. 'I really thought I was dying – it certainly felt like it.'

'I can't understand why yer didn't knock on the wall for Peggy? Yer should never have let yerself get so bad without asking someone to help yer.'

'Well, I thought after the first day it would get better, and the next day I thought the same. But yesterday I felt too bad to knock for anyone. I was so weak with going to the lavvy and vomiting, I didn't have the strength to get off the couch. I was frightened, queen, 'cos I really thought I was a goner.'

'Ah, yer poor love.' Kate gave her a hug. 'Anyway, let's see if I can get yer down the yard. One thing about it, sunshine, it's a beautiful morning.' She helped Winnie to her feet but the older woman's legs buckled and Kate let her fall back on to the couch. 'I've got a brainwave, we'll use the brush as a walking stick. I'll hold yer tight on one side, and yer can use the brush for support with yer other hand.'

They were halfway down the yard when Kate burst out laughing. 'I've just been thinking about a saying Monica has when she trips up, and I only hope it doesn't apply here. She calls it going arse over elbow.'

It was only a half chuckle, but when Kate heard it, she felt heartened. 'Actually, I'm being very kind to me mate, telling yer that, because she's not so refined. What she really says is, "arse over bleeding elbow". And she doesn't care who hears her, either. Sometimes I don't know where to put me face.'

They reached the lavatory at the bottom of the yard, and Kate opened the door. 'D'yer want me to help yer with yer knickers?'

'No, I'll manage.'

'Then take the brush with yer to help yer keep yerself steady.'

After closing the lavatory door, Kate flew up the yard to put the kettle on to make a pot of tea. She wanted to be home by eight to make sure the children got their breakfast, and to be certain Billy hadn't got a tidemark big enough for the *Queen Mary* to sail in.

In the kitchen Kate found the tea and sugar and raised her eyes to thank God there was just enough milk left in Monica's jug for a cup of tea. She put a light under the kettle, set a cup and saucer ready, then flew back down the yard. 'I'm outside when ye're ready, sunshine.'

The wooden door was pushed open, and there stood Winnie with both hands around the top of the brush for support. 'Well, where there's a will, there's a way.' Kate just couldn't hold the laughter back. 'Oh, if only yer could see yerself, sunshine. I know I shouldn't laugh, that to you it's not funny, but yer put me in mind of a nosy, lazy woman, standing gassing to a neighbour while leaning on the brush instead of using it on her step.'

'I'm glad yer haven't got a camera, queen, 'cos I haven't got me best dress on, and I haven't had me hair Marcel-waved.'

'No, but ye're showing a bit of knicker, though, yer brazen hussy.' Kate found it easier going back up the yard because the brush was proving to be a blessing. When they were back inside the house, she led Winnie to the couch. 'You sit there, sunshine, and I'll get yer a bowl of water to wipe yer hands and face over. Then yer can eat the porridge before it gets cold.'

Winnie grabbed her arm as she went to walk away. 'Ye're spoiling me, queen.'

'I hope ye're not complaining! Make the most of it while yer've got the chance. I've often wished I'd been born into a rich family, so I could be waited on. Like yer see in the pictures where Claudette Colbert has this beautiful negligee on, and sweeps across the room to where her maid is running a bath for her. But some people are born lucky and others are not.'

'If Claudette Colbert could see you, she'd be the jealous one, 'cos ye're far more beautiful than she is. And I bet she's not as kind as you.'

Kate put her hands on her hips. 'Just listen to the pair of us, and we've got the cheek to talk about people what jangle. We've had a go at Claudette Colbert and we've never even met the woman. She's probably a very nice person.'

Time is marching on, she thought, and made a hasty trip to the kitchen to pick up the bowl of warm water and the flannel and nice scented soap. 'Here yer are, sunshine, give yerself a wipe over while I make the tea.' She reached the kitchen door, then turned back. 'Eh, how come yer've got scented soap? I've never had any since the kids were born! Proper posh, that's what yer are, just like our friend Claudette.'

Winnie was wiping her face and neck with the warm flannel. 'I mugged meself at Easter. I had no one to buy an egg for, so I mugged meself. And I don't use it every day, mind, only now and again, 'cos it's got to last.'

'And I've got to be home for eight to see to the kids. So I'll take the bowl out now, sunshine, and pass yer the porridge. While ye're eating that, I'll make yer a cup of tea, then I'll have to vamoose. But Monica will be here at nine to see if yer need anything.'

'There's no need, queen, I'll be all right now.'

'Of course yer won't be all right now! Ye're as weak as a flaming kitten, and it'll be a few days, getting some goodness down yer, before yer'll be anywhere near all right.' Kate's hands went to her hips. 'D'yer hear me, Mrs Woman? Me and me mate are going to look after yer whether yer like it or not. And this afternoon we'll be coming to visit so we can give yer the news we were going to give yer last night, only yer'd gone and got sick on us.'

'What news is that, queen?'

Kate put a finger to her lips. 'I can't tell yer that without me mate being here or she'd have me guts for garters.'

'How did yer think Winnie looked?' Kate asked as she walked towards the main road with her friend. 'I was wondering whether we should call the doctor in, just to be on the safe side.'

'I don't think there's any need for that, and I'm bloody sure Winnie wouldn't thank yer if a doctor walked in on her.' Monica shook her head. 'No, girl, let's give it a day or two and if she's no better, then it'll be time to call someone in. What we've got to do meanwhile is feed her up with the likes of rice pudding, sago, and custard. Just for the next day or two, until her tummy's settled down. Then she can go back to eating what she usually eats.'

'She's terribly thin, though, sunshine, not a pick on her. I know she's always been thin, but not like she is now.'

'Three days of being sick can take the weight off yer like nobody's business, girl, take it from me. But she'll be a bit better each day, you'll see.' Monica glanced sideways. 'By the way, have yer told her about the wedding yet?'

'No, I haven't, except to say we had some news for her. I wouldn't tell her without you being there, so I said we'd call this afternoon.'

'Yeah, she told me. That's why she's asked me to get a pint of milk in with the other bits she's asked for. And d'yer know what I've been thinking, girl? Listen and see if yer agree with me. She must be missing her nightly jug of stout if she's been getting it every night for years, and stout is reckoned to be very good for yer. I mean, they recommend pregnant women to drink it because of the goodness there is in it.'

'Yes, I've heard that, sunshine. I tried it meself when I was carrying our Nancy, but it was too strong for me, I didn't like it.'

'But yer agree with me that it would do her good?'

'It would probably do her the power of good! Certainly wouldn't do her no harm.'

'Then yer wouldn't mind going down to the pub with her jug, and asking them to fill it?'

'What! I'm not walking into no pub full of men and asking the barman to fill a jug with milk stout! Only loose women go in pubs on their own, and I'm not having meself looked over by a gang of boozers. John wouldn't like it, either!'

'But yer wouldn't be on yer own, girl, I'll come down with yer.' There was a wicked gleam in Monica's eyes that Kate couldn't see. 'So how does that suit yer?'

'Oh, I wouldn't mind the two of us going in, we wouldn't be so conspicuous.'

'I think yer misunderstood me, girl! I didn't say I'd go in the pub with yer, I said I'd go down with yer. I meant I'd stand outside.'

Kate gasped. 'Well, yer know what yer can do, Monica Parry, yer can sod off! How soft you are – waiting for me outside indeed! Yer must take me for a right lemon!'

172

'Ha-ha-ha, ooh, ha-ha-ha.' Monica doubled up. 'I knew that would get yer going. I told Tom this morning yer'd lose yer rag. Honest, girl, yer'd fall for anything.'

Kate really got on her high horse now. 'Oh, and why, pray, were you and yer husband discussing me? Have yer got nothing better to do?'

'Well, there's not much to talk about at seven in the morning, is there? Me and my feller were sitting facing other, chewing toast, and I suddenly understood why people say the gilt soon wears off married bliss. Anyway, for the sake of seeing Tom look halfway awake, I told him I was going to pull your leg. And I told him what yer reaction would be. He didn't believe yer'd fall for it, but he doesn't know yer like I do.'

'Ye're a holy terror, Monica Parry, and one of these days I'll get me own back on yer. The thing is, I'm not as devious as you.' Kate could see the joke now and was dying to laugh, but she thought she'd drag it on a bit longer. 'Yer see, sunshine, all is pure to the pure, and I have a very pure mind.'

'My God, girl, if yer had yer hand on yer forehead, and put on a sad face, yer'd be a dead ringer for Mary Pickford. In that picture where her cruel landlord has thrown her out of her house and she has nowhere to go. It's cold, the wind is blowing, and snowflakes are beginning to fall. She's desperate, lost the will to live, when along comes Charlie Chaplin and rescues her from a fate worse than death.'

Kate began to clap her hands. 'That's the best performance yer've ever given, sunshine, it's no wonder the people are standing in the aisles shouting for an encore.'

'Ah, it's so good to meet someone who appreciates my artistic talents. You are a lover of the arts, I take it?'

'Oh, most definitely! *King Lear*, *Midsummer Night's Dream*, oh, I practically know all of Shakespeare's work off by heart.'

People going past were glancing with curiosity at the two women who were holding on to each other while laughing their heads off. It seemed to be infectious because the scene brought a smile to many faces. And even if there were a few miserable souls who found it hard to laugh, the two women didn't care. They were having their funny half-hour and folks could like it or lump it.

'Come on, sunshine, let's get our shopping in. I don't want to be out too long, 'cos I've still got some ironing to do.' Kate squeezed her friend's arm. 'I enjoyed that laugh, it was just what I needed. Now comes the serious business of what to get for the family's dinner. I'm not getting fish, not after what happened to Winnie. I know the man in the fish shop wouldn't have sold any he thought was off, but nothing keeps for long in this hot weather. So I think we'll have a salad. Lettuce, some tomatoes, four eggs, and either corned beef or brawn. And a nice crusty loaf from the home-made baker's.'

'Yer know, yer must be a mind-reader, 'cos that's exactly what I had in mind for our dinner. They say great minds think alike.'

'You are one big fibber, Monica Parry! Yer had no idea what yer were getting to eat. At least, not until I told yer what we were having.'

'D'yer know what I do fancy, girl?' Monica licked her lips. 'A custard from the baker's to have with our afternoon tea. Doesn't the thought of them make yer mouth water?'

'I won't let me mind dwell on them long enough for me mouth to water, 'cos I can't afford one. It's the girls' birthdays at the weekend, and I need every penny to buy Nancy's cards and presents.'

'I'll mug yer to a custard,' Monica said. 'Life is a bit easier for me money wise with only having Dolly, a couple of coppers won't skint me.'

Kate shook her head. 'No, don't tempt me. Yer know I've got a sweet tooth and love cakes and sweets, but what I can't afford I'll do without. Thanks all the same, sunshine, it was a very generous offer.'

'Well, Winnie asked me to get some biscuits so I'll get custard creams, 'cos I know they're yer favourites. And two custard creams are as good as one custard.' Monica jerked her head. 'Who am I trying to kid? I'd rather have a custard any day! But if me best friend is fasting, then I'll suffer with her. On one condition though. That you go in the baker's for our two crusty loaves so I won't be tempted. Yer know I've got no willpower.'

'When yer've got no money, yer've got to have willpower, sunshine. I don't let me mind dwell on things I know I can't afford. And if we don't get a move on, I'll not get the rest of me ironing done before it's time to go to Winnie's.'

'Yer want us to leg it, do yer, girl?'

Kate chuckled. 'I haven't legged it since I was our Nancy's age. In fact, apart from two women our age looking ridiculous going hell for leather down the road, I'd have no breath left by the time we got to the shops.'

'Let's try a nice sedate pace then, eh? Not fast and not slow. But keep in mind that yer've got yer ironing to do, and I told Winnie we'd be there around half-two to three o'clock.'

'Right, I've made a mental note of it. And here's our first port of call for the lettuce and tomatoes.'

When the friends walked into Winnie's that afternoon, they were surprised to see her wearing one of her dresses. 'Yer didn't go up the stairs for that, did yer?' Kate asked. 'Why didn't yer stay in yer nightdress, yer'd have been more comfortable?'

'I had big hopes and big ideas, queen. I wanted to look respectable for yer coming, so I told meself I'd be able to get up the stairs as long as I clung to the handrail. But I'd only got as far as the bottom of the stairs when I knew I wasn't going to make it. Still, I can be bleeding stubborn when I set me mind on anything, so I went upstairs on me bottom. It was quite easy really, I just pushed meself backwards up each stair. And when I took me nightie off an' put this dress on, I felt really pleased with me little self. Anyone would think I'd swum the Channel, I was that proud of meself.'

'Yer could have fallen and broken yer bleeding neck!' Monica's voice was high but not with anger so much as fear of what could have happened. 'These stairs are so steep they're deathtraps at the best of times.'

'Well, I'll be honest with yer, queen, coming down wasn't nearly as easy as getting up. I stood on the landing and looked down the stairs and, d'yer know what, the bottom stair seemed miles away. After I'd called meself for all the stupid cows going, I wondered how the hell I was going to get down. Still, I couldn't stay up there all day, could I? So I did no more than drop to me knees, rolled on to me backside, and shuffled forward. And that's how I came down, on me backside and shuffling.'

'I hope ye're not thinking of sleeping in yer bed tonight, sunshine, because if yer do, then I won't get a wink of sleep for worrying about yer. Yer'd be asking for trouble.' Kate was really concerned. What would happen if the older woman had an accident and no one knew? It didn't bear thinking about. 'Yer'd be better putting yer nightdress back on and settling down on the couch. Ye're asking too much of yourself, need more time to get some strength back. Maybe the day after tomorrow, all being well, me and Monica will walk yer to the bottom of the street and back, for a bit of fresh air.'

'I've learned me lesson, queen, I won't be trying anything until I'm fit enough.' Winnie rested her head back on the pillows. 'It's fair taken it out of me, and I'll not try it again. Stubborn I might be, stupid I ain't.'

'I got the custard creams yer asked for, girl, so I'll put the kettle on to make us a drink. And while I'm waiting for the water to boil, I'll put a rice pudding in the oven.' Monica had it all worked out. 'If we leave it in for two hours on a low light, it should be nice.'

'Yer won't forget to put a blob of butter in it, will yer? And I've got some nutmeg to sprinkle on the top. That's the way I like it. When it's cooked, yer can't beat the skin on top.'

'Listen to me, girl.' Monica stood in front of the couch wagging a finger. 'You go and teach yer grandmother how to milk ducks! I'll have yer know I make the best rice puddings in Liverpool! Renowned for them, I am.'

Winnie grinned. It was nice to hear voices and laughter in the house. It was usually so very quiet you could hear a pin drop. 'Okay, queen, keep yer hair on. How was I to know yer were the best rice pudding-maker in Liverpool?'

'If you two are going to make a song and dance about rice puddings, and who makes the best, I think I'll make a start on the tea,' Kate said. 'Otherwise we might find out that Monica makes fairy cakes so light yer have to hang on to them or they'd float off the plate.'

Monica barred her path. 'Ye're only jealous, girl. And there's nothing worse, to my mind, than having a mate what's envious. So sit down and give yerself a good talking to, while I get about doing what's necessary.'

When they were finally settled with their cups of tea and a custard cream biscuit in the saucer, Winnie asked, 'What was the news yer had for me, queen? I hope it's something nice to cheer me up.' Then as the words left her mouth she realized they might sound insulting to the two women who had been so good to her. 'Not that you two don't cheer me up, ye're like a breath of fresh air.'

'Thank you for the compliment, sunshine, but me and Monica have been glad to help. And we'll do the same tomorrow, and the next day if necessary.'

'Kate, are yer ever going to bleeding tell me what the news is that yer have for me? I've missed knowing what's going on in the street.'

'Okay, sunshine, but I'll let Monica tell yer her bit of news first. And if that doesn't cheer yer up, then nothing will.'

Monica grinned. She was slowly learning that helping someone in distress does have its reward. It makes you feel good. 'My feller Tom is going to get yer jug of stout for yer tonight. We thought yer'd been missing it, and anyway it'll do yer good. A jug of that and yer'll be ready to fight Popeye.'

'Oh, queen, that's really good of him. I have missed it something terrible, I think it's what keeps me going.' Winnie gave a deep chuckle. 'But I can hardly go down to the pub on me backside.' Once again she chuckled. 'Not that I hadn't thought about it, mind.'

'Well, I'll take the jug home with me and bring it back full about half-eight. And if yer want a laugh, my feller said I've got to go down to the pub with him, 'cos if I don't he's going to lose valuable drinking time.'

'Oh, dear, we can't have that, can we?'

'That's something I'm giving careful consideration to,' Monica told her, tongue in cheek. 'If I start letting my feller boss me around, heaven knows where I'd end up. So we'll wait and see what tonight brings. But whatever happens, girl, yer'll get yer milk stout.'

'Don't yer be falling out with yer husband because of me!' Winnie didn't know about Monica having her tongue in her cheek, you see, and didn't want to be the cause of man and wife having a row. 'It wouldn't kill me if I didn't get the ruddy milk stout. I can wait until I'm on me feet again, it'll only be a few days.'

Kate tutted. 'Monica Parry, can't yer see Winnie thinks ye're serious? Go on, tell her yer've got the softest, most easy-going husband yer can imagine.'

'Yer've already told her, girl, and I hate repeating meself. So why don't yer just go ahead and tell Winnie your news.'

178

Kate rubbed her hands, a smile on her lovely face. 'I think this is wonderful news, and I'm dying to see your face when yer hear it. D'yer remember me telling yer about Margaret Blackmore being in the family way, and that the boy responsible was denying all knowledge of it? And how Betty and her husband were out of their minds with worry?'

'Of course I remember, queen, and I was really angry that the lad had let her down. They're a good family, the Blackmores, all of them, and they don't deserve that.'

'Well, there've been some changes there. The lad met Margaret coming out of work one night, told her how sorry he was for lying, and went with her to see Mr and Mrs Blackmore. And although there's a lot more gone on, like Greg's mam not being too happy about it at first, he's proved he's got more backbone than we all gave him credit for. He asked Margaret to marry him, and Betty's making all the arrangements for next week. It's going to be a register office wedding, but that's what Margaret wants. She's right because the priest wouldn't marry her at the altar, not in her condition, and she'd have to wait weeks for the banns to be read, by which time she'd be showing. So I think it's best for all concerned. It won't cost nearly as much in a register office, and they don't need any frills and flounces.'

Winnie leaned forward. 'Oh, that is certainly good news, that is, queen! Oh, I'm so glad for Betty, and the girl of course. I wonder what made the boy change his mind? I'm glad he has, for everyone's sake.' Her eyes were eager. 'Go on, I'm sure there's more yer've got to tell me.'

'Not until we have a chance to talk to Betty. She should have all the details by now, so we might call there tonight or tomorrow.' Kate sat up straight and folded her arms neatly across herself. 'Monica and I have been invited to the house to toast the bride and groom. We might even go to the register office so we can give some moral support and throw confetti.'

'I'll be better by then, queen. If you and Monica don't mind, I'd like to come with yer. I don't get to go many places now, so it would be like a day out for me.'

Without even exchanging glances, Kate and Monica spoke as one. 'Of course yer can come.' They burst out laughing and Monica said, 'I told yer great minds think alike, girl, and that proves it.'

Then Winnie asked something that took Kate by surprise. 'So yer've met Greg Corbett now, then?'

Kate stared at her as though she didn't understand what she'd been asked while her brain told her she would have to tell a lie. It would grieve her to lie to this woman, though. 'What makes yer say that?'

'Well, with yer being invited to the house for a drink, I thought yer must have met him.'

Monica could see Kate's dilemma, and knew how her friend hated telling lies. Even if they were only white ones. 'We've never met him, it was Betty who invited us. Margaret knows but I don't know about the lad. As far as we know there'll only be the two families there, and me and Kate. It's in such a rush, no one has had time to save up and money is tight.'

'Yer'll know him when yer see him even if only by sight. He lives a few streets away.' Winnie hadn't noticed Kate's red face and carried on. 'I've seen him around a lot over the years, mostly when he was going to school. In fact, I've seen him twice in the last few weeks. With the weather being so good, I've taken to going for a walk in the early evening, so the day doesn't seem so long. Time drags when yer live alone and are sitting talking to yerself. Anyway, I've seen Greg Corbett a couple of times, getting off the tram at about a quarter-past six on his way home from work.'

'Then we probably have seen him,' Monica said, hoping to glean some more information. 'I mean, the tram stops practically at the end of this street!'

'Oh, not this stop, queen, it's the next one he gets off. It's nearer his home.'

'Well, our curiosity will be satisfied when we meet him. He probably knows us by sight as well.'

Kate jumped to her feet. 'Anyone want another cup of tea?'

Chapter Thirteen

'Shall we get the same scent for both of them or not?' Kate and Monica were looking in the window of the chemist's shop. 'If we get them different, it could cause friction if one would rather have had what the other one's got.'

'Get them the same, girl, then there's no argument. I like the sound of the sweet-pea the best, what d'yer think?' This was a bit of selfishness on Monica's part because she liked the smell of sweet-pea and might have the occasional dab behind the ears. 'Or would yer rather have the violet?'

Kate shook her head. 'No, I think the sweet-pea. Let's buy it and get it over with, then we can go for the hankies.' As they walked into the shop she said, 'Just think, sunshine, this time next year they'll be leaving school.'

'Yeah, we'll be in the money then, girl, with a few bob extra every week. Mind you, to hear our Dolly talk, she's going to break eggs with a big stick. What she isn't going to do with her pocket money is no one's business. I heard her talking to your Nancy last night and they have visions of long stockings, high heels and lipstick. I didn't disillusion them, it's best to let them find out for themselves.'

'They're no different from what we were at their age,' Kate said. 'I know I had big ideas, but in those days the wage for a fourteen year old was three shillings. Out of that I got sixpence pocket money.' She smiled at the assistant behind the counter. 'Two bottles of the sweet-pea toilet water, please. And can you put them in separate bags, they're for presents.'

When they were outside the shop again, Monica said, 'The wage is only five bob now for school-leavers. Yer'd have thought it'd have gone up more than that in the last twenty years, wouldn't yer?'

'It doesn't seem to make any difference, sunshine, because when wages go up so do rents and the price of food. We just can't win.' She looked sideways at her friend. 'But don't yer start on yer pet subject of the rich getting richer and the poor getting poorer. Let's think of nice things, like our daughters' birthdays.'

'How about me having a tea for them on Saturday, and inviting Winnie to come up? She should be fit by then, and it's only a matter of walking a few yards.'

'She'd love that. As she says, she seldom goes anywhere.' They were passing the sweet shop and Kate remembered they needed cards. 'We'll get them now, while we think on, and we may as well get a wedding card for the bride and groom.'

'It's one thing after another, isn't it, girl?'

'Ye're not kidding! By the time we've got the cards and the hankies, I'll be skint! We'll be living on bread and dripping until I get John's wages on Saturday.'

'What are yer going to do about Greg Corbett? The lad won't know whether he's supposed to know yer or not!'

'I'm going to the tram stop tonight. As soon as John steps foot in the door, I'll be off. I should be in time for Greg getting off the tram. The poor lad will probably have a fit when he sees me, but I can't help that. And it'll be another worry off me mind.'

'What are yer going to say to him?'

'I dunno, sunshine, I'll play it by ear. It went off all right last time, so there's no reason why it shouldn't this time. In fact, it'll be a doddle this time 'cos it's not as serious. Two minutes, that's all it'll take to tell him he's never seen me in his life before. Now that's not difficult, is it?'

'Not the way you see it, no! But I wouldn't be taking it so calmly, and I'm a damned sight more hard-faced than you are.'

Kate laughed. 'Yer like to think yer are, but ye're not that tough. Yer don't frighten me, anyway, even when yer get on yer high horse.'

'Don't be getting too cocky, girl, 'cos yer've never seen me when I'm in a real temper. That's when I start throwing pans and crockery around. They're aimed at Tom's head, but I'm a lousy shot and they usually hit the wall. And if I can't hit a standing target at only three feet, I'd be no good to Robin Hood and his Merry Men. In fact, if they let me loose with a bow and arrow, he wouldn't have any men left.'

Kate looked at her with surprise. 'What made yer think of Robin Hood, sunshine? Yer mind must have been miles away!'

'Ah, well, it's like this, yer see, girl. Most people have their favourite film or stage star, and mine is Robin Hood. I fantasize about him something rotten. How he'll come along on his horse and carry me off. I'd go willingly as well, he wouldn't have to drag me.'

'Some imagination yer've got, Monica Parry! We've gone from our daughters' birthdays, to Greg Corbett, and from there to Sherwood Forest and Robin Hood. Yer've got me dizzy trying to keep up with yer.'

'Tom doesn't have any trouble keeping up with me. In fact he's a great admirer of Robin because of the favours he's done him. Yer see, some nights, when I'm half asleep, I imagine Tom is Robin. And as my feller will tell yer, he has more fun in bed those nights than on any other. He's even thinking of buying a picture of him and putting it on the wall opposite our bed, so it's the last thing I look at before I close me eyes. Naturally I'll think I'm in Sherwood Forest and get very loving and passionate, and Tom'll think it's his birthday.'

Kate was shaking her head and tutting. 'Monica Parry, don't yer think it's about time yer grew up?'

'Not bloody likely, I'm having too much fun! Tom thinks I've forgotten about it the next morning, but I haven't. I just act daft, ask him if he's got a tanner to spare, and he hands it over like a good little boy. So, yer see, Robin Hood is doing both of us a power of good. Yer want to try it yerself sometime.' Monica bit on the inside of her lip to stop a smile appearing, before she said, 'On second thoughts, I don't think yer should bother. I believe yer favourite film star is Charles Laughton, and *he* couldn't arouse passion in anyone.'

'I never said Charles Laughton was me favourite film star! I said he was a good actor, that's all. I don't know any that I'd go crazy over.'

'Then borrow mine, girl, and give John a treat. All yer've got to do is close yer eyes and think Robin. Yer can think of his Merry Men as well, if yer've got the energy, but if yer take my advice yer won't be so greedy.'

Kate tilted her head. 'Have yer ever thought of seeing a doctor about these fantasies of yours? He can maybe give yer something to cure yer.'

'Cure me? I don't ruddy well want to be cured! I want to live my life to the very full while I'm still young enough to enjoy it. I don't want to be a sour-faced stick-in-the-mud like some folk I know.'

'Is that a hint, sunshine?'

'Now, if I thought yer were a stick-in-the-mud, would I be offering to share me heart throb with yer? No, friends should share and share alike, so I'll put in a good word for yer.'

'Be an angel and leave it for a few weeks, will yer? I'm awful busy right now. In fact, to be absolutely truthful with yer, my John would knock spots off your Robin. In a straight contest, he'd win hands down.'

'I know that, girl, yer don't have to tell me. So I think I'll forget all about Robin and share your feller with yer.'

'Some hope you've got! Anyway, sunshine, we've spent about ten minutes in Sherwood Forest so would yer mind if we put a move on and make up the time? And I can get things straight in me head so I know where I'm working. I'm going to see Greg, you're going to Betty's to find out what the arrangements are, and Tom is getting Winnie's milk stout for her. Have I got it all right?'

'Dead on the nose, girl, dead on the nose.' Monica's tummy began to rumble. 'That's hunger pangs. I'll have to have a piece of bread when I get in to keep me going until dinnertime. I'll have a round of toast, I think, it's more filling.'

'The way we're going on, no one will be getting any dinner. Let's put a move on.' Kate's legs picked up speed. 'We'll keep our news until the morning, if yer don't mind. John was moaning last night that he seldom sees me so to keep him happy I won't go out after I've seen Greg. But we'll do the usual tomorrow. Me at Winnie's for half-seven, and you at nine o'clock. Then you and me can meet at my house around ten o'clock for a cuppa and a long chat. Is that all right with you, sunshine?'

'Yeah, that's fine. I hope yer get on all right with Greg and he's nice about it.'

'Of course he will be, I'm expecting him to be as nice as he was last time. If not I'll call for reinforcements to help. That means you, Monica Parry. But if all goes well, I'll expect yer at my house at ten in the morning, bursting with news.'

'And I'll expect a biscuit with me cup of tea. Let's act like the toffs, even if it's only for an hour or so.'

Kate was waiting at the door when John came home from work. 'I've got to go out for a few minutes, sunshine, but I've left the dinners on plates, and Nancy will see to yer. I'll tell yer about it when I get back.' She stepped down on to the pavement and grinned up at him. 'Don't time me, love, 'cos I'll be more than a few minutes. More like twenty, I think.'

She was already walking away when John said, 'I don't know, this is a fine welcome after working all day. No kiss, nothing!'

'I'll make up for it later, I promise.' Kate was afraid of missing the tram Greg should be travelling on, and walked quickly down the street and turned the corner on to the main road. When she reached the tram stop, she felt conspicuous and moved to stand in the shelter of a shop doorway. She didn't have long to wait until a tram came trundling along towards her. When she saw the young man step down from the platform, she came out of the doorway. 'Hello, Greg, I've been waiting for yer.'

The lad smiled in recognition at first, as though he was really pleased to see her. Then the smile disappeared as he wondered what she had in store for him. Things had settled down now with Margaret's family and his own, and were running smoothly. He hoped nothing was going to change that. 'I didn't expect to see yer again.'

'It's all right, sunshine, I haven't come to cause trouble. It's just that Mrs Blackmore has invited me and me mate in for a drink after yer wedding, and I didn't want yer to get a shock when yer saw me. But nobody knows I've ever spoken to yer, and what I told yer is a secret between you and me. So all yer have to do is pretend we're meeting for the first time. I promise no one will ever know it's not the truth.' Kate smiled. 'I'm delighted you and Margaret are getting married, and I wish yer all the luck in the world. So now yer can take that worried look off yer face, 'cos I'd like us to be friends.'

Greg's face cleared and the smile came back. 'Thank you, I'd like us to be friends too, because I think me and Margaret will need friends pretty soon.'

'Oh, yer won't be short of friends, sunshine, I can promise yer that!' Kate held out her hand. 'Let's shake on it, then, before I have to run home to see to my family. But we'll meet again when yer get married, and I hope it's a lovely day with clear blue skies.' She moved away from him and half turned. 'Ta-ra, sunshine.'

Kate was a block away before Greg realized he was still watching her. Then he turned into the entry that would take him to his home, though it wouldn't remain so for long. Although he'd miss his mam and dad, he was looking forward to marrying Margaret and living with her and her family. He went around there every night, and got on really well with Mr and Mrs Blackmore. They were a lot nicer to him than he deserved, the way he'd behaved at the start.

As he lifted the latch on the yard door, he tried to remember the name of the woman who'd met him at the tram stop. She had told him her name the first time they met, but he couldn't for the life of him remember. He hoped she meant it about being friends because there'd be a lot of tongues wagging in the next few weeks, and he and Margaret would need friends. Maybe not him so much because he'd be at work all day. Mr Blackmore said to take no notice of anyone because it would only be a nine-day wonder, but his wife didn't agree. She said the gossips would have a field day. They liked nothing better than a juicy bit of scandal to get their teeth into. They'd keep it up until something else came along to claim their attention, and their tongues.

Monica, with Winnie's jug in hand, had to skip to keep up with her husband's long strides. 'It's bleeding ridiculous, me having to come with yer. What's the harm in yer going in the pub that yer go in every night, without fail, and asking them to fill the jug for a friend?'

'In the first place, how daft I'd look walking down the street with a ruddy jug in me hand! I'd get me leg pulled soft. Especially asking them to fill it with milk stout!'

'Ah, poor you, me heart bleeds for yer. I'll come in the pub with yer, but don't yer dare try and pretend I'm not with yer, 'cos I'll make a holy show of yer.'

Tom chortled. 'Yer would, too!'

'You bet I would!' They came to the front door of the pub and without giving her husband time to think, she linked his arm and pulled him through. Straight to the counter she marched him, and put the jug on the bar. 'My feller was too embarrassed so I had to come with him.' She gave the barman a sly wink. 'Will yer put a pint of milk stout in there, please?'

'What's the matter with Winnie, isn't she well?'

Monica was taken aback. 'How did yer know it was for Winnie?'

The barman lifted the jug and said, 'I've been filling this every night for about five years. I wondered what had happened to Winnie the last few nights, I've missed her.'

'She's been a bit off colour,' Monica told him, giving her husband daggers. 'And me and me mate have been helping her out.'

Tom was beginning to feel a bit of a heel. 'I'm here every night, how come I've never seen her?'

'She comes to the back door. She's a smashing little woman. If I'd known she wasn't well, I'd have taken the jug up for her. She loves her milk stout.'

Monica put sixpence on the counter but the barman waved it aside. 'Tell her this is on me. And if she wants it delivering tomorrow night, I'll be only too happy to oblige.'

'Now that's real kind of yer,' Monica said, picking up the coin. 'It's a pity others are not as thoughtful and kind as you are.'

Tom screwed up his face. 'Okay, yer've made yer point, don't go on at it like a ruddy dog with a bone. I'll get Winnie's milk stout tomorrow night.'

'Oh, ye're a little love.' Monica gave him a kiss on the cheek and grinned when there was a rousing cheer from his mates. 'See, yer'd have been less embarrassed if yer'd walked in with the jug.' And the smile was still on her face when she let herself into Winnie's house.

John waited until the children were in bed before asking, 'Are yer going to tell me the truth about where yer dashed off to? I know Nancy fell for the tale about yer going to see Mrs Cartwright, but I didn't.'

189

So Kate explained where she'd been, and why. 'Now are yer satisfied, sunshine, or do yer need evidence?'

His brown eyes twinkled. 'I'll tell yer what, love, it's only because this Greg is nineteen that I haven't slapped him across the face with me leather gauntlet and challenged him to a duel. Pistols at dawn, in Walton Park.'

Kate was chuckling inside. 'But yer haven't got any leather gauntlets.'

'That wouldn't stop me, I could borrow our Nancy's woollen ones.'

'Yer haven't got no pistol either.'

'Are you trying to put me off fighting for me honour?'

Kate raised her brows. 'And yer'd have to take a day off work and they'd dock it out of yer wages.'

'Ah, now that is something I would have to take into consideration. So instead of a duel with pistols, in Walton Park, you ask him to come down our entry one night and I'll clock him one. That way me honour will be preserved.'

'Wait until yer meet the lad, yer'll like him, he's nice.' She saw the look on his face and nodded. 'I know, he got a girl into trouble. But he's not the first and he won't be the last. Yer can't hold that against him for the rest of his life. When yer meet him, yer'll know what I mean.' Kate suddenly remembered something and her hand went to her throat. 'Oh, my God, I bought our Nancy's birthday presents and cards today and shoved them in the sideboard cupboard, intending to take them up to our bedroom when I got the dinner on. Then I went and forget all about them. Did yer see her go near the sideboard, or did she say anything to yer?'

'She didn't say anything, love, and I didn't see her near the sideboard. She helped with the washing up, then went next door to play with Dolly.'

'I'd better get them out now before I forget to take them upstairs with me again.' Kate opened the sideboard cupboard and took out two small paper bags and three loose cards. 'They're not much but they're all I could afford. I'm sure she'll like them.'

When John leaned forward, his eyes were bright. 'Well, it's not often I have the money to buy anything for the kids, love, but I risked a tanner on one of Bill's tips yesterday, and the horse romped in at four to one. So I got me tanner back, plus two bob winnings.'

Kate tutted. 'Yer know I don't like yer gambling! What would yer have done if the horse had lost? I can't help yer with tram fare 'cos I'm skint.'

'I wouldn't have told yer if the horse hadn't won, love, I'd have cut down on the tram fare by walking half the way to work.' He laced his fingers together, and those big brown eyes of his were asking for her understanding. 'Yer can't blame me for wanting to buy me daughter a birthday present, can yer? I never have any money to buy either of the kids anything, and I feel I'm not a good father to them in that respect.'

Tears came quickly to sting the back of Kate's eyes. She left her chair to sit on her husband's knee. 'What are yer talking like that for, John Spencer, when ye're the best father any child could ask for? Yer give Nancy and Billy much more than money can buy. Yer give them love, yer protect them when they need it, and yer make them feel happy and contented. They love the bones of yer, idolize yer. And ye're not only the best father in the world, ye're the best husband. I wouldn't swap yer for a big clock or all the tea in China.' She gave him a noisy kiss on his lips. 'Now, if that isn't enough to make yer realize what yer mean to all of us, then I'd say yer were fishing for compliments.'

His two hands went around her slim waist. 'What sort of a kiss was that? I want a proper wife to loving husband kiss, so how about it?'

Kate prised his hands from her waist. 'The place for a wife to loving husband kiss is in the bedroom. So I'll make us a cuppa and we'll have an early night. What d'yer say?'

John left his chair with alacrity. 'I'll put the kettle on and see to the tea, you take those presents upstairs before yer forget them in yer haste to get to me body.'

Kate chuckled. 'With yer black hair, yer do look like Robin Hood now as I come to think of it. Funny, I hadn't noticed it before.'

'What's Robin Hood got to do with anything?'

'Nothing, sunshine! It was just something Monica said. I can't remember how it came about, but I bet as soon as I get in bed and close me eyes, it'll come to me.' Kate picked up the paper bags and cards and hurried to the stairs before her husband asked her what she was laughing at. And the two shillings he'd won on the horses, well they'd discuss what he wanted to do with it when they were holding each other close between the sheets.

'Next Thursday! Ooh, that's quick, isn't it?' Kate's eyes widened. 'I was hoping to be able to buy them something – nothing expensive, perhaps a towel or pillowcase. But Thursday is me hard-up day.' She pondered for a while. 'Mind you, I could use a couple of coppers out of the two shillings John gave me to buy a present for Nancy.' She tapped a finger on her chin. 'How much would a decent-sized towel cost? We could buy one and give it from both of us.'

'The market is the cheapest place, girl. They sell pillowcases and towels, and yer'll not get them cheaper anywhere else.'

'That's a good idea! I might see another decent second-hand dress for Nancy. She could do with one, heaven knows.'

'We'll go tomorrow if yer like,' Monica said. 'And Winnie seems a lot better today, d'yer think going to the market would be too much for her? Yer know what it's like when it's crowded and people are pushing and shoving. And there's getting on and off the tram.'

'We can go down after and ask her. It would do her the world of good to get some of this sunshine on her face, and fresh air in her lungs. But like yer say, I don't know whether it would be too much for her. She's the only one who can tell us that.'

'By the way, girl, I was telling Betty about Winnie being off colour and asked if they'd mind if she came to the register office with us, as a break for her, like. Betty was all for it. I had no idea they were so friendly, but she said she's known Winnie for years and has a lot of respect for her.'

'Monica, yer wouldn't ever tell anyone what Winnie told me, would yer? Yer see, I've told lies to her and Greg. I told both of them that, apart from meself, there's not a soul knows about the entry business.'

'I haven't repeated one word of it to anyone, not even Tom. And I'm surprised yer felt yer had to ask me that, girl, after us being mates all these years.'

'I'm just frightened of being found out.' Kate sighed. 'My mam, God rest her soul, always used to say: "Never tell a lie, sweetheart, because one always leads to another. And no one likes or trusts a liar." It wouldn't be so bad if Greg found out, 'cos he's told plenty of lies himself. But Winnie would be so upset, I'd never be able to look her in the face again.'

'Don't be getting yerself all het up, girl, it's not good for yer indigestion or yer complexion. And when yer get to our age, we've got to start taking care of ourselves.'

Kate was thinking of the conversation yesterday, and said, 'Yer don't have to worry about Robin Hood, 'cos he only ever sees yer in the dark.'

Monica narrowed her eyes. 'Yer didn't tell your feller about me fantasies, did yer?'

'No, I didn't. I just told him, as we were going to bed, that I'd never noticed before how alike him and Robin Hood were.'

Monica feigned great curiosity. 'And did it do yer any good, girl? Was that your bed banging against our wall I could hear?'

Kate's face went crimson. 'I should have known better than to mention the words bed or bedroom to you.'

'I don't know what ye're blushing for, girl! Ye're married to the ruddy man, aren't yer? He's not yer little bit on the side! And from what I could hear, yer were enjoying yerself last night.' Monica, of course, hadn't heard a thing, but she loved to see how easy it was to embarrass her mate. 'What's yer problem? A good night was had by all, so, as my old mam used to say when everything was rosy, "Bob's yer uncle and Fanny's yer aunt." '

The friends knocked on Winnie's door to let her know they were coming before they let themselves in with the spare key they had. They found her in the kitchen waiting for the kettle to boil.

'Things are looking up, eh, sunshine?' Kate kissed her cheek. 'Yer must be feeling better today.'

'Well, if I don't exercise me legs, queen, they'll give up on me altogether. I need to keep them moving to remind them what they're there for.'

Monica squeezed behind Kate to get to the stove. 'I'll see to the tea, girl, you go and sit down and have a chat to Kate.'

But the older woman was determined to be up and about as soon as possible. She'd never get her strength back if she lay on the couch day and night. 'No, queen, I'll make the tea. No offence, like, not after yer've both been so good to me. God knows where I'd have been without yer. But I want to start moving around, building meself up, so I can go out under me own steam. Another day or two and I'll be running around like a two year old.'

'Oh, we were hoping yer'd be able to come out with us tomorrow!' Kate kept her face expressionless as she waited for Winnie's reaction. 'That's what we've come down for, sunshine. Me and Monica are going to the market tomorrow, and we were wondering if yer felt able to come with us? We'd give yer an arm each, but yer know how crowded the market can get. Then there's getting on and off trams . . .'

Nothing would have put Winnie off that. The thought of getting out of the house was tempting enough, but to be going somewhere with friends, well, it was many years since she'd had such a treat. 'Oh, I'll be fine, queen! It's just the sort of tonic I need. But yer've got yerselves to think of. I might be a burden and spoil yer day out.'

'Listen, girl, when I take our Dolly out and she becomes a burden, I buy her a lollipop and sit her on a wall somewhere until I've done me shopping.' Monica looked into Winnie's eyes. 'Me and Kate between us could manage to lift yer on to a wall. All I need to know now is what colour lollipop would yer like?'

Winnie closed her eyes and frowned, for all the world in deep thought. 'Mmm, I think I'd settle for a pink one.'

'Take no notice of me mate, sunshine,' Kate told her. 'If yer do get tired we could ask one of the stallholders for the loan of a chair so yer could rest yer legs for a while. I've seen them do that a few times, they're very obliging.'

The kettle began to whistle, and Monica lifted it from the stove and poured some of the boiling water into the brown earthenware teapot. 'Will you go and sit down out of me way? I'll bring the cups through when the tea's had time to stand for a while. One thing I can't abide is weak tea.' She shuddered at the thought. 'Might as well be drinking water.'

With Monica's hand in her back, propelling her forward, Winnie said, 'The milk is in the pantry, queen, it's cooler there.'

'Winnie, I know where yer keep everything! I'm as much at home in this kitchen as I am in me own.' She gave a broad wink. 'I have to admit, though, that yours is far more organized than mine is.'

'That's because I've only got meself to worry about, queen. The house doesn't get untidy when there's only one person living in it.'

'Don't keep her talking, fetch that blinking tea in,' Kate said, not wanting Winnie to become sad because she had no family.

'You've got a little bit of news for her, so don't keep her waiting.'

Winnie's face did contortions, and because she hadn't worn her false teeth since she became sick, she looked hilarious. 'Ooh, er, what news is that, queen?'

'It's not for me to tell yer, sunshine, Monica should have that honour. But I think yer'll be thrilled to bits with it.' Kate kept her smile back. 'It's definitely something that calls for yer to wear yer false teeth. And the way I see it, like yer legs, if yer don't wear them, they won't know what they're there for.'

Before she allowed her smile to show, Winnie put a hand over her mouth to hide her toothless gums. 'Yer'll have me wearing lipstick next.'

'It's a good job yer haven't put any lippy on yet,' Monica handed over a cup and saucer, 'because it would all be on the rim of the cup by the time yer'd drunk that.'

'The day yer see me wearing lipstick, queen, is the day yer can send for the men in white coats to cart me away. Tell them they won't need straitjackets, though, 'cos they could pick me up with one hand.'

'Let's hope that doesn't happen before next Thursday, girl, 'cos I'd hate yer to miss the wedding.'

'I've been thinking about that, and I'm worried they'll say it's cheeky of me to just turn up without being asked.'

'It's only in a register office, sunshine, it's not like a church. Besides, Monica can tell yer something about that.'

Monica nodded. 'Yeah, I told Betty yer were coming with us, and she was over the moon. Said she's looking forward to yer being there.'

Winnie looked from one to the other of the two friends. And forgetting all about her teeth still being in a glass in the kitchen, she smiled. 'D'yer know, I've got a lot to thank that fishmonger for, haven't I? He did me a good turn, selling me fish what wasn't fit to eat.'

Chapter Fourteen

As the tram trundled towards the stop nearest to Great Homer Street, Kate said, 'I'll go to the front so I can get off first and give yer a hand, sunshine.' She turned her head to Monica, who was sitting on the seat behind. 'Yer'll watch her down the aisle, won't yer?'

'Of course I will, bossy boots.' Monica rolled her eyes. 'It was a complete waste of breath, yer telling me that. D'yer think I'd have got off and left Winnie sitting there?'

'Yeah, it did sound a bit bossy. I'm sorry, sunshine, I didn't mean it to come out like it did.' Kate swung her legs round to the aisle, where it would be easier to stand up, and held on to the back of each seat she passed to avoid losing her balance as the tram swayed from side to side.

The conductor was busy talking to the driver when he saw Kate walking towards him. 'Ay, get a load of this, Ted. She's a good looker if ever I saw one.' His chuckle was thick, as though his lungs were tarred from the cigarettes he smoked one after the other. 'Now, if my missus looked like that, it would be a pleasure to go home.'

Kate stood on the platform holding on to the grip bar and enjoying the warm breeze that fanned her face. As soon as the tram came to a shuddering halt, she swung herself down from the platform to wait for Winnie. 'Don't try and step down, sunshine, it's too high. Just hold yer arms out and I'll lift yer down. Don't worry, I'm stronger than I look.'

Seeing this beautiful woman with her arms outstretched brought out the he-man in the conductor. He was a real show-off who fancied himself with the women and he wasn't going to

197

miss this chance of showing off his prowess. He placed his hand on the older woman's shoulder and said, 'Stay there, love, I'll lift yer off.'

Winnie found herself being carried through the air on to the pavement, all the time thanking the Lord she'd remembered to put her teeth in. 'Thank you, lad, ye're a real gent.'

After receiving a dazzling smile from Kate, and giving her a smarmy one in return, the man squared his shoulders and stuck out his chest. 'It was my pleasure.'

With the idea of swinging himself back on to the platform, Tarzan-like, the conductor reached out his hand to grab the rail – and found Monica blocking his way. 'Can yer move out of the way, love, so we can get on with our journey?'

'Oh, I thought yer were helping ladies down, and I was hoping yer could do the same for me.' Monica tried not to show her dislike for the man who was obviously a womanizer. After all, he wouldn't have been so quick to help Winnie if he hadn't had his eye on Kate. One look at her and he was practically slobbering at the mouth! She pitied his poor wife. 'Yer see, I've got a corn on me little toe and it's giving me gyp.'

Normally the conductor wouldn't have thought twice about telling the stupid woman to go to hell, but with Kate still on the pavement he tried to keep his calm. 'I'm sorry, love, but ye're hardly an invalid. And ye're not as light as the little woman, either! I don't want to do me back in 'cos the wife wouldn't like that.'

Monica had a few sarcastic remarks on her tongue, to take the man down a peg or two, but she never got the chance to use them. By this time the driver had lost his patience. 'Have yer any intention of getting back on this bloody tram? If we're late back at the terminus it'll be your fault and I'll report yer to the inspector.'

Before stepping down on to the pavement, Monica smiled sweetly at the conductor who was now red in the face. After he'd rung the bell to send the tram on its way, he said, 'Ay, Ted, yer spoilt me chances there. I bet yer any money she'd have come if I'd asked her to the pictures one night.'

'Yer wouldn't have stood an earthly with that one, she could afford to be choosy with her looks. And why the hell don't yer stop going to the flicks, 'cos they're giving yer big ideas? Last week yer said a pretty girl had told yer yer look like Cary Grant. But from where I'm sitting yer look more like Charles Laughton when he was the hunchback in that film I saw last week.'

'Jealousy won't get yer anywhere, Ted. I can't help it if the women fancy me, can I? I think it's me dark eyes and me tall figure.'

'Sod off, yer big-headed bugger! I'd pity yer, but I'll save me pity for yer wife 'cos she must lead a dog's life.' The driver twisted the handle on the steering wheel and the tram began to slow down. 'Next stop coming up. And yer'd better go upstairs and make sure every passenger has a ticket in case an inspector decides to make a spot check.' He grinned when he heard the conductor running up the stairs. 'Silly bugger! A wife and five kids, and he hasn't bloody well grown up yet.'

'In the middle, sunshine, and yer can link us,' Kate fussed. 'Remember, if yer feel in the least tired, just tell us and we'll stop.'

Winnie was already feeling shaky on her legs, and wondering if she hadn't rushed things too much. Perhaps she should have been content to potter around the house for a day or two. Still it was too late now, she'd have to grin and bear it. And it was nice to feel the sun on her face and have a friend walking on either side of her.

'Shall we look for a stall selling towels and pillowcases first, girl?' Monica glanced across at her mate. 'I managed to scrounge two bob off my feller last night so we've both got the same.' She chuckled. 'It was like getting blood out of a stone, he didn't want to part. It took all me powers of persuasion and a threat that I'd go off Robin Hood if I didn't get the money. I got it in the end, but I'll swear he was in real pain when he passed it over. He didn't see it as two bob, he saw it as eight pints of bitter going down the drain.'

'I was going over it in bed last night and thought it might be nice to buy them one big white fluffy towel so they could use it for bathing the baby. Or, if yer like, we could get two small ones instead.'

Winnie had been following the conversation. 'Are yer talking about a wedding present for Margaret?'

'Only a little something, sunshine, a kind of gesture. They probably won't be getting many wedding presents because nobody knows. So me and Monica thought we'd buy her something between us.'

'I'll give yer something towards it, queen,' Winnie offered. 'After all, I've known the family for years.'

'No, there's no need for that,' Monica said quickly. 'Yer must have a hard time managing to keep yer head above water on the few bob widow's pension yer get.'

'I get a small pension from where me husband used to work. It's not much, but I'm glad of it. It keeps the wolf from the door.' Winnie pressed on their arms. 'I don't spend much, I've learned to be very thrifty, and I manage. As long as me house is clean, there's coal in the yard, me rent book is clear and I've enough food to keep me from starving, then I've got no worries.'

'I think yer could teach me and Monica a lesson on how to make the money stretch out, sunshine, we're both hopeless. But I think you are a little wonder.'

'Then let me share the cost of whatever yer buy for the young couple, please, queen? I'd really like to.'

The two friends exchanged glances, and silently agreed she would be upset if they refused. 'If it'll make yer happy, girl, then we'll gladly let yer share,' Monica said. 'And we'll put your name on the card with ours.'

The market was busy and bustling, but not as crowded as it would be on a Saturday, so the threesome were able to look at the goods on display without having to fight for a place near the front. They came across a stall selling linen goods, towels, and other items. Kate noticed there was a chair standing by the stallholder who was busy shouting encouragement to people passing to come and see his wares, which were not only the cheapest in Liverpool but in the whole country. He seemed a pleasant enough bloke, and because she was concerned for Winnie, Kate wondered if it would be cheeky to ask for a loan of the chair for ten minutes. The older woman hadn't complained, but her face was pale and she looked tired.

The stallholder saw three potential customers and wandered over to them. His motto was never to let a customer go past without trying to sell them something. 'Can I help you good ladies? Yer won't get the same quality of goods on any other stall. Second to none, and I dare anyone to prove otherwise.'

Kate took advantage of his eagerness to make a sale. 'Do yer think I could borrow yer chair for ten minutes, for me friend? She's tired, and it would be nice if she could rest her legs while me and me mate are looking for what we want. The journey's been too much for her, and a few minutes' sit down would be a blessing.'

The chair was quickly handed over, and after Kate had placed it where Winnie wouldn't be in the way, the older woman sat down with a grateful sigh. 'Ooh, that's better, queen, me legs were just about to buckle under me.' She nodded her head towards the stallholder. 'Thank you, lad, I'm happy now.'

'The name's Harry, sweetheart, and I'm glad to help. You stay there until yer feel able to walk. Take an hour, if yer want to.'

Monica leaned towards Kate and whispered in her ear, 'I hope he doesn't think we've got money to burn. Stay here an hour! Some hope he's got.'

'Yeah, he's in for a disappointment,' Kate whispered back. 'But I'm not going to tell him we've only got three bob between us. So let's stretch it out for as long as we can, for Winnie's sake.'

'Only three bob!' Monica pulled a face. 'I bet he wishes all his customers spent that much. Three shillings is a lot of money to him.'

'And me!' Kate could sense the stallholder coming towards them. 'Have yer got any nice towels? We want a big white one to give as a present to someone who's expecting a baby. Nice, but not too expensive.'

Harry pointed to a trestle table running along the far side. 'All the towels are over there, girls, so go and have a dekko. Ye're bound to find one to yer liking 'cos I've got them in all sizes and colours. They're good quality, and marvellous value for money.'

Kate glanced over to where Winnie was sitting, watching with interest the goings-on at the nearby stalls. She seemed all right, but Kate was loath to leave her. 'You go and have a dekko, sunshine, I'll stay here with Winnie.'

'Okay, girl, I'll be back in a couple of minutes.' Monica raised her eyebrows to the watching stallholder. 'Yer won't mind if I bring one or two over for me mate to see, will yer, Harry? I promise I won't run off with a few stuffed up me dress.'

The stallholder chuckled. 'Yer've got a nice slim figure now, missus, so I don't think yer'd get away with being six months pregnant when yer come back.'

Monica answered his chuckle with one of her own. 'Ay, now, it all depends who I meet on the way round there. If he's like Robin Hood, well, anything might happen.'

Kate could feel her face colouring. Why had her friend ever told her about what she got up to in the name of the film star? 'Go and get the towels, sunshine, and don't keep the man talking when he's got customers waiting on him.'

Harry had seen the customers, and knew them well enough to know they'd spend half an hour picking things up off the stall, inspecting them as though they intended to buy, then say they'd be back on Saturday when they'd had their husbands' wages. They did come back occasionally, he'd grant them that, but they were never going to make him rich enough to retire. And that was his one ambition in life, to retire while he was still young enough to enjoy the lie in every morning. Getting up at six, hail, rain or snow, was getting him down.

But as Harry started walking towards the two middle-aged customers, he saw a sight which pulled him up in his tracks. A man about his own age, or even younger, was using a white stick to feel for obstacles on his left side, while a woman was holding his right elbow and guiding him safely past the stalls and shoppers. And the sight gave Harry pause for thought. Why the hell am I always moaning? he asked himself. I don't know I'm born compared to that poor soul. I've got me health and strength, I can see the blue sky and the sun, and those colourful flowers on the next stall but one. And when I get home I'll be able to see the faces of my wife and children. I'm a miserable bugger, I should be thanking God for me blessings instead of moaning. I should be thanking him for being alive, 'cos there's plenty in the cemetery who'd be glad to swap places with me.

Harry watched the blind man until he was out of sight. Then he took a deep breath and walked towards the two ladies with a broad smile on his face. 'Good morning, ladies, isn't it a beautiful day? Makes yer feel glad to be alive.'

Kate was standing by Winnie's chair, and it was like being in the picture house watching a film. 'Yer could spend a day just sitting here watching the different types of people, couldn't yer, queen? Some with happy faces and a spring in their step, and others slouching along with the worries of the world on their shoulders.'

'I was just thinking the same thing, sunshine,' Kate said. 'I bet the stallholder has plenty of tales to tell his wife every night.'

'Well, it takes all sorts to make a world, queen, we can't all be alike.'

Just then Monica came bounding up to them, her face one big smile. 'Look at these, girl, yer wouldn't know which to pick.' She held up a large white towel which looked nice and soft. Then she showed them a smaller one in white. The rest of the towels on her arm were different colours, blue, pink and yellow and some with stripes. 'They're a real bargain, girl, yer couldn't fall out with them.'

'How much?' Kate asked, crossing her fingers. 'Tell us the price of the big white one first, 'cos I think that's the best one for a present.'

'One and six, girl, and on the price list they call it a bath sheet. The small towels are only ninepence each. The coloured ones are only a tanner, they're cheaper than the white.'

'Ooh, they are a bargain,' Winnie said, feeling the quality of the large towel. 'We could get one large and two small, that would be a good present.'

Kate nodded. 'I'll say! What do you think, sunshine?'

'If I was choosing for meself, I'd chose a coloured towel any time, they don't show the dirt as much as white. But for a present, yeah, I think one large white, and two small. That comes to three bob, so it's just right. Mind you, if we can rustle up another tuppence we could manage a flannel, as well. They've got them in white and every other colour yer can mention.'

'Shall you and I go a penny each, then? A penny's not going to make much difference to what we can buy the girls, and it would be a nice finishing touch to the present. What do you say, Winnie?'

'I think they'd be a very welcome gift. It will be something for her to start her bottom drawer with.' Winnie gave a little sigh. 'She's doing things back to front but nothing can change that now, so everyone should pull together to help her and the lad.' She opened her purse and took out a shilling. 'Here's my contribution.'

'Thanks, girl, I'll go and see the bold laddo now and ask him to sort things out for us.' Monica approached the stallholder from behind and pulled on his short white linen coat, an unusual outfit for a man with a market stall, but ideal for the hot, sunny weather. 'Can yer serve us now, Harry, we know what we want.'

And wasn't he delighted with the sale. Business hadn't been very good so far, and he'd feared he was in for a quiet day. But to his great surprise, the ladies he'd been chatting to had spent two shillings, and now a three-shilling sale! Things were looking up. As he was in a benevolent mood, he didn't charge for the tuppenny flannel. 'Yer can have that on the house, ladies, for being good customers.'

'Oh, it's very kind of yer,' Kate said. 'We really appreciate that, and next time we need anything we'll know where to come for it. Good value for money, and service with a smile.'

'If yer friend wants to sit for a bit longer that's all right with me, she's welcome. And I won't charge, even though it's one of the best seats in the stalls.'

'Oh, no, lad, I'll be all right now,' Winnie said, using the seat of the chair to push herself up. 'That little rest did me the world of good, I'll be fine until I get home now.'

Feeling more than satisfied with their purchases, the three women bade the stallholder goodbye and set off on their second mission.

'Are yer sure ye're feeling up to it, sunshine?' Kate asked. 'Me and Monica want to look at a second-hand clothes stall, but we won't be long. We got a few bargains there a couple of weeks ago, and we're hoping to be lucky again today.'

'I'll be fine, queen, I'm sure I'll last out until we get home. So you and Monica do what yer want to do and don't worry about me. If I was feeling groggy I would tell yer. I wouldn't just collapse at yer feet.'

Monica pulled them to a halt. 'This is the stall, girl, and there's not many people around it. We'll find yer a good speck and yer can lean on the stall. That should take some of the weight off yer legs.'

'Here yer are, sunshine, yer've got a good space for yerself. You lean on there while me and Monica delve into those heaps of clothes. I know they look like rags, the way they're all jumbled together, but we were surprised what we found last time. I'm keeping me fingers crossed we come up with something for the girls to wear on their birthday.'

Kate left Winnie leaning on the stall while she rummaged through the first mound of clothes. She couldn't see anything that took her eye, so moved to the next lot. Before long her sharp eyes spotted material that looked attractive. Of course it could be a pinny, or a blouse, but as she pulled at it she was hoping it was something worthwhile. Her hopes rose when she found it was a dress, and she fell for it right away. It was pink and white gingham and looked just the right size for Nancy. She held it up and could see no tears in it or signs of wear. 'Ay, Monica, come and look at this! I'd say it looks about right for Nancy, and it's in good nick. Washed and ironed, it would look lovely, just the job for wearing in this hot weather.'

Monica eyed the dress with more than a touch of envy. 'Ye're not half bleeding lucky, girl, I'm sure ye're in league with the devil.' She examined the dress and could find no fault. 'That's just the ticket. Now yer can help me find one for our Dolly.'

'Wait until I show this to Winnie first, then I'll help yer.' Kate turned, holding the dress aloft, and bumped into her neighbour. 'Ooh, I was coming to yer, sunshine, yer should have waited for me. What d'yer think of this dress for Nancy?'

'I was too nosy to wait, queen, because I could see the material of the dress but not the style. I've always loved gingham since me ma used to make me dresses of it when I was little. That just puts me in mind of it. I was only young, but I can remember she put a bit of starch in the water when she washed them because she said they ironed up lovely after they'd been starched.'

'I wouldn't have thought of that,' Kate said, folding the dress over her arm. 'But I'll have a go and see how it turns out.'

'How much is the dress?' Winnie asked.

'I haven't got a clue, sunshine, and I won't ask until I've helped Monica find one for Dolly. If we buy two, we're likely to get them a bit cheaper.'

The stallholder came towards them, her hands in the wide pocket of her apron. She looked to be about sixty, the same age as Winnie but carrying a lot more flesh. She had a black knitted shawl across her shoulders, which was the uniform of a Liverpool Mary Ellen. Her face was lined and weatherbeaten with being out in all weathers. She came from market stock, it was in the blood. Her mother had worked the stall before her, and her grandmother before that. Nodding to the dress on Kate's arm, she said, 'That will cost yer a tanner, queen, 'cos it hasn't got a break in it. Came from a good clean house in one of the posh neighbourhoods.'

Winnie's eyes widened. 'Ooh, that's a bargain, queen! I don't suppose yer've got anything for an old fogey like meself, have yer?'

'Ay, less of the old, missus! I'd say yer were about my age, and I don't consider meself an old fogey. My old ma is ninety, and believe me she'd still be down here every day if we let her. Rules the bleeding roost, she does, thinks me and me sisters are still kids and we still have to do as we're told.'

Monica could hear the conversation from where she was rooting for a likely dress for Dolly. It intrigued her and she joined her neighbours. 'Ninety, did yer say? That's a good age. I lost my mam, God bless her, when she was in the prime of life. Does yer ma still manage to get around and look after herself?'

'There's always one of me sisters with her to make sure she doesn't try anything like standing on a bleeding ladder to clean the windows. But we let her do what she can because when the day comes when she's not able to do anything, well, that will be the day me ma gives up on life.'

'Those are my thoughts exactly.' Winnie nodded knowingly. 'That's why I'm not going to sit with me feet up every day, just waiting for the Grim Reaper to pay me a visit. I hope I'm out enjoying meself the day he knocks on me door.'

'This conversation is getting too cheerful for my liking,' Kate said. 'Come on, Monica, I'll help yer look for a dress. And we can look for one for Winnie at the same time.'

'I'll tell yer what, you and yer mate go about yer business and I'll give Winnie a hand.' The stallholder jingled the coins in her apron pocket and raised her eyebrows enquiringly. 'Yer don't mind me calling yer Winnie, do yer?' Without waiting for an answer she went on, 'I've got no customers at the moment, it's like a bleeding graveyard. I don't know where everyone's got to, they must all be skint. So I've time to look for something suitable for yer. I've got a sackful of ladies' clothes under the trestle, I'll empty it in front of yer and we can go through it together.'

'That's very kind of yer.'

'Listen, queen, there's one thing my old ma has always drummed into us. She says, "If yer can't spread a little kindness as yer pass down the path of life, then don't expect kindness at the end of it." And I think she's got it just about right.'

Winnie was thinking how wise the old lady was as she watched the stallholder cross to a trestle table opposite and pick up a sack. It looked bulky, but it couldn't have been heavy because the woman carried it with ease. 'Here we are, queen, let's see if we can find yer something to wear to the ball.' She smiled, showing that two of her teeth were gold. 'The name's Sarah Jane, by the way.'

The two women delved into the pile, picking out colours or patterns they thought suitable. And when Kate and Monica returned triumphant with a dress for Dolly, their pleasure was nothing compared to Winnie's. Her face was aglow and her eyes shining with delight. 'Just look what I've got, queen.' She gave the skirt she was holding a good shake before putting it to her waist. It was a full tartan skirt, in squares of green, navy and black, and had heavy pleats all around. 'Anyone game for an Irish jig?'

The stallholder looked as pleased as her customer. She and Winnie had got on like a house on fire. 'I think yer mean a Scottish reel, queen, those are the colours of a Scottish clan. It's good heavy material, that is, the wind will never blow it up. But if yer intend doing a jig in it, make sure yer've clean bloomers on.'

'That's up to me legs, Sarah Jane. I'll have to wait until they decide they're strong enough for a knees-up, then I'll show yer a nifty bit of footwork. And Sarah Jane has found me a navy blue blouse to go with it!' Winnie was talking fifteen to the dozen now in her excitement. 'I could wear them for the wedding, couldn't I, queen? The skirt needs a wipe down with a wet cloth and then a good press with the iron. The blouse I'll wash in the sink when I get home. And I bet they'll both come up as good as new.'

Her two friends and the stallholder laughed at her enthusiasm. Kate was quite touched, she'd never seen the little woman so happy. 'All yer need is a Scottish piper to walk in front of yer, sunshine, and that would be a sight worth seeing.'

It was then Winnie noticed the dress over Monica's arm, and was instantly full of apologies. 'Oh, I'm sorry for going on about meself, queen, I've been selfish. I haven't even asked to see the dress yer got for Dolly.'

'This is what I got, girl, and I'm tickled pink with it.' Monica held up a cotton dress with a blue background covered in white spots. Like the gingham dress, it had a plain round neck, short sleeves and a full, flared skirt. 'I can't wait to see our Dolly's face when she sets eyes on it. She'll be that thrilled, I bet she'll even offer to wash the dishes for me.' She looked over to the stallholder. 'Is this sixpence, like the one me mate's got?'

'Yes, queen, they're both the same price. And I don't think yer can argue over that, 'cos they're worth the money.'

'I wouldn't dream of arguing with yer, girl, we've definitely got ourselves bargains.'

Sarah Jane had told Winnie she'd only charge her ninepence for both the skirt and blouse. While they'd been sorting through the clothes, they'd been busy talking, and the stallholder had discovered the little woman was a widow like herself. But Sarah Jane was lucky because her mother was still alive and she had two sisters, a brother, and loads of nieces and nephews, whereas her customer had neither kith nor kin. But she couldn't be generous with everybody as the stall didn't make that much money, and there were times when she had to keep telling herself that charity begins at home.

But Sarah Jane had grave misgivings about the tartan kilt. The woman was too old and small to wear a kilt, and apart from its being too heavy for her, she would look out of place in it. She didn't have the heart to say anything, though, because Winnie had been so pleased. It wasn't up to her to tell her customers what to wear, even if she did like them. So the stallholder was relieved when she heard one of the friends, the one with the face of an angel, speaking.

'We saw a dress over there we thought yer'd like, sunshine. A cotton one in a deep blue, just the job for this weather. Yer'd be sweating cobs in that skirt, 'cos the material is wool and very heavy. Ideal for the winter, but far too heavy for this weather. I think so, anyway. But if that's what yer want, then you go for it, sunshine, because if we talk yer into anything yer'd call us fit to burn when yer got home.'

Winnie was beginning to look doubtful. She lifted the arm the kilt was draped over, and nodded. 'I think ye're right, queen, it is heavy. And I'd probably look a stupid nit in it, anyway, 'cos it nearly comes down to me ankles.' Then she brightened up. 'I could always cut a bit off and put a hem on, then I could wear it in the winter. What d'yer think, ladies?' Her eyes swept over the three women. 'And I don't want yer to tell me what yer think I want to hear, I want the plain, unvarnished truth.'

'You buy the skirt and blouse, girl, and do as yer say, alter it to fit yer for the winter.' Monica turned to Kate, while Sarah Jane looked on with interest. 'Will you tell her, or d'yer want me to?'

'You tell her, sunshine, and see what she says.'

'Well, it's like this, yer see, Winnie, me and Kate were going to buy the cotton dress for yer. We thought it would look nice on yer for the wedding. But we didn't bring it over with us, 'cos we wanted to ask yer first, in case yer were insulted.'

Sarah Jane couldn't let that go without chipping in. Her back straight and her head held high, she said, 'Why would she be insulted? I wear clothes off me own stall, I'm not too proud, so why should yer friend be? Nah, she's like meself, I bet she'd never look a gift horse in the mouth. Would yer, queen?'

'I'm not proud not at all,' Winnie said. 'But I couldn't let you two buy a dress for me, it wouldn't be fair, 'cos yer've got to watch yer pennies with a family to look after. Besides, yer've done enough for me over the last week, waiting on me hand and foot.' She was in a dilemma now, wondering whether she should just take the skirt and blouse and not bother even looking at the dress. Then again, her friends might be upset if she didn't at least look at it. 'I'll tell yer what, if Sarah Jane doesn't mind, I'll have a look at the dress. And if I like it, I'll buy it instead of the skirt.'

'I'll go and get it, I know where to put me hand on it.' Monica was off like a shot and back within seconds, holding the blue dress in front of her. 'There yer are, girl, and I bet yer'd look a treat in it.'

'Hang on a minute, sunshine, just hold yer horses,' Kate said. 'There's a catch to it, I'm afraid, Winnie. Yer only get the dress if yer let me and Monica pay for it. For heaven's sake, it's only coppers, we're not talking shillings or pounds. And I'll tell yer this, I wouldn't refuse if someone wanted to buy me a dress.'

'There yer are, queen.' Sarah Jane folded her arms and nodded her head, sensing victory in the air. 'Yer'll only upset yer friends if yer refuse, and I'm sure yer don't want to do that after they've been so good to yer.'

Winnie felt as though she was floating on cloud nine. A skirt and blouse, a dress, and to top it all off, she'd made a new friend in Sarah Jane. The stallholder had told her to come down any time she had nothing to do. Never mind if she didn't want to buy anything, they could have a good natter. 'And if I'm busy, yer can keep yer eye on the customers. We get some right scallies down here, especially on a Saturday when we're rushed off our feet. They'd nick the clothes off yer back if they could, the thieving swines. And I can't be watching everyone, I'd need eyes in the back of me head and in me backside.'

So Winnie, all smiles, promised she'd be down to help out. A promise she meant to keep.

Chapter Fifteen

'I'll fill the sink and put all the dresses in, save me dragging the dolly tub out.' Kate sat back in her chair and breathed out. 'God, but it's hot. I feel as though I've done a day's hard work instead of walking round a market enjoying meself.'

'I could have gone straight home, yer know, queen,' Winnie said, 'instead of sitting here, drinking yer tea and getting waited on.'

'Ay, don't be saying that!' Monica shook her head. 'Ye're making things bad for me by saying we're putting on her! When I come in tomorrow for me morning cuppa, I bet she'll give me cow eyes and start feeling sorry for herself.'

'Oh, it's different for you, queen, yer've been mates with Kate for donkey's years. But I hope I haven't been a nuisance to yer, or spoilt yer day out? I wouldn't want to do that, and I did me best to keep up.'

'Of course yer weren't a nuisance, we enjoyed having yer with us.' Kate started to collect the cups and saucers. 'Besides, there was method in me madness, sunshine, I needed yer here to tell me how much starch to put in the rinsing water. Left on me own, I'd probably put too much in, and the dresses would come off the line as stiff as a board. They'd be able to stand up for themselves.'

'Yer'll not get the five dresses in the sink, girl,' Monica said. 'Yer'll have to do them one at a time.'

'Go and teach yer grandmother how to milk ducks, Monica Parry! The sinks are deep, as yer ruddy well know, and I'll easy get the dresses in. They're only ruddy cotton!'

'Okay, girl, take it easy, I can see yer hair falling out from here! God, ye're not half touchy, it doesn't take much to make yer lose yer rag.'

'Only scorching hot weather, sunshine, and a mate that thinks she always knows best.' Kate reached the kitchen door with the cups and saucers, and turned her head to smile at her neighbour and best friend. 'I must admit ye're right most of the time, but not always.'

Monica faced Winnie across the table, and jerked her head towards Kate's disappearing back. 'She was on the point of praising me then, but thought better of it in case I got a big head. Now can yer imagine, even in yer wildest dreams, me with a big head? The very idea is preposterous.'

Kate's head quickly reappeared. She feigned surprise, with her eyes and mouth wide open. 'What did yer say the idea was?'

'Preposterous, girl!' Monica winked at Winnie, and in an exaggerated whisper told her, 'She might have the looks but she certainly hasn't got the brains. Pig ignorant, she is.'

Kate moved quickly to the sideboard. From a drawer she took a piece of paper and a pencil. 'Write it down for me, clever clogs.'

Monica's nostrils widened and her lips narrowed as she shook her head slowly for several seconds. 'The very idea of yer thinking I can't spell preposterous is preposterous in itself, and I refuse to satisfy yer childishness.'

Winnie was looking from one to the other. She was getting used to the friendly arguments between the two pals, but she wasn't sure whether it was always in fun. She decided on this occasion it would be best to be diplomatic and stay neutral. So, while her head turned from one to the other, her face remained impassive.

'Ye're only saying that 'cos yer can't spell it,' Kate said. 'I've got threepence left out of me money. It's yours if yer spell preposterous for us.'

Monica grinned. 'Money for old rope, that is. Pass the pencil over.' Convinced no one would be any the wiser she began to write. And as she wrote each letter down, she spoke it out aloud. 'P-r-e-p-o-s-t-e-r-u-s.' She handed the paper over to Kate, then turned her palm face up. 'I'll have the threepence now, girl, in case yer forget to give it to me later.'

Kate didn't look at the paper before asking, 'I gather the bet goes both ways? That I get threepence off you if yer've spelt it wrong?'

'Of course, girl, that goes without saying.' Monica was very confident. She often pulled the same trick on her husband. She'd think of a big word, one which she didn't know how to spell herself, and have a bet with him. And he was bloody hopeless at spelling, was Tom. 'Go on, have a look at the paper and yer'll see I've spelt it right.'

Kate intended to turn the tables on her mate. 'I don't think either of us should be the judge, it should be someone impartial. How about you, Winnie, are yer any good at spelling big words?'

'Oh, I don't know about that, queen, it's forty-five years since I left school. Besides, I don't want to be piggy in the middle with you two.'

'Don't be daft, girl,' Monica said, convinced the older woman wouldn't be able to spell the word, not after leaving school forty-five years ago. 'We're not kids, neither of us will cry if we lose. Tell her, Kate.'

While her friend's eyes had been off her, Kate had sneaked a look at the paper, and trying to sound as if she couldn't care less, said, 'Don't let that worry yer, sunshine, we're big girls now. But I wouldn't like to put yer in a spot if yer don't know how to spell it, 'cos it is a big word. So if yer don't want to get involved then we won't mind.'

'Oh, I know how to spell it, queen! I used to be top of the class in English, and yer seldom forget what ye're taught at school. Besides, me hobby is doing crosswords, and yer have to know how to spell to get them right.'

Monica's heart sank. She had only her own knowledge of the English language to rely on, and she was no good at school and had never done a crossword in her life. But then neither had Kate so they were level pegging there. 'Pass the paper over, Kate, and let her have a look. And don't worry, Winnie, we won't be tearing each other's hair out.' Just for bravado, she added, 'I won't, anyway, 'cos I know I can't lose.'

'Here yer are, sunshine, see what yer think.' Kate was determined not to smile yet even though she was certain she'd won. 'Take yer time, to make sure.'

Winnie took a look at the paper, her eyes instantly seeing the mistake but her head not wanting to. 'I'm not sure . . . I think yer'd be better asking someone else. Anyway, why do yer play these stupid bleeding tricks? What difference does it make whether yer know how to spell it or not? It's not going to change yer ruddy life, is it? Why don't yer just tear the piece of paper up and forget all about it?'

'No!' Monica's voice was high. 'That would only spoil our fun! If Kate and me didn't act daft, we'd never get a laugh out of life. And seeing as we've had a good morning out, got what we went out for, nobody's going to get in a paddy if they lose.'

'Oh, okay then, but don't blame me.' Winnie looked at the slip of paper again. 'I think there's a letter missing.'

Kate allowed her smile to appear as she nodded her head. 'Yes, there is a letter missing, sunshine, but don't say what it is or she'll say we're in cahoots with each other.'

'How do you know there's a letter missing?' Monica demanded. 'Yer haven't even seen what's on the paper!'

'Yes, I have, so there! I sneaked a look when yer head was turned. And so yer won't think there's anything dodgy going on, before Winnie says what she thinks is the missing letter, I'll write it down on a piece of paper. Then yer can't say we cheated.'

When it came out that both Kate and Winnie said the letter 'O' had been missed out, Monica wouldn't have it. She kept repeating the word slowly, to prove she was in the right. '*Preposterus* . . . that's how yer say it, and that's how yer spell it. I don't care if yer bring the cleverest bugger in Liverpool here, I'm not going to change me mind.'

'If I knew the cleverest bugger in Liverpool, sunshine,' Kate said, 'd'yer think I'd be living next door to you!'

The two women were laughing so much they didn't hear the knock at the door. It was Winnie who cocked an ear. 'There's someone banging hell out of yer door, queen, and it sounds urgent.'

Kate put a hand on Monica's arm. 'Shush, for a minute! Winnie said there's someone at the door.'

Her neighbour's loud guffaws ceased and she wiped the back of a hand across her eyes. 'Whoever it is means business, girl, they'll have the door in if yer don't get out there and answer it. And if it's someone selling pegs, tell them we don't need none.'

'Put those bags in the kitchen for us, in case I have to ask whoever it is in. I don't want the whole street to know I buy me clothes from Paddy's Market.' As Kate reached a hand out to open the door, she heard Monica say, 'She's proper posh is my mate. Yer can take her anywhere and she won't make a show of yer.'

So there was half a smile on Kate's face when she opened the door to the woman who lived opposite. 'Hello, Maggie, have yer been knocking long? Me and me mates were . . .' She suddenly noticed the woman was agitated. Her hands were being clasped and unclasped, and her face was drained of colour. 'What is it, sunshine?'

'It might not be anything, Kate, and I'm sorry to bother yer, but I didn't know who else to turn to.' Maggie Duffy glanced back to the opposite side of the street. 'I was standing at the sink peeling potatoes when I saw a man on Miss Parkinson's yard wall. It happened so fast, I didn't get a proper look at him before he'd dropped down into her yard. But he must be up to no good, otherwise why didn't he knock on her front door? And at her age, the shock of seeing a stranger in her yard, or in her house come to that, well, it would kill her.'

Maggie's next door neighbour was a spinster of eighty years of age. Her name was Audrey Parkinson, but to everyone in the street she was Miss Parkinson. She was a very refined, well-spoken lady, who was respected by everyone. She still kept her house like a little palace, and the only time she allowed anyone to help her was when she needed something from the corner shop and there were children playing in the street. She would ask them kindly if they would go on a message for her.

By this time, Monica and Winnie had come to stand behind Kate. 'Are yer sure, Maggie?' Monica asked. 'It wasn't the coalman, was it?'

Kate tutted. 'The coalman, in this weather? And can yer see Tommy climbing over a wall?' She shook her head. 'No, we'd better do something. Yer hear some terrible things these days, he might be breaking in to rob her.'

Monica pushed herself to the front. 'The only way to find out what's really going on is to go over and see. Standing here yapping is not going to get us anywhere. I'll go the back way with Maggie, and you and Winnie go to the front, Kate, and knock on the door. Whoever he is, he's bound to make a run for it, through the front or the back.'

'I'll get me rolling pin, just in case,' Kate said. 'If he tries anything, I won't hesitate to use it. I'll clock him one over the head.'

It was easy to talk bravely, but not so easy when it came to the crunch. Kate watched Monica and Maggie disappear down the side entry, and when she'd given them enough time to get to Miss Parkinson's yard door, she took Winnie's arm and they crossed the street. She was holding the rolling pin tightly in her hand. 'I won't have the nerve when the time comes, sunshine, I'll probably run a mile.'

'Then pass that over to me, I won't be afraid to use it,' Winnie told her. 'If it is a robber in there, I'll break his bleeding neck for him. If he's frightened the old lady, or harmed her, I'd swing for the blighter.'

Kate looked down at the other woman who was about six inches shorter than her, and as thin as a rake. Especially after the bout of sickness she'd just had, she wouldn't have the strength to wield the rolling pin. She had the guts and the will to do it, but not the power.

'No, I'll be all right, sunshine. If I see a strange bloke running out of this house, me temper will boil over and I'll forget I'm frightened.' Kate was about to lift the knocker when she heard a sound from within and pressed her ear close to the letter box. 'I can hear Miss Parkinson shouting at someone to get out, so here goes.' She raised her hand to the knocker and whispered to Winnie, 'Be on yer guard, sunshine.'

No sooner had the sound of the knocker died away than the front door burst open and a burly man charged out. He was so quick, Kate was taken aback and not fast enough with the rolling pin. The man would have got clean away if Winnie hadn't stuck her leg out and tripped him up. He fell face forward, and before he knew what had hit him, Winnie was sitting on his back. He was struggling violently and Kate could see her friend was no match for him, that he could easily shift her off his back. So she lifted the rolling pin and hit him on the head with it. She didn't hit too hard, she didn't want to kill him and go to jail. At the same time she was shouting for Monica. She always felt safer when her mate was with her, as though she would be protected from harm.

As Monica and Maggie came running from the entry, doors were beginning to open along the street and women, alerted by the urgency in Kate's voice, were running towards them. 'In the name of God,' Monica said when she saw the size of the man Winnie was sitting on. 'The size of him to her! She's a bloody hero!'

'I only tripped him up, queen, it was Kate who knocked him out.'

Maggie stepped over the man who was slowly coming round. 'I'm going to see how Miss Parkinson is. Will one of yer go for the police?'

Two of the neighbours volunteered while the rest stayed put, hoping that the man would make a move and they'd have an excuse for kicking him. They had no time for robbers in this neighbourhood where money was scarce and many people were living hand to mouth. They'd share their last penny with someone who was starving, but a robber would get little sympathy from them.

The man was slowly coming round. His eyes were open and he tried to twist his body over, but there were many willing hands and feet to teach him that if he knew what was best for him, he'd stay still. One of the women took the rolling pin from Kate's hand and waved it in front of his eyes. 'One wrong move out of you, yer thieving bastard, and yer'll be getting another taste of this.'

Maggie came to the front door. 'Miss Parkinson is real shook up, but he never laid a finger on her, thank God. He's got her purse, though, and some jewellery she kept in a box in the sideboard. What she's most upset about is that one of the rings belonged to her mother, it's nearly a hundred years old. Crying her eyes out she is over that ring.'

There were angry murmurs from the women. 'Tell her we'll get everything back off him,' Kate said, feeling heartbroken for her. If he hadn't been caught, the man would have got away with the thing that probably meant more to the old lady than anything else in the world. He'd have sold it, or pawned it, for coppers, when to Miss Parkinson it meant more than anything money could buy. Never once would he have thought of the heartache and misery he'd brought her. Kate looked at Monica. 'Keep yer eye on him, sunshine, while I feel in his pockets for his ill-gotten gains.' The first pocket in his jacket gave up the old lady's purse which was quickly handed to Maggie to take into the house. There was nothing in the other pocket of his jacket and Kate sat back on her heels, reluctant to reach into his trouser pockets. 'Has anyone ever seen this bloke around here before?' She watched each head shake. 'I wonder if his wife knows what he gets up to, putting the fear of God into old people and stealing their belongings? If she does, then she's worse than he is.'

'What about the jewellery, girl?' Monica asked. 'It must be in his pockets.'

'There's nothing else in his jacket pockets, sunshine, and I don't feel inclined to put me hand down his trouser pockets.'

This brought forth a few titters. But not from Monica. 'Get up, girl, for heaven's sake, and let me have a go. My stomach isn't as delicate as yours.'

One woman bent down to whisper what else Monica could do while her hand was in his trouser pocket, to punish him, like. But her suggestion wasn't acted upon. 'I'll be in and out before yer know it, girl, I'm fussy where I put me hands.'

There were gasps of astonishment when Monica's hand reappeared clutching a gold chain and a string of pearls. On the gold chain there hung a heart-shaped locket which caused one of the women to say, 'The swine! I bet there's photies in there, of her mam and dad, and he was going to pinch them off her.'

'I haven't got the ring, but he must have it somewhere because he didn't have time to stash it away. But I can't reach down to the very bottom of his pocket because his whole weight is on it. So would a couple of yer lift this side a little, just enough for me to get me hand in? Not too much, or yer'll topple Winnie off.'

'Nothing would topple me off, queen, I'm here till the bobby comes and puts handcuffs on him. And I hope he doesn't do it gentle, either!'

There were more gasps when Monica's hand emerged holding two gold watches, a gent's and a lady's. 'Ay, girl, just look at these! Will yer go and ask Miss Parkinson if she had a gent's watch?'

Kate was back within seconds. 'She didn't have any watches, sunshine, so God knows where he got them from.'

'Some other poor bugger's house.' One woman, Tessie by name, was bending down to shake her fist in the man's face. 'I wish the men were home from work, they'd soon teach yer a lesson.'

'I still haven't got Miss Parkinson's ring,' Monica said. 'It's definitely not in any of his pockets, but where the hell could he have put it?'

'I used to know a robber once.' This came from a neighbour of Winnie's whose name was Sally. 'He used to live in the same street as me before I got married. And I remember someone saying that robbers usually have pockets sewn on the inside of their jackets. So it's worth a try, lass.'

And Sally was right. The robber did have a pocket on the inside of his jacket, and in it were nestling two rings and a bracelet. Monica looked down at them in the palm of her hand, and said, 'My God, he must have robbed a few houses to get this lot. I wonder which ring belongs to Miss Parkinson?'

The man lying flat out on the pavement felt a lightening of the weight on his back and knew Winnie was leaning forward to look at the rings. His luck was in, this was the perfect opportunity. He'd lose the loot which had been going to keep him on Easy Street for a few months, but at least he'd be away from these women who frightened him more than any man he'd ever had to tackle. None of them knew him because he didn't live in this neighbourhood so they wouldn't be able to give the police his name.

Instinct or second sight warned Winnie the prisoner was about to make a run for it. She was ready for him. He rolled his body from side to side to try and shake her off, but little as she was she clung on, even if she did end up lying face down across his stomach.

Sally raised her foot. 'You try that again, buggerlugs, and yer'll feel this. I've got steel toe-caps, so yer can imagine what harm a hard kick from them would do.'

'Ay, if he tries that again, I want the lot of yer to pin him down.' Monica couldn't believe she was holding in her hand jewellery worth hundreds of pounds. She'd never owned anything in her life that was worth more than a few bob. Except for her wedding ring which she remembered had cost ten bob, a lot of money in 1920. 'I'll take these in to show Miss Parkinson, so she can pick out hers.'

'I thought the police would be here by now, sunshine,' Kate shouted after her. 'I wish they'd hurry up, this feller is giving me the creeps.'

Monica turned at the front door. 'I don't think he's very fond of you, either, girl, 'cos I can see a swelling on his head.'

'If it wasn't for getting into trouble with the police, I'd give him a few more swellings,' Tessie said. 'In places where he'd be too bleeding well ashamed to show to anybody. He'd not be able to sit, stand nor lie.'

There were murmurs of agreement, and as more women joined the group, the chattering became louder, making the robber sorry he'd ever set foot in the neighbourhood. He'd be in for a slanging match with his wife, too, if he ever got home. She'd be expecting money from him so she could go to the shops. He never, ever hung on to any of the stuff he stole but took it straight to a pawnshop whose proprietor was as dishonest as himself. He'd hand the goods over and the pawnbroker would take out his magnifying glass to satisfy himself the articles weren't paste before passing the cash over the counter. He never asked questions, didn't want to know where anything came from.

'Miss Parkinson's got everything back that he stole. The necklace with the locket on and the string of pearls were hers, and one of the rings is the one that belonged to her mother. She feels a lot better now she's got them back, but it'll take a while before she feels safe in her own bleeding home again.' Monica aimed a kick at the man's thigh. 'I won't repeat what I'd like to do to you, yer slimy excuse for a man, but yer can tell us where yer robbed the other stuff from and we'll get it back to its rightful owner.'

When he didn't answer, Monica held out both hands to show the other women what he'd taken from some other poor soul. 'Just look at these! Two solid gold watches, the most beautiful bracelet I've ever seen, and a diamond ring. Somewhere in the city of Liverpool, right now, there are heartbroken people missing these, and I think the queer feller, that piece of scum on the ground, should be made to tell us where he got them from, so we can return them and put the owners out of their misery.'

'Ay, out, here come Grace and Tilly, and they've got a bobby with them.'

The group fell silent and shuffled back a few steps. They'd been brought up to respect the police, the same as they did doctors, priests or ministers. And this particular policeman had stripes on his uniform which meant he was no ordinary bobby. The women were impressed.

Sergeant Geoff Bridgewater was in his mid-forties, and had been in the police force for twenty years. At six foot two inches, and broad of build, he was a man it would be foolish to pick a fight with for you would never win, as many a member of the criminal world had found out to their cost. He had seen many sights in his years of being a policeman and thought nothing would surprise him any more. But the picture before him now would stay in his memory for a long time. A man of probably the same height and weight as himself was stretched out, face down, on the pavement, and there was a slip of a woman sitting on his back. Ten other women hovering nearby were standing guard. It was like a scene from a Laurel and Hardy film, and if he'd been watching it in a picture house, he'd have laughed his head off. But from what he'd been told, this was no laughing matter.

'Well, well, what have we here?' The sergeant ignored the prisoner for several reasons. First he could hardly question a man who was flat on his face with a woman sitting on his back, and secondly, he wouldn't get the truth anyway. 'Which one of you ladies can tell me what happened?'

'The woman next door saw the start of it, I'll give her a shout.' Kate held on to the side wall while she leaned inside the hallway. 'Maggie, can yer come out a minute? The police are here and want to know how it happened.'

Maggie came out, thinking all this excitement was too much for her. Many more days like this and she wouldn't live to tell the tale. 'I was peeling me spuds by the sink, and I happened to look out of the window and saw a man sitting astride Miss Parkinson's wall.' She was doing her very best to speak posh. 'That's the name of the lady what lives here, and she's eighty years of age. Well, I was fair flummoxed, I didn't know what to think. One minute he was on the wall, the next I heard him dropping into her yard.' Whenever Maggie saw a policeman she thought of trouble. Not that she'd ever been in trouble, nor had any of her family, thank God, it was the uniform that put her in mind of it. To stop her hands from shaking, she folded her arms and hoisted her bosom. 'I didn't know where to turn, 'cos there wasn't much I could do on me own, so I ran across the street to Kate's house and told her. And she'll tell yer what happened after that because I'm not thinking straight. It's the shock, yer see.'

'I understand, and I'll take your particulars down later. Thank you.'

When Kate told him there were four women involved in catching the robber, the policeman said he thought it better to question them in Miss Parkinson's house, later. 'A police van will be here any minute to take our friend here to the station for questioning. Then, if Miss Parkinson is up to it, I can take down all the details.'

'Look what I've taken off him.' Monica held out her hands. 'These were in his pockets along with what he'd pinched off Miss Parkinson. She's got all her stuff back, but he won't tell us where he robbed these from so we can give them back to their owner.'

'I'm afraid I'm going to have to take them off you, they're evidence. But we will find the rightful owner, I promise.'

'Did yer say there was a Black Maria coming, sir?' asked Grace, getting excited because she'd never seen one in their street before and she'd enjoy seeing what they were like inside.

The sergeant nodded. 'It should be here any moment.'

Grace turned to her neighbour. 'I won't come home yet, Tilly, but you can go if yer want. I'm not going to miss seeing that bastard being put in a Black Maria.' Then she lowered her voice. 'And I want to see them putting handcuffs on him.'

'What makes yer think *I'm* going to miss all the fun!' Tilly's tongue came out to blow a raspberry. 'Yer can sod off, Grace, I'm staying put.'

The sound of a motor engine set all heads turning. 'Ah, here it is.' When the van stopped where the sergeant pointed his finger, the women moved as one. Everyone had seen a Black Maria and knew it was for carrying prisoners, but they'd never been close to one before. The two bobbies who stepped down were amazed by what they saw. It was the talk of the station for days. Not when Sergeant Bridgewater was around, though. He frowned and asked if they didn't have something better to do. He thought if they found it so funny, they should enjoy the joke in their own time. Like he did.

'Have you brought a property bag with you?'

'Yes, Sarge, and a report sheet.'

'Good! Get them for me before you remove the prisoner. I'm going to be busy here for a while, so put him straight into a cell and I'll interview him myself when I get back to the station. There's no hurry, he won't be going anywhere for a long time.'

Sergeant Bridgewater didn't go straight into Miss Parkinson's house but stood and watched as the prisoner was lifted to his feet handcuffed, and put in the back of the van. Never once did he lift his head to look at the women. But, oh, how they enjoyed watching him. They called him names that turned the air blue, and would have battered him if it hadn't been for his two escorts. They even ran after the van for a short distance, banging on the sides and cursing him for robbing the poor. The sergeant made no attempt to stop them because he thought they deserved that much leeway. They had prevented a robber from stealing from one of their own.

'Now I'm going to ask you to go back to your homes, ladies, except for the four who were involved in apprehending the prisoner. And I want to thank you for showing your concern for an elderly person, and for being so public-spirited. Without you, he would be robbing another innocent person right this minute.'

'That's what neighbours are for,' Kate said, 'to help each other when needed. We'd be a poor lot if we'd sat on our backsides and did nothing.'

'Hear, hear!' This came from most of the women. And Tilly added, 'We're always on the look-out for each other in this street, but after today we'll be keeping our eyes peeled.'

'That's good to hear.' Sergeant Bridgewater turned to go into the house, got as far as the step, thought of something and turned back. 'By the way, ladies, I'll be back to see Miss Parkinson tomorrow, after I've interviewed the prisoner. I will tell her what has happened, and what will happen, and I'm sure the information will be passed on to you. Good afternoon.'

Kate was about to follow Monica and Winnie into Miss Parkinson's house when Sally caught her arm. 'Proper gent, he is, Kate. Treated us with respect, not like a gang of kids without a brain between us. You tell him we appreciate that.'

'Yer haven't got yer eye on him, have yer, sunshine?' Kate grinned. 'Don't be greedy, yer've already got one feller.'

'I'd swap my feller for him any day,' Sally said. 'Tell him I'm a smashing cook, good at housework, and would wait on him hand and foot. Now, no man could refuse that.'

'I won't tell him, Sally, 'cos it might embarrass him.' Kate leaned forward and in a loud whisper said, 'What I will do, though, sunshine, is keep me eye out for your Bill coming home from work tonight. And I'll tell him how lucky I think he is to have a wife what waits on him hand and foot.'

'What! I don't wait on *him* hand and foot, it's the other way around! So don't yer be causing bleeding trouble, Kate Spencer, or I'll be having sharp words with yer.'

As Kate stepped into the hallway, she heard Tilly saying, 'Sally, yer live in a blinking world of yer own, you do, yer silly faggot! What d'yer mean by saying Bill waits on yer hand and foot? That's a bleeding lie if I ever heard one.'

Chapter Sixteen

Sergeant Bridgewater straightened his notebook on his knee before replacing the top on his fountain pen. 'That's fine, ladies, you've been very co-operative. I wish I could tell you what will happen now, but until I've interviewed the prisoner with one of my senior officers there's little I can say. The man will have to appear before a court for sentencing, and in my opinion will be sent to jail for a considerable time. But that is for the judge to decide.'

Kate, who had been sitting on the floor next to Miss Parkinson's chair, scrambled to her feet. 'The one thing I will regret all my life is that I didn't hit him a couple more times with this.' She waved the rolling pin with a flourish. 'I'd feel as though I'd got me own back on him for what he put Miss Parkinson through.'

Monica grinned at the officer as she got to her feet to stand beside her friend. 'Yer wouldn't believe, would yer, with the face she's got what makes her look like an angel, that she could be so bloodthirsty? It just goes to show, like my old ma used to say, yer should never go by a person's looks, they can be very deceptive.'

'I feel the same as Kate,' Maggie Duffy said. 'I can count on one hand the times in me life I've ever wanted to raise me hand to anyone in anger. But, by God, I felt like raising it to that man. It doesn't bear thinking about what would have happened if I hadn't seen him on the wall! Miss Parkinson would have been no match for him. He could have felled her with one blow.'

Miss Parkinson, always neat and tidy, and still looking elegant in her eighties, was well-spoken and very articulate. 'It was my

229

own fault, I should keep the kitchen door bolted. I shall be more careful in future.'

'Yer shouldn't have to keep yer door bolted, queen!' Winnie's voice told of her anger. 'This is your home and he had no right to come in uninvited, to steal from yer.'

'That is quite true,' Sergeant Bridgewater said, nodding in agreement. 'However it is always best to be careful, especially about yard and back doors. Not that anything like this is likely to happen again, burglaries are rare in this area. And I can say for certain that the person you apprehended today, you will never see again.'

'Will yer let us know how yer get on with him?' Kate asked. 'We'd all like to hear what his punishment will be, and also if yer find out who that other jewellery belongs to. If we know it'll go back to whoever owns it, at least the story will have a happy ending for someone.'

'I'll be calling back because there may be further questions I need to ask. I'll have some information on the prisoner, if nothing else.'

'Thank you, the whole street will be interested to hear.' Kate bent to put a hand on Miss Parkinson's arm. 'I'll nip over after we've had our meal tonight to make sure ye're all right. I'll tap on the window first, so yer'll know who it is.'

'I've told her to keep the poker at the side of her chair, so she can use it to knock on the wall if she needs anything,' Maggie said. 'But it would be nice if yer popped in tonight, Kate, and I'll be here first thing in the morning.'

'We'll organize something,' Monica said. 'We can take it in turns between the three of us.'

'Four of us,' Winnie said, her mouth set in determination. 'I can give a hand. Yer've been helping me over the last few days, I know what a comfort it is to have people calling when yer live on yer own. So count me in for a visit any time yer like.' She saw Kate raise her brows. 'Oh, I know that sounds like the blind leading the blind, but I'm a lot better today and will be even more so tomorrow.'

'Okay, sunshine, have it yer own way. Now let's be making tracks or there'll be no dinner on the table tonight!'

Goodbyes were said, then the three friends hurried across the cobbled street. 'This has been a day and a half, this has,' Kate said. 'I feel worn out yet I haven't done anything! And I'll never get those dresses washed now, there won't be time before the kids come home. I'll have to hide them until tomorrow.'

'Give the dresses to me, queen,' Winnie said. 'I'll have them washed and dried before bedtime. I've got no one to worry about coming in for a meal, so I've got time on me hands.'

'What! Yer first day out, and all hell's broken loose! It's been far too hectic for yer today, yer'll be worn out.' They were standing outside Kate's house, and she was surprised to see the front door ajar. She'd been so concerned when Maggie knocked to tell her about the man on the wall, she'd run out without thinking. 'I'll do them first thing in the morning, sunshine, don't you be worrying yer head about them.'

Winnie chuckled. 'I'm not a bit tired, queen, I've had a good sit down on that bloke's back for half an hour. Go and get the dresses and I promise I won't kill meself washing them. Go on, do as yer granny tells yer or the kids will be home from school before yer know it.'

Monica pulled a face. 'It's five dresses, girl, not one! What's the use of us telling yer to take it easy, and then palming our washing on to yer?'

'If I didn't want to do them, or feel up to it, then I'd soon tell yer. All the excitement seems to have done me good, I feel better for it.'

Mindful that Nancy would be home soon, and that one of the dresses was to be a surprise for her birthday party on Saturday, Kate gave in. 'Okay, yer talked us into it. But I won't ask yer in the house now, if yer don't mind, 'cos I'll have to go like the clappers to get the dinner on in time. I'll fetch the clothes out for yer.'

When Winnie took hold of the bundle of clothes, she said, 'With a bit of luck I'll have them on the line while there's still a bit of a breeze. It'll give me something to do while I'm waiting for me tummy and me heart to calm down after all the excitement.' She shook her head. 'There's some rotters in the world, isn't there? Fancy a big feller like that robbing an old lady! I hope they lock him in a cell and throw away the key.'

'Oh, I agree with yer, girl!' Monica said. 'If it was up to me, I'd put him in a room with half a dozen women and let them loose on him. He'd think twice about doing it again.'

'I'm going to love yer and leave yer,' Kate told them. 'I'll have to run around like the Keystone Cops to get things looking halfway normal for John coming home.'

'He won't expect everything to be spot on, queen, when yer tell him about Miss Parkinson's lucky escape. I bet he'll be flabbergasted.'

'Flabbergasted or not, sunshine, he'll want a cooked dinner after working all day. So I'll say ta-ra until tomorrow.'

When Kate disappeared into the house, closing the door behind her, Monica clicked her tongue on the roof of her mouth and shook her head slowly. 'I don't worry about my feller as much as Kate does about hers. If the meal's not on the table on the dot, she's a nervous wreck. Anyone would think John was a bully, yet he's the most mild-mannered man yer could wish to meet. She started off being too soft with him, and now she can't stop. It's not John's fault, Kate's only got herself to blame. I don't have no bother with my feller. If the dinner's not ready, he'll sit and read the *Echo* with never a peep out of him.'

'Everyone is different, and it wouldn't do for us all to be the same, queen. It would be a miserable world if we were. But I was like Kate with my husband. I used to watch for him through the window, and his dinner would be on the table and his slippers by

232

his chair. Of course there was only the two of us, so we looked after each other.' Winnie held the bundle of clothes to her chest. 'I'd better make a start on these. It won't take me long 'cos they're only cotton. I'll put them to steep in warm water while I make meself a cuppa. So I'll see yer tomorrow, queen, ta-ra.' Winnie had turned to walk away when she remembered something. 'Oh, Monica, will yer thank yer husband for getting me milk stout but tell him I'll go for it meself tonight? The sooner I get back in me routine the better. But I am beholden to him.'

Monica waved and called, 'I will tell him, but I think ye're daft. Yer should let us wait on yer for another day or two. Ye're too ruddy independent.'

'As long as I'm able to look after meself, queen, I'll do it.' She saw Nancy and Dolly turn into the street. 'Here's yer daughter with Nancy, so we're just in time. Ta-ra!'

Kate was regretting telling the family about the excitement because their dinners were left untouched as questions flew across the table. John was red in the face with anger. 'What sort of a man would pick on an old lady?' He shook his head vigorously. 'No, I'm wrong to call him a man, 'cos no man I know would stoop so low. He's a coward, through and through.'

Billy's eyes were like saucers. 'I wish I'd been here, I'd have had a go at him.'

'Did Mrs Cartwright really sit on him, Mam?' Nancy was picturing the scene in her mind. 'She's very brave, 'cos I wouldn't have, I'd have been too frightened.'

'She's not only brave, she's ruddy quick! I thought the bloke would go out the back way when he heard us knocking at the front, and I wasn't expecting him to come bursting out. I had the rolling pin in me hand, but before I knew what was happening Winnie had tripped him up and was sat on his back. She moved like greased lightning, I've never seen anything like it! When I hit him with the rolling pin, he'd already been caught. Still, I must have dazed him because after a while a big lump came up on the top of his head. It bought us some time so Monica and Maggie could get round to us.' Kate closed her eyes to visualize it more clearly in her mind. 'No one thought it funny at the time, and of course it's a very serious matter and not to be laughed at, but the policeman's face was a picture no artist could paint. I knew he was having a hard job to stop himself laughing. After all, yer've seen the size of Winnie – four foot ten and weighing about six stone at the most. The bloke she was sitting on was six foot at least, and could have picked her up with one hand as though she was a feather. It must have looked comical to anyone arriving on the scene, a burglar who'd been caught by a gang of women who were in the mood for lynching him. Yer see, all the neighbours came out when they heard the commotion, and were so angry they were calling the bloke every name they could think of, and kicking him into the bargain.'

John still looked concerned. 'Is Miss Parkinson all right?'

'She was in a real bad state at first, shaking and crying her eyes out 'cos the thief had stolen a ring that had been her mother's. That's besides her purse and two necklaces. But when Monica went through the bloke's pockets, everything he'd stolen from her was there. She seemed to calm down a bit then. But I'm going over when we've finished our dinner, just to make sure she's fit to leave in the house on her own.'

'She'll have to be watched very closely, love,' John said. 'A shock to the system like that would affect anyone, even a young person. At her age it could bring on a stroke, or even a heart attack.'

'She'll be well watched, don't worry. There's four of us going to take turns sitting with her until we think she's over the shock. But as it's my turn tonight, can we please get on with our dinner? It's cold now, and if it's left any longer, it won't be fit to eat at all. And yer know I can't abide wasting food.'

* * *

'How did yer find Miss Parkinson?' Kate asked Monica the next morning. 'I thought she was coping well last night, but John said the shock wouldn't really hit home for a few days. He put the fear of God into me, saying it could bring on a stroke or a heart attack.'

'He's right, girl, it has been known to happen. Delayed shock, that's what they call it. But Miss Parkinson seems to have a very strong constitution, let's hope she gets over it without any ill effects.' Monica was standing on Kate's step, thinking of the work she'd have to face when she got home. 'I'll have to go, girl, I haven't done a hand's turn yet. The dust will be meeting me at the door, and there's a stack of dishes in the sink. Give me an hour to sort meself out, then yer can make a pot of tea for us to drink while we make a list of the extra shopping we'll need because of the party tomorrow. I got a three bob sub off my feller, we can get some of the food in.'

An hour later Kate had just opened the door to Monica when the knocker sounded again. 'Oh, I wonder who the heck this can be? I hope it's not trouble.'

'If it is, girl, chase it. We've got enough to be going on with,' Monica called as she pulled out a chair. 'And if it's the rag and bone man, tell him we've got plenty of those as well.'

Winnie smiled up at Kate. 'I heard that, queen, and though I might look like a rag and bone man, I'm just the opposite this morning. I come bearing gifts.' She lifted her arms to show Kate there were two dresses draped over each. 'Am I welcome?'

'Oh, sunshine, they look brand new! Of course ye're welcome, come on in. Yer must have smelt the tea 'cos it's just been made.'

When Monica saw the dresses she jumped to her feet. On impulse she threw her arms around the older woman. 'Ye're as welcome as the flowers in May, girl!'

'Ay, watch it! I've been an hour ironing these, and I don't want them full of bleeding creases, thank you.'

Kate took two dresses from her and passed one over to her

mate. 'That's Dolly's, so treat it gently.' Then she held up her own daughter's dress. 'I'm not kidding, they could pass for brand new! Yer've worked wonders with them, sunshine! No one in a million years would think they'd come out of a pile of second-hand clothes.' Kate really was amazed at the transformation. 'The girls will be over the moon. I bet they spend most of Saturday parading up and down the street, swanking, so everyone will see them.'

'If I didn't know better, I'd swear they'd just come off a hanger in TJ's.' Monica was equally delighted. 'There'll be no holding our Dolly back, she'll be showing off like no one's business. I don't mind telling yer they wouldn't have looked like this if I'd washed them. Me and the iron don't get on very well together.'

Winnie was well pleased with the praise, and the fact she'd been able to repay a little of the kindness shown to her by these two. 'I put bit of starch in the water when I rinsed them, and as I told yer, Kate, it makes all the difference. Puts a bit of life back into the material.'

'I'll remember that in future,' Kate told her. 'Now I'm going to put this on a hanger in the wardrobe in our bedroom, 'cos I'm dying to see what the one I got for meself turned out like.'

'Have yer got a spare hanger to put this on?' Monica held out Dolly's dress. 'So it doesn't get creased and Winnie tells me off.'

'I haven't got a spare hanger! What d'yer think this is, sunshine, a ladies' fashion shop? I think there's three hangers in the wardrobe, or it could be four, and all the clothes we possess are on those hangers, all on top of each other.'

'Okay, girl, keep yer hair on! Blimey, anyone would think I'd asked yer for the loan of ten bob, the way ye're carrying on.'

'Oh, no, if yer'd asked me for the loan of ten bob, I'd have burst out laughing. That really would have been funny.'

Monica grinned. 'Yeah, it was a bit far-fetched, wasn't it? Anyway, I'll take Dolly's dress home now, while ye're pouring the tea out, and I'll hang it over my clothes on one of the three hangers we possess.' She winked at Winnie who was taking it all in. 'What it's like to be hard-up, eh, girl? I don't suppose Sarah Jane will have any second-hand hangers, will she?'

'I didn't see none, queen, but then I wasn't looking for them. I will ask, though, next time I go down.'

When Monica had left with the dress draped carefully over her arm, Kate sat down facing Winnie. 'Listen, I wish yer'd take things easy for a few days. Yer didn't give yerself long enough to get better, to get some strength back. Don't go overdoing things, for heaven's sake, or I'll blame meself if yer go down sick again.'

'It wouldn't be your fault, queen, I'm old and ugly enough to look after meself.' Winnie pursed her lips. 'No, yer can rest assured I won't wear meself out. But it wasn't overwork what made me sick, it was that bleedin' fish. Next time, I'll make sure I smell before buying.'

'Just make sure yer put yer feet up for an hour twice a day, instead of running around like a twenty year old. Look after yerself, sunshine, and yer'll live to a ripe old age.'

'I'm not daft enough to let meself get sick again, not when I've got things to look forward to. And I've got you to thank for that, sunshine, 'cos without you I wouldn't have the party tomorrow. Then there's the wedding next Thursday, I'm really excited about that. And as soon as me legs feel strong enough, I'll be going to give Sarah Jane a hand at Paddy's Market.' Her top teeth dropped and she quickly adjusted them with her tongue before saying, 'The way things are going, I'll have to buy meself a bleeding diary. I'll have as many engagements as the Queen herself.'

'Somehow I don't think hers will be as enjoyable as yours, sunshine. She'll be with a load of stiff, la-di-da toffs, who speak frightfully far back and don't know no jokes.'

'Ye're right there, queen, 'cos I used to work in a shop before I got married, and the wife of the man what owned it, she spoke so far back I had to go to the bottom of the street to hear her. And the best of it was, she was only born in a two-up-two-down like meself. But to hear her talk, yer'd think she wasn't only born with a silver spoon in her mouth, but a whole bleeding canteen of cutlery!'

Kate's chuckle was hearty. 'I bet yer were a real live wire when yer were young, 'cos yer've still got that mischievous glint in yer eye. And I bet yer led the lads a merry dance.'

'Ye're not far wrong there, queen, I had a marvellous time from when I was fifteen and me ma let me go to the local dances. I had plenty of partners and could dance the feet off any of them.' Winnie's smile faded a little, and there was a catch in her voice. 'That is until the night I met a boy with hair the colour of midnight, eyes that yer felt yer could swim in, and a smile to charm the birds off the trees. I fell for him hook, line and sinker. Never looked at another boy after that. Never danced with one either, 'cos Stan was very jealous and stuck to me like glue. And I lapped it up, queen, 'cos he was the only boy I'd ever wanted.'

'Then yer must have some wonderful memories,' Kate said. 'Not everyone in life finds someone to love the way you and Stan did, so yer must treasure those memories.'

'I keep them close to me heart, queen, that I do. Never a night goes by that I don't lie in bed and go over the good times we had. When Stan first died, I used to cry me eyes out and sit rocking in me chair every night, too afraid to go to bed because I knew I'd only make meself worse, missing his arm around me waist and us cuddling up together. I saw his face everywhere . . . on the ceiling, walls and mirrors. I'd have given anything to die so I could be with him. But they say time is a great healer, and they're right. I didn't think so for the first two years, but then I made meself put the sadness behind me. Instead of being unhappy whenever I thought of him, I started to remember the way he used to laugh at me jokes, and how he'd lean forward to knock his pipe against the fireplace. So many good things to remember, queen, and I take them to bed with me every night, so I never feel lonely now.'

'Ye're going to have me bawling me eyes out in a minute, sunshine. But I've got to say I think yer've been a little brick, the way yer've kept yerself busy, making sure yer house is like a new pin and offering a helping hand when needed. And yer don't do things by half, either, it's always the whole hog. Proper little live wire, yer are. I'm a lot younger than you, but yer can leave me standing.'

'If I didn't keep meself on the go, queen, I'd just fade away. And I've no intention of doing that, not while me diary is so full of engagements.' Winnie nodded to the dresses. 'Go and hang Nancy's up, then yer can have a look at yer own. I think you and Monica will be pleased with the way they've turned out.'

'Well, talk of the devil and he's bound to appear!' Kate said when her mate came back in. 'Winnie was just saying she thinks we'll be pleased with the dresses.'

Monica clicked her tongue. 'D'yer mean yer haven't hung that dress up yet or poured the tea out? I dunno, you two can't half talk. I thought I was bad enough, and my feller thinks I'm the world's worst, but you beat me by a mile.' She held out her hand. 'Here, give me my dress and I'll try it on in the kitchen.'

'I'll hang Nancy's up then I'll join yer,' Kate said, as she took the stairs two at a time. 'And if we don't come out of that kitchen looking like Jean Harlow and Maureen O'Sullivan, then someone's in for it. I won't say who, but they'll be the only one in the room besides you and me, sunshine.'

Her arms free now, Winnie folded them and sat back in the chair. She wouldn't admit it but she was feeling a bit tired. She'd been using two flat irons on the dresses, and they were heavy to take on and off the gas rings. Perhaps when she'd finished here she'd go home and put her feet up on the couch for an hour. Then she heard peals of laughter coming from the kitchen and a smile crossed her face. What were they up to now? She was soon to find out.

Kate came through the kitchen door, and the sight of her sent the little woman into pleats of laughter. She had her right hand on her hip and her left at the back of her head, and walked slowly, her body swaying from side to side, like she'd seen them do in the pictures. Her brown eyes looking through half-closed lids made her look sultry and passionate. Glancing at Winnie over her shoulder, she pursed her lips and blew a kiss in the air before walking over to stand by the window and await the entrance of her friend.

And what a grand entrance it was. Monica had surpassed herself. When Winnie saw the spectacle she nearly chocked. A mop head covered Monica's hair and fell around her face, and half a wooden peg had become a cigarette holder and was held shoulder-high between two fingers. Her movements were slinky and exaggerated, the expression on her face that of a hard-boiled gold digger. Taking a puff from an imaginary cigarette in the pretend holder, she bent down and blew invisible smoke towards Winnie before swaying her way to stand next to Kate.

'Oh, my God!' Winnie rocked back and forth with laughter. 'I don't know whether yer look like two women of ill-repute plying yer trade down on Lime Street, or two of them mannikins.'

The two friends joined in her laughter. 'Oh, dear,' Kate said. 'We might not have any money, but we certainly do see life.'

'Yer don't need money to enjoy yerself, girl, as long as yer can see the funny side.' Monica grinned over to where Winnie was drying her eyes. 'I didn't quite catch what yer said. Who did yer say we looked like? And I don't mean the trollops on Lime Street.'

'Them mannikins, queen, yer know who I mean. They show off clothes for the rich people to buy.'

'D'yer mean fashion models, sunshine?' Kate asked. 'Like in

George Henry Lee's and the posh shop at the bottom of Bold Street?'

'She means no such thing,' Monica said. 'She said mannikins and she meant mannikins. Don't be trying to confuse her.' She suddenly noticed Winnie's attention was no longer on her or Kate, but on something she could see happening outside the window. 'What have yer seen, girl, a ghost?'

'No, it's the police officer knocking on Miss Parkinson's door. Oh, now the door's been opened and he's stepping inside.'

'Oh, flipping heck, look at the state of us!' Kate tutted. 'I really want to see him to find out what's going on. I hate to miss anything.'

'If we put a move on, girl, we won't miss anything. Two minutes and we could be back in our old working clothes.' Monica pulled the mop head off and grinned down at it. 'Yer probably look better on me than me own hair does, but I'm afraid we must part even though parting is such sweet sorrow.' She pretended to kiss the mop while wiping a tear away. 'I would give yer a hug, only I can see in me head Kate washing the floor down with yer. And that's not a very romantic thought.'

Kate clicked her tongue. 'There are times when I seriously question your sanity, Monica Parry. But right now we don't have time to mess around, so let's take these dresses off and get ourselves over the road, on the double.' On her way to the kitchen, she asked Winnie, 'Are yer coming with us, sunshine, or will yer wait here until we come back?'

'Neither, queen, I'm going home. Yer told me to put me feet up for an hour every day, and that's what I intend doing. I'm sitting with Miss Parkinson this afternoon, so I'll find out from her then what's happening to that swine of a man.'

Kate soon came out of the kitchen wearing her old dress and patting her hair into place, and was quickly followed by Monica. 'Yer might as well come out with us, then, so I can lock the door behind us. But don't forget it's the girls' party tomorrow

241

afternoon, and ye're an invited guest. About three o'clock, eh, Monica?'

'Yeah, that's about right. It's not a posh do, yer know, Winnie, so yer won't need to wear that tiara ye're always talking about. Yer'll be getting a dripping sandwich and a fairy cake, and if yer luck's in we might run to a cream slice.'

'I'll not be worrying about the food, queen,' Winnie said, following the two friends out of the front door. 'It's the company I'm looking forward to.' She turned right to walk down to her own house while the two other women crossed the cobbles to the house opposite. She grinned when she heard Monica shout after her, 'And yer can keep yer eye off my feller as well, 'cos he's spoken for.'

'Ye're a spoil-sport, Monica, that's what yer are. I've a good mind to wear me tiara after all, and it would serve yer right if your feller took a liking to me. Especially if I'm wearing me new dress as well, which will knock spots off yours.'

Kate had already disappeared into Miss Parkinson's, but Monica stayed long enough to call, 'My dress hasn't got no spots on, girl, so yer'd have a job.'

Winnie saw a hand come out of the front door and grab Monica's arm. And she heard Kate hiss, 'Will yer grow up and behave yerself, sunshine, and stop showing me up? Honest, I can't take yer anywhere.'

Chapter Seventeen

'We won't stay long, Miss Parkinson.' Kate was concerned for the elderly lady who was looking very tired. 'We'll just hear what the officer has to say, then we'll leave yer in peace.'

'She never slept a wink last night, so she tells me,' said Maggie Duffy from next door. 'If she'd knocked, I would have come and stayed with her. But she's too ruddy stubborn and independent.'

'You need your sleep, Miss Parkinson,' Sergeant Bridgewater said kindly. 'If I were you, I'd accept all offers of help. For the time being anyway, until you're back to your old self.'

Miss Audrey Parkinson knew they all meant well, and their offers of help were given genuinely and generously. But this was the first time since her childhood that she hadn't been able to attend to herself and her affairs and she suddenly felt very old, frail, and afraid of the future. 'I'll have a few hours' sleep on the couch this afternoon,' she murmured.

'Yer'll have a full night's sleep in bed as well,' Maggie said, determination written all over her face. 'Whether yer like it or not, I'm staying. I'll bring the alarm clock to make sure I'm awake in time to get my feller up for work. So we'll have no excuses or arguments, if yer don't mind. Now I think we should all be quiet and hear what the officer has to say.'

But old habits die hard, and the old lady couldn't change the way she'd been brought up. She had guests, and they must be treated as such. 'First, perhaps the officer would like a cup of tea?'

That sounded good to the sergeant. Tea out of a decent cup, instead of the stewed brew they served up at the station in chipped mugs, sounded very tempting. 'If it's not too much trouble, I would be delighted. It would wet my whistle before I proceed to tell you of developments since I was last here.'

Maggie jumped to her feet. 'I'll see to it.'

'I'll give yer a hand,' Kate said. She was about to follow Maggie into the kitchen when she had a thought. 'Excuse me, officer. Mrs Parry there is my neighbour and best friend, but although I hate to say it she's also very nosy. So if she starts asking yer questions, will yer tell her to wait until we're all sitting together?'

Monica's tongue clicked in protest. 'Why did yer bother saying yer were me mate when yer knew yer were going to tell him I'm a nosy cow? Some mate you turned out to be, I must say! Yer've really hurt me now, I'm cut to the quick.' Putting on a sad, badly-done-by expression, and shaking her head, she said, 'I am, Miss Parkinson, I'm cut to the quick.'

A faint smile crossed the lined face. 'For years I've watched you and Kate, been a spectator to your comings and goings. In fact you have entertained and amused me almost from the time you both moved into the houses opposite me. I've often thought you were having a serious argument, only to watch in amazement as you've fallen into each other's arms, laughing your heads off. Neither of you would ever really do anything to hurt the other. So don't be trying to fool Sergeant Bridgewater.'

'Do you mean to say that me and me mate have been entertaining you for nearly twenty years! Well, if we'd known, we would have been selling tickets! Tuppence for a matinee and threepence for the first house in the front row of the stalls. And that would have been dirt cheap considering yer were sitting in the comfort of yer own home, no tram fares to pay, and no shoe leather used either!'

The sounds coming from the kitchen were of laughter mixed with the rattle of cups and spoons being placed on saucers. As he listened and smiled, Geoff Bridgewater was wishing all his calls were as pleasant as this. More often than not when he knocked on a door it was to tell some poor family that there'd been an accident and someone they loved was seriously ill in hospital. Or, worse still, had died. How he hated his job when he had to do that! Even though he told himself a hundred times that it was a service that had to be done, and someone had to do it, well, he wouldn't be human if it didn't get to him sometimes, would he?

Maggie came bustling in carrying a tray, her face wreathed in smiles. 'I'm not going to tell lies and say I haven't often watched you two through me window, but that's as far as I'll go 'cos I've got a feeling Monica's going to ask for back payments on the street entertainment.'

'She would if she was let,' Kate said, following up with a plate of arrowroot biscuits. 'But the officer hasn't got time to waste, so let's give him a chance to tell us what he came for.' She took a cup and saucer from the tray and handed it to him. 'Help yerself to sugar and milk.'

The four women made themselves comfortable before looking at him with eager anticipation. When he'd taken several sips of the hot tea, he placed the saucer carefully back on the tray and took out his notebook. 'The prisoner's name is Richard Willis, and he's not from this area. I can't give you his address, but I can say he lives on the other side of Liverpool. He's known at several police stations there, and has served one prison sentence of two years for burglary. That doesn't mean he's only offended the once, far from it. It's his livelihood, he makes a damn' good living out of it, but the police have not been able to catch him a second time until now as he never leaves any clues. He's known as Tricky Dicky 'cos he's very crafty. Never works in his own area where he'd soon be recognized, and always gets the lay of the land before attempting to break into a house. He'll pick on someone he thinks lives alone and is vulnerable. Someone like Miss Parkinson. He'll pick them out at the shops and follow them home, watch the house for hours to see how many live there.'

When the officer leaned forward to pick up his cup again, Kate said, 'Well, the crafty beggar! But if yer know all this, why hasn't he been caught before?'

There was a deep chuckle from the policeman. 'Because he's never had four women waiting for him to come out of a house before! He only robs elderly people because they can't hang on to him or give a very good description. If you had searched him a bit more yesterday, you'd have found a pair of gloves tucked down the front of his trousers. That's why he never gets caught, he never leaves a fingerprint for the police to go on. In police stations around the city, they know about a string of robberies they suspect are down to him because of what we call his MO – that means his method of operation – but you can't charge a person with a crime if you have no concrete proof.'

'Do you think he's been watching me, then?' Miss Parkinson's voice was shaky. She found the thought of someone following her every movement terrifying. 'I'm sure I would have noticed if I was being followed.'

'Not with Tricky Dicky you wouldn't. He's a professional, been doing it since he left school. He wouldn't have got away with it for so long otherwise. Crooks don't very often go on for years without being caught.'

'People who buy from robbers are as bad as those who actually do the stealing,' Miss Parkinson said. 'They must know how upset people are when anything precious is taken from them. Apart from it being a sin.'

'Oh, Tricky Dicky hasn't been selling around the pubs like most petty thieves. We managed to get quite a lot out of him, the Inspector and myself. He was under the impression that if he co-operated it would serve him well when the case comes up in court, and we didn't tell him otherwise. He told us where the other items of jewellery were stolen from so we'll get them back to the owners today. And one man, who he called a "fence", took everything he had to offer. Nothing ever went to his home, nor did he try to sell it to neighbours. But no amount of coaxing would get him to tell us who that "fence" is. Perhaps when our man's in court he might change his mind and spill the beans. Anyway, officers will be out in force now, visiting jewellers and pawnshops, to see if they have any of the items we have listed as stolen.'

'When is this bloke, this Tricky Dicky, going to court?' Kate asked. 'I wouldn't mind being there to hear what his punishment is to be.'

'He'll be going before a magistrates' court tomorrow, but that is only a formality, to set a date for the trial. Until then he'll be kept in custody. If you wish I'll let you know the date of the hearing and you can sit in court to hear what his fate will be. But I can assure you he'll be going to prison for a long spell, probably four or five years.'

'He deserves more than that for what he's done,' Maggie said. 'All those people he's robbed over the years, I haven't got no sympathy for him.'

'I'd like to go to the court, just to pull faces at him to let him know what we think of him. I'm good at curling me lip and sneering when I put me mind to it.' Monica gave a demonstration. 'I've never been in a court in me life, so it would be interesting.'

'I believe ye're not allowed to speak in court,' Kate told her. 'At least from what I've seen at the pictures. D'yer think yer could keep quiet for a couple of hours, sunshine?'

'Ay, ye're asking for it, you are, girl! Getting a little bit too big for yer boots and being sarky. If the police officer wasn't here, I'd say yer were bleeding well showing off. But seeing as he is, I won't say it until he's gone.'

Sergeant Bridgewater gave a rumbling laugh. 'I'm well used to choice words, ladies, and have often used them myself. Not at home, mind you, because my wife disapproves. But in my job, with the things we see, well, we'd have to be saints not to come out with the odd swear word. It helps to relieve the tension, let off a bit of steam.'

Monica gave Kate a dig in the ribs. 'Did yer hear that, girl, what the officer said? That it does yer good to let off steam? Well then, perhaps yer'll understand why I sometimes say a word that makes yer look down yer nose at me. I do it to relieve the tension.'

'If you say so, sunshine, but how come, before the officer mentioned the word tension, I'd never heard yer use it before? And I bet after a night's sleep yer'll have forgotten it when yer wake up in the morning.'

'Oh, no, I won't, girl, 'cos I'm going to write it down as soon as I get in the house. I may get more sympathy from my feller if I tell him I'm suffering from tension.' Monica was laughing inside at what she was going to say next. She knew her mate had a tendency to blush at the least thing, so she said, 'I won't tell him I'm suffering from tension on one of Robin Hood's nights, though, I'm not going to cut off me nose to spite me face.'

Kate left her chair so quickly it would have fallen backwards if Maggie hadn't caught it in time. 'Monica, I think it's time we left, so Miss Parkinson can have some peace.' She patted the old lady's hand. 'We'll be back later to sit with yer. Try and have some sleep before then, 'cos yer won't get much rest when me mate here starts. Once she opens her mouth, she forgets how to close it.'

'No, I don't, girl, not any more.' Monica knew Kate would start on her when they got outside, and was dying to laugh. 'My feller showed me how to close me mouth last night. All I have to do is put me hand under me chin, press up, and hey, presto! I was as quiet as a mouse all night, honest!'

Kate grinned. 'Then who was it I heard shouting that the kettle was boiling and would someone please see to it?'

'Ah, yer can't count that, girl, 'cos if I hadn't yelled, there'd have been no arse left in the ruddy kettle.'

'That does it!' Kate said. 'Up yer get, and home we go. And no messing either.' She gave the sergeant a wink and a smile. 'Sometimes I don't know what to do with her. She's worse than a child that's out of control. At least with a child yer can smack them, but if I smacked me mate, she'd smack me back, twice as hard.' She pulled Monica from her chair, saying, 'Be a good girl and say ta-ra to everyone.'

Monica went into her little girl act, with her head hanging down and her tongue sticking out of the side of her mouth. 'Ta-ta, everyone, I'm going out with me mam now. She taking me to the park so I can have a go on the swings and roundabout.' Sucking her thumb now, she waved. 'Ta-ta.'

Kate was laughing when she said, 'I could take yer to the park and leave yer there! Come on now, sunshine, and stop acting daft.' She was pushing Monica towards the door when Miss Parkinson spoke.

'Kate, if you're going to the shops, would you be kind enough to post a letter for me?'

'Yes, of course I would. Have yer got it ready?'

'Yes, but I haven't got a penny stamp. The letter's to a niece of mine in Essex whom I haven't seen in twenty years because of the distance. But we keep in touch with Christmas and birthday cards.' The old lady ran a veined hand across her forehead as she sighed. 'After what happened yesterday, and the fact that I've now turned eighty, I have decided it's time to put my affairs in order. As Celia is my only living relative, there are things I would like to discuss with her.'

All three neighbours showed surprise because Miss Parkinson had never mentioned a relative. But no one voiced their thoughts. 'I'll put a stamp on, sunshine, and pop it in the pillar box. It will catch the one o'clock post so she should get it in the morning.'

'Thank you, you are very kind. The letter is on the sideboard. And if you'll pass me my purse out of the drawer, I'll give you the penny for the stamp.'

Kate waved a hand in the air. 'Don't worry about the penny, for heaven's sake! I'm not so hard-up.' She picked up the envelope from the sideboard. 'It will be on its way to her this afternoon, and with a bit of luck she'll be reading it this time tomorrow.' She bent down and kissed her neighbour's wrinkled cheek. 'Me and Monica have some shopping to do so we'll love yer and leave yer. But we'll be back later.'

After more farewells, the friends pulled the front door shut behind them, then linked arms to cross the street. 'I was real surprised when she said she had a niece, she's never mentioned it before. I always thought she was alone in the world.'

'She might as well be if she only sees the niece every twenty years,' Monica said. 'Mind you, I haven't a clue where Essex is, only that it's a long way away.'

'It must be, or they wouldn't have left it so long to see each other.' Kate inserted the key in the lock and pushed the door open. 'Now let's get cracking with that list of shopping we need or the morning will be over before we know it.' She saw an expression on her friend's face which she recognized straight away. 'Oh, no, sunshine, we haven't got time for a cuppa now so don't be asking.'

Monica muttered under her breath, 'Miserable bitch.'

Kate spun around. 'What did yer just say?'

Her friend raised her brows. 'I didn't say nothing, girl!'

'Oh, yes, yer did, I heard yer! Yer called me a miserable bitch!'

Monica's face was a picture of innocence. Pressing a hand to her side and looking really put out, she said, 'I said I had a stitch! Stitch, girl, not bitch! Yer want yer ears washing out, yer bad-minded so-and-so.'

Kate stood with her head tilted. She managed to keep the laughter from her face, but not from those deep brown eyes which were shining with mirth. 'You must think I came over on the banana boat, sunshine. I may be hard-up but I'm not ruddy well hard of hearing, so don't be telling lies.' Her hands went on her hips. 'When yer go to confession, do yer tell the priest about all the lies yer tell? I don't think yer do or yer'd be in the church till they closed, saying all the prayers he'd given yer as penance.'

'Nah, me and Father Kelly are like this.' Monica crossed two fingers of her right hand. 'He understands me and we get on fine. I never get any more than three Hail Marys.'

'That's because yer tell him ye're as pure as the driven snow, that's why.'

Monica held up one hand in surrender. 'D'yer know what, girl? In the time yer've taken to tell me what a heathen I am, yer could have had the kettle on and boiled.'

Then, as though there hadn't been a word spoken since they entered the house, Kate said, 'That's a good idea, sunshine! You see to the tea while I find a piece of paper and a pencil.'

'I can't wait for the party tomorrow,' Nancy said, wriggling on the wooden chair because she couldn't sit still. 'Or to see what I've got for me birthday.'

'It's not really a party, sunshine, more of a tea. And although circumstances don't allow for big expensive presents, I think yer'll be quite happy with what yer get.'

'Yeah, I know I will. It doesn't matter what it is, it's the thought of opening it up that I like, it's exciting.' Nancy had little appetite for her dinner tonight. All she could think of was that after tomorrow she'd be in her teens. And this time next year she'd be looking for a job. 'Is Dolly getting the same as me?'

'Well, me and yer Auntie Monica thought that if yer didn't both get the same, there'd either be a crying match or blue murder. So we settled for a quiet life.'

Billy tried to curl his lip into a sneer, but although he thought he looked like James Cagney, he actually looked as though there was a bad smell under his nose. 'I don't want no party for my birthday. It's daft sitting around a table eating jelly creams and fairy cakes, and pretending to be enjoying yerself. That's more for little kids, and I'll be eleven! I'd rather have the money so me and Pete can go to a matinee and see a cowboy film.'

'Oh, well, you're easily satisfied, sunshine!' Kate said. 'Instead of costing me and yer dad about five bob, it'll only cost us coppers. Tuppence to get into the pictures, and a penny for a bag of sweets. That's a load off me mind.'

Billy's eyes nearly popped out of his head. 'I didn't mean I didn't want presents, Mam,' he spluttered, 'only no party. Or tea, as yer call it. But I want me presents, same as our Nancy, or it wouldn't be fair.'

Kate shook her head and tutted. 'I thought it was too good to be true. It's just a pity your birthday is two weeks away, or we could have had the one party for both of yer. Nancy and Dolly, and you and Pete.'

'Ah, ay, Mam! I'm not sitting at the table with two girls!' Billy couldn't find the right words to say how disgusted he was that his mam would even think of it. 'And if I told Pete, he'd think I'd gone doolally. He'd run a mile from a girl, he can't stand them.'

'Yer don't know how lucky yer are, son, to get presents and have the chance of going to a party,' John said. 'When I was your age, there was no such thing because me ma couldn't afford it. We were lucky if we got one decent meal a day. And when me dad died, and there was no money coming in, me ma took in washing to help with the rent money. She also scrubbed steps and cleaned windows, all to fetch in a few bob. She had it hard, did my ma, until our Alan left school and got a job. Then the year after I left school, and I'll never forget how proud I felt on the day I gave me ma me first wage packet. I'd seen the way she'd had to struggle to bring me and our Alan up, and even though we were only earning buttons, we were both glad we could help her out. I thought the world of my ma. If I could, I would have given her the world.'

Nancy kicked sideways and caught her brother on his shin. 'Yer see how lucky we are? So stop yer moaning and think of someone else for a change.' For good measure, she added, 'Me and Dolly don't want yer at the party anyway 'cos ye're a misery guts and would spoil everything.'

'All right, let's not have an argument at the dinner table.' Kate turned to her husband and changed the subject. 'It's a pity your Alan lives so far away, it would be nice if the families could meet up more often.'

'Where is it Uncle Alan lives?' Nancy asked. 'I know I've asked yer loads of times but I keep forgetting 'cos it's a funny name.'

'I don't think the people who live in Ormskirk think it's a funny name, sunshine. We're used to the areas of Liverpool 'cos we were born here,' Kate said. 'But a stranger to the city might think Bootle a funny name. Or the Dingle, Seaforth, Orrell Park, Fazakerley or Vauxhall! They'd all sound strange to someone who doesn't live here. They're built-up areas 'cos we live in the city. Yer Uncle Alan and Auntie Rose live in the country surrounded by farms and green fields.'

'D'yer think we'll ever go there one day, Mam?' Billy asked. 'I mean, when we've got the money. I've never seen what it's like in the country.'

'Ye're not the only one, sunshine, 'cos neither have me or yer dad. It's not for want of being asked, either, 'cos yer Uncle Alan always asks in his letters. And when we've got a few bob to spare, we'll surprise him and Rose one day, and turn up on their doorstep.'

'I'll be working next year, Mam, so yer'll be a bit better off then.' Nancy's eyes slid sideways to where her brother sat. 'And I know it's a long way off, but in a couple of years our Billy will be working as well, and yer'll never be hard-up then.'

The boy had been deeply moved by what his dad had said about his own mother. Billy felt that perhaps he didn't show enough appreciation for what his own mam did. He wouldn't want her to think he didn't love her. 'Yeah, I'm going to be like me dad. When I hand me first wage packet over, I'll stick me chest right out with pride. And yer never know, one day, when I'm a man, I might hand yer me wage packet with one hand, and the world with the other.'

Kate leaned forward to ruffle his hair. 'Me and yer dad are going to be all right in our old age, aren't we? You'll be there to look after us.'

'And I will,' Nancy said. 'We'll pay yer back for all the years yer've looked after us. In the meanwhile, our Billy can get some practice in by being nice to his sister. It's not my fault I've been born a girl, and brothers and sisters are supposed to love one another.'

Billy rolled his eyes. 'She's getting soppy now.'

'No, I'm not! We *are* supposed to love one another.'

'Okay, then, if it makes yer happy, I do love yer. But if yer'd been a boy, I'd have loved yer even more.'

John winked at his wife. 'Perhaps we shouldn't have had any children at all. We could have had a cat or a dog, they don't take much looking after. Don't answer yer back, either.'

Billy wrinkled his nose. 'Pete's mam has a cat, and it's a mangy-looking thing. It doesn't half make the house smell as well. So I think yer did the right thing in having me and our Nancy instead of a cat.'

'We had a cat when I was a little girl,' Kate said. 'It was all pure white. I used to wash it and wrap it in an old piece of sheet, stick it in the pram and take it for a walk. And d'yer know, that cat was just like a baby, it loved being taken for a walk. Mind you, people got a shock when they pulled the cover back expecting to see a bonny baby.'

The idea tickled Billy. 'I bet they said, "Isn't he like his father?" That's what all women say when they see a new baby. They coo over it, and say, "Ooh, isn't he the spitting image of his dad?" Or, "She's got her mother's nose and chin." When, as far as I can see, all new babies look alike. Can't tell one from the other.'

'A mother can always tell her own baby, son. Even if yer put a hundred in a row, she'd be able to pick her own out.'

'Especially if they were all crying.' John chuckled. 'Women seem to have a sixth sense over their babies, they know them by smell, looks and sound. Yer'd never fool a woman over which was hers. She's just like a homing pigeon who can fly thousands of miles and still find the right roof to come down on. It's never ceased to amaze me, that.'

'Blimey, we've covered some ground in the last half hour,' Kate said. 'We've got Nancy and Billy working, been to Ormskirk, spoken about brotherly love, crying babies and homing pigeons. That's a wide variety of subjects, no one could say we were dull. But all good things come to an end and now it's time to come down to earth, clear the table, then wash the dishes. Hands up all the volunteers.'

Chapter Eighteen

It was half-past two on Saturday afternoon when Kate answered a knock on the door and found Winnie looking up at her. 'I wasn't expecting you, sunshine, I thought yer were going straight to Monica's.'

'I'm a bit early, queen, and I thought she would be busy and not want me sitting there gawping. I've been keeping Audrey company for a couple of hours while Maggie did her shopping, and didn't feel like going home.'

'Well, don't stand there, come on in.' Kate held the door wide. 'We've got half an hour before we go next door. There's no way I'd go early either 'cos I'd get the height of abuse, and she'd have me guts for garters.'

Winnie stepped into the hall and whispered, 'That dress looks really bonny on yer, queen, the colour doesn't half suit yer.'

Kate grinned. 'Ye're looking very fetching yerself, if I might say so. This is the first time I've ever seen yer without a coat on, and yer look great! Yer should do it more often. And yer were right about showing me and Mon up in yer dress, yer'll put us both in the shade.'

'Who is it, Mam?' Nancy called. 'Is it for me?'

'No, it's Mrs Cartwright, and we're coming in now.'

Winnie clasped her hands together when she saw the young girl looking very pretty with her face aglow. She quickly remembered she wasn't supposed to have seen the dress before. 'Oh, yer look lovely, pet! That dress really suits yer, is it a new one?'

Nancy did a little twirl. 'It's me birthday present off me mam and dad, and I'm really made up. It was a lovely surprise.'

'Ye're getting more like yer mother every day, pet. Yer'll be a real beauty like her.' Winnie nodded a greeting to John. 'Ye're well blessed with the women in yer life, John, yer must be very proud.'

'That's putting it mildly, Winnie.' He was feeling quite emotional at the sight of his wife and daughter looking so pretty. He wished he could afford to buy them the clothes they deserved, but they never asked for anything or complained. 'Yer see, they're not only beautiful on the outside, they're beautiful inside as well.'

'Ah, that's a lovely thing to say, Dad!' Nancy ran to put her arms around him. 'There's not another dad in the world as good as you. Or as handsome.'

'Ay, we're going to a birthday party, and we should be happy and laughing,' Kate said. 'If yer keep that up yer'll have me bawling me eyes out.'

'It's a good job our Billy's not here.' Nancy took a fit of the giggles. 'He'd have dashed out to the yard and pretended to be sick down the grid.'

'Well, now, pet, if Billy was here and I told him he'd be a fine figure of a man when he was older, and as handsome as his father, he'd be walking ten feet tall.'

John ran his fingers through his thick mop of dark hair before hooking a thumb in each side of his braces and stretching the elastic. 'At last the compliments are coming my way. Keep it up, Winnie, and I'll not be able to get through the door without bending me head.'

'Come off it, John Spencer, ye're bigheaded enough as it is.' Kate glanced at the clock. 'Another ten minutes before me mate will let us in. So tell me, Winnie, since when have yer been calling Miss Parkinson by her first name?'

'Don't forget I've known her for many years, queen, and we always called each other by our first name. Then one day a shopkeeper called her Mrs Parkinson, and she got quite snooty with him. "I am Miss Parkinson, if you don't mind." Now there were a few neighbours in the shop at the time, including meself,

257

and afterwards we all started to give her her full title. But when we're on our own, she's never got anything but Audrey off me.'

Kate tilted her head, her lips pursed. 'I wouldn't have had her down as an Audrey. More of a Hannah or Amelia. I bet she was a looker when she was younger, 'cos the signs are still there. And she holds herself well, very elegant. I'm surprised she's a spinster. The men in her day must have all been blind.'

'Oh, she had plenty of chances, queen, I know that for sure. Even in her fifties there were a few men after her from where she worked, and they were men in good positions who could have given her a comfortable life. But for some unknown reason she wasn't interested and sent them all packing.' Winnie shrugged her shoulders. 'I often wonder whether she ever regrets not getting married, 'cos it's been a lonely life for her since her parents died.'

'Did you know she had a relative, a niece or cousin?'

'Celia, yeah! I met her once, about twenty years ago. Nice woman, she is, about the same age as meself. Like Miss Parkinson, she's very well-spoken.'

'It's funny, isn't it, 'cos I'm not a snob, but every time I'm over there I watch me Ps and Qs. I don't do it anywhere else.' Kate's laughter bubbled to the surface. 'Not that it makes much difference, 'cos while I'm trying to be something I'm not, me mate stays her own sweet self and comes out with whatever comes into her head. If she swears, and someone doesn't like it, then it's just too bad for them.'

'Monica entertains more than she upsets, queen, so enjoy her and to hell with everyone else. And she's kind-hearted, too, as I've had cause to find out over the last week. What more could yer ask in a friend?'

'Not a thing, sunshine, I know when I'm well off.' Another quick look at the clock told Kate it was just on three o'clock. 'We'd better get moving. Yer see, my entertaining, kind-hearted mate said not a minute before, nor a minute after. Otherwise she'd get a cob on, and no one should have a cob on at a party. But it wouldn't be her fault if she got a cob on, it would be ours, so she doesn't advise us to be early or late.'

'Blimey! All that without taking a breath,' John said. 'I think you and Monica make a good team. Both of yer can talk the hind legs off a donkey.'

Nancy was quick to defend. 'Me mam doesn't talk a lot!'

'Take no notice of him, sunshine, 'cos he knows damn' well that if I didn't talk this house would be like a graveyard. Him and Tom never have much to say for themselves.'

'That's because we don't have a chance to get a word in edgeways. Yer must admit, love, that there's not a man born who could out-talk a woman.'

'We'll discuss that in more detail after the party. We should be back in about two minutes 'cos Monica threatened to lock us out if we were late.'

Nancy was out of the door before you could say Jack Robinson. She couldn't wait to see Dolly's dress, to see if it was nicer than hers. Not that it could be, 'cos hers was really lovely and she was delighted with it. She'd have been next door hours ago to show it off, but her mam said it would be much better to arrive for the party in it. More grown-up, like.

'The birthday girl is excited,' Winnie said, linking Kate and leaving the house a little more sedately than the young girl. 'Ah, what it is to be young, eh, with yer whole life ahead of yer?'

'Yeah, I remember when I was her age, I had such hopes and such dreams. Like wanting to be a film star or a singer on the stage. I didn't have the sense to realize I can't even sing in tune, never mind going on the stage.' Kate was laughing when she stood on the step next door. 'I can just about manage "Any Old Iron" or "Down By The Old Bull And Bush".'

'I'm sorry, but we don't want no drunks in here.' Monica stood before them with her arms folded and a look on her face which said she wasn't going to let them pass. 'Now sling yer

259

hook, the pair of yer, before yer feel me boot up yer backside. I don't know what the world's coming to, women of your age drunk.'

'Behave yerself,' Kate said. 'We've only had two bottles of stout and two glasses of sherry. It would take more than that to make me drunk.' She hiccuped several times, then crossed her eyes and pretended to sway from side to side. Her words slurred, she said, 'I can hold me drink, I can.'

Monica chuckled. 'Ay, girl, if I didn't know better, I'd believe yer! Ye're good at taking a drunk off. Yer can make that yer party piece in future, like when we come to your house at Christmas for a knees-up.' She winked at Winnie before saying, 'Yer want to get in there early, girl, and put yer name down for an invite. She gives smashing parties, does my mate, I'll say that for her.'

Kate quickly sobered up. 'Who said I was having a party at Christmas? Yer know what yer can do, don't yer, Monica Parry? I'm not having no party, so yer can forget it. I had it last year and it's your turn next time.'

Tom's loud voice bellowed, 'The way ye're going on, Christmas will be come and gone and yer'll still be standing there yapping about whose turn it is! Get inside before the jellies melt and the milk turns sour.'

To which Monica replied, 'The only sour thing in this house is your bleeding face! And I don't know what yer want us to come in for 'cos it's not as if yer were worried about missing anything. And I'm damn' sure it's not 'cos yer've got a funny story to tell us that will make us roll about laughing.'

'No, it's nothing like that,' Tom shouted back. 'It was to remind yer that yer didn't give me back the three bob yer borrowed off me yesterday.'

Monica's face was comical. Her eyes and mouth opened as wide as they'd go. Then she tapped the side of her nose and whispered softly, 'Listen to this, girls, and see if yer don't think I'm a genius.' Her eyes filled with mischief, she called, 'Ah, now, light of my life, yer wouldn't spoil yer daughter's birthday party by talking about who owes what, would yer? Why, that nice dress she's got on, what I bought with the money yer gave me, was supposed to be a present from you. And if that dress hears yer asking for yer money back, it'll fall to pieces.'

They could hear the girls giggling, then Dolly, with her mother's quick wit, said, 'Ah, ay, Dad, yer can't give me a present and then ask for yer money back! That's mean, that is. And if me dress falls to pieces like me mam said it would, then I'll be left standing here in me vest and knickers.'

'That's my daughter, a chip off the old block.' Monica jerked her head. 'Come in, girls, and I bet yer any money he's squirming in his chair, the miserable sod.'

But far from squirming, Tom greeted the women with a huge grin. 'I must want me head testing 'cos I fall for it every time. By my reckoning, I've bought that dress twice over.'

'No, yer haven't, sweetheart.' Monica pretended to gush. 'I wouldn't pull a trick on yer like that. I was just telling me mates that ye're the love of me life, and I wouldn't swap yer for anyone, not even Robin Hood. But just so yer know where yer stand, I'll tell yer. With the two lots of money yer gave me, or what I borrowed, well, I bought the dress with one lot, and with the other I bought all the food for the birthday party. So we're all very grateful to yer for the cakes, jellies, lemonade and sandwiches. It's a pity there's no milk stout or sherry for the ladies, but we can't be greedy, so yer won't hear us complaining.'

'I know I won't hear yer, 'cos I won't be here! I'm on me way to the pub for a pint with some of the lads. I'm getting from under yer feet so yer'll be free to jabber as much as yer like.'

'Oh, that's come in very handy, sweetheart, light of my life! I'll come down with yer and yer can pass me three bottles of milk stout out.' She raised her eyebrows at Kate and Winnie. 'Don't yer think I'm lucky having a husband who's one in a million?'

'Far be it from me to come between man and wife,' Kate said, 'but I think yer've got a husband that's too soft with yer.'

'Oh, thanks a bundle, girl, and here's me thinking yer were me mate! Ye're standing in my living room, here by invitation to a birthday tea, and ye're insulting me all ends up! I think ye're just jealous 'cos I've got a very accommodating husband.'

Tom put a hand on each arm of his fireside chair and pushed himself to his feet. 'I wouldn't argue with her, Kate, 'cos yer won't win. I only do it as a point of principle, not because I think I stand a snowball's chance in hell of winning.' He ran a finger down Monica's cheek. 'Yer'll have to do without the milk stout, love, because I'm not made of money. Yer've bled me dry, and I can't give what I haven't got.'

'Oh, aye, give us the old sob story. Yer've got no money, but ye're on yer way down to the pub for a few pints with yer mates. Pull the other leg, it's got bleeding bells on.'

'Sit down, then, and I'll oblige.'

'What d'yer want me to sit down for, yer daft nit! We're supposed to be having a party, in case yer've forgot.'

'That's all right, I'll get out of yer way.' Tom knew he was flogging a dead horse because he'd never got the better of his wife yet. But thinking of the saying that God loves a trier, he decided to have a go. 'I was only trying to do as yer asked.'

'What d'yer mean, do as I ask? I haven't asked yer to do nothing!'

'Yes, yer did! Kate and Winnie will vouch for that, they must have heard yer.'

Monica put a finger to her temple. 'He's going crazy, I never asked him to do nothing.'

Tom bent closer, so their noses were nearly touching. 'Yer told me to pull the other leg 'cos it's got bells on. Well, I could hardly do that when yer were standing up, could I?'

'Oh, very funny, I don't think! Now toddle off to the pub before I change me mind and come down with yer.'

He didn't need telling twice. And he walked quickly, knowing his wife was quite capable of following him. Not that he objected to buying three bottles of stout, but the extra money he'd given to Monica had left him skint. Well, almost skint. He'd made sure he'd kept enough back for his nightly pint. It wasn't as though he was starving his family or they were going round in rags. A pint would be the last thing on his mind if that was the case. But he had to draw the line somewhere with Monica or her spending would get out of hand. He was too soft with her as it was. However, when she looked him straight in the eye, he couldn't refuse her.

When the door had closed on her husband, Monica waved to the chairs set around the table. 'Sit down, folks, and make yerself at home.'

'Let me wish Nancy and Dolly a happy birthday first, and tell them how pretty they look.' Winnie reached for her handbag which was hanging in the crook of her arm. 'And give them their birthday cards.' She handed an envelope to each of the bright-eyed girls. 'Have a lovely day, darlings, and thank you for inviting me to yer tea party.'

'Ooh, another card, Dolly,' Nancy said. 'That's five each we've got.'

'Yeah, isn't it the gear!' While Nancy was opening her envelope with care, Dolly was too impatient and tore at hers. As she pulled the card from the tattered remains of the envelope, a silver sixpence fell on to the table. 'Yer've dropped a sixpence, Mrs Cartwright.' She picked up the coin and held out her hand. 'It must have fallen out of yer handbag.'

'No, queen, it's a little present for yer. Nancy's got one too. It's not much, but yer can buy yerselves some sweets with it.'

The next minute Winnie was fighting for breath as she was hugged by two excited and thankful girls who were each trying to pull her their way. 'Oh, thank you, Mrs Cartwright, ye're very kind.'

'Okay, kids, just settle down and I'll make the tea.' Monica got as far as the kitchen door, stopped for a second, then turned around. 'I'll make the tea in a minute, I've just had a thought that tickled me fancy. In me mind I could see my feller walking down the street.' She moved to the centre of the room, her face creased in laughter lines. 'Pretend I'm him, and I'm talking to meself.' Her head down, which was a habit of her husband's, she slowly walked the length of the room. 'Now, this is where yer have to use yer imagination. "It's a lovely day in the middle of summer, and the sun is cracking the flags. And what are those stupid women arguing about . . : who's having the ruddy Christmas party! I'll never understand the female sex if I live to be a hundred." '

Kate chuckled. 'D'yer know, I could see Tom in me head then. But I'll tell yer what, he was right, we *are* stupid. And you are wrong, sunshine, 'cos I am definitely not having a party at Christmas. So I hope your feller doesn't tell John as soon as he claps eyes on him that we are.'

Dolly heaved a sigh. 'Ay, Mam, do yer think we can have our birthday party, please, 'cos me and Nancy are hungry? Yer can talk about Christmas later. Say in four months' time.'

'Yer can't be that hungry or yer tongue would be hanging out and yer tummy rumbling. But I can see Winnie eyeing the cakes up, so I suppose I'd better put a move on.'

'The table looks a treat, queen, and I can see everything is home-made.' Winnie nodded in approval. 'Yer must have worked hard this morning.'

Monica carried on the conversation from the kitchen. 'Don't take any notice of my feller saying I never stop talking, girl, 'cos I can shift when I want to. I started just after he left for work and finished just before he got back. And when he saw the table all set out, he just said, "That looks nice, love." I could have hit him, 'cos he probably thought I'd knocked it all together in half an hour.'

'I think yer've done very well, sunshine, the food is a credit to yer. And yer never told me yer were making a birthday cake, it's a lovely surprise. Nancy has never had her name on a cake before, have yer, sunshine?'

'I've never had a birthday cake before, have I, Mam? Auntie Monica has been very clever making it herself.'

Monica came through carrying the teapot and stand. 'It was nothing, no trouble at all.'

'Oh, you big fibber, Mam!' Dolly wagged a finger. 'If it was no trouble, why were yer swearing when yer were trying to ice the names on? Yer should have heard her, Auntie Kate, she called that poor cake all the names under the sun.' She tossed her head, sending her shoulder-length, mousy hair into waves which fanned her face. 'If I'd been that cake, I'd have upped sticks and left home.'

'But ye're not, and yer didn't, so let's start. Help yerself, Winnie, don't sit there all ladylike or yer'll be left with the crumbs. We don't stand on ceremony here, so dig in.'

Kate looked confused. 'Haven't yer forgotten something, sunshine?'

'What's that, girl?'

'The birthday presents, yer daft nit!'

It was Nancy's turn to look confused. 'I thought the dresses were our presents, Mam.'

'They are the main ones that yer dads bought yer, but there's a couple of little ones off me and Auntie Monica that she seems to have forgotten about.'

Monica's eyes rolled. 'There's a good excuse for me, I have been very busy and I've got to admit they slipped me mind.' She made haste to the sideboard cupboard and took out the wrapped parcels containing the toilet water and the hankies. 'I'm sorry, girls, but better late than never.'

The delight of the girls brought smiles to the faces of the adults. Scent was what grown-up ladies wore, so this was a definite sign they were growing up. Within no time the room was smelling of sweet-peas and the amount they were putting on the lace hankies and dabbing behind their ears meant the bottles would last them no time. But Kate and Monica thought it was a small price to pay to see such happiness on their daughters' faces.

Winnie proved to have a good appetite, which meant she was back in better health. Doing as she was bid, she tucked in with gusto. In fact, it was a pleasure to see how much she enjoyed the food. After sampling several sandwiches, she reached for a fairy cake. On her first bite, a look of bliss came over her face and she declared, 'This is the lightest and best bleeding fairy cake I've ever tasted.'

Monica stuck out her chest and looked very smug. It was about time someone congratulated her on her skill in the kitchen. Tom and Dolly just took her for granted. 'I've been wondering if Betty would like me to make her a few cakes for after the wedding, 'cos she'll have enough on her plate then without baking.'

'Oh, sunshine, I'm sure she'd be really grateful,' Kate told her, while counting in her head how many cakes there were left on the plate. There was more than enough for another one each, and then there was the sponge birthday cake. 'It's good of yer to think about it. And I'll give yer a hand, even though yer wouldn't let me help yer today.'

'I'll slip down in the morning, it'll be one worry less off her mind.' Monica nodded. 'Yeah, I'll do that.' She bit her tongue just in time to stop herself from asking Kate how she was getting on with the matinee coat. Last time she'd asked, a couple of days ago, her mate had said she only had to sew the sleeves in, and it would be ready in plenty of time. The one she herself had been knitting was finished and was now on the bottom of the wardrobe wrapped in tissue paper.

Nancy had been trying to get something off her chest for the last half hour, but couldn't pluck up the courage. However, seeing how quickly the plate was emptying, it was a case of now or never. 'Auntie Monica, could I take one of the cakes for our Billy, please? I feel a bit mean for leaving him out.'

'Yer don't need to, girl, 'cos I've stashed a few in the pantry for him and Pete. I know he acts like a tough gangster but he's still a kid at heart, I wouldn't leave him out for the world. They'll get a piece of birthday cake as well.'

Nancy gave a sigh of relief. 'Thank you, Auntie Monica, him and Pete will be made up.'

'Yer thought of everything, sunshine.' Kate smiled across the table at her best mate. 'I am beholden to yer.'

'I'll remind yer of that near Christmas,' Monica said, tongue in cheek. 'I might even offer to make the cakes for yer Christmas party!' Before Kate could come back with anything, she carried on, 'When we've finished eating and the dishes are washed, we'll have a game of I Spy.'

'I'm being spoilt,' Winnie said, adopting a posh voice. 'A party today, and a wedding to look forward to on Thursday. My life is one whirl of social engagements and I really could do with a secretary to keep a diary because I would be very upset if I let anyone down.' Her eyes dropped to her dark blue dress. 'I could do with a maid to see to me clothes as well, 'cos this is the only dress I've got and haven't I only gone and spilt some red jelly on the bleeding thing.'

The laughter floated through the open window to where Billy was playing ollies in the gutter outside. His finger bent ready to flick at the marble, he looked at Pete with disgust written on his face. 'Can yer hear that? And I bet it was some daft joke that wasn't funny at all.'

'Yeah,' Pete agreed. 'My mam's the same, she'll laugh at anything whether it's funny or not. But come on, it's your turn!'

Chapter Nineteen

'Do I look all right for a wedding?' Monica asked, twirling around. 'It's because I know where this dress came from that's giving me doubts.'

'Don't act daft, yer look fine!' Kate clicked her tongue. 'No one else would ever guess we got them from a second-hand stall. And even if they did, why worry? As long as yer feel good, that's all that matters. And I think yer look lovely.'

'It's all right for you, yer'd look a million dollars if yer wore a sack. Everyone is that busy looking at yer face, they don't notice what yer've got on.'

'Now ye're being silly, sunshine, 'cos yer only have to look in the mirror to know yer can hold yer own with anyone. If I thought yer looked a sight in that dress, I'd say so, 'cos ye're me mate. But yer don't, yer look great.'

'Where's Winnie got to? She should be here by now. I don't want to be late.'

'Calm down, sunshine,' Kate said. 'She'll be here any minute. And we're not going to be late, we'll be there well before the bride and groom arrive with their families.'

Just then there was a knock on the door and Kate went to answer it, saying, 'I bet this is Winnie now.'

The little woman passed Kate with a grin on her face. 'I'm dead excited, aren't you?'

'Another minute, girl, and yer would have been dead,' Monica told her. 'We should be on our way now!'

'No, we've plenty of time, queen, I went out to get these for us.' Winnie brought her hand from behind her back clutching three pink carnations. 'I thought it would be nice if we looked the part.'

'Oh, I take it all back, girl, ye're forgiven.' Monica took one of the flowers, saying, 'Betty did say she'd get flowers for us, but I told her not to bother, she had enough on her plate. But I'm glad yer got these, though, Winnie, we'll look more dolled up with them on our dresses.'

'The man in the shop didn't have no bleeding pins, though, 'cos he said they were for button-holes and didn't need pins. Proper cocky about it he was, too! If I'd had time, I would have clocked him one.'

'I've got some safety pins, sunshine, so don't worry, it's any port in a storm.' Kate rooted through the sideboard drawers and came up with two safety pins. 'I could have sworn I had more than that.'

'Well, as yer said, queen, it's any port in a storm so I'll use the pin I've got in me knickers.'

Both the younger women gazed at her in horror. 'Yer can't take that out of yer knickers! Suppose they fall down when we're walking down the street?'

'Or worse still,' Kate said, 'when we're in the register office? I'd die of humiliation if that happened.'

Monica was beginning to see the funny side. 'We'll pretend we're not with her, girl, and if her knicks do fall down, I'll say in a loud voice, "Well, I've heard of a fur coat and no knickers, but never a second-hand dress and no knickers." '

'They won't fall down, yer silly buggers, 'cos they've got elastic in. I only keep the safety pin as a precaution, like, in case the elastic snaps.' Without further ado, Winnie turned her back on them, lifted her clothes, then turned around holding a pin shoulder high. 'There we go, all ready for the off. And don't worry. If the elastic does snap and me knickers fall to the ground, I won't make a fuss, I'll just step out of them as though nothing's happened, roll them up and stick them in me handbag. No one will notice a thing.'

'Except we'd know that the woman walking between us is

knickerless.' Monica was thinking that if Tom didn't laugh when she told him about this little episode, then she'd know for sure he had no sense of humour. 'What happens if yer fall flat on yer face and yer clothes come over yer head? The whole world would see yer backside then.'

Winnie's shoulders were shaking. 'No, they wouldn't, queen, they'd think it was the sun rising.'

'I'd run off and leave yer if a crowd gathered,' Kate said. 'I'd want the ground to open and swallow me up.'

'If there was a crowd gathered, queen, and yer ran away, I'd tell them yer'd pushed me over and pinched me knickers. And when they'd all run after yer, calling yer a thief, I'd pick meself up and carry on to the wedding. I wouldn't let nothing spoil this day for me, knickers or no knickers.'

'We'll worry about that if it happens.' Monica moved a leaf on the carnation to cover the safety pin. 'I've got no worries, I can just enjoy meself with nothing on me mind. I took the cakes down to Betty, and on the way back I got meat and potato pies from the home-made shop for tonight's tea. I'd already told Tom to see to Dolly if I wasn't back in time. It won't hurt him to see to his own meal for once. In fact, it'll do him a power of good.'

Kate waited until her friends were standing on the pavement, then she pulled the door behind her and gave it a push to make sure it was shut tight. 'It was a real brainwave of yours to get some pies for me, sunshine, to save me worrying. I've left a note for John telling him to see to himself and the kids. And, oh, what a glorious feeling it is, knowing there's no need to rush back or keep looking at the clock all the time. Freedom, wonderful freedom!'

They walked to the tram stop and were pleased to see a tram trundling towards them. 'That's what yer call good timing.' Monica said. 'You hop on first, Winnie. Age before beauty and all that.'

But Winnie didn't hop on board, she put a hand over her mouth instead. 'Oh, my God, the elastic has snapped.'

'Oh, no!' Kate was mortified. 'We'd better let this tram go and catch the next. Yer'll have to sort yerself out, but God knows how.'

With a cheerful chuckle, Winnie hopped on board and turned to grin at her friends. 'Only kidding, queen, everything is safe.'

The conductor came behind her and growled, 'Make up yer mind whether ye're coming or going, missus, 'cos we haven't got all day.'

As her friends climbed on to the platform, Winnie was gazing at the man through narrowed eyes. 'I've seen you somewhere before, but for the life of me I can't think where!' Then she snapped her fingers. 'I've got it! Ye're the spitting image of the feller in the shop where I bought some flowers. He was a miserable bugger, too!'

Monica thought that was hilarious and laughed all the way down the aisle. But Kate didn't like unpleasantness of any kind, and sat in a seat next to the window so she could look out and avoid meeting the conductor's eye. She only hoped they could get to the register office without any further mishaps. But Monica and Winnie were both unpredictable, so perhaps that was asking too much.

'It's a miserable place, isn't it?' Monica said, looking around the entrance hall of the register office. 'Not the happiest place for a wedding.'

'It's also for births and deaths,' Kate reminded her. 'Yer can't expect to hear music playing when a lot of people who come here have had a death in the family. They'll have a special room for weddings, I'm sure, and it will be nicer than this.'

'Let's go and stand outside and wait for them there,' Winnie said. 'This place would give yer the willies, it's so dark. But the sun is shining outside.'

The three of them trooped out and leaned against the wall. 'They're late,' Monica said. 'They should be here by now.'

'For heaven's sake, will yer stop moaning?' Kate sighed. 'Ye're finding fault with everything. Cheer up, or yer'll put a jinx on the wedding.'

'They're here now.' Winnie was hopping from one foot to the other with excitement. 'They're in that taxi that's just stopped.' She started to run out of the entrance gates, with Kate and Monica in hot pursuit.

Greg stepped out of the taxi first, and held out a hand to help Margaret who was looking very pretty in a lilac dress and wide-brimmed straw hat, and carrying a small posy of lilac flowers. They could see she was nervous, though, because her lips were quivering and her hands shaking. Kate's heart went out to her, she looked so timid and afraid. But Greg was very attentive and held her elbow while the two sets of parents stepped out of the black taxi. He kept looking down at Margaret, smiling and talking softly to calm her.

'Ah, the poor girl looks terrified,' Winnie said. 'It takes me back to me own wedding day when I was a bundle of nerves.'

'She's a pretty girl, isn't she?' Monica said. 'I didn't realize before how good-looking she is. And he's handsome enough to be a film star. They make a fine couple, even if they are doing things back to front.'

'Keep remarks like that to yerself, sunshine, at least until we get home. The bride and groom will both be embarrassed enough as it is, knowing that we know they've had to get married. Don't spoil the day for them.'

Betty waved when she got out of the taxi, and shouted, 'We'd better go straight in, we're cutting it fine. Come on, follow us.' She urged Greg's parents forward. 'I'll introduce yer to me friends later.'

And they certainly had cut it fine because as they walked through the entrance a voice could be heard calling, 'Mr Gregory

Corbett and Miss Margaret Blackmore, will you come this way, please?'

The room they entered wasn't as dismal as the entrance hall, but it was definitely lacking in one respect and that was flowers. There wasn't one in the room apart from those worn by the wedding party. But the man who conducted the ceremony was pleasant in his own way, and did his best to put Margaret and Greg at their ease. It was a very simple ceremony, cold even, but the mothers of the bride and groom were too busy crying to notice. Kate and Winnie shed a few tears, but Monica refused to cry. She preferred to put up with the lump that was forming in her throat.

'I now pronounce you man and wife. You may kiss the bride.'

That was when Monica's lump dissolved into tears. The newly married couple looked so young and so shy, you would have needed a heart of stone not to feel for them. But Greg behaved perfectly, bending down to brush his new bride's lips with his own. Then Betty and Jack Blackmore hurried to kiss their daughter and shake hands with their new son-in-law, followed closely by Maude and Albert Corbett. They weren't allowed long for congratulations because the registrar wanted the necessary forms signing. After that Betty called her three neighbours over to introduce them to the groom and his parents.

Kate's heart was thudding, but when Greg shook her hand she smiled and said, 'I didn't think I knew you, but I have seen you around.'

His handsome face seemed to relax now the part he'd been dreading was over. 'Yes, I've seen you around, too. I believe ye're coming back to the house for a drink?'

'Yes, me and me two mates. We'll be neighbours of yours when yer move in with the Blackmores.' Kate tried to put him at his ease. 'Yer know the one yer were introduced to as Monica? Well, watch out, she's a holy terror. She'd pick a fight in an empty house, and that's a fact.'

'You cheeky article!' Monica looked put out. 'Take no notice of her, Greg, because behind that pretty face she's a dangerous woman. Don't trust her as far as yer can throw her.'

Greg, his arm around Margaret's shoulders, glanced down at Winnie. 'Which one is telling me the truth? Or are they having me on?'

'They're both telling yer fibs, lad, take no notice of them. It's me what's the devil in disguise, they're angels in comparison.'

Greg looked down at the little woman who only came up to his chest. 'Oh, I think I can handle you. What d'yer say, Margaret?'

The bride looked a little more settled now, and managed a shaky smile. 'Even I could handle Mrs Cartwright, there's nothing of her.'

Betty put a hand on Winnie's shoulder. 'You tell them, girl, that good stuff comes in little parcels.'

Winnie's eyes slid sideways. 'Aye, so does poison, Betty. But we'll stick with what you said, I don't want people pointing at me behind me back and saying I'm poison. If it got to the wash-house, they wouldn't let me in. Or if they did, the place would go dead quiet when I walked in and the women would steer clear of me. That's what poison does for yer.'

The registrar approached the group. 'I'll have to ask you to leave now, we have another wedding in five minutes.'

Outside the building, Greg said, 'I'll keep an eye open for a taxi and flag it down.'

Monica had a question that had been bugging her. 'How did six of yer get in that taxi? I thought the most they were allowed to carry was five people.'

'They do, really,' Jack Blackmore said, 'but the driver was very helpful when he knew it was a wedding. We were a bit squashed, but it was only a ten-minute ride, if that!'

'That's the mystery solved, then. I couldn't make it out when yer appeared one after the other. I thought it was one of those tricks magicians play. You know, where the people go round the back and keep coming through the door.'

Albert Corbett started to enjoy himself. His wife might be a nervous wreck, worrying about losing her beloved son, but the lad was only going a few streets away. And if all the folks around there were as funny and friendly as these three, their son would be well catered for.

'We'll leave yer, then, and go for the tram,' Kate said. 'We'll see yer back at the house.'

'You will not!' Betty was determined. 'The very idea! We'll get two taxis and all go home in style. It's not every day yer daughter gets married, so we might as well push the boat out and do it proper.'

The first taxi took Greg, Margaret and her parents, and a couple of seconds later a second taxi was flagged down. The three friends shared this with Maude and Albert Corbett. When Winnie sat back in the seat, her legs were so short her feet dangled in mid-air, but there was a fixed smile on her face as she inwardly gloated. This was what she called living it up, and she intended to make the most of it because she may never have the opportunity again.

Kate, hoping to break the ice, said, 'They made a very handsome couple, didn't they? I thought they looked well together.'

Maude Corbett sniffed up. She was sad inside because her son would never again sleep at her house, or come in from work to find his dinner on the table waiting for him. But she had to admit that he seemed to be really fond of Margaret, and they did indeed make a lovely couple. 'Yes, they seem well suited. Greg is very mature for his age, and understands what his responsibilities are.'

'And she's a nice lass.' Albert knew his wife would go on forever about how good her son was, and although he loved Greg just as much, she had to learn that he was married now and

275

his wife must never be made to feel left out. 'We've got to know Margaret well over the last couple of weeks, and I think she'll make him a good wife.'

'Oh, she will,' Kate said. 'Because her parents have set her a good example. She's kind, capable, and not afraid of work. I reckon she'll make a marvellous wife and mother.'

'Aye.' Albert was holding his trilby between his legs and running a finger around the brim. 'Me and Maude were shocked at first, but we've come round to it now. We're looking forward to having a grandchild.'

Winnie could see that Greg's mother hadn't come to terms with it as easily as his father, and felt a certain pity for the woman. So she shuffled to the edge of the seat and spoke directly to Maude. 'That's one thing I'll regret all me life, that me and me husband never had any children. Because I think Grandma is one of the nicest words yer'll ever hear.'

'Ay, hang about a bit,' Albert said, 'what about Granda? Don't we men get a look-in?'

'Oh, yeah, yer come in handy for rocking the pram or giving the baby a dummy.' Winnie chuckled. 'But yer all run like hell when it comes to changing a dirty bleeding nappy.'

The ice was well and truly broken when they saw Winnie's screwed up face as she held an imaginary dirty nappy between two fingers. By the time the taxi stopped outside the Blackmores' house, Maude and Albert were no longer strangers to the other three.

Kate pulled Monica and Winnie aside as Greg's parents entered the house, and quickly said, 'I know we said one of us would go round for the presents, but on second thoughts it might be embarrassing for everyone concerned if we give them now. The presents are all for the baby, and they've only just got married.'

'Ye're right, girl,' Monica said, while Winnie nodded. 'Come on, let's go in or they'll wonder what's keeping us.'

'Yer've done well, Betty,' Maude said, her eyes running over the table laden with food. 'Yer must have been up at the crack of dawn to make this lot.'

'I had help, Maude, I can't take all the credit. Monica and Kate did all the baking, I only made the sandwiches with Margaret's help.'

'Yer've got good neighbours, lass.' Alfred dropped into a chair, crossed his legs and felt quite at home. The room was cosy, comforting and welcoming. 'Ye're lucky.'

Maude's nostrils flared. 'Are yer going to leave that trilby of yours in the middle of the couch? Other people want to sit down, yer know.'

Her husband jumped to his feet. 'I'm sorry, I never thought.'

'That's all right, Albert.' Betty moved like a flash and whipped up the hat. 'You make yerself at home, and we'll have no cross words today.'

As soon as the hat disappeared, Greg led Margaret to the couch where they sat holding hands and gazing into each other's eyes. This certainly didn't look like a shotgun wedding, the bridal pair appeared to be really in love.

'Me and Monica will see to the tea, Betty, you rest yer feet. We know where everything is, so don't be flapping about.'

'What can I do to make meself useful?' Winnie asked. 'I don't want to be standing here like a lemon.'

'Yer can pass the plates and serviettes around, sunshine.' Kate couldn't help laughing inside when she thought of the look on the little woman's face as she'd pretended to hold a dirty nappy at arm's length. It had put a smile on Maude's face, too, which was a blessing. 'Then yer can hand the sandwiches around.'

Winnie turned to Betty and spread her hands. 'If I'm going to wait on, I want one of those frilly aprons like they wear in the Kardomah and Reece's. When I do a job, I like it done proper, no half measures.'

'I've got just the thing!' Betty looked very pleased with herself. 'Come upstairs with me.'

After a few minutes the loud laughter that came down the stairs was so infectious everyone had a smile on their faces. 'What's the wife up to now?' Jack said. 'I bet her and Winnie are planning something.'

And sure enough, when Winnie came down she was wearing a short white pinny trimmed with lace and matching head-piece, just like the waitresses in Reece's. Her face was deadpan, as though being a waitress was her usual job. Even when Kate and Monica came out of the kitchen to join in the laughter and clapping, the little woman kept her face straight. 'If you will all take your seats, I'll serve you,' she said.

Greg and his new bride were in stitches. This was just how it should be when two people got married, friends and laughter all around them. It was the best present they could get. Now Winnie was into her stride, she showed what a bright little spark she was. 'I'll serve the bride and groom first, 'cos that's only etiquette. And in case ye're ignorant and don't know what that long word means, I'll tell yer. It means good manners. And how do I know that? Because I'm not just a pretty face, yer see.' She stood in front of the bridal pair, who were shaking with laughter, and said, 'If yer'd put yer bride down now, Mr Corbett, I'll put a plate in yer hand for yer to put a sandwich on. The kitchen staff will be serving tea.' It was then that she spied two bottles on the sideboard. 'Oh, dear, how remiss of me. I almost forgot that we should first lift our glasses in a toast to the happy couple. The wine waiter for the occasion is Mr Jack Blackmore, and I'll leave you in his capable hands until you are ready to eat.'

To everyone's amusement, Winnie walked over to the sideboard, took off her cap and apron, and then turned to face them with a huge grin on her face. 'This is me being a guest, now, so I don't have to be polite to yer or speak in me posh voice.' With hands outstretched she appealed to those who were hanging on her every word, 'What I'd like to know is, how do these toffs manage to talk posh all the time? If it was me now, well, I couldn't be . . .' She saw Kate's set face and said, 'Ah, I know what yer were thinking, queen. Yer thought I was going to say I couldn't be arsed, didn't yer? But I wouldn't dream of saying that in front of company, I've got better manners than that. I was going to say, I couldn't be bothered.'

And so it was that Winnie was the life and soul of the party, aided and abetted by Kate and Monica. The house was filled with joy and merriment. No awkward silences between the young couple today. They held hands whenever they didn't have a plate in them, and laughed until the tears fell. The sadness, hurt, anger and animosity of the past weeks were forgotten now, and they would look back on their wedding day as being a very happy one. So, too, would Betty and Jack Blackmore. They could hold their heads high now, and when the whispering and nudging began would ignore those who had nothing better to do than gossip.

And as glasses were raised, Maude and Bert Corbett were realizing they hadn't lost a son. Greg would only be a stone's throw away from them, and they could see him whenever they liked. They had gained some good friends, too. Already the two families were talking about which house to have Greg's birthday party in. And nobody in the room that day was in any doubt about the true feelings the young bride and groom had for each other.

The three women linked arms as they walked up the street later on. 'Ay, I haven't half enjoyed meself,' Winnie said. 'And I've got you two to thank for getting me an invite.'

'That was the best thing we ever did, girl.' Monica squeezed her arm. 'Yer didn't half liven the proceedings up.'

'I'll say! Yer were the star of the show, sunshine,' Kate said. 'And I for one will never have a party without inviting you.'

'Ooh, yer've got yer feet in there, girl, without a doubt.' Monica's face did contortions. 'Yer don't have to worry about Christmas now, yer'll be coming with us to the Spencers.'

'Don't you start that again, Monica Parry, or I'll spit! Will yer get it through yer head that I am not having the Christmas party this year! That is definite, that is, so yer'd better start getting your guest list ready. And on the top of that list yer should have all the Spencers and Winnie Cartwright.'

'To save any argument, I'd have yer all down to my house,' Winnie said, 'but I've only got three cups and saucers to me name, and three plates. Yer see, I've never had any call for more so it seemed a waste to buy them.'

That got through to Kate, but she wasn't prepared to give in just yet. 'Don't you worry, sunshine, wherever the party is, you'll be top of the guest list.'

They came to a stop outside Winnie's house. 'Here yer are, girl, home safe and sound.'

'Oh, I promised Maggie Duffy I'd sit with Miss Parkinson for a few hours, to give her a break. So I'll walk up with yer.'

'Would yer like me to come with yer to see if she's all right?' Kate asked. 'I could give John a knock and tell him, he won't mind.'

'No, I'll be fine, you go home to yer family. If anything untoward happens, I'll be over like a shot. I'm usually practical if anyone is sick, and not the type to panic, but I think I might in the case of Audrey.' Winnie stepped off the pavement, saying, 'I'll give yer a knock later, when Maggie takes over, and let yer know how she is. And thanks again for today, it was a real pleasure and I appreciated it.'

'Ye're welcome, sunshine, it was a treat to have yer.'

Monica nodded in agreement. 'The star of the show, yer were, girl, and I bet everyone there would agree with me.'

Winnie was pleased with the compliment. 'I'll see yer later, ta-ra for now.'

* * *

'So it went off all right, did it?' John asked, happy to see his wife. It had seemed strange coming home from work and her not being there. 'Yer had a nice time?'

'Everything went off beautiful. Greg's mother was a bit miserable at first, and I thought she was going to spoil the whole day. But two minutes in the taxi with Winnie and she was laughing her head off. What an asset that little woman is. She may be small, but by God, she's all there. The day wouldn't have been the same without her. Oh, we'd have had a nice time, and the bride and groom looked very posh, as yer would expect, but the reception afterwards would have just been tea and talk.' Kate couldn't speak without doing the actions, and her impersonation of Winnie had John, Nancy and Billy in stitches. Well, it showed she'd done a good job when Billy decided it was better than playing ollies with his mate.

'And who is having the party at Christmas, Mam?' Nancy asked. 'Yer can't expect Mrs Cartwright to if she's only got three cups and saucers.'

Kate chuckled. 'I wouldn't put it past yer Auntie Monica to offer to lend her enough to have the party in her house. But I wouldn't dream of letting her, it costs too much money.'

'Why don't you and Auntie Monica toss a penny for it?' Billy thought he was brilliant to think of that. He'd bet no one else had. 'That would be fair, then.'

'I'm not tossing any coin, sunshine, 'cos with my luck Auntie Monica would have a double-headed penny.'

John, whose fireside chair faced the window, leaned forward. 'Here's Winnie crossing the street now, and she's coming here.'

Kate's chair toppled to the floor as she jumped to her feet. 'Oh, my God, there must be something wrong with the old lady.'

'I'll open the door, Mam,' Nancy said. 'You sit down before yer faint.'

'Is yer mam in, queen?' Winnie asked. And when the girl nodded, she said, 'Could I see her for a minute?'

'Come in, sunshine.' Kate's hand was fluttering at her throat with nerves. 'I hope it's not bad news yer bring, not after such a nice day.'

'No, it's not bad news, queen, nothing like it. In fact, it's excellent news for Miss Parkinson, she's over the moon.'

Kate took a deep breath and let it out slowly. 'Then in future, when ye're running across the street to my house, would yer mind doing it with a smile on yer face so I know everything in the garden is rosy?'

'I can't go through life with a smile on me face, queen, or folk will think I've lost the run of me senses. But I'll try and remember to have one when I'm near your house. Will that do?'

Kate picked up her chair and sat down. 'That'll do fine. Now what's brought yer hot-footed over here?'

'Well, Audrey – I mean, Miss Parkinson – has had a letter from her niece in Essex, to say she's coming here on Saturday. And as it's such a long way she wants to stay until Monday and hopes her aunt has a spare bedroom. Now, we all know she's got a spare bedroom, and we all know it's spotlessly clean like the rest of the house, but Miss Parkinson has got herself in a state about it 'cos she said it's weeks since she shifted the furniture to brush underneath. And I remember her niece, she's very posh. So as I didn't want Miss Parkinson fretting and making herself ill, I volunteered to give her a hand tomorrow. And I knew you and Monica would be the last people on earth to see an eighty-year-old woman left high and dry with the worry, so I volunteered you two as well.'

Kate studied Winnie's earnest face and burst out laughing. 'Ye're a ruddy hero, you are, sunshine! But how can I refuse when yer've entertained us for most of the day? Of course I'll help, and I'll slip and ask Monica. I know she won't refuse, so yer can count on both of us. But don't forget tomorrow one of us has to take the presents round to Margaret and Greg.' Kate thought it best not to say much more about these or the children would be wondering about baby clothes being given as presents on a wedding day. 'Never mind, I'll sort that out. What time do yer want us in the morning?'

'How about ten o'clock? That'll give yer time to tidy up, queen, and make yer beds.'

'We'll be there, I promise.' Kate cupped her chin in her hand. 'Yer know, sunshine, for someone who was at death's door last week, yer've made a marvellous recovery.'

'Fancy yer saying that, queen, when I was only thinking the same meself. Next time I go in that fishmonger's, I'll be really nice to him 'cos of the difference he's made in me life. I might even go as far as to give him a kiss.' Winnie's eyes became slits. 'No, on second thoughts I'd better not or I'd be smelling of bleeding fish all day.'

Chapter Twenty

Monica walked up Kate's yard the next morning at half-past nine. Seeing her mate at the sink, she rapped on the window. 'Are yer respectable?'

'Now wouldn't it be too ruddy bad if I wasn't, eh? Of course I'm respectable, like any self-respecting woman of my age would be this time of the day. What made yer think I wouldn't be?'

'Well, the milkman's got his eye on yer, and yer never know. Even yer best mate doesn't tell yer everything.'

'I'd have a job to have a secret affair with any man, you living next door to me. I bet yer even know what I had for breakfast.'

'Give us a hard one to test me brain, girl, that one's too easy. Yer had toast, as yer always do. We can smell it, like you can smell ours. I don't know why they bothered putting walls between the houses, 'cos we can hear every word yer say, as well as smell the aroma of what ye're having to eat.'

'At least yer can't see us with no clothes on when we're getting into bed.' Kate wiped her wet hands on a towel hanging behind the kitchen door. 'Unless yer've drilled a hole in the bedroom wall, and I wouldn't put that past yer.'

Monica's throaty chuckle should have warned Kate so she could have put her hands over her ears. 'If I made a hole in the bedroom wall, girl, it would have been for your benefit. I'm not selfish, and don't see why you shouldn't share my nights of passion. Especially when Robin Hood is at his finest.'

'Monica Parry! Yer'll be the death of me yet, you will. Talk about a one-track mind isn't in it.' Kate was shaking her head and her lips were in a straight line, but inside she was chuckling. 'Don't yer ever say anything like that in front of John or I'll die of embarrassment.' She walked through to the living room, leaving Monica to follow. As she reached to pull one of the dining chairs from the table, she tilted her head. 'What nights does Robin Hood usually come?'

'Every Saturday.' Monica sat facing her. 'Every bleeding Saturday, as regular as clockwork. He's too tired every other night, or else he's got to be up early the next day for work. But he's got no excuse on a Saturday, so I have me wicked way with him then.'

'If the poor man had known what he was getting when he married you, he'd have run a mile.' Kate leaned her elbows on the table. 'Anyway, enough of your love life, how did yer get on at Betty's? Did they like the presents?'

'Greg and Margaret weren't in, they've both gone to work. They need every penny they can get and couldn't afford to take another day off. They're saving for a cot and pram, so Margaret is keeping her job on until she begins to show. Betty was made up we bought them presents, but although she was nosy, she wouldn't open them 'cos she said it would be a nice surprise for them to open the parcels themselves. She said she'd thank you and Winnie herself when she sees yer, but until then I was to tell yer she was very grateful.'

'It was a good day yesterday, wasn't it?' Kate said. 'I really enjoyed meself.'

'Yeah, it was a cracking day.' Monica cocked her head to one side. 'Yer know, girl, I was wrong about Winnie, saying she was nothing but a jangler. And you were right about her, she's a little smasher.' Her eyes full of devilment, she went on, 'Oh, I was telling Tom about what she got up to, and some of the things she came out with. And d'yer know what he said?'

'No, what did he say, sunshine?'

'He said to tell yer not to forget to ask her to yer party at Christmas, 'cos she sounds as though she'd make it go with a swing.'

'Aye, and I bet I know who put him up to saying that, soft girl. But it won't do yer no good, I'm determined it's your house this year.' Kate pushed her chair back. 'Come on, I told Winnie we'd be over the road by ten o'clock. I'd like to be finished by twelve so we can get to the shops before they close. What say you and me do a bedroom each, and Winnie can do the stairs? That shouldn't take us more than an hour, then we could give her yard and lavvy a good brush and clean.'

'Yeah, it'll be a doddle with three of us. It'll give Maggie a break, too, because she's been tidying up for the old lady and doing her shopping. She's been a good neighbour.'

'Yes, she's a good scout is Maggie. She'd be the first one to lend a hand to anyone in trouble, and she'd lend yer her last ha'penny.' Kate went to untie the back of her pinny, then changed her mind. 'I may as well keep it on, seeing as we intend to get stuck in over there. No point in getting me dress dirty, is there, sunshine?'

'No point at all, girl, that I can see. Shall we make tracks? The sooner we start, the sooner we'll be finished. But I'm going to have words with our friend Winnie. I don't want her volunteering us willy-nilly. I don't mind Miss Parkinson, because it's in a good cause, but she could put us down for scrubbing steps or red-raddling window sills the length of the street. If we're not careful, it could get out of hand.'

'Oh, I don't mind,' Kate said. 'When we get old, we might be glad of someone to give us a helping hand.'

'You and me will look after each other, girl, as long as we're able. And when we're not, we've got daughters who will see us right.'

They stepped on to the pavement opposite, and Winnie had the door open before the sound of the knocker had faded away. 'I'll say this for yer, ye're punctual workers. Clocking in dead on time so yer won't have any money docked out of yer wages.'

Miss Parkinson looked neat and tidy as always. Her white

hair was combed back from her face and rolled into a bun at the nape of her neck, dress immaculate and highly polished shoes so bright you could see your face in them. But she seemed a little flustered. 'It really is kind of you, but I think it's asking too much. You have your own homes and families to look after without having me as an extra burden.'

'Nonsense!' Kate bent down to kiss her cheek. 'It's not heavy work, your house is spotless as it is. But seeing as ye're having a visitor to stay, we'll give everywhere a good going over and it will put yer mind at rest.'

'Kate is right. If yer haven't seen yer niece for twenty years, yer want everything to be spick and span. Just imagine if she looked under the bed and saw a pile of fluff. Well, it would put her off, wouldn't it?' Monica patted Miss Parkinson's thin hand. 'With the three of us, we'll have it done in no time. We'll be that quick, if yer blink, yer'll miss us.'

'I've got all the dusters and floor cloths ready, and brushes and buckets.' Winnie seemed to be in her element. 'I brought me own brush and mop and bucket so we can get through it quicker.' She gave a cheeky grin. 'So there's no excuse for being held back by lack of cleaning materials.'

'Would you not like a cup of tea before you start?' Miss Parkinson asked. 'The cups are all ready in the kitchen.'

'Not just yet, sunshine, thank you.' Kate spoke for all of them. 'We'll get cracking for an hour, then have a tea break. So, let's get started, girls, all hands to the pumps.'

Monica gave Winnie a wink and a dig in the ribs. 'Ay, who made her supervisor? She's not half pushy, giving orders out. We should have taken a vote on it.'

'I don't want to be supervisor anyhow,' Winnie said. 'Too much responsibility for my liking. And I'm too small anyway. If I gave one of yer an order, yer'd belt me one.'

Monica gazed at Kate. 'Right, that leaves you and me. So what's it going to be? Me on the brush and you on the mop to start with, then we'll swap over when necessary?'

'Suits me, sunshine, whatever yer say.'

'Ay, what about me? I know I'm little, but I'm not that ruddy little yer can't see me! Where d'yer want me to start?' Her chest swelling, Winnie announced grandly, 'But I have already done the kitchen and pantry. I was up early, so rather than sit doing nowt, I came up and got a head start on yer.'

'We'd be very much obliged, Mrs Cartwright, if yer would do the stairs,' Kate said. 'Then after we've had a break, we can see to windows, yard and lavatory. So, come on, heave-ho me hearties.'

And the three women worked like beavers, stopping only for a cup of tea at eleven o'clock. Maggie Duffy came in when they were halfway through, to see if they needed a hand. But she was told she'd done more than her share and was sent packing.

'I feel really guilty sitting here listening to you doing my work,' Miss Parkinson told the three women as they stood before her. They had done the house from top to bottom and there wasn't a thing out of place or a speck of dust anywhere. The furniture and windows were shining, and the hearth and grate cleaned and black-leaded. 'You've worked very hard, I don't know how I'm ever going to repay you. And I have to tell you that you have put my mind at rest. You see, I last visited my niece over twenty years ago, but I remember she lived in a large house in a very good area. Now, I am not a snob, I really don't mind her thinking I'm the poor relation, but I would hate her to think I was too poor to keep my home clean.'

'I'm sure your niece is very nice and will certainly not think of you as the poor relation.' Winnie had known this woman long enough to say what she thought. 'If she does, then she is not worth bothering with.'

'Celia is far from being a snob, she's a very sweet and gentle person. And she knows this house because she has been here, so it won't be strange to her. But I'm sure you'd be the same if you were having a visitor to stay, you'd want the place to look its best. And while I do as much as I'm able in keeping everywhere clean and tidy, age has caught up with me and I find I can't cope like I used to.'

'If I get to eighty and look like you, Miss Parkinson, I'll be very happy.' Kate could see Monica nodding in agreement. 'Yer don't look yer age, and as far as I know yer've never had any real health problems.'

'No, God has been very good to me. I've been blessed with good health and very good neighbours. I can't thank you enough for the way you've worked for the last few hours, I can assure you it is much appreciated.'

'It was done willingly, Audrey, and as long as it gives yer peace of mind, it was worth it.' Winnie undid the ties on her wrap-around pinny. 'Maggie's coming in to see to some lunch for yer so we'll love yer and leave yer. But I'll be in again about seven, to make sure everything is as it should be.' She turned to her two friends. 'I know ye're going down to the shops. I'll nip home with the bucket and things then walk down with yer.'

Even though they were only going across the street, Miss Parkinson came to the door to wave them off and repeat her thanks. As she closed the door behind her, she sighed. Getting old stopped you from doing so many things, but she was lucky compared to some. Not many women lived to be eighty, so she mustn't grumble.

With the mop and brush in one hand, and a bucket in the other, Winnie marched across the road like a soldier going to war. The fact that the bucket was banging against her leg didn't seem to bother her at all. 'Well, that's a good job done, that is.'

'Let me carry the bucket, sunshine, or yer leg will be black and blue.'

'No, I'm going straight home now so it's not far. I won't be long, I'll just tidy meself up and come to the shops with yer. That's if yer don't mind?'

'Ye're as welcome as the flowers in May, girl.' It took Monica all her time to stop herself from laughing at the little woman who looked so comical. 'As long as yer don't bring the bleeding brush and bucket along with yer.'

'I'm making us a cuppa before we go out, sunshine,' Kate told her. 'So if yer hurry, yer'll be in time for one.'

'I'll be as quick as I can, queen.' Winnie made as much haste as was possible with the bucket banging against her leg making a clanging sound. They could hear her saying, 'Sod the bleeding thing. I'll kick it down the yard when I get it home.'

Monica went in a pleat. 'D'yer know, girl, if I could play the spoons I could harmonize with her. And with you making music on yer comb, we could go busking by Lime Street station and rake the money in.'

'I wouldn't get no tune out of my comb, sunshine,' Kate said as she opened the door. 'It's only got about three teeth left. I keep meaning to buy meself one, but as soon as I put it in the drawer I forget about it until the next time I need to comb me hair.'

'I'll buy yer one for Christmas. They've got them in Woolies in nice cases with a little mirror in. I'll bring it with me on Christmas Day.'

'I'll let that pass, clever clogs, 'cos you'll get fed up with talking about this party sooner than I will.' Kate went straight through to the kitchen. 'I'll see to the tea, but we'll have to be sharp drinking it or by the time we get to the shops they'll be closed for dinner.'

Monica followed her out. 'I'll wash me hands and face at yer sink, if yer don't mind. Me dress will do, no one will see the splashes on it. Oh, and I'll have to borrow yer comb, even if it has only got three teeth in.' She cocked an ear. 'There's a knock at yer door, girl, it'll probably be Winnie.'

As she struck a match and held it to the gas ring, Kate said, 'Yer've made yerself at home getting washed here and combing yer hair, anyone would think it was your house. So yer can go and open the ruddy door for yer cheek.'

Monica chucked her under the chin. 'Temper, temper! I'm going, yer don't have to get all het up about it.'

Winnie grinned up at Monica when she opened the door. 'Who's getting all het up, queen, and why?'

'It's your mate and mine, Winnie. She thinks I'm taking advantage of her home, but she gets funny moods like that, I don't take a ha'porth of notice of her. Now, if I was taking advantage of her very handsome and attractive husband, then she'd really have something to moan about.' Monica gave a cheeky wink. 'The trouble is, he thinks the sun shines out of her backside.'

Kate's head appeared over her shoulder. 'There's a pot of tea made, and if it's not drunk within the next fifteen minutes it's going down the grid. I'm not missing the shops because you two feel like a gossip. You have been warned.' With that her head disappeared and Monica leaned down to haul Winnie into the hall. 'When she uses that tone, girl, she means business.'

'Which shops are yer going to?' Winnie asked as they reached the main road. 'I want to nip along to the fishmonger's. Not to buy anything, like, 'cos I'm off fish while this hot weather's on even though it is Friday. I want to see the bloke for two reasons. One, to tell him off for selling me rotten fish and making me ill, but also to thank him 'cos that piece of rotten fish has made all the difference to me life.'

Monica screwed her face up before saying, 'Let me get this straight. Ye're going to thank the bloke for making yer ill?'

'Yeah, if yer put it like that, queen. But I'll tell him off first, 'cos if it hadn't been for you two, I could have died. And I wouldn't have liked that.'

'Me and Monica don't go to the same fish shop as you, and I know yer've been going there for years. But yer only ever say "the bloke", sunshine, yer never call him by name.'

'I think his name's Bert, but I've only ever called him "lad". He's nice enough, but he should suffer a bit for what he put me through. He's got a nose, he should have smelt the fish was off.'

'You go on then, sunshine, and yer can catch us up in Irwin's, the bread shop or the greengrocer's. We'll watch out for yer.'

When Winnie walked away, she broke into a hop, skip and jump. And as Monica watched her retreating back, she said, 'It would be worth following her, girl, 'cos I'd like to see how she can tell a bloke off, then in the next breath thank him for the same thing. I think we're missing a good laugh.'

'Yer'll have more of a laugh when she's telling us about it, sunshine, 'cos we'll get every word and every action. The woman is a born comedienne and doesn't know it.'

The two friends were in the greengrocer's when Winnie caught up with them. They'd just been served with lettuce, spring onions and tomatoes when her face appeared between them. Monica couldn't wait to be told what had transpired, so she asked, 'Did yer get it all off yer chest, girl? Tell him everything yer wanted to, did yer?'

'Only half of it, really, queen. Yer see, with it being Friday, fish day, the shop was packed. And I couldn't talk to him when he was run off his feet, especially about selling me rotten fish 'cos the shop would have emptied in no time. I wouldn't like to take his livelihood away from him when he's got four kids.'

'Yer mean, yer went all that way and didn't say a dickie bird?'

Kate interrupted. 'Can we talk outside, please, instead of cluttering this shop up?'

Monica, impatient as always, marched Winnie outside. 'Now, am I right in saying yer went all that way and didn't open yer mouth?'

'Of course I said something, queen, I'm not daft enough to run all that way for sweet bugger all.'

'Oh, that's good,' Kate said, 'what did he have to say?'

'Well, he didn't say nothing, queen, 'cos he was too busy. So I stood just inside the door and shouted at the top of me voice, "Thanks very much, lad, yer did me a big favour." And he waved to me.'

'Did yer tell him why yer were thanking him, girl?' Monica's mind was working overtime. 'I mean, if yer didn't, he'll be racking his brains all day, wondering what yer were on about!'

'Well, queen, I'll tell yer how I worked it all out when I saw the shop so full. I didn't want to stand waiting when I wasn't going to buy owt so after careful consideration I thought of a way of killing two birds with one stone.' Winnie hitched up her bosom. 'If I thanked him and then skedaddled, he'd spend the rest of the day giving himself a headache wondering what he'd done that I'd thank him for. So, yer see, the headache would be my revenge for selling me the rotten fish and making me sick. Don't yer see, queen, I've thanked him and punished him all in one go. Now we're quits.'

With a perplexed look on her face, Kate said, 'I suppose there's some logic in all that, but I'm blowed if I can see it. When I get home, sunshine, I'll give it some thought and I'm sure I'll see your point.'

'Oh, I can see it, and I think it was very clever of yer. The work of a genius.' Her face deadpan, Monica asked, 'So yer didn't buy any fish, then, even though it is Friday?'

'Not bleeding likely I didn't, not when I'm enjoying meself so much.'

'What are yer having to eat, then?'

'I haven't thought about that, queen, but I couldn't eat meat 'cos it would stick in me throat and me ma would turn in her grave.' Winnie looked thoughtful for a few seconds, then asked, 'What are you having?'

Kate could see her mate's tummy shaking, and knew she'd egg Winnie on so she could have a laugh. She wouldn't mean anything by it, it would all be in fun, but they'd both had enough laughs at Winnie's expense for one day. 'Me and Monica are having salad. We've just bought lettuce, onions and tomatoes, and we're going to Irwin's for a tin of John West's pink salmon.'

'Well, I declare! Yer'd never believe it but that's exactly what I was telling meself as I was walking back here. "Winnie," I said, "why don't yer buy yerself a tin of pink salmon, seeing as yer don't fancy fresh fish?" And you've just said the same thing. Now, if that's not coincidence I don't know what is.'

'And did yer tell yerself yer'd have lettuce and tomatoes with it?' Monica asked. 'And perhaps the odd spring onion?'

'No, I will not tell a lie, queen, I never gave a thought to spring onions. And I do like them, even if they do rift on me and give me indigestion.'

'We'll give yer a couple of lettuce leaves, a tomato and a spring onion, sunshine, save yer going back in the shop.' Kate was laughing to herself because she was about to make Monica pay for her entertainment. 'We don't mind, do we, sunshine?'

'If I don't watch out, Kate Spencer, yer'll be making me into a saint. And I don't want that, 'cos saints are not allowed to swear or speak ill of anyone. Besides which, I can't play a harp and I'd look stupid with a halo.'

'If God doesn't have the sense of humour yer say He has, then yer stand little chance of ever finding out whether yer'd suit a halo or not.' Kate held a bent arm out to Winnie. 'There yer are, sunshine, I told yer she wouldn't mind. So stick yer leg in and we'll go to Irwin's. You buy yerself a small tin of pink salmon and me and my kind-hearted mate will sort yer out with the other things for a salad.'

'Would yer like us to give yer a slice of bread and butter each?' Monica asked. 'Then that's yer whole meal sorted out for yer.'

Kate's mouth opened wide in horror. Fancy insulting the little woman like that! But when she looked at Winnie it was to see her chuckling happily. 'That would be nice. Yer did say butter, didn't yer, queen? 'Cos I can't stand that margarine stuff, I only like the best.'

'Yer can sod off, Winnie Cartwright, what's good for me and my family is good enough for you. Take it or leave it.'

'Oh, I'll take it, queen! Butter would have been nice, but when I'm eating it I'll close me eyes so I don't see the colour. Because the colour is a dead give-away, yer know. Butter is a nice light creamy colour, and margarine is yellow.'

Monica muttered, 'Some people are never bleeding satisfied.'

'Isn't it nice to be on our own for a while?' John asked. 'I love the bones of the children, yer know that, but I seldom have yer to meself. Even if we don't speak, I get a kick out of watching yer sewing, or sitting with yer head cocked listening to the wireless.'

Kate was sitting in a fireside chair on the opposite side of the hearth. 'Well, I like that! Yer spend most of the time with yer head stuck in the *Echo*!'

'It might look like that, love, but me eyes have a mind of their own and they keep straying to you. I read the same lines over and over again until I lose interest. It's much nicer just to sit watching you. Ye're a feast for my eyes.'

'Oh, lord, don't start going all poetic on me or I'll never get this sock darned. Billy needs it for tomorrow because he hasn't another that doesn't have a ruddy big hole in the heel. How he wears them out so quick is a mystery to me. And his trousers are the same. I'm putting patches over patches now.'

'Well, hurry and finish the sock before the kids come in. We can sit on the couch for half an hour, holding hands like we did when we were courting and yer mam and dad had gone to bed.' He laughed at the memory. 'Though yer dad never gave me half an hour, did he? He was knocking on the bedroom floor with the heel of his shoe after ten minutes. Which I took to be a pretty broad hint that it was time for me to be on me way.'

'He was no different from any other father. Since time began, fathers have always tried to protect their daughters from men with only one thing on their mind.'

John groaned. 'There goes me quiet romantic half-hour. Monica's just passed the window.' The knock came before he got the last word out. 'And I think she's got someone with her.'

Kate quickly put the darning down at the side of her chair and jumped to her feet. 'Fold the paper and put it away, sunshine, make the place look a bit tidy.'

When she went to answer the door, John shook his head. There wasn't a thing out of place in the room, so how could one evening paper make it untidy? Women. They were hopeless for making more work for themselves.

While the evening paper was being pushed under the cushion of her husband's chair, Kate stood on the top step with her hand still on the lock and a look of total surprise on her face for Monica was accompanied by Margaret and Greg. 'Well, this is a surprise! But ye're very welcome, please come in.'

John jumped to his feet when the visitors entered the room, and was equally surprised when they were introduced as Margaret and Greg, the newly weds. They weren't a bit what he'd thought they'd be like. He'd imagined Margaret to be outgoing and a bit rowdy, but she was just the opposite. And the same with Greg. He hadn't been expecting such a quiet bloke whose voice was soft, handshake firm, and eyes and face open and friendly. John remembered then what his wife had said. Just because a young couple had got themselves into trouble, it didn't mean they weren't nice people.

Kate waved to the couch. 'Sit down and make yerselves comfortable.'

Monica leaned against the sideboard with her arms folded, looking very pleased with herself. She'd been caught on the hop when they'd knocked on her door, but unlike her mate didn't worry what the room looked like. She was glad the couple had called, and when they said they wanted to see Kate as well it gave her an excuse to get out of the house for a while.

'We won't stay, Mrs Spencer, we just came to thank you for the presents.' When Margaret sat down, Greg sat as close to her as possible and reached for her hand. If words could be put to that action they would be: Anyone who says anything to upset my new wife will have me to reckon with. 'They're lovely and we're very grateful.'

Greg nodded. 'It was a nice surprise, we weren't expecting anything.'

'I'm sorry it wasn't more,' Kate said. 'But it was all a bit of a rush.'

'I've told her we're going to keep on knitting for her.' Monica felt she'd been quiet long enough. 'By the time the baby's born, they'll be well equipped for it.'

A flush came to Margaret's face, and Kate was sorry her friend had mentioned the baby. Still, the sooner they were able to speak about it openly, the sooner the couple would start looking forward to it. 'Yer've got time for a cuppa, haven't yer? Monica can give me a hand, it won't take long.'

'I'll help.' Margaret smiled at Greg and took her hand back. 'All girls together in the kitchen, so we can talk about yer.'

'Okay, come on, sunshine, we'll have a little gossip while we're waiting for the water to boil. Leave the men to get to know each other.'

While Monica was chatting to Margaret, Kate kept her ear cocked for any sound from the living room. And when she heard John asking, 'Where is it yer work, Greg?' a smile crossed her face. The two men would get on like a house on fire, she knew.

Chapter Twenty-One

Kate was on her hands and knees scrubbing the front step on the Monday morning when she heard footsteps crossing the cobbles. She turned her head to see Maggie Duffy coming towards her. Sitting back on her heels, she put the scrubbing brush into the bucket of water. 'Good morning, Maggie. Yer gave me a fright at first, I thought there was something wrong with Miss Parkinson. But I can tell by yer face yer haven't come with bad news.'

'No, the old girl is fine, she's enjoyed seeing her niece. Celia took a taxi early this morning to catch a train at half-nine.'

'Yes, I saw her leaving when I was putting breakfast out. That was a hell of a big case she had, considering she was only stopping for two nights.'

'Oh, she didn't bring that with her, she only brought a small weekend case. The big one she took back belonged to Miss Parkinson.' Maggie glanced across the street to the old lady's house and could see her peeping out behind her curtains. 'I don't know much more really, but we'll soon know how things went. She's asked if you and Monica will go over this morning, and Winnie and myself, 'cos she's got something to tell us.'

'Ooh, er, that sounds mysterious, I wonder what it is?'

'I honestly couldn't tell yer. I've got me suspicions but I'm not saying anything because I'm probably miles out. Anyway, will yer see the other two for us?'

Kate nodded. 'I'll just finish me step, then give them a knock. What time did she say she wanted us to call?'

'Whenever is convenient for yer. How about half-ten?' ·

'Suits me, sunshine, and I don't think me two friends have got any pressing engagements at that time. So we'll see yer later, Maggie.'

Kate wrung out the floorcloth in the bucket, then wiped it over the step. It looked a treat now, all snowy white. But that wouldn't last long once Billy came home from school. She was tired of telling him to step right up into the hall when anyone with half an eye could see the step had just been cleaned with a donkey stone. But when her son was dashing out to play, his mam's step was the last thing on his mind.

The perspiration was trickling down Kate's face and she wiped a hand across it before getting to her feet. It was going to be a scorcher today from the look of things, and while it was no weather to be working in, she hoped it kept up because the schools closed on Friday for the long summer holidays. In weather like today's the children would be quite content to spend a day in the park with some sandwiches, a bottle of water and a ha'porth of lemonade powder.

After stretching her back and arms, Kate lifted the heavy bucket and placed it inside the hall. Then, using the door frame as a lever, she pulled herself over her nice clean step. She'd give herself a swill at the sink, and take her pinny off before knocking next door and then going down to Winnie's. She wondered what Miss Parkinson wanted to see them for, then decided it was probably just to tell them how she'd enjoyed having her niece there, and how they'd talked about old times.

She was emptying the dirty water from the bucket down the grid when she heard the sound of someone walking down the yard next door. 'Is that you, sunshine?'

'That's a bloody daft question, girl, who else could it be? It's not me the milkman's got his eye on.' There was a familiar sound of the lid on the bin set in the yard wall being banged down. 'Of course, I could have died in the night and come back as a ghost to haunt yer.'

'There's one way of finding that out for sure, sunshine.' Kate was smiling as she imagined the look on her mate's face. 'Give yerself a good, hard pinch. If yer can't feel it, then yer did die in the night and yer are a ghost.'

There came a loud yelp, then Monica's voice. 'Bleeding hell, I hurt meself then. But I suppose it was worth it to prove to meself that I'm still well and truly alive.'

'That's good, 'cos I'd hate to take a ghost over to Miss Parkinson's with me, it would frighten the old lady to death.'

'What are we going over there for?' Then before Kate could answer, there came a groan. 'Don't tell me, girl. Her niece was a dirty, untidy beggar and she wants us to clean the house from top to bottom again? Well she'll have to wait until the sun goes down, I'm afraid, 'cos I'm sweating cobs as it is.'

'No, nothing like that, sunshine. At least I don't think so. Maggie came over as I was doing the step and said Miss Parkinson wants to see you, me, Maggie and Winnie. She's got something to tell us.'

She could hear Monica's throaty chuckle, then her mate said, 'Ay, the invitations are coming thick and fast these days. I wonder why we're so popular all of a sudden?'

'I think it's only so she can tell us about her visitor. After all, she doesn't see many people in her life, so when she does it's a big thing.'

'Have yer told Winnie yet?'

'Ay, give us a chance, missus! I've only just finished scrubbing me step, and with the heat I'm worn to a frazzle.'

'Serves yer right for being so fussy. I'm not doing any scrubbing in this heat, me step can be as black as the hobs of hell for all I care. So if yer like, I'll slip down the entry to Winnie's and give her the message. She'll be tickled pink.'

'If yer would, sunshine, I'd be grateful. I'm going to swill meself down in cold water to cool off and get rid of the smell of perspiration. I think I'll change me dress as well, to smarten meself up. That new one will do me more good in this weather than hanging in the wardrobe. I may as well get the wear out of it.'

'I should think so, the price yer paid for it!' Both women burst out laughing. Then Monica said, 'Never you mind, girl, we'll be in the money one day and then we'll go down to Blackler's and buy a dress we really like, not one we've dragged out of a pile of second-hand clothes.'

'I don't mind wearing a second-hand dress, sunshine, I'm not too proud. Besides, the ones we got from the market are nice, and no one would know we hadn't bought them new.'

'I'm not bothered meself, either, girl, I'm quite happy with my lot. One thing I would really like, although I don't suppose it'll ever happen, is to go away on holiday. I wouldn't care where it was, Blackpool, Wales or even Sefton Park, as long as I got waited on and didn't have to do no housework, no washing or ironing, for a whole week. Just imagine it, girl, a whole week with nowt to do but enjoy ourselves.'

'Oh, I'm coming with yer, am I?'

'Well, yer don't think I'd go anywhere without yer, do yer? I haven't been further than the corner shop without yer in the last, what, eighteen years? So I certainly ain't going to start now. All we need, kid, is the money.'

'That's the story of my life, sunshine. A little bit of extra money would cure all my wants.' Kate remembered then the woman who lived on the other side of Monica, Thelma Robson, the biggest gossip imaginable. Neighbours could often be heard talking freely in the street, but the mere sight of Thelma sent everyone quiet until she was out of earshot. 'I think we should be getting ready, sunshine. Besides which, it doesn't pay to let the whole street know our business. Many a secret is let out of the bag by someone standing the other side of the wall.'

'Oh, Thelma isn't standing the other side of the wall, girl, she's watching us from her back bedroom window. She's even opened it a bit so she can hear what we're saying. She wouldn't sleep tonight if she thought she'd missed something.'

The two mates both looked up at the aforementioned window, and were just in time to catch the eavesdropper letting the curtain fall back into place. 'I wouldn't be arsed, would you, girl?' Monica raised her voice. 'I've got more to do with me time.'

'Make a move, sunshine, or we'll be late. Nip down for Winnie and knock on me window when ye're ready, I'll come straight out.'

Winnie looked bright and eager when Kate joined her and Monica on the pavement. 'D'yer know, queen, all these invitations are wearing me out. I think it's a bit late in life for me to stand the pace of constant parties and weddings,' she said jovially.

As Kate led the way across the cobbles, she said, 'I wouldn't knock it, sunshine, or yer'll put a jinx on yerself.'

'How d'yer mean, queen, I'll put a jinx on meself?'

'I mean the invitations will dry up, and yer'll be left in yer old routine.'

'Then from now on my lips are sealed.' And to prove she meant it, the little woman clamped her mouth tight shut. But it didn't last long because her bottom lip was soon pushing at her false teeth which were biting into her gum. 'Sod that for a joke, I'll take me chances with the ruddy jinx. Not that I know what it is, like, but I'll be on the lookout for it.'

Maggie opened the door to them. 'I think you lot can smell tea a mile off. I've just this very minute brewed up.'

'Ah, ye're a good 'un, sunshine,' Kate said. 'A woman after me own heart.'

Maggie lowered her voice. 'Miss Parkinson is like a cat on hot bricks waiting for yer. Whatever it is she's going to tell us must be important.'

They trooped into the living room one after the other, reminding Kate of when she'd done something wrong in class and had to go to the headmistress for a ticking off. 'I hope ye're not having a birthday party or getting married, Miss Parkinson, 'cos Winnie has just been saying she can't keep up with all her social engagements.'

The old lady smiled. 'I'm afraid my news isn't so exciting. But I'll wait until you are all sitting down with a drink in your hands.'

Winnie made for the kitchen. 'I'll give Maggie a hand.'

When they were all seated, Miss Parkinson leaned forward in her chair. 'You know my niece has been here for two days, and we've had some long talks. She doesn't like the idea of me living on my own now, not after what happened when that man broke in, and she wants me to go to live with her and her husband in Essex. I wasn't for the idea at first, it would be quite a wrench to leave this house after twenty-five years. But the more I gave thought to it, the more I began to see how right she was. They have a large house, their children are all married, and I would have my own bedroom and living room. And they would be close in case I was ill and needed attention. At my age, that is something I really do have to bear in mind.' It was clear the old lady was feeling emotional, but even though her voice was quivering she carried on. 'So when the rent man comes this afternoon, I will be giving him a week's notice. My niece is coming back on Saturday and is taking me to Essex on Sunday. One of her sons is driving her up in his car so I won't have the upset and inconvenience of railway stations and trains.'

You could have heard a pin drop in the room, it was so still. This quiet, reserved gentlewoman had lived in the street longer than anyone else, it just wouldn't be the same without her. But no one would say those words because they would start the tears flowing. In the end, it was Winnie who broke the silence. 'I think ye're doing the right thing, Audrey. We'll all miss yer, and we really don't want yer to go, but it is much better for you to be living in a house with relatives than staying here alone.' She sniffed loudly. 'It's yerself yer've got to think about, and yer wellbeing. Another thing, I bet yer niece has got a nice big garden.'

'Yes, that was one of the things that Celia used to persuade me. When the weather allows, I can sit out amongst the trees and flowers.' She smiled, adding, 'With a wide-brimmed straw hat on my head to keep the sun from my face.'

'It sounds as though yer'll be going to a lovely place, and yer'll want for nothing,' Kate said. 'But the street won't be the same without yer, and I'll miss waving to yer through the window.' She sighed. 'But it would be selfish to want yer to stay when yer niece can offer yer so much more. A life without worry or loneliness.'

'How are they going to get yer furniture down there, Audrey?' Winnie wanted to know. 'It would cost a small fortune to hire a removal van to take it down to Essex.'

'I'm not taking the furniture, Winnie. All I'll need are the things that were left to me by my parents. Things that are very dear to me. Celia took some of them with her this morning in a suitcase, but not all of them as she would never have managed. Family portraits, ornaments, glassware, jewellery and linen . . . many things my parents left to me. The furniture was theirs also but I will have no need of it. I'll have everything else safely wrapped and ready when she comes back on Saturday.'

Miss Parkinson paused for a while, her eyes sweeping over the furniture, fireplace and windows. How it would tug at her heart to leave this small house. But she knew her niece was right, she could no longer live alone with no family close to her in times of sickness. 'That's why I wanted to see you. You have all been very good to me, the best friends I've had. I want you to share what is left in the house between you. The furniture, curtains, and any other things I may be leaving. Because I know you so well, I know there will be no jealousy or bickering. I would be very happy if you would do that, rather than everything be left for the tenants who will be given the house when I leave.'

'Oh, dear, I'm going to cry.' Kate thought her throat would burst open from the lump that had formed. 'It's so sad, after all these years.'

'Take a mouthful of tea, girl, that'll stop yer from crying.' Monica didn't hesitate to tell someone else to stop crying, even though she was near to tears herself. 'The last thing Miss Parkinson wants is four grown-up women bawling their eyes out.'

'Oh, listen to hard-hearted Hannah!' Winnie always thought she herself could take things without letting them upset her. But she was finding out now that she couldn't, not when it came to someone she'd known, admired and been friends with for nearly half a lifetime. She glared at Kate, her eyes telling her she mustn't dare cry or she'd set them all off.

'I'll miss yer, love,' Maggie said. 'We've got on well together, with never a cross word between us. I can't imagine anyone else in your house.'

'I'm sure you'll get very nice people in,' Miss Parkinson told her. 'The landlord won't rent it out to riff-raff.'

'I hope not.' Maggie's eyes went to the ceiling. 'Or I'll be looking for a new place meself.'

'Don't be such a pessimist, Maggie.' Winnie looked at Kate. 'Ay, queen, what will she bring down on herself if she's not careful? Is it a minx?'

'No, sunshine, it's a jinx. But yer mustn't take that seriously, 'cos I only said it in jest.'

'Yer've got nothing to worry about, Maggie,' Monica said. 'Yer'll never get anyone as quiet as Miss Parkinson, but ye're bound to get a decent family. After all, we haven't had a bad family in this street, not since I've lived here anyway. We've got nosy beggars, and we've got gossip-mongers and those who like a bit of tittle-tattle, but I've never known there be real trouble in the street, like fighting.'

'Yer forgot to mention the drunks who crawl home singing at

the top of their voices,' Kate said. 'I've been woken up a few times by them.'

'Yer get that in every street, and it's only on a Saturday night.' This came from Monica who was pretty lenient with drunken men. She reckoned they'd worked hard all week and deserved one night's pleasure. 'They don't do no harm.'

Kate chuckled. 'D'yer know Ben, our next door but two neighbour? Well, last Saturday night he had his arm around the lamp-post, singing to it.'

'I didn't hear him,' Monica said. 'And that's very unusual 'cos I've got perfect hearing. What was he singing?'

'I don't know the name of the song, sunshine, something like his hat being on the side of his head.' Kate scratched the tip of her nose. 'What was the other one now? Oh, I know, it was "The Talk Of The Town".'

'Oh, that's one of me favourites, girl, I'm sorry I missed that. I'd have gone out and sung along with him.'

Kate was made up that everyone was looking more cheerful now, and she herself was laughing inside. 'I don't think yer'd have been able to harmonize with him very well, sunshine, 'cos yer'd have been looking down at him. Yer see, while he had his arm around the lamp-post, the rest of his body was in the gutter.'

'Kate Spencer, yer've been having me on! And here was me thinking I'd give Ben a knock and tell him to give me a wire next time he was street singing, and I'd join him.'

This exchange was a little light relief after hearing Miss Parkinson's news, and every face now wore a smile. 'This is what I'll miss most, having a jolly good laugh. I'm afraid Celia doesn't have the quick wit of a Liverpudlian,' she said. 'But you will all keep in touch with me by letter, I hope, to keep me up to date with what's going on in the street?'

Winnie nodded. 'We'll take turns writing to yer, so yer'll get one letter every week. But we'd expect a reply.'

'Yes, of course, it will give me something to look forward to. True friendship lasts a lifetime, and you have all been true friends to me.'

'Have yer got plenty of paper for wrapping yer ornaments and china in?' Kate asked. 'I've got a couple of *Echo*s at home if yer want them?'

'I'd be grateful because I don't have a newspaper delivered now. My eyesight has failed a little, and reading the small print was a strain. The wireless has been my source of news for the last few years, and I do enjoy the mystery plays.'

'I'll bring the papers over to yer when me and Monica get back from the shops,' Kate said. 'And I'll help you pack, if yer like?'

'No, it will give me something to do. Thank you all the same, dear, but I've got all week to do it.'

'I'll come to the shops with yer, queen, if yer don't mind me tagging along,' Winnie said. 'I might get some idea on what to have for me dinner from you two.'

But Audrey had other ideas. 'If you're going to the shops, Winnie, would you buy something for my lunch? Perhaps some nice boiled ham from Irwin's? And it would be nice if you would have lunch with me. We could talk over old times and be company for each other. I would like that very much, but of course you may have other plans?'

'Now as it happens, there's nothing in my diary for today so I would be delighted to have lunch with you.' Winnie was so proud she grew at least six inches, upward and outward. 'What else would yer like me to get from the shops?'

'Would you fetch my purse from the sideboard drawer, please, and you'll find a notepad and pencil in there as well. I'll make a list of the shopping I would like.' With the pencil poised, the old lady spoke aloud as she wrote down her list. 'Six ounces of boiled ham, some tomatoes and cucumber, a small home-made cottage loaf, and while you're in the confectioner's you could get two cream cakes.' She took two half-crowns from her purse and held them out. 'That should more than cover it.'

Winnie shook her head. 'Seeing as I'll be eating half, I'll go half with the money. I'll just take one half-crown.'

'You most certainly will not! I invited you to lunch, Winnie, and I wouldn't dream of allowing you to pay for it. You're to be my guest.'

A short time later, when the three friends were walking to the shops, Monica said, 'Ye're a jammy beggar, you are. What have you got that me and Kate haven't?'

'More than twenty-five years of friendship, queen. Me and Audrey have been good mates, and I'm really going to miss her when she goes.'

'Then make the most of the next few days, sunshine.' Kate put her arm across Winnie's shoulders. 'Enjoy yer meal, talk about the good old days, and be happy in each other's company. But remember, it's not the end of the world, yer know. Yer can write to her every week to give her all the news from the street. Yer'll have plenty to tell her about. What's happening in the lives of her old neighbours, and what the people are like who take over the tenancy of her house. She'll be interested in that. And trains do run to Essex, yer know, yer don't have to be cut off from each other for ever.'

'Oh, that would be wishful thinking, queen, 'cos I'd never have the money for that. Much as I'd like to go, the lack of money would hold me back.'

'With your luck, girl, I wouldn't rule anything out.' There was no sarcasm in Monica's voice, only fondness. 'If yer keep yer eyes down when ye're walking, I bet one day yer'll find a ten-bob note in the gutter. That would well pay yer train fare to Essex.'

'If I walk everywhere with me head down, queen, I'm more likely to wrap meself around a bleeding lamp-post than find a ten-bob note. But I'll take heed of what yer said, and although

I won't walk with me head down, I will walk with me eyes peeled. And if I happen to find a pound note, instead of a ten-bob one, I'll take you and Kate to Essex with me, that's a promise.'

'It won't seem the same without the old lady,' John said that night. 'She always waits for me coming home from work, either at the door or the window, and I always get a wave.'

'All the neighbours feel sad about it, particularly Maggie Duffy and Winnie. Maggie's worried about what sort of neighbours she'll get, but I can't see the landlord putting anyone in that isn't decent. Bill the rent collector got a shock when he was told this afternoon, he seemed quite upset. Mind you, he's been calling there for twenty years and was fond of Miss Parkinson. And as he said, she was a marvellous tenant, never once missed a week's rent in all those years. The rent book was always ready on the sideboard for him, with the exact money on top. There's not many in this street that can say that. Bill said she was a real lady.'

Nancy was sad because she was very fond of the old lady whom she often called on to see if she wanted any messages. She'd never known anyone speak as nicely as Miss Parkinson, even her teacher, and she never swore or shouted in the street. 'She'll be very sad when she leaves, Mam, 'cos she's lived here so long and everyone in the street likes her. I won't half miss her.'

'We all will, sunshine, but when yer think about it, it is best for her. Living alone in that house, she could be ill and no one would know. Yer wouldn't find her knocking on Maggie's wall in the middle of the night, she'd be too proud. And she must be lonely at times with no one to talk to. Where she's going, she won't ever be lonely again, or frightened living on her own. So we must be glad for her.'

'It's very good of her to leave her furniture for the four of you.' John pushed his empty plate away and left his chair to move to his favourite fireside one, where he would light up and enjoy one of the five Woodbines he smoked each day. 'It must be good furniture, because she seems to have come from monied people.'

'I imagine they left her well provided for, and Winnie said she receives a small pension from where she worked. I don't know about the furniture because I've never taken much notice, but she does have some good jewellery and paintings she's taking with her. And I'm glad about that, 'cos it means she doesn't need to be beholden to her niece, she can be independent.'

John drew on his cigarette and blew a smoke circle in the air. As he watched it rise to the ceiling, he asked, 'So she's leaving on Sunday?'

Kate nodded. 'Early on Sunday. Maggie said she'll leave the key with her, to return to the rent man, so we can all go in later on and sort out what's what. We'll not be able to go in after that because it would mean Miss Parkinson owing another week's rent. Not that I think for one minute Bill would worry, and he doesn't come till the afternoon anyway. But Maggie promised the old lady we'll do what we have to do on Sunday.'

'Can I come in with yer, Mam?' Nancy asked. 'I can help yer.'

'No, sunshine, no children. If you came then Dolly would want to come too, and we'll be much quicker on our own.'

'If you go, I'm going,' Billy growled. 'I've as much right as you have. Besides, you've been inside the house loads of times, and I've never been in once.'

'There's no need for an argument to develop because neither of yer is coming! Good grief, we're only going to look at furniture, it wouldn't interest yer in the least.'

'You heard yer mam,' John said, 'so not another word on the subject.'

* * *

At eleven o'clock on the Sunday morning, the four women stood in the middle of what used to be Miss Parkinson's living room. Maggie shivered. 'The room looks as sad as I feel, as though it's missing her already. I hardly slept a wink last night for thinking about her. Honest, no one could have had a better neighbour.'

'It'll take us all a long time to get used to not seeing her again. But we'll have to keep telling ourselves she'll be much better off there than here.' Kate looked at their three glum faces. 'She'd never have felt safe, not after that swine broke in. So we've to stop feeling sorry for ourselves, which is what we are doing, and sort the rest of her things out before the key's to be handed in tomorrow.' She looked around the room. 'Apart from little knick-knacks, this place is fully furnished. Any family could walk in and set up home without having to worry about furniture.'

'It's good stuff, too!' Maggie said. 'And the bedrooms are the same. The beds still have the bedding on them.'

'Well, where shall we start?' Monica asked. 'And who's going to be referee if it comes to fisticuffs when two of us want the same thing?'

'I'd rather do without than argue over the old lady's belongings when she's only been gone a couple of hours.' Kate looked hard at Monica, daring her to disagree. 'Let's try and be as ladylike as she was.'

'Eh, don't be giving me cow eyes, girl, I can be a lady when I like. I promise I won't hit anyone hard, just a gentle tap.'

'Before we start,' Maggie said, 'Miss Parkinson has left something for each of us as a token of her gratitude for the help we've given her over the years. They're in the sideboard cupboard, but they are all wrapped up and strict instructions were given that they weren't to be opened until we got home. Oh, and we're to be careful because they are breakable.'

'She's thought of everything, hasn't she?' Winnie was feeling very low in spirits. She'd stood at the window for an hour this morning, and when the car had pulled away from her old friend's

311

house, had hurried to the front door for one last wave as it went past. Now she wanted to be away from here as quickly as possible. 'Let's start in this room and see how we get on. There's the sideboard, table and chairs, sofa, small side table, the fireside chair, the companion set in the hearth, the coal scuttle, picture on the wall, four ornaments, and the curtains and nets. So who wants what?'

'We'll let you go first, sunshine, seeing as she was a good friend of yours. What in the room would you like best?'

'Her fireside chair, if no one minds.'

'It's yours,' Maggie said. 'Now who goes next?'

'You're next,' Kate insisted. 'That's only fair.'

So the sideboard went to Maggie, the table and chairs to Monica, and although Kate didn't let it show, the one thing she wanted was the one left after they'd all chosen – the couch, or, as Miss Parkinson called it, the sofa. The one at home had the springs sticking up and wasn't a bit comfortable, whereas this one was in excellent condition because it had rarely been used. And she got the brass companion set because she was the only one who didn't have one at home. The rest was easy, an ornament each, picture to Maggie, coal scuttle to Winnie, and front and back curtains to split between Kate and Monica.

Upstairs, each bedroom contained a double bedstead with mattresses filled with kapok, both still made up with their bedding as though someone would be sleeping there tonight. Winnie didn't want anything from upstairs because, as she said, she had enough at home at last her lifetime. She sat in the fireside chair and stroked its arms. She'd have this to remember Audrey by, and would take good care of it.

Upstairs, Maggie said she'd like one of the beds with its bedding as the ones at home had seen better days. The bed in the back bedroom would be left with its bedding until they decided what to do with it. Monica asked for one of the wardrobes, and Kate was delighted to be allowed to have the five-drawer tallboy.

Maggie said she'd take all of the things out of the kitchen home, too, so they could share them out. 'I'll take them out the back way and up our yard. That way, no one will see what's going on. We don't want to start tongues wagging.'

'And what about the furniture?' Kate asked. 'Shall we tell the men to leave it until it goes dusk? Say nine o'clock?'

'Yeah, it shouldn't take too long with three of them doing it. Your feller won't mind if he's a bit late for his pint, will he, Monica?'

'It's just too bad if he does, 'cos I'm not asking him, I'm telling him. But can we take our presents out of the sideboard now? I can't wait until it gets dark.'

While Maggie was taking the well-wrapped parcels out, Winnie asked, 'Would one of the men carry the chair down for me later, please? I'd never make it on me own.'

'John will, sunshine. He'll be happy to 'cos I think he's got a soft spot for yer.'

Chapter Twenty-Two

John came through from the kitchen on the Monday morning drying his face and neck on the towel he'd taken from the hook behind the kitchen door. He glanced around the room and heaved a big sigh. 'What are yer going to do with the old couch, love? We can't put up much longer with being cramped like this, it's hopeless trying to squeeze between the two of them. And it's not only a nuisance, the room looks terrible!'

'I don't need you to tell me that, sunshine!' Kate put a plate of toast down in front of him. 'And don't forget, when you go out to work, yer can forget it for the day, while I'm lumbered with it.' She poured out two cups of tea and sat facing him. Without telling him, she'd the alarm clock ten minutes forward last night so they could have some time together. 'And the kids have started their six weeks summer holiday, so yer can imagine what it's going to be like when they get up.'

'What are yer going to do with the old one anyway?'

Kate took a bite out of the piece of toast. 'I know it's not much good with the springs gone to pot, but there may be some poor soul glad of it. There's a second-hand furniture shop in Scotland Road, and I've seen the bloke picking furniture up with his horse and cart. I'll go along there when the children have had their breakfast and ask him. If I tell him I don't want any money for it, he might take it. At least, I'm keeping me fingers crossed he will.'

'That couch of Miss Parkinson's is in good nick, and it's nice and comfortable, too!' John wiped away a trickle of margarine from his chin. 'The room will look grand when the old one goes. Mind you, we've had our money's worth out of it. We've had it over fifteen years, with the kids climbing all over it when they were younger, and it was only cheap when we bought it. So we can't grumble, it doesn't owe us anything.'

'I'll miss it when it goes even though it is murder to sit on. It was the first piece of furniture we bought when we got married so I feel a bit sentimental about it.'

'I bet Miss Parkinson feels the same as you, she's bound to miss the things she's had around her for so long. So before yer start getting soppy, think of her.' John glanced at the clock on the mantelpiece and took a quick swallow of tea. 'Either that clock's wrong or the alarm is wonky. I'd better get a move on, I don't want to be late.'

'No, yer won't, sunshine, 'cos I set the alarm ten minutes early so I could have some time with yer before the kids get up. The clock on the mantelpiece is right, yer've time to eat yer breakfast without gobbling it down.'

He grinned at her across the table. 'You sly little minx! Why didn't yer tell me?'

'There'd be no use in doing it if I was going to tell yer, yer daft nit! All yer'd have done would be to turn over and go back to sleep.'

'Oh, no, I wouldn't!' His eyes held that look that never failed to warm her. 'I can think of more pleasant things to do with an extra ten minutes in bed than turning over.'

She tutted. 'Honest, at this time of the morning yer should be thinking about work and not bedroom antics.'

'I'm in the prime of life, sweetheart, not an old codger living on memories.'

Kate chuckled. 'Monica told me the other day she can hear everything that goes on through the wall, even what we say. Now if she heard what's been said in the last few minutes, she'd have her ear to the wall wishing she could join in. I call her a sex maniac, but she says she's just a normal hot-blooded woman.'

'I hope yer don't discuss our love life with her? What happens in the bedroom between a man and his wife should be secret.'

'Oh, yeah, I go blabbing to everyone in the street! Haven't yer seen the looks they give yer as yer pass them? They all think ye're a dirty old man.' Kate's laughter was infectious. 'Can yer see me discussing our love life with anyone? Or listening to anyone discussing theirs?'

'Monica does, from the sound of things.'

'She talks about it, yeah, but only because she likes to see me blushing. And she doesn't half pile it on! Tom would have to have the strength of an ox, and the stamina, to be the passionate lover she says he is. She's all talk, is my mate, just to get me going.'

'Much as I don't feel like it, love, I'd better get going meself.' John pushed his chair back, then curling his fists, put them on the table and leaned forward. 'If Tom knew what his wife lets out of the bag, he'd never walk up this street again. He'd use the back entry to get to the pub every night.'

'Don't you ever dare say one word to him.' Kate's lips set in the thin line that told her husband she was deadly serious. 'There'll be holy murder if yer do, I'll never speak to yer again.'

John was shaking with mirth as he struggled into his short working jacket. 'Well, it goes without saying, love, that if yer murder me, yer wouldn't be able to speak to me again. Unless yer went to one of those spiritualist meetings.'

'Fat chance of that! But don't ever say anything to Tom, it wouldn't be fair on him or Monica. Not that I really think he'd get upset or worry, 'cos he's as soft as putty with her. She can wrap him around her little finger.'

'Oh, and I suppose you can't wrap me around yours? I've been spoiling yer from the day I first clapped eyes on yer. But I don't earn the money Tom does. If I did, yer'd get it all – and all my love along with it.'

'Don't be running yerself down, sunshine, 'cos ye're not on a good wage. We manage all right.' Kate followed him to the door and lifted her face for a kiss. 'Love is far more important to me

STROLLING WITH THE ONE I LOVE

than all the money in the world. You're my man, and I love yer to bits.'

'Yer can tell me and show me how much tonight.' He began to walk away. 'I'll see yer the usual time, sweetheart, ta-ra.'

Kate closed the door and leaned back against it for a few seconds to savour those few minutes she'd had with the man she adored. Then she entered the living room and groaned. She'd have to do something with the old couch today, they couldn't live like this. She couldn't even get around the furniture to dust or polish, it was hopeless. Then a smile crossed her face. What a lovely, ready-made excuse that was. And the hot weather was on her side, 'cos they hadn't lit a fire for weeks, so the hearth was clean and tidy.

A sound from above had her moving to the kitchen to start on the children's breakfast. As she did, she spoke aloud. 'Anyway, I'm not the only one in a mess. Monica's got an extra table and four chairs in her living room. She'll be keen to get them out of the way, so she can come to the second-hand shop with me.'

Nancy stood in the doorway rubbing sleep from her eyes. 'Who are yer talking to, Mam?'

'Meself, sunshine, as usual. And the walls, of course, I spend a good part of me life talking to them.'

'I thought it might have been me dad, that's why I came down, so I could give him a kiss.'

'He's gone to work, sunshine, yer missed him by five minutes. But yer shouldn't have got up so early, why didn't yer have a nice lie-in?'

'Once I wake up I can't go to sleep again, and there's not much fun in looking up at the cracks in the ceiling. Besides, me mouth is dry, I want a drink.'

'If ye're desperate, the tea in the pot will still be warm. Have some of that while I'm making some toast and a fresh pot. Was there any sound of Billy waking up?'

A gruff voice answered, 'There wouldn't have been if she

hadn't woke me up.' Billy stood on the bottom stair which faced the kitchen. 'She sounded like a baby elephant crashing through the jungle.'

Nancy sighed at the exaggeration. 'I bumped into the tallboy, that's all! A baby elephant indeed. How would yer know that when yer've never seen one? Yer must have some vivid dreams if yer know the sound of animals in the jungle.'

Billy stuck his tongue out. 'I've seen them on the pictures, so there! I know what sounds they make. Elephants and monkeys.'

'Well, sit down and yer sister will pour yer a cup of tea out. I'll have yer toast made in about five minutes, if I'm left in peace.'

Nancy brought two cups out of the pantry under the stairs and filled them with tea from the pot on the table. 'Why didn't yer say lions and tigers as well?'

'I won't do them, not when you can do them better than me.'

'I can't make animal noises, yer daft nit! I don't want to, either, 'cos girls wouldn't make fools of themselves like lads.'

Billy had a devilish grin on his face because he thought he had her now. 'Yer *can* make animal noises! Yer make them every night when ye're snoring yer head off and keeping me awake. Yer do a good lion one, it sounds just like the real thing. In fact, the first time I heard it, I really thought there was a lion in me room.'

Kate came through with two plates of toast. 'Don't tell me I've got six weeks of you two bickering at the table every morning, 'cos I couldn't stand it. And I bet the person who said that children should have six weeks summer holiday was a man. One who went out to work every morning and left his poor wife to cope. Then he'd come home at night and wonder why she complained. Just like a man, that!' She picked up the teapot and took it through to the kitchen. 'A fresh brew will be up in a minute.'

'Don't yer be picking a fight over nothing at all, our Billy.' Nancy kept her voice down. 'It's not fair on me mam, she'll have a headache every day.'

'Well, I won't if you won't. Is that a deal?'

Nancy nodded. 'It's a deal.'

'What are you two plotting now?' Kate put the chrome stand down, then placed the teapot on it. 'Ye're not thinking of blowing up the Houses of Parliament, are yer?'

Now Billy wasn't very good at history, only the parts he liked. But to show he wasn't exactly thick, he chose one of his favourite characters. 'Now I could do that, if Dick Whittington would take me to London with him.'

Nancy slapped him on the back. 'Very good, our Billy! I wouldn't have thought of that.'

Kate decided not to say that of course Nancy wouldn't have thought of it because she knew Dick Whittington had nothing to do with Bonfire Night. But if she took the side of one of her children, then fireworks would soon be flying. So she led them on a different track. 'Are you two playing out this morning? I've got to go and see a man about having the old couch taken away, I'll probably be gone for an hour or so.'

'Will Auntie Monica be going with yer?' Nancy asked. ''Cos she said last night they couldn't move with all the furniture they've got in the living room.'

'I'm hoping she comes with me, sunshine, to help me talk the man into picking all the stuff up with his horse and cart. She's much more persuasive than me, is yer Auntie Monica. The poor man would stand no chance with her, she'd talk him to death.'

'Mam, when we've had our breakfast and washed up, can we have another look at the present Miss Parkinson left for yer?' Nancy leaned forward and coaxed, 'Please, Mam, we didn't get a proper look at it last night?'

'Oh, all right, but yer mustn't touch anything. It's the best china yer can buy, sunshine, and it's also very old. That means it's probably worth something, and I'd be devastated if any of it got broken.'

Billy became very interested. This might be something he

could brag about to Pete. 'How much d'yer think, Mam?'

Now Kate loved the bones of her son but she wasn't blind to his failings, one being that he couldn't keep anything to himself. His mate Pete probably knew everything that went on in this house, including how many blankets they had on the beds. 'Not enough to make us rich, son, it's more sentimental value because of the china's age. And as it's been in Miss Parkinson's family for about fifty years without being broken or chipped, I'd hate it to come to any harm while it's in our care.'

'I'll be careful, Mam,' Nancy said. 'I only want to look at them properly.'

'Okay, I'll get the things out while you clear the table. And you can get off yer backside, Billy, don't sit and watch yer sister doing all the work.'

Miss Parkinson's present to each of her four neighbours was exactly the same. She had split a full twelve-setting dinner service into four, so they each got three cups, saucers, side plates, tea plates and dinner plates. They were in the finest china Kate had ever seen, of pure white with a gold rim. Besides that the old lady had split a full canteen of cutlery between them, all solid silver. At least Tom said the hallmark proved they were solid silver, but how he would know that was anyone's guess. He could be right, though, because the knives and forks were very heavy and ornate.

Nancy gazed in wonder as her mother set the china out on the table. The pieces were so pretty and so fragile. The girl stared at them for a while before plucking up the nerve to ask, 'Can I pick one of the cups up, Mam, please? If I promise to be very careful, would yer let me hold one in me hand?'

Kate placed one of the cups on a saucer and passed them over. 'Only for a minute, sunshine, then they're going away again.'

'I don't want to hold one,' Billy said, looking at the finely curved handle on the cup. 'And yer wouldn't get a proper drink of tea out of that, either! The size of them, yer'd be lucky if yer got a mouthful. And I'd have to put me hands around the cup, 'cos me finger wouldn't go through the handle.'

'I'm glad about that, sunshine,' Kate said, smiling at him. 'They're too delicate for a man's hand.'

That made Billy's face light up, as his mother had known it would. He'd swagger around all day now after that compliment. Heaven help poor Pete, he was in for an earache.

'That's all, I'm going to put them away again. And as yer can see, they've got plenty of paper around them to stop them from getting broken. So I'm warning both of yer, do not go in that part of the sideboard without asking me. Now I know yer both always do as I say, but this time I'm really serious. I want to keep them safe so I can pass the china down to Nancy when she gets married, and the silver cutlery to Billy. My mam, and yer dad's, they didn't have nothing to pass down to us because they were working-class people, like ourselves. All they worried about was paying their way and being out of debt. So you two will be very lucky to have these lovely things passed down to yer.'

While Nancy clasped her hands together in delight, Billy's face creased and his chest expanded. And once again Kate thought, Poor Pete. He'll have an ache in both ears today.

She stood up after closing the sideboard door. 'Right, who's going to get washed at the sink first?' When Nancy's hand shot up, her mother said, 'Go on, then, sunshine, and Billy can go after yer. By the time I go next door to see about getting the furniture moved, yer should both be washed and dressed and I can see to meself then.' She hadn't got as far as the front door before she had a thought which turned her back into the living room. 'Billy, because yer don't have to go to school, it doesn't mean it's all right to have a tidemark, yer know. And when ye're washing the tide out, don't forget yer have ears as well.'

Her son grinned. 'I'll be that clean when yer come back, yer won't know it's me.'

321

Nancy winked over her brother's head. 'D'yer know what I wouldn't put past him?'

Kate shook her head. 'No, sunshine, what wouldn't yer put past him?'

'Cutting his ears off to save himself the trouble of washing them.'

Far from being put out, Billy thought that was hilarious. 'Yeah, that's a good idea! Yer could roast them, Mam, and give them to Nancy for her tea, seeing as it was her idea.'

'Well, this is a very pleasant conversation for this time of the morning, I don't think! It's a good job I've had me breakfast or yer'd have put me off. Now when I come back from Auntie Monica's, I want yer both to be sitting quietly, looking nice and clean and being very friendly with each other.'

'I promise I won't raise a finger to her, Mam,' Billy said. 'After all, she is me only sister, and 'cos she's a girl, and not as strong as me, I should be nice to her.'

Kate clicked her tongue on the roof of her mouth and called back, 'Don't be going overboard, son, or I might get the idea yer don't mean it.'

With her arms folded, a habit she couldn't break, she reached Monica's house. She rapped the knocker for the second time then heard a tap on the window and saw Monica peeping out. 'Open the door, I haven't got all day.'

'Yer'll have to go around the back, girl.' Her friend was waving her arm in the direction of her yard. 'Go on, girl, round the back.'

'Why can't yer open the door for me?'

'I can't get to the bleeding door, soft girl, 'cos I've got two bleeding tables and eight chairs, stopping me. I've also got big ruddy bruises on me legs, and in places I won't be able to show anyone except my feller.'

Kate nodded and motioned that she'd go back home and come up Monica's yard. And while she was doing this, she was chuckling away. Her mate seemed to be in a right state, so she shouldn't be difficult to talk into going to the second-hand shop. She'd be glad to get rid of her old dining suite.

'Yer've been quick, Mam!' Billy was taken by surprise. 'Usually when yer go to Auntie Monica's, though yer always say yer'll only be a few minutes, we don't see yer for an hour.' He chortled. 'What's the matter, Mam, has Auntie Monica got a sore throat or the measles?'

Sharing his humour, Kate said as she passed him, 'Neither of those, sunshine. Yer auntie couldn't open the door to me because eight chairs stood in her way.'

Nancy was in the kitchen drying herself. 'Ooh, I know she got a set of chairs and a table, but eight chairs! Her room must be worse than this.'

Kate was halfway down the yard when she heard Billy saying, 'They'd come in handy at Christmas to play musical chairs.'

And then Nancy's infectious giggle. 'Go and ask her to hang on to them, then.'

'Oh, we're in a right state, girl! Just look at the place!'

'It's no worse than mine, sunshine, with the two couches. But I'm hoping to get rid of me old one today, we can't carry on the way it is.'

Monica never seemed to lose her temper or her cool, but right now she was red-faced, breathing heavily and in a proper mood. 'Those chairs are going out in the yard, right now, I can't stand this! If it rains it's just too bad.'

Kate didn't tell the truth, the whole truth, because she knew the best way to get around her mate. 'I'm going to the second-hand shop in Scotland Road to see if the bloke will pick me couch up today. He's got a horse and cart, if I ask him nice he might do it.'

'Well, you selfish so-and-so! Just thinking of yerself and to hell with everyone else.'

The trick had worked and Kate didn't feel bad about being

crafty because Monica was always pulling stunts on her. 'Well, come along with me and ask if he'll take yer table and chairs. It's no good just looking at them and moaning or they'll still be here this time next week. Anyway, it's up to you, but that's what I came to tell yer. I'm going to get meself ready now 'cos if I get there early he might be able to pick it up today.'

'I'll be ready in fifteen minutes, girl, and I'll come with yer. Two voices are better than one, aren't they?'

'They sure are!' Kate told her, while thinking her mate's voice was better than twenty others any day. 'I'll scram, then, and get meself ready.'

'Auntie Kate,' Dolly said, 'is Nancy up yet?'

'Yeah, she's just finished getting washed. Yer can go in there and sit with her if yer like, but leave it until yer mam's coming out, to give our Billy time to get washed.'

'I'll give him time to get out, Auntie Kate, never mind get washed. He's a right tease, always pulling our legs. And he's nearly as big as me. If I gave him a clout he'd probably give me one back.'

'And so he should!' Monica said, rubbing her leg after banging it on a chair. 'Yer have no right to clout him, so he has my permission to clout yer back.'

'Ay, missus, our Billy knows better than to clout anyone, least of all a girl! So don't yer be leading him into bad habits.' Kate rubbed her hands together. 'Right, I'll be off, and I'll see yer in fifteen minutes, sunshine. And don't worry about the state of the room, leave it as it is, like I am. We can give them a thorough going over when we get back to normal. Which will be tomorrow, I hope. Anyway I'm off. See yer, Dolly, ta-ra.'

The two friends stepped down from the platform of the tram right outside the second-hand shop Kate had in mind. 'That's handy, isn't it, sunshine? Off the tram and right into the shop. We may as well go straight in and get it over with, what do you say?'

'Yeah, may as well, girl. You can go first, seeing as yer've only got the couch and it was your idea anyway.'

'But yer will come to my aid if I need it, won't yer? It was you what said two voices are better than one. And, sunshine, let's both be as sweet as honey and try and get round the man.'

'I don't want to be that sweet, 'cos then we'll make him sick. But I will be nice and only put my twopennyworth in if I think ye're not getting anywhere.'

When Kate pushed open the shop door, a bell on the top rang and both women nearly jumped out of their skin because it was so loud. Before they had a chance to look around, a man suddenly appeared before them. He seemed to come from nowhere and reminded Kate of the genie in Aladdin's lamp. 'Holy suffering ducks, yer frightened the life out of me! Where did yer spring from?'

The shopkeeper, a middle-aged man with a pleasant smile, waved his hand towards the back of the shop which was filled with furniture of every description. 'I have an office of sorts at the back, and a mirror on the wall which allows me to see customers as they open the door.' He gave a wry smile. 'And the ones who are not paying customers, but try and whip something out without being seen. We don't get many of them, though, and I can see it certainly doesn't apply to you ladies. So, how can I help yer?'

Kate took a deep breath. She'd been rehearsing on the tram, but it was much easier there than here. 'One of our neighbours has moved away and she gave me and me friend some of her furniture. I got a couch, which means I've got that and me old one. I wanted to know if yer'd do us a favour and pick up me old couch? It hasn't got a tear in it, but I've got to say a couple of the springs have gone. It might do some poor soul, though, 'cos I have heard that some families are sitting on orange boxes.'

The man, whose name was Sol Greenberg, asked himself how he could refuse someone with a face like hers and replied,

'I'll come and have a look at it this afternoon if yer like?'

'Oh, that would be smashing, thank you!' Kate was delighted, but she had to think of her friend as well. 'My friend here, she's me next-door neighbour, I think she has something she wants yer to look at, but I'll let her tell yer.'

Monica gave him her best smile. 'I'm in a worse state than Kate, 'cos I've got an extra dining table and four chairs. So if ye're coming next door, would yer take a look at them for me 'cos we can't move in the living room?'

'What condition is the old dining room suite in?'

'D'yer want a lie or the truth?'

Sol chuckled. 'Which would yer prefer?'

'Well, seeing as yer'll see it for yerself later, there's no point in lying. So, like me mate's couch, it's seen better days. But there's no legs missing, nothing like that. And again, as me mate said, there's probably some poor family would be glad of it. We don't want no money off yer, we just want to get them out of the house. Isn't that right, girl?'

'That's right, sunshine, we don't expect to be paid for them. But they would probably have lasted us a few more years if we hadn't been given something in better condition, so I think someone will be glad of them.'

'What made yer come here?' Sol asked. 'I don't think yer live around here 'cos I've never seen yer before.'

'We're only three tram stops away,' Kate said, hoping the distance wouldn't put him off. 'And I know yer've got a horse and cart 'cos I've seen yer name on the side of the cart.' Without warning a scene flashed before her eyes. It was Miss Parkinson's back bedroom with the bed still made up. 'Would yer mind if me and me mate went outside for a minute? I've just thought of something.'

'Not at all, I'll wait for yer.'

'What's got into yer?' Monica asked as she was pulled out of the shop to stand on the pavement. 'Yer haven't changed yer mind, have yer? Because I haven't, I want my room clear as soon as possible.'

'That's not why I brought yer out. I was thinking about that good bed in Miss Parkinson's back bedroom. He'd pay quite a bit for it and all the bedding. We could send the money to her, or buy her something with it.'

'But we can't get back in the house, yer know that. If we were caught, we'd have to pay a week's rent.'

'The rent collector doesn't come until this afternoon. The man could have it out by then and no one would know any different. I'd rather do that than leave it there for strangers to have, or to be thrown in the entry by whoever takes over the house.'

'The feller in the shop couldn't do all that before the rent man comes! He's not going to run out straight away because we ask him to. I'd say forget it, girl, there just isn't the time.'

'Let's ask him!' Kate said. 'If he says he can't come until this afternoon then well and good, we'll forget about it.'

'On your own head be it, girl, but I'll go along with yer. Let's see what he says.'

Monica left the talking to Kate because she thought it was a waste of time. After all, the man must have things arranged for today, he wasn't standing in the shop just waiting for them to turn up. But much to her surprise Sol was interested when told the bed was in excellent condition and came complete with bedding. And when Kate explained how important it was to get it out of the house as soon as possible, he said, 'I can close the shop for an hour and bring my assistant with me. Between the two of us, we can have the bed dismantled and out in the entry in fifteen minutes.' He took a fountain pen from his waistcoat pocket, a small notebook from his jacket pocket, and handed them to Kate. 'Write your name and address down, and we'll be there within the hour.'

Chapter Twenty-Three

'I can't let yer have the keys to the house, love, I've got to hand them to the rent collector when he comes.' Maggie didn't like refusing Kate, but she had told Miss Parkinson she wouldn't let anyone in the house after Sunday. 'And what would the neighbours think if they saw yer? Yer know what some of them are like, they'd spread the word that yer were stealing furniture.'

'I'm not asking for meself, Maggie, I'm not wanting to gain by it. But yer must admit it would be nicer to buy something for Miss Parkinson with the money we got than it would be to leave that bed for strangers who probably wouldn't appreciate it.'

Monica thought it was time to add her weight. She wasn't for the idea at first, but the more Kate had explained it to her, the more it appealed to her. 'Yer needn't give us the front door key, girl, just the back door. The men can carry it out through the entry and no one would be any the wiser.'

Maggie was torn. 'Are yer sure they won't come to the front door?' Even after emphatic nods from her two neighbours, she wanted further assurance. 'And the money would go to Miss Parkinson?'

'Well, I have thought of something she'd like better than the money,' Kate said. 'We could buy her something to remind her of the street she lived in for so many years. Say a photograph of the street which showed her old home? We could put it in a frame and then she'd be able to stand it on the mantelpiece, or a little table, where she'd be able to look at it whenever she wanted. I'm sure she'd be delighted.'

Maggie saw Winnie walking up the street and felt a sense of relief. 'Let's ask Winnie what she thinks.'

'What is this?' The little woman looked from one to the other. 'A mothers' meeting for fathers only? Or can anyone join?'

Kate quickly explained what was in her mind, and Winnie was all for it. 'Give them the bleeding key, Maggie, and if the rent man comes and catches them redhanded, why worry? I'm blowed if I can see Bill having any objection anyway! And if he did then I'd soon sort him out. The ruddy bed belongs to Miss Parkinson, it's not as if we're stealing it. And I think it's a jolly good idea that Kate's had. Audrey would be absolutely delighted if we sent her a photo of the street.'

That decided Maggie. She went into the house for the back-door key. 'Pass it over when yer've finished, Kate, and try and have the bed out as soon as you can. I'll feel better in me mind then.'

Winnie walked between her two friends as they crossed the cobbles. 'What have you two been up to, why have yer been up to it, and where did yer get up to it? And in future, when there's anything exciting happening, call for yer Auntie Winnie and take her with yer.'

'I'd hardly call it exciting, sunshine, more a case of necessity. I've got to get rid of me old couch 'cos we're overcrowded, and Monica's got that extra dining-room suite. We wanted them moving today, and if the man does as he promised, they'll be gone in an hour.' Kate felt in her pocket for the front-door key. 'Yer can come in if yer want, but it'll be a squeeze.'

'We'll be all right, won't we, girl?' Monica said. 'Both of us are thin.'

Kate let out a gasp. 'What d'yer mean, both of yer? Why don't yer go to yer own house, Monica Parry, and sit there in discomfort, instead of crowding mine even more?'

'Ye're bound to be making a pot of tea, girl, so don't be so bloody miserable! An extra cup isn't going to skint yer. Besides, our Dolly's probably in yours with Nancy, so if I went home I'd be all on me lonesome.'

329

'Why don't yer both come down to mine?' Winnie asked. 'I'll make yer a nice pot of tea and yer can sit in comfort. Except not on me new chair, that's not for visitors, it's purely for my own use.'

'We can't, sunshine, 'cos the man will be here any minute. But thanks all the same. Can yer hear the silence from me mate? She wouldn't dream of inviting us into hers.'

'Yer should know by now that I don't insult easy, girl, so I don't know why yer bother. Get that ruddy door open, me throat is parched.'

Kate had the key in the lock when Winnie said, 'There's a horse and cart coming up the street, queen, will it be coming here?'

'Oh, thank God for that! Ooh, they'll have the couch out in no time, and I'll have me room back to normal.'

'Yer house will be better than normal, girl, 'cos yer've got that nice new sofa.' Monica waved to the two men sitting on the long seat in front of the cart. 'I'm going to be as nice as pie to these two, 'cos I'll never be so glad to get shut of anything in me life as those ruddy chairs and the table.'

'I'm glad to see them 'cos it saves me making a pot of tea. Unless the men want one, of course, I will ask them.' Kate's face showed how happy she was. 'When they've gone I'll make a pot, and I'll even let both of yer sit on me sofa. As long as yer wipe yer feet first.'

'Oh, that's a good one, queen! Yer've bucked up since yer saw the horse and cart, haven't yer? Yer were looking down in the dumps before.'

They could hear the man holding the reins calling 'Whoa' to the horse and were amazed the animal was so obedient. It stopped right outside Kate's house and shook its mane as if to say, 'Well, here I am, what have yer got for me?'

'Is it your house first, Mrs Spencer?' Sol Greenberg jumped down from his seat, leaving the reins to hang loose. 'The couch, isn't it?'

'Yes, please, I'll just make sure there's nothing under the cushions.' While Kate fussed, thinking they'd have a job on their hands trying to manoeuvre the heavy couch through the front door, it was all in a day's work to the two men and they had it on the cart in no time. She walked behind them, explaining they'd have to get the bed out of the house the back way, and the easiest way to do that would be to take the horse and cart down the side street and stop at the top of the entry.

Sol smiled and nodded. He'd worked in the second-hand shop since he left school at fourteen and only had to look at an item to know the best way to move it. The shop had belonged to his uncle then, but when he'd retired he'd let Sol rent it off him until the lad had saved enough to buy him out.

'We'll do your neighbour's dining set first, then we'll talk about the bed.'

When the two men were clearing Monica's furniture out, Kate and Winnie crossed over to the side entry and let themselves into Miss Parkinson's house by the back door. While they were waiting for the men to come, they spent the time stripping the bed and folding the sheets and blankets neatly, ready for carrying out.

'These are marvellous quality. Just look at the fine linen sheets and pillowcases with a pattern in each corner,' Kate said. 'My sheets are so old and been washed so often yer can see through them. And I bet that feather eiderdown would keep yer as warm as toast in bed in the winter.'

'Audrey never bought anything but the best. It was what she was used to, her parents were quite well off.'

'But how did she come to end up in a two-up-two-down in this street, sunshine? I know I live in the street, and I'm not ashamed to say so, but yer could tell right away that Miss Parkinson was different. She was a class apart from anyone else.'

'I can tell yer about her 'cos she's not here now, queen, and I know ye're not one for jangling. Yer see, Audrey was used to a better style of life, but when it came to money she was very shrewd. Her parents left her with a nice home and a healthy bank account, but where many a woman would have kept up that lifestyle, Audrey had more sense. She realized that when she stopped working, there would be no money coming in, and to maintain a big house just for herself was not practical.' Winnie gave a corner of the eiderdown to Kate so she could help her fold it. 'Don't forget we're talking about thirty years ago, so what money she had would have well gone by now. I mean, she didn't know she'd live till she was turned eighty, but I remember her once saying that if she was careful, what she had would last her her lifetime. The upkeep of this small house was a drop in the ocean to what she'd been paying in her parents' old home. So I think she did the right thing coming here, and she never regretted it. Nor did she feel she'd lowered her standing. Audrey was no snob.'

'We'll buy her something soon and send it to her, so she knows she's not forgotten.' Kate put her arms around a pile of bedding and lifted it from the bare mattress. 'Let's take these down, save the men a job.' When they were on the landing, she looked over the pile at Winnie. 'I'll go first, sunshine, and you follow. Yer know how shallow the stairs are, so be careful.'

They laid the bedding on the draining board and leaned back against the sink. 'Doesn't the living room look empty and sad, as though it's missing her? It's happened so quickly me brain won't take it in.'

'Don't be getting yerself upset, sunshine, because she's probably living in the lap of luxury, being waited on hand and foot, with someone there all the time to talk to.' To take Winnie's mind off missing her friend, Kate changed the subject. Her head tilted, she asked, 'Ay, I wonder how much he'll offer for all this? What would you think it was worth?'

'Well, I wouldn't let it go for coppers because it's all good quality stuff. And it's almost brand new!' Winnie was still thinking of her old friend, and intended fighting her corner. 'Yer can leave that side of it to me, queen, if yer like. I'm not too bad at haggling.'

'Oh, I'll be glad to! I'm hopeless at it. If it was left to me, I'd take his first offer without a murmur. I've got no backbone, yer see, sunshine, I'm a real coward.'

'Of course ye're not! Ye're just too much of a lady to argue over money.'

They heard footsteps coming up the yard and Kate opened the door. 'Yer said yer'd be quick, Mr Greenberg, and yer've certainly been that.'

Sol jerked his head to where his assistant was standing. 'Bill does all the donkey work, I just give the orders.'

'I won't believe that for one minute. I saw the way yer were both handling that ruddy big couch, and there's no doubt ye're good at yer job.' Kate waved a hand at the two piles of bedding. 'We stripped the bed to save time. As yer can see, the sheets and pillowcases are all in the finest linen without a break in them. In fact yer could almost sell them as new, they've hardly been used. And the eiderdown and pillows are not kapok, they're all feathers.'

Sol knew quality when he saw it. His trip had certainly been worthwhile. 'Can we go upstairs and see the bed? I believe there's a deadline to getting it out of the house.'

Kate led the two men upstairs while Winnie followed behind. The women stood by the wall to allow room for the two men to lift the mattress and examine the springs. Sol was thinking this bed was better than the one he was sleeping in at home. And from what he'd seen of the bedding downstairs, it was of far superior quality than the linen he was used to. Selling and buying second-hand furniture was a living and he didn't do too badly out of it, but he'd never be rich enough to buy what he was seeing in this house. His wife would be over the moon with it.

'How much do yer want for the bed and the bedding?' he asked. 'Have yer got a figure in mind?'

This was where Winnie stepped in. 'As it's you what's buying, it should be up to you to say what yer'll give for it.'

Sol stood away from the bed, and with chin in hand gave the appearance of giving the matter some considerable thought. But what he was really thinking was that he and his wife would be sleeping in this bed tonight. 'I'll give yer one pound five shillings for the lot.' And without giving the two women time to answer, he went on, 'And three shillings for the old couch. It's well past its best, but I can probably sell it.'

'What about me mate Monica?' Kate asked. 'She'd do her nut if she thought I'd got something and she didn't.'

'I've already given Mrs Parry three shillings. Like your couch, her dining suite was well worn and not worth any more.'

Kate was overjoyed, and knew Monica would be tickled pink. But Winnie, her eyes narrowed, was ready to bargain over Audrey's bed. 'I think that bed and bedding are worth thirty bob of anyone's money! All of it is good quality and almost new.'

Sol puckered his lips once again. After a few seconds of deep contemplation he appeared to come suddenly to a decision. 'Okay, yer twisted me arm, thirty bob it is. Now me and Bill will dismantle the bed and get it down to the entry. But before we do, I'll give yer the money I owe yer. Thirty bob for the bed and three shillings for the couch.'

Kate took the money with a smile. 'We'll wait for yer downstairs. I've got to make sure the door's locked before I hand the key over to a neighbour.'

Monica was waiting outside the house for Kate and Winnie to come through the entry. She was quick to note that, like herself, the other two were wearing smiles and looking pleased with themselves. 'Not bad, eh, girl? I've got me room back to normal, and three bob into the bargain. I wasn't expecting any money, I would have been happy just to get rid of me old stuff.'

'Me too, sunshine,' Kate said. 'It seems too good to be true, 'cos I thought he might charge us something for taking the furniture away.'

'Oh, he's not that daft, queen, he's a businessman and can't afford to do favours, even for nice-looking women. He'll double the money he gave you for yer furniture, yer can bet yer sweet life on that. A nice bloke, very obliging, but he has to make a living.'

'Ay, how did yer get on with him over Miss Parkinson's bed? Did he give yer a good deal on it?'

'I'm going to let Winnie tell yer, sunshine, 'cos she did all the negotiating over that, and she did far better than I'd have done.'

'He offered twenty-five bob for the bed and bedding, but I could see he was impressed with it so I got him to cough up thirty shillings. So yer see, queen, it was a good day all round!'

Monica was very impressed. 'Go 'way! Ay, that was good, that was.' She slapped Winnie on the back. 'Nice work, girl, yer did well. Now we can get something decent to send to Miss Parkinson.'

'She didn't do well, she did marvellous! I'd have taken the twenty-five bob and thought I'd got a good deal.' Kate rubbed her hands together. 'I'm going in now to straighten me living room out. John will be as pleased as Punch that the old couch has gone.'

Monica laid a hand on her arm. 'I've straightened yer room out, girl, and it looks a treat. I've even put the kettle on and got the cups ready. So shall we go in and relax, and celebrate with a nice cuppa?'

'Ye're a cheeky article, Monica Parry! Why didn't yer put the kettle on in yer own house for a change?'

'Oh, I hate change, it upsets me whole routine. So lead the way, girl, and we can toast our success.'

'Are Nancy and Dolly in?' Kate just happened to catch the smug expression on Monica's face, and thought, Oh, aye, what's the queer one been up to now? 'I know that look, missus, and it usually means trouble. So answer me question, are Nancy and Dolly in?'

'No, girl, they're not!' Monica stuck out her tongue. 'I've sent them to the cake shop for three cream slices for us to have with our cuppa. And out of the shilling I've given them, I've told them to buy themselves a pennyworth of sweets and to give Billy a penny to buy him and Pete some gobstoppers.'

Kate slowly licked her lips. 'A cream slice each?'

Her mate nodded. 'So perhaps yer won't begrudge us sitting on yer new sofa while we drink the tea ye're going to make us.'

'Yer shouldn't be spending yer money on me, queen,' Winnie said. 'Yer should see to yer family first.'

'Winnie, sunshine, yer don't know my mate where money's concerned,' Kate told the little woman. 'She can't keep hold of it, it burns a hole in her pocket. But seeing as she's already gone and done what she shouldn't have, then we'll accept her generosity with thanks and enjoy the nice surprise. Now can we go in instead of standing in the street as though we haven't got a thing to do.'

Kate was on the step when Monica said, 'It can be your turn to buy the cakes tomorrow, girl, it'll give us something to look forward to.'

'Not on your life, sunshine! I've got more to do with me money than buy cakes, much as I love them. It's Billy's birthday next week, and although he doesn't want much, just enough money so he can mug Pete to a matinee and a bag of sweets each, it doesn't mean I can go mad because I've got a few bob I wasn't expecting.'

Two women passed by on the opposite side of the street and waved across. Kate called a greeting and waited until they were out of earshot before saying, 'Can we carry on with this conversation inside the house, please?'

She was surprised and delighted to see how neat and tidy the room looked. You could see her new sofa in all its glory now, and it looked real posh. 'Yer've done well, Monica, me room looks a treat.'

'I wouldn't have done it if I'd known I was going to get a lecture on being a spendthrift. Do a good turn and yer get told off for it!'

'Yer don't need me to give yer a lecture on money, yer know yerself it goes through yer fingers like water. And I only do it for yer own good, 'cos after all, yer are me mate.'

'Okay, girl, don't get yer knickers in a twist, I haven't taken the huff. I just thought while we had a few bob we weren't expecting, we could go mad and break eggs with a big stick.'

'Not me, sunshine, I've already decided that I'm starting Christmas clubs in all the shops, so I won't be worried sick when the time comes and I haven't enough money to buy all the extra food and presents. I'll open the clubs with this money, and each week from now until Christmas I'm putting something in each. Even if it's only tuppence, it'll all mount up over a few months.' Kate's face broke into a smile. 'Lecture over. Now, would my guests like to sit on my new sofa while I make them a pot of tea?'

'Ay, girl, she's letting us sit on her new sofa, that means she really loves us.' Monica gave Winnie such a hard dig in the ribs, the little woman almost lost her balance. 'And please note, it's not a couch, it's a sofa.'

'If that dig in the ribs had been a bit harder, queen, it would have been a bleeding hospital bed for me, never mind a posh sofa. Fair knocked the wind out of me it did.'

'Oh, I'm sorry, girl, I don't know me own strength, that's my trouble. But I'll tell yer what, I'll let yer choose which end of the sofa yer want to sit on. Now I can't be fairer than that, can I?' Just then Nancy and Dolly passed the window, and Monica flew to the door. 'Did yer manage to get three cream slices?' The two young girls nodded, and passed over a white bag which Nancy had carried very carefully.

'We're going to the park, Auntie Monica, will yer tell me mam so she doesn't worry? And I'll find our Billy to give him his penny.' Nancy, by far the more sensible of the two girls, handed a threepenny bit over. 'That's all the change there is out of yer shilling, I'm afraid.'

'That's all right, girl, I've already been taught the error of me ways by yer mam. But I'm thick-skinned. Rolls off me back like water.'

'Don't forget to tell her I've gone to the park with Dolly, will yer? She worries if she doesn't know where me and Billy are. But we'll both be in at dinnertime because we'll be starving.'

The women had decided that a new sofa wasn't the place to sit eating a cream slice oozing out at the sides so they moved to sit at the table. Their faces were blissful as they bit into the cakes. 'I take everything back that I said to yer, sunshine, because this is a little bit of heaven.'

'So that means yer'll be forking out for three tomorrow, does it?'

'No, it does not! Much as I'd like to mug yer, I can't afford to be generous. There are more important priorities than cakes. Such as clothes for the kids and food for the table. That's why I always quicken me pace when I'm passing a cake shop. I love them, but I have to leave them. Sad, but true.'

'Well, I've only spent ninepence, so I can join the clubs with yer. I know the sweet shop has already started, 'cos I saw Mrs Robinson getting her card filled in last week. And Bob in the butcher's, he has one all the year round. Who else were yer thinking of, girl?'

'Sid in the greengrocer's. So apart from the cake shop and groceries from Irwin's, I'll be covered for everything. If I really tighten me belt, I could even put a couple of coppers in their clubs, then I'd only have clothes to worry about.'

'Ye're starting yer worrying early, aren't yer, queen? It's nearly six months off.'

'I swore I wouldn't leave things until the last minute like I did last year. I'd rather start too early than too late.'

'It's not worth me worrying about Christmas clubs, queen, not with only meself to see to. Christmas Day is just like any other day, 'cos what's the use of buying a turkey just for one?' Winnie realized she was probably sounding sorry for herself, so she grinned. 'I don't mind being on me own, I'm used to it now. I get a few extra pints of milk stout in, and they cheer me up and put a smile on me face.'

Kate felt a rush of sympathy. No one should be alone on Christmas Day. 'Yer can come here for yer Christmas dinner, sunshine, we'd love to have yer.'

'No, queen, I wasn't fishing for an invite. I don't mind being on me own, I've got the wireless for company. You see to yer family, I'll be fine.'

Kate then told a lie. 'I had every intention of asking yer, sunshine, it wasn't just a spur of the moment thing. After all, it's only a few extra roast potatoes, no trouble at all.'

'Ay, now, that's a brain wave for yer!' Monica said to Winnie. 'Then yer could stay for the party at night.'

Even Kate had to smile at the hint. Then she pretended to let out a weary sigh. 'D'yer know, sunshine, if yer keep that up, yer'll wear me down.'

'That is the general idea, girl, but it's like flogging a dead horse. If yer don't hurry up and give in, then I'll be wearing me bleeding self out! So much so, yer'll have me thinking it would be a lot less hassle if I had the ruddy party at our house!'

'We've got six months to go before we need worry about that, so can we change the subject and talk about Miss Parkinson's present? I honestly believe the best thing we could give her would be a photograph. In fact, I started getting ambitious when that man gave us thirty bob for her bed and bedlinen, and thought we might have enough for two photographs. One of the street, and another of her house with her four neighbours standing nearby. Not in front of her house, that would spoil it, but by Maggie's window.'

'It sounds a good idea, girl, and I can't think of anything she'd like better. But who is going to take the photographs?'

'It would have to be a professional,' Winnie said. 'We don't want anything amateurish or cheap-looking.'

'Well, don't look at me!' Kate pulled a face. 'I've never held a camera in me life. And I don't know anyone who's got one.'

'Me neither,' Monica said. 'And it would be daft to use her money to buy a camera.'

'The only professional I know of,' Winnie said, 'is the shop in London Road called Jerome's. But I don't know whether he goes out to take photos of streets. He has a studio and takes portraits of people. I've often looked in his window and seen some lovely photos in frames. Some are of wedding groups, some of whole families. But apart from that I haven't a bleeding clue. Except yer can have yer photo taken for a shilling, and threepence for every extra copy. How I know that is an old friend of mine had hers taken. She had to wait a week before she could pick it up, but it was nice and she was over the moon.'

The soft icing on the top of the cream slice had made Winnie's false teeth all sticky, she had to keep pushing the top set back into place with her tongue. 'Don't ever get false teeth, queen, hang on to yer own as long as yer can. These are nowt but a bleeding nuisance.' She waited a second to make sure the teeth were securely anchored, then went on. 'The friend did tell me that she was pleased with the end result, but having it taken was a nightmare. The man tells yer how to pose, and she said she felt a right nit.'

'We wouldn't have that trouble with the street, sunshine, it's not got any eyelashes to flutter. But how do we find out about this Mr Jerome?'

'I don't know whether that's his name, queen, it's just got Jerome's over the shop. We'd have to go down to London Road, to the shop, and ask whoever is there if they do outside work. That's all I can think of.'

Monica swivelled sideways on the chair and crossed her legs. 'I can't see him refusing 'cos thirty bob is a lot of money and not to be sniffed at. I wouldn't mind taking two photies for that sort of money. He'd be a fool to turn it down, unless he's loaded and can afford to be choosy about what he does.'

'I'll have a word with Maggie, see how she feels about it. After all, she has as much right to her say as we have. If she thinks it's a good idea, then perhaps the three of us can get the tram to London Road this afternoon and see what we can come up with. Is that okay with you two?'

'Fine by me, queen!'

Monica clicked her tongue. 'I think we should send you in first, girl, seeing as ye're the nicest looking. I'll only come in if the going gets rough and yer need a bit of support.'

Winnie chuckled, dislodged her teeth, pushed them back with her forefinger, then carried on with the interrupted chuckle. 'Well, we've got a nice-looking one in case he's swayed by looks, a straight-talking one in case he's swayed by argument, so can I be the one with a hard luck story in case he's swayed by pity?'

Chapter Twenty-Four

Kate said goodbye to Monica and Winnie and carried her basket of shopping through to the kitchen. She rubbed her arm and stretched it a couple of times to get the circulation going. The basket was heavy with potatoes and veg, and although the shops weren't a long way off, its weight had pulled on her muscles. She was about to empty the contents when there was a rat-tat on the knocker. At first she thought one of her mates had forgotten something, then she remembered it was the day for the rent man.

The rent book, with the money on top, was on the sideboard and Kate picked it up as she made her way to the front door. 'Hi, Bill, I just made it back in time. I'd forgotten it was Monday until Winnie reminded us.' She passed the book and money over. 'Five minutes later and I'd have missed yer.'

The collector grinned. 'I know yer've been to the shops, Kate, 'cos I've just bumped into Mrs Cartwright. She's dashed home to pick up her rent and said she'd catch me up. I told her to leave it until next week because I know she wouldn't do a midnight flit. But yer know what she's like, always pays on the dot.'

'She's not the only one, Bill, I've never been behind with me rent. I'd rather go without food than miss that. I had it drummed into me when I was a kid by me ma. She used to say yer could go without food or coal, but yer couldn't go without a roof over yer head. And her words have always stayed with me.'

'I wish all the tenants were like that.' Bill entered the payment in his ledger, filled in her rent book and passed it back. Then he lifted the flap and dropped her money into the large leather bag which hung in front of him from the wide leather straps around his shoulders. 'Mind you, some poor buggers can't pay up every week, and I have a lot of sympathy for them. With the man of the house being out of work, they're living on the poverty line. The women earn a few bob doing cleaning jobs, or taking in washing, but that's not enough to keep the wolf from the door. The boss isn't very happy when he sees arrears in me book, but I can usually talk him round. He's not a bad landlord, or a bad boss to work for.'

'I wonder how long Miss Parkinson's house will be empty for?' Kate asked. 'I hope it's let to a decent family.'

'I know there's two families after it now, but more than that I can't tell yer. It'll be taken in the next week, that's for sure, because unlike some houses that come empty, it won't need fumigating. It's ready for a family to move into.'

Kate shivered. 'Yer mean, they sometimes have fleas and bugs?'

'And yer can add the word filth. Yer wouldn't believe the state some people leave their houses in. I'd be ashamed of meself.' Bill lifted the strap which was digging into his shoulder. 'Anyway, I'll let yer know next week if I find anything out.' He began to laugh. 'Here comes Mrs Cartwright, her book and money clutched in her hand. I'll walk down to meet her, save her being breathless.'

'I'll get in and sort me washing out. Ta-ra, Bill, see yer next week.' Kate closed the door quickly, knowing she ought to put a move on. She was meeting her two mates again in an hour to go to the photographer's in London Road, and she wanted to get the dinner prepared by then. And wash a pair of Billy's trousers and get them on the line to dry. He only had two pairs, one slightly better than the other, but the pair she wanted to wash had a hole in the backside you could put your fist through. It would take some doing to get a patch to cover it, but needs must when the devil drives. There were boys playing in the street with holes in their socks and trousers, but she didn't want her son to be one of them. Anyway, she'd peel the spuds and carrots first, then put the trousers in steep while she made herself a quick cuppa.

* * *

ᕐ'Well, this is it.' Winnie pulled her two friends to a halt outside a shop that looked quite bare compared to the other shops in the busy shopping area of London Road. They'd passed T. J. Hughes, where the huge windows were displaying clothes, china, bedding, shoes, and lots of other things which could be bought inside. The windows of Brown's, the jeweller's on the other side of the main road, were bright with sparkling diamond, ruby and sapphire rings, gold necklaces and bracelets. But the window the three friends were looking in had just two small photographs, both of young women, and one huge family portrait showing a mother, father and three children. They all looked stiff as though terrified to move, but it was a definite eye-catcher. Whoever had taken it was a true professional.

'I bet that one cost a few bob,' Winnie said. 'Can't yer just imagine it hanging in a posh drawing room over the fireplace, or in a hallway?'

'Yeah, it shows what yer can do if yer have money.' Monica was eyeing the clothes on the people in the portrait. 'Those dresses on the kids and the mother must have cost a small fortune. My feller would have to work a full year to buy us clothes like that.'

'Money is the root of all evil,' Kate said. 'It can buy yer anything in the world. Take yer to any place in the world where yer want to go. But it can't buy yer health or happiness.' She moved away from the window. 'Well, shall we all take a deep breath and go in?'

'After forking out on tram fare, I'm not backing out now. So as you're nearer the door, girl, just push it open and me and Winnie will follow yer in.'

They found themselves in a waiting room with half a dozen chairs set against the wall upon which there was a notice which asked them to sit down and they would be attended to as soon as possible. So, a little disheartened, the women looked at each other, shrugged their shoulders and sat down. Their bottoms had no sooner touched the chairs when a door on the opposite wall opened and two young women came out, each holding an envelope in one hand, and a photograph in the other.

'God, I look terrible!' girl number one said. 'Look at the state of me hair, and me eyes look as though they're popping out of me head.'

'Swap over and let's have a dekko.' This was girl number two. After a quick scrutiny, she pulled a face. 'They're not bad, Alice. I mean, we're not exactly film stars, are we? The man can't make us look like something we're not.'

Alice clearly thought her looks deserved more than that. 'I don't think they're very good of either of us, they don't do us justice.'

'I bet we'll think different when we see them in daylight. It's too dark in here to tell, let's go outside.'

'I can't see how bleeding daylight can make them look like Jean Harlow,' Winnie said with a grin. 'If it did, I'd never go indoors.'

Just then the door opened again and a man came out. He was of medium height, smartly dressed, with thick black hair and an efficient manner. 'Good day, ladies, what can I do for you?'

When her two mates remained silent, Kate said, 'I don't know whether yer can do anything, it might not be in your line, but there's no harm in asking.' She quickly filled him in with all the details of what they wanted and why.

'I'm afraid it isn't in my line,' the man said, 'but I do know someone who does take the kind of photographs you're after. He works as a press photographer, most of his work is for newspapers and magazines. I could give you his telephone number and you can ring him and see what he says.'

'That wouldn't do much good because none of us has a telephone.' Kate felt like Little Orphan Annie, as poor as a church mouse. 'Perhaps you have an address where we could contact him?'

The man's eyes never left her face. Her two friends might not have been there for all the notice he took of them. He was thinking that with her beauty she would take a marvellous photograph. He could work wonders if she would sit for him. With her bone structure, the wide deep brown eyes and sweeping black eyelashes, she was the perfect model.

Kate began to grow embarrassed under the man's searching eyes and lengthy silence. 'It doesn't matter if yer don't have an address, we'll try somewhere else.'

'I'm sorry, I was thinking. I will ring him from here for you, explain what you require and ask if he's interested. Oh, and if you give me your name and home address, and he agrees, I can perhaps get a date and time he will be able to call. Would that help you?'

'That's very kind of you, and yes, it would be a great help.' Kate kept her eyes off her neighbour when she gave the man Monica's name and address. 'We would be very grateful.'

When the door had closed behind him, Monica said, 'Well, I like that, I must say! The cheek of you, Kate Spencer! Who said yer could give him my name and address?'

'He had me all hot and bothered, the way he was looking at me! I didn't think yer'd mind, sunshine, but if yer do, I'll tell the man when he comes back.'

'There was no harm in him, queen. He was probably interested in yer because yer do have the looks of a film star.' Winnie was nodding as though she had read the man's thoughts. 'I bet he'd like to take yer photie to put in his window.'

Monica's throaty chuckle warned Kate she wasn't going to like what was to come. 'Or perhaps he'd like one to hang over his bed.'

'If you mention the words bed or Robin Hood, so help me, sunshine, I'll walk out of this shop and leave yer to it.'

Monica blew out, making her lips quiver, then leaned towards Winnie. 'Yer know her trouble, don't yer, girl? No bleeding sense of humour.'

'Would it be asking too much to see if we can behave like ladies when the man comes back? He'll think we've been dragged up from the gutter.'

'Considering me and Winnie haven't opened our mouths, if he gets the impression we're as common as muck, then it's you what's done it, girl, not us.'

'He's taking a long time, I wonder if he can't get hold of the other chap?' Kate said. 'I hope he can, 'cos if the bloke takes pictures for the papers and magazines he'll be used to doing outside work like streets and things. Then again, he might charge the earth for what we're wanting. Expenses for travelling, plus his time, plus everything else . . . he might be out of our league altogether.'

Monica once again leaned towards Winnie. 'As well as having no sense of humour, she's a bleeding pessimist. Always expects the worse.'

'I most certainly do not!' Kate was emphatic. 'I always look on the bright side, I never look for trouble.'

They hadn't heard any footsteps so when the door suddenly opened they all sat up straight as though they'd been caught in the act of being naughty. Once again the photographer's eyes went straight to Kate. 'I managed to get hold of him. He'll be at your house tomorrow at ten o'clock, if that's convenient? If not I'm to call him back with a time that suits you.'

'Tomorrow is fine.' Kate jumped to her feet. 'And we'd like to thank you very much for your trouble. You have been kind.'

'Before you go, can I ask if you've ever sat for a portrait, Mrs Parry?'

Kate blushed when she heard Monica giggle, and was really expecting her mate to say she was the real Mrs Parry, and no, she hadn't had her portrait taken. 'No, I haven't,' said Kate finally when her friend did not speak up. 'I couldn't afford to because I have a husband and two children to feed and clothe.'

'Oh, I wasn't touting for business, Mrs Parry, I wouldn't expect you to pay. But I would very much like to take your photograph, for free, if you would allow me to display it in my window. I would, of course, give you a print for yourself.'

Kate backed away from him and bumped into a chair. 'Oh, I couldn't do that, me husband wouldn't like it. Besides, what would the neighbours say if they passed yer shop and saw a photograph of me in the window? They'd wonder where I got the money from, and say I was getting too big for me boots.'

Monica could see her friend was getting flustered, and although she couldn't understand why, it wasn't in her to stand back and not lend some moral support. 'Can me friend have some time to think about it? After all, yer've taken her by surprise and she's very shy at the best of times.' She cupped Kate's elbow. 'Let her give it some thought when she gets home and has a talk with her husband. She'll come and tell yer if she changes her mind.'

Winnie then cupped Kate's other arm and she was marched out of the shop like a prisoner between two guards. When she felt the pavement beneath her feet, she turned on Monica. 'Why did yer tell him I'd think about it? Yer know damn well I wouldn't dream of doing what he asked.'

Monica let go of her arm and faced her. 'It's up to you what yer do, girl, but the way ye're carrying on, anyone would think the man had insulted yer instead of paying yer a compliment. If it had been me, I'd have jumped at the chance.'

'For what it's worth, queen, I agree with Monica,' Winnie said. 'Not that he'd be likely to want a photie of my ugly mug. But yer could have had a smashing professional photie taken, like the one in the window of the family, and it wouldn't have cost yer a penny. Most people would give their eye teeth for such a chance.'

Monica's laughter rumbled in her tummy. 'Ay, girl, they'd

have had to have the picture taken before they parted with their eye teeth. It wouldn't be good for the man's business to have a gummy woman as a sample of his work.'

'Listen, yer can both talk until ye're blue in the face, but I won't change me mind. How soft I'd look with people gawping at me through the window. Can yer imagine what the neighbours would say? I'd be the talk of the wash-house.'

'And how many of our neighbours d'yer think stroll down London Road looking into shop windows? Particularly that window. They'd consider having their photo taken a luxury. They've got more on their mind, like where's the next meal coming from, or how much longer their kids' shoes will last without the soles falling off. I doubt if anyone yer know would ever see yer photograph.'

Kate shook her head. 'John wouldn't like it at all. He'd be dead against it.'

'Are yer going to tell him, so he can make up his own mind?'

'Waste of time, that would be, I know what he'd say.'

'Oh, queen, yer can be as stubborn as a mule sometimes.' Winnie had always thought Kate was the most beautiful girl she'd ever seen, and when she grew older, how nice it would be for her and her family to have a photie to look back on. 'When yer get home, and yer nerves settle down, think it through properly because yer may never get another chance. And I've got a feeling John and the children would be delighted.'

Kate blew out her breath impatiently. Deep down, she knew that her friends were saying what they thought was best for her, but she was still unnerved by the memory of the man's searching gaze and so she stuck to her guns. 'I'll never sit and have my portrait taken so let's leave it at that. Can we please get home? Me throat is parched and I'm dying for a cup of tea.'

Monica and Winnie looked at each other, shrugged their shoulders and linked Kate's arms as they walked towards the tram stop.

* * *

›The subject wasn't mentioned on the way home, and Kate become more relaxed. 'Don't forget, that bloke's coming at ten in the morning so put yer best bib and tucker on and don't be late.' They had turned into their street and she saw something that had her tugging at her friends' arms. 'Ay, Sergeant Bridgewater's at Maggie's door! Come on, let's make a dash for it, I want to find out what's going on so we can tell Miss Parkinson.'

'Hello, ladies! I was just keeping Mrs Duffy informed on how the case is progressing. Now you're here, it will save me knocking on your doors and having to repeat it. But first, I must say what a surprise it was to find out Miss Parkinson had moved. I'm told she has gone to live with family where she'll be well cared for, so it's maybe for the best. If the offender had not pleaded guilty, we may have needed her as a witness. However, even if he changes his plea to not guilty, which sometimes happens, we still have you as four good witnesses.'

'What's happening with this Tricky Dicky, is he in jail?'

'He's still in custody but he's due in court on Wednesday which is what brings me here. I wasn't aware that Miss Parkinson had moved and wanted to give her the chance of attending. And, of course, any of you ladies who might want to find out what happens to villains like Richard Willis.'

'He will be sent to jail, won't he?' Monica asked. 'I'd hate to see him getting away with it.'

'There's no doubt he will be sent down. I couldn't tell you for how long, it depends very much on the judge. Some are more lenient than others.'

'I don't fancy sitting in a courtroom,' Kate said. 'But I would like to know what happens to him so we can let Miss Parkinson know that the monster who frightened the life out of her is being punished. We are going to keep in touch with her, yer see, we're not going to forget her, not after all those years.' Kate then went on to tell the sergeant about the photographs they were arranging to have taken, to remind her of her old home and her nearest neighbours.

'That's a lovely thought,' the officer said, 'I'm sure she'll appreciate them. And if none of you fancy sitting in court, and I don't blame you because it could take up most of your day, then I'll make it my business to call again and let you know the outcome of the trial.'

'It won't take all day, surely?' Winnie looked surprised. 'I thought it would be over in an hour or so, 'cos if ever there was an open and shut case, this is it. There were at least twelve witnesses, apart from Miss Parkinson.'

Sergeant Bridgewater shook his head. 'If his is the first case to be heard, then it could be over and done with by late afternoon. If not, it could be carried over to the next day. Some people find the workings of a court very interesting and are frequent visitors, but I don't think you would. In fact, you would probably find it maddening because Richard Willis will have a barrister whose job it is either to get him off or to try for the most lenient sentence possible. You would find that very hard to swallow.'

'Ye're not joking,' Maggie said. 'I'm afraid I'd be standing up and telling that barrister what I thought of him. That thief needs to be in jail, not only to teach him a lesson but because he needs to be punished. She's a real gentle old lady is Miss Parkinson, and wouldn't hurt a fly.'

'Hear, hear!' Monica said. 'I'd batter him meself if I could get me hands on him.'

'He won't be very popular in prison, ladies, I can assure you. There are some old lags in there who won't take kindly to a man who picks on old people to rob from. It's funny but criminals have their own code of practice. They think anyone harming children or old people is worse than a murderer. Don't ask me how they reach that conclusion, but it's true.'

'I'd be happy if they just frightened him, like he did Audrey,' Winnie said. 'I wouldn't want them to murder him, even though I felt like doing it meself at the time.'

'I'll have to get home and put the dinner on, then look for me children,' Kate said. 'But yer will let us know the outcome, won't yer, Sergeant?' She waited for his nod, then crossed the street with Monica and Winnie following behind. She turned when they reached the other side, lifted her hand, and said, 'Before yer ask, no, yer can't come in for a cuppa. I've the dinner to see to, the kids to find, a pair of our Billy's kecks to iron, and patching and darning to do. So leave me in peace until ten o'clock in the morning when I want to see yer all dolled up in yer finery.' She suddenly put a hand to her mouth. 'Oh, God, I forgot to tell Maggie! She'll go mad if we turn up in the morning with a photographer and she opens the door to us in her pinny and mobcap.'

'I'll nip over and tell her, queen, and I'll see yer in the morning.' Winnie looked knowingly at Monica. 'And you'll see her in the morning, won't yer?'

'My God, talk about "here's yer hat, what's yer hurry" isn't in it!' Monica's eyes rolled to the heavens. 'For the first time in me life I feel not wanted.'

'You fibber!' Kate inserted the key in the lock. 'I've told yer hundreds of times ye're not wanted, but yer don't take no notice. That doesn't mean I don't love yer, though, or you, Winnie. I love the bones of both of yer. Ta-ra for now.'

It was ten minutes to ten when the photographer knocked, and Kate was glad she'd made the effort to be ready early, and have the children organized. They'd been sent out to play but told not to leave the street under any circumstances. When they wanted to know why, she'd tapped her nose and said they'd find out later, if her idea came to fruition.

'Mrs Parry? My name's Will Conley, I'm the photographer,' her visitor introduced himself.

'Come in, please, my friends will be here any minute. And I'm not Mrs Parry, I'm Mrs Spencer. Kate Spencer. There was a mix up yesterday and yer were given me next door neighbour's name.' Kate waved him to the sofa, her pride and joy. 'Before they come I'll explain what we want and why.' This she did very quickly. 'But we haven't a clue what your charges are and whether we can afford yer.'

'To cover me time, travel, films and developing, I charge ten shillings a photograph. Is that within your limits?'

Kate nodded, thinking what a pleasant young man he was. 'I was wondering if we could have a few children playing in the photo of the street? The lady we're sending it to would know the children and it would make it more interesting for her. My son and his friend are eleven, they spend their spare time in the gutter playing ollies, we could easily include them. And my daughter and her friend, Mrs Parry's daughter Dolly, could be playing with a skipping rope.'

Will Conley's laughter was hearty. 'You wouldn't like a job, Mrs Spencer, would you? I could do with an assistant with a bit of imagination.'

Kate's hand went to her throat. 'Have I been too forward, trying to teach you your job?'

'Not at all! I think your suggestion would be fine. Where are the children now?'

'They won't be far away. I told them to stay near, but didn't tell them why. Shall I go and bring them in?'

'No, I'll come out with you, to get a feel of the street.' His eyes widened in surprise when Kate took her shoe off and banged on the wall. And he roared with laughter when she said, 'That's to let me mate know we're ready. The Indians had smoke signals and drums, but we manage very well with a shoe.'

The next hour was very exciting and pleasant for the four women and children. Kate was afraid Billy would want to show off and sit up and look at the camera, instead of pose with head down and finger out to strike the ollie. Pete thought it was like being in a film, and he did everything he was told to do without a murmur. They were in the gutter outside the Spencers' house, and Nancy and Dolly were a little higher up the street with their skipping ropes. There weren't many neighbours out with it being quite early, but when Will took the photograph, there were two women walking down, one walking up, and lower down a man walking a dog. Will said he was very pleased with the shot. The four friends weren't outside, of course, they were watching through Monica's window.

'Where do you want the other one taking?' Will asked. 'Outside the house directly opposite?'

'No, that's my house,' Maggie said. 'Miss Parkinson's is the one next to mine, on the right. But it looks so different to when she lived there, 'cos there's no curtains at the window.'

Will had enjoyed his hour here, and he wanted to help. 'I can always touch it up, if you'd like me to?'

'How d'yer mean, lad, touch it up?' Winnie asked.

'Well, I can't make it exactly as she had it with curtains and nets, but as yer really don't see the draw curtains from outside, I can make it look as though there are nets up.'

'That would be wonderful if you could,' Kate told him. 'She'll have happy memories of that little house, and I'd hate her to be sad about how it looks now.'

'Let's go over and you can tell me where you want to stand. And because of your reasons for wanting the photographs, I will only charge you seven and six for each. That's fifteen shillings for the two.'

As they crossed the cobbles, Kate pulled on Monica's arm. 'I wonder what he'd charge for copies? I'd love one of each, how about you?'

'Ooh, yeah! Especially the one with Dolly on. I'd frame it and stand it on the sideboard, so when she grows older, she'll be able to look back and see what she was like as a kid.'

'Well, I've done my share today, sunshine, so you can take it from here. Ask him nicely how much he'd charge for copies.'

'I heard that, queen,' Winnie said in a low voice. 'Count me in.'

But in the end it was Kate who asked. Will had just taken a photograph of the four women standing between Maggie's house and the empty one, making sure he got all of Miss Parkinson's house in, and as Kate was nearest to him it was to her he spoke. 'I hope you'll be pleased with the end result, Mrs Spencer, I'm pretty sure you will be. It will take a few days to develop them, and I'll drop them off to you when I'm in the area.'

A little nervously, she asked, 'Do I pay yer now or when yer bring the photographs?'

'Never pay in advance for anything, Mrs Spencer. You pay when you and your friends have looked at and approve them.'

'Well, me and me friends were wondering how much yer charge for extra prints? Yer see, we'd all like one of each, on top of the ones for Miss Parkinson.'

'That would make another eight prints.' Will Conley looked doubtful. The photographs he took weren't like the ones taken by an ordinary Brownie camera, they were six by eight and on good quality paper. 'That's a lot of prints, Mrs Spencer.'

'Look, instead of haggling, and pussyfooting about, why don't we tell the man what we can afford?' Monica faced him. 'Ye're charging fifteen bob for the two we asked for, and that is less than yer usually charge for which we're grateful. Altogether we've got thirty shillings, so how far would that go towards the extra prints?'

'That would cover them, Mrs Parry. Expenses, everything.'

Even if he wasn't going to make very much on the deal, the smiles on the women's faces more than made up for it. But there was one little matter he must put straight to ease his conscience. 'Mrs Parry, don't you think we should tell Mrs Spencer that I had knocked on your door first, and you said not to tell her that, 'cos it was a little joke yer were playing on her?' He grinned into Kate's surprised face. 'I knew you weren't Mrs Parry, and if the joke fell flat, I don't want to get the blame for it.'

Kate looked at her friend and shook her head. 'Yer'll get me hung one of these days, you will, with yer little jokes. But I suppose it was me own fault so I'll let yer off. And you, Mr Conley, I'll let you off, too. It's not your fault I've got a holy terror for a mate.'

Will grinned. 'So when you open the door to me, in a few days' time, you won't have a bucket of water in your hand to throw over me?'

'I don't play tricks like that on people. Yer see, I wouldn't think it was funny.'

'I'd think it was hilarious,' Monica chuckled. 'Mind you, I wouldn't do that to someone like yerself who's over six foot, I'd pick on a little 'un like Winnie, here.'

'Oh, aye, well, yer might find yer'd picked on more than yer bargained for.' Winnie quivered, putting those watching in mind of a bird ruffling its feathers. 'I may be little but I make up for it in other ways.'

'I can vouch for that,' Maggie said. 'I've seen Winnie standing up to a woman twice her size, and coming off best.'

Will put the strap of his camera bag over his shoulder, saying, 'I'm on my way, before Winnie wants to prove she can lick a six-footer. Being tall doesn't make you a hero.' He smiled at each of the ladies. 'I'll see you in a few days' time. Goodbye until then.'

'What a nice man,' Maggie said. 'A real gent if ever I saw one.'

'I agree,' Kate said. 'A really nice bloke. And we're getting all those pictures for the exact money we got for the bed.'

'Hang about a bit, missus, where do I come into this?' Monica asked. 'I'm the one what got him to give us them cheap. So don't yer be taking all the praise, Mrs Parry!'

'I'll kill yer for that, sunshine, 'cos yer made a fool of me. I told him when I let him in that I wasn't Mrs Parry, and the poor man must have felt awful pretending he didn't know.' But Kate couldn't keep her feeling of joy back any longer. Lifting her skirt, she began to hum a tune as she danced an Irish jig. She was joined first by Winnie, who felt as happy as she did after six milk stouts, and then Monica lifted her skirts and knees, and because she didn't know any Irish songs that you could jig to, she decided that 'When Father Painted The Parlour, Yer Couldn't See Pa For Paint' was as good as any.

Maggie wasn't as outgoing as her three neighbours, but now she said to herself as she lifted her skirts, 'If yer can't lick 'em, join 'em!'

Chapter Twenty-Five

It was on the Thursday morning that Will Conley called to Kate's house with the photographs. They were in a large buff envelope, and as he handed it over, he said, 'I hope you and your friends will be pleased.'

'Ooh, I'm so excited!' Kate was like a schoolgirl who had been offered a treat. 'But I don't want to take them out of the envelope yet, not until all me friends are here.' She laid the envelope down on the table as carefully as if it contained the crown jewels. Then, much to Will's amusement, she took off her shoe and banged on the wall. She waited three seconds and then banged again. She grinned as she bent to put her shoe back on. 'One knock means when you're ready, two knocks mean it's important, so I'll open the door for Monica.'

Monica came dashing in, still with her pinny tied around her waist. She groaned aloud when she saw Will. 'Why didn't yer tell me yer had company? Look at the flipping sight of me!'

'How can I tell yer that with a shoe? Anyway, take yer pinny off and nip down for Winnie while I fetch Maggie. And don't stand gabbing, I'm dying to see the photographs.'

Monica saluted. 'Yes, boss, all right, boss, three bags full, boss.' With that she took to her heels to deliver the message.

Kate had her foot on the step when Maggie's door opened. As she closed it behind her, she explained, 'I saw him knocking at yer door, love, so I thought I'd save yer a journey and yer shoe leather.'

Five minutes later the four women were standing at the table looking down at the envelope while Will sat with his fingers crossed that they wouldn't be disappointed. He didn't think they would be because he was pleased with the way the photographs had turned out.

'Well, are we going to stand here all morning looking at the bleeding envelope?' Monica tutted. 'It's your house, girl, and it's your table, so open it up! It won't bite yer! And be quick, before we all die of curiosity.'

'Don't you dare die in my house, Monica Parry, I won't have it. If yer think ye're going to peg out, have a little consideration for me and go outside to do it.'

Winnie got tired of waiting and picked up the envelope. 'Just in case she does, I think she should be allowed to see the photies first. Yer know what I mean, like, queen, we'd be granting her her last wish.' With that the envelope was tipped up and there was a flurry of photographs. Then came the jostling as hands reached out to claim two each.

'Oh, my God, look at our street!' Winnie was amazed. 'It's just like it is, I'd know it anywhere.'

This brought a titter. 'Well, yer'd have something to say if it looked like County Road, wouldn't yer, sunshine?' Kate's eyes were taking in her daughter and son, and she felt a swell of pride. 'Isn't it wonderful what a camera can do? Oh, I'll have to get this framed and stand it where it can be seen.'

'Or hang it on the wall, queen, that's a good place.' Winnie was holding a print in each hand. 'Wait until Miss Parkinson sees them, she'll be really pleased.'

'Yes, the only thing that mars the one of her house is the four ugly buggers standing near it.' Maggie didn't really think that, she thought she came out very well. Just wait until her husband saw it, he'd be flabbergasted. 'And yer did well with the windows, lad, yer really would think there was nets up. How did yer manage that?'

'Trick of the trade,' Will said, very happy with the reaction of the ladies. 'And I think all four of you look very attractive and glamorous.'

'There yer are,' Monica said, nodding her head at Kate. 'I told yer he was a gent, didn't I? And he's proved it by making us look like film stars.'

'I dunno, the one on the end looks like King Kong.' Winnie put her eyes close to the photograph, then pretended to be shocked with an exaggerated backward stagger. 'It's me! I can tell by me dress! What have yer done to me, lad?'

Monica went one better. 'I don't know what you're moaning about, look at me! He's given me a moustache and beard!'

Kate looked across to Will, who seemed content and pleased with himself. 'I've got to say yer've done a really good job, and as yer can tell, me and me mates are more than satisfied. We've never had our photograph taken before so we'll be spending the next half hour going over every detail. So would yer like a cup of tea while ye're waiting, or are yer rushing off to another job? If ye're in a hurry, I can pay yer now, save yer waiting.'

'I'm all right for half an hour, and I'd love that cup of tea you kindly offered.' Will was experiencing a feeling of peace and wellbeing. It wasn't often his clients were as entertaining and humorous as these ladies. His next assignment was a large warehouse on the Dock Road. He wouldn't get much of a laugh out of bricks and mortar.

'If I made you a cup of tea and left me mates out, there'd be holy murder and the air would be blue. But as I'm not well off for decent cups and saucers, I'm going to have to ask me neighbour and best mate if she'll help me out. Go on, Monica, be an angel and nip home for some. Oh, and will yer bring some milk with yer, please?'

'Well, I'll be blowed! How's that for cheek? If I want a cup of tea I've got to bring me own cup! Oh, and milk! I don't suppose yer'd like me to bring sugar as well, would yer?'

Kate grinned. 'No, I'm all right for sugar, sunshine, but it was thoughtful of yer to ask. A plate of biscuits would be very welcome, though.'

'Ooh, that's nice,' Winnie said, pulling out a chair and sitting down. 'I'm glad yer came, lad, 'cos now we can have a little tea party. And yer deserve it, 'cos there's few people round here ever had their photie took, and you've done a real good job.'

The other women voiced their agreement, then Monica made off to pick out any cups she could find with a handle and free from chips and cracks plus whatever biscuits she could rustle up. She'd be lucky if she could find any biscuits in one piece, 'cos she usually bought broken ones from the corner shop. Still, she might find the odd one, and she'd make sure it went on the bloke's saucer before the women started to help themselves.

Five minutes later, Monica stepped down on to the pavement with two cups and saucers in one hand, and a plate of mixed broken biscuits in the other. Then she looked at the open door and wondered how she was going to close it. Help arrived in the shape of Sergeant Bridgewater. He hurried across the cobbles after seeing her dilemma, and was about to relieve her of the plate of biscuits when she said, 'Close the door for us, please, and I'll carry these. What brings yer down here anyway?'

'The trial was yesterday and I did promise to let you know the outcome.'

'Oh, yeah, I'd forgotten about that. Don't tell me yet, come in next door. All my friends are there and we can hear it together.'

There was a loud babble of voices as they walked into the living room but it died down when they saw who Monica had brought in with her. 'Look who I found,' she said, handing over the crockery to Kate. 'And finders are keepers, so keep yer hands off.'

'Hello, Sergeant.' Kate's eyes darted around the room. 'I know me place looks untidy, but it's only because half the street are here.'

Geoff Bridgewater chuckled when he heard the loud objections. 'I believe the lovely ladies enhance the room. But I forget my manners, I see we have a gentleman in the company too.'

When Kate introduced the two men, Will jumped to his feet, an act noted by the women who were to say later that it was a pity all men, including their own, weren't so hot on good manners.

When the officer was seated, Kate handed him one of each of the photographs. 'These were taken by Mr Conley, and we'll be sending them to Miss Parkinson in the next day or two. Haven't they come out well?'

'Excellent! She will be delighted, I'm sure. And when you write, you can tell her how the court case ended. That's what I came to tell you, as I promised.'

'Don't tell us yet, wait until the tea's poured out. It's been made for a while, and it'll be stiff if we don't drink it now.' She jerked her head at Monica, and as the two women walked into the kitchen, everyone heard her saying, 'I hope yer've brought two cups with handles and no chips.'

The loudest laugh came from the sergeant who, when handed a cup and saucer, said, 'All present and accounted for. One handle and no cracks or chips.'

'It's a good job I'm not proud,' Kate said. 'When yer've got two youngsters in the house, yer can't expect things to last forever.'

'I'm surprised yer didn't get two out of the set Miss Parkinson gave yer, queen,' Winnie said. 'Then yer could have been really proud.'

'Not on your life! If any got broken I'd never forgive meself.'

'I'd have given yer one to make it up, 'cos I haven't anyone to hand mine down to. Not like you and Monica. And you, of course, Maggie.'

'I wouldn't have let yer use yours, sunshine! She was a good friend of yours, and I know yer'll treasure them. And one day, someone may come into yer life that yer'll grow fond of, and yer'll be glad yer didn't give them away.' Kate took a deep breath, blew out, and said, 'Well, I can't help it if I'm soft-hearted, can

I? Anyway, Sergeant, I know yer haven't got all day to sit listening to nattering women, so d'yer want to tell us what happened in court? And by the way, Mr Conley will know what ye're talking about because I told him what had happened.'

'Well,' the officer put his saucer down on the table, 'you'll be glad to know that Richard Willis is today beginning a six-year sentence in Walton Jail.'

'Ooh, er, did he get six years?' Kate, like her friends, was surprised. 'I didn't think he'd get that long, more like two.'

The officer nodded his head. 'He would have been sent down for two or three years if Miss Parkinson had been his only victim. But in the other house, where the rest of the jewellery was taken from, he used force on the occupants. They are an elderly couple who happened to come home from a shopping trip while Tricky Dicky was in their house, ransacking the place. The husband tried to stop him, but at his age didn't stand a chance against a much younger man who was desperate not to be caught. The old man received a punch which knocked him to the floor where his head caught the edge of the fireplace. The wife started screaming, hoping to alert the neighbours, but she was pushed with some force on to the sofa while Mr Willis made off with his haul. And it was some haul – the items were worth several hundred pounds each. It was thanks to you that everything he stole from the old couple was returned to them, but that made little difference to the judge. Because of the force used, and the physical and mental suffering of the victims, Willis was sentenced to six years with the recommendation he serve the full term, without any time off for good behaviour. So, fortunately, Tricky Dicky will be out of action for that time. And I hope it will teach him that crime doesn't pay.'

'Oh, I am glad,' Maggie said. 'That should learn him a lesson.'

'I hope he doesn't have a cushy time in there because he deserves to suffer.' Winnie was thinking of her old friend. 'If it hadn't been for him, Miss Parkinson would still be living in that house across the way. The swine might not have got away with any of her belongings, but he'd taken away her peace of mind and the pleasure she got out of her little house. If it was up to me, I'd have hung, drawn and quartered him.'

'When you write to Miss Parkinson, will you please send my kindest regards?' The sergeant was mindful that he was on duty, and although he would be happy to spend an hour or two in the company of these friendly, happy women, he really should be back at the station doing the job he was paid to do. 'And I wish her every happiness in her new home.'

'I will,' Kate promised. 'And I'll tell her how kind yer've been in keeping us informed about the trial. I won't say too much about it, though, in case it brings it all back and upsets her.'

Will stood up, running two fingers down the creases in his trousers. 'I'll leave with the officer because I don't want to be late for my next appointment. But it has been a pleasure meeting you, and I hope our paths cross again some time.' He took out a business card from the pocket of his waistcoat and handed it to Kate. 'In case you ever need me again, you can contact me on that telephone number.'

'I'll make sure that Kate mentions you as well, lad,' Winnie said, with a determined nod of her head because she'd taken a liking to the young man. 'And she'll tell our friend how yer went out of yer way to make sure the photies turned out well, just for her.'

Kate saw the two men to the door. When she came back into the living room it was to find her three neighbours seated at the table conducting a lively conversation. 'I hope you lot are not making yerselves too comfortable, 'cos I've got work to do!'

'Trust you to want to put a damper on things.' Monica's eyes rolled to the ceiling to show her mate how disgusted she was. 'This has been the most exciting morning we've had since we came to live in the street. We'll probably never again have two important visitors like we've just had so let's make the most of it. Try to relax, for God's sake, girl, and sit down and have another' cup of tea.'

Kate put her hand to the teapot. 'We can't have another because it's gone cold. And I can't stand cold tea.'

'Me neither, queen, I can't stomach it.' Winnie pushed her chair back. 'That's why I put the kettle on while yer were showing the men out. It should be about boiled now, and there's still a few broken biscuits left. So while I see to it, you sit yerself down and take the weight off yer feet. After all, queen, it is your house.'

'I was beginning to wonder!' Kate looked at the photographs spread across the table and said, 'Yeah, to hell with the work. If it doesn't get done today, there's always tomorrow. And it has been an exciting morning, hasn't it? I'm surprised neither of the kids has been in, they must have seen Will and the officer coming up the street. I mean, yer could hardly miss them, they'd stick out a mile. There's no men in this street wear a policeman's uniform or carry a big camera bag over their shoulder.'

'Ah, well, yer see, girl, that will be because when I went home to fetch the cups and saucers, I told the kids to make themselves scarce until we called them in.' Monica spread her open hands. 'It would have been like bedlam with them in here. The men couldn't have had a cup of tea in peace, and the photographs would have been ruined with dirty fingermarks all over them. So let's have just a little time on our own to talk over events and have another look at the photographs, eh? Indulge ourselves for once. Then I'll give the kids a shout.'

'Okay, yer talked me into it.'

Monica grinned. 'That's the style, girl, that's the spirit!'

Kate bit on the inside of her bottom lip to keep a smile back. 'There's just one thing, though, sunshine.'

'What's that, girl?'

'Next time, can we have the style and the spirit in your house, please?'

* * *

ꞌJohn walked up the street on his way home from work with his jacket draped over his arm. It had been like an oven in work today, and he felt drained. But at the sight of his daughter and son bounding towards him, their faces aglow, he forgot some of his weariness.

'You two look very pleased with yerselves, have yer lost a ha'penny and found a tanner?'

Billy, hands and knees filthy with kneeling in the gutter, couldn't get the words out quick enough. 'Yer should see the photies, Dad, they're smashing. Me and Pete playing ollies, and yer can tell it's us.'

'And what about you, Nancy, are you pleased?'

'Oh, not half, Dad, they're great. Me and Dolly were standing up, pretending to be skipping, so yer can see all of us. Me mam said she'll let me take it in to school after the holidays, to show the teacher and me friends.'

'I'll look forward to seeing them, if they're so good.'

'We'll be famous, won't we, Dad?' Billy was walking backwards so he could see his father's face. 'I don't mean like film stars, but there's not many people round here got themselves on a big photo. And they are big, Dad, not fiddling little things. They're whoppers, aren't they, Nancy?'

'That's not half an exaggeration, even for you, Billy! Take no notice of him, Dad, they're not whoppers. They're not small, like, but don't expect to see photos the size of the *Echo*.'

'Has Pete seen himself?'

'Yeah, and he's not half swanking about it. He wanted to take it to show his mam, but my mam wouldn't let him in case it got dirty. Like she said, if anything happens to the photographs we'll never get any more 'cos they cost too much money. But she's promised to take it round to Pete's tonight, so his family can see it.'

Kate was waiting on the step. 'I suppose he's told yer? If he hasn't, yer'll be the only one in the street 'cos he's told everyone' else. Even those what weren't interested and didn't want to know, he followed them to their houses and told them anyway!' She stepped back into the living room and held up her face for a kiss. 'Mind you, I'm delighted meself, and I think you will be too!' Then her eyes narrowed when she noticed how worn out her husband seemed. 'Yer look all in, sunshine, do yer feel all right?'

'I'll feel a bit better when I've had a swill. It was so hot by those machines today, I've been sweating like no one's business. All the men were complaining but there's little the manager could do, bar open the doors, which he did. When the sweat's running off yer all day, it's bound to make yer feel weak. I'll be fine when I've washed meself down.'

After raising a finger, and giving them a look that told the children to be quiet, Kate followed John into the kitchen. She was concerned for him, he did look drained. 'Shall I boil yer some water to get washed, sunshine?'

'No, love, cold water should do the trick. And tomorrow, I don't care what yer say, I am not going to wear a vest under me shirt.'

'I don't blame yer, in this weather. But as soon as it turns cold, the vest is going back on. I don't want you laid up with pneumonia.'

John felt a little refreshed as he sat down for his meal of mashed potato with liver and onions though he still felt weary and promised himself a very early night in bed. But right now he could sense the impatience and excitement of his children as they sat restlessly at the table. No matter how lousy he felt, he could never disappoint them. Heaven knows, it wasn't often they had something so exciting and unusual happen to them. They were probably the envy of every child in the street. 'This smells nice, love, I'm going to enjoy it. But can't I see these famous photographs first? I don't want to be shovelling me food down in me haste to feast me eyes on them.'

Billy swivelled on his chair, ready to dash to the sideboard, but Nancy held him back by the collar of his shirt. 'Oh, no, yer don't! It's my turn to do a little bragging. Anyway, I'm the eldest and I should go first.'

Billy looked put out. 'Being the eldest doesn't give yer the right to be first. That means I'll always be last, and that's not fair. Tell her, Mam, that's not fair.'

'To keep yer both quiet, and to be fair, I'll get the photographs and give yer one each to show yer dad.' Kate opened the sideboard cupboard and took out the envelope. 'But I really think the two of yer should have more sense now, ye're not little kids any more.'

'Ah, we don't argue much, Mam,' Nancy said. 'Our Billy's nice to me more often than he's horrid.'

Billy didn't have an answer for that because he didn't know whether it was a compliment or not. So for once he bit on his tongue, and when his mother handed him a photo, he didn't forget to thank her. And he was glad he'd kept his mouth shut when his sister said, 'Let him give them both to me dad, otherwise our dinners are going to be cold.'

'They're a good size, aren't they?' John was pleasantly surprised, he hadn't expected anything so professional. And his heart skipped a beat when he saw his wife's lovely face. 'You've come out very well, love, and so have yer mates. You're the best-looking, though.'

'Right this minute, I bet Tom is telling Monica exactly the same thing,' Kate said. 'Yer know the old saying about beauty being in the eye of the beholder.'

'I know, love, beauty comes in all different forms. Someone can have a wonderful personality, have the ability to make you laugh or have a marvellous caring nature. In the eyes of the person who falls in love with them, they will be beautiful.'

While Nancy thought that what her dad said was really nice and romantic, it was all going over Billy's head. Why were they gabbing about nothing in particular instead of looking at the other photo, which he thought was the best and most important?

John didn't disappoint either of his children. And he didn't have to pretend to be pleased, because he really was. Looking down at the street he lived in, and seeing his two children playing in that street, well, it was something he would never have dreamed of happening. 'I can honestly say I didn't expect anything like this, they really are very good. I know they cost thirty bob but it was cheap at the price.'

Billy couldn't sit still any longer. He rounded the table to kneel down at the side of his dad's chair. 'Look, there's me finger ready to flick the ollie! It looks dead real, doesn't it, Dad? And there, yer can even see the tear in Pete's trousers!'

'I've got a feeling Pete's mam won't be as happy as we are about that photo. I only hope she's got a better sense of humour than I think she has. Otherwise when I knock on her door tonight, she might clock me one. Still, I'll have Monica with me for support, so it's two against one. Or one and a half against one, 'cos I'm no good when it comes to trouble,' Kate said.

'Pete's mam is all right, she'll be made up,' Billy said. 'She knew he had a tear in his trousers, she told me. But his only other pair were in the wash.'

'Okay, that's enough for now, get back to yer seat,' Kate said. 'The dinner is probably not fit to eat now, but it's a case of Hobson's choice 'cos I've nowt else.'

John put the photographs back in the envelope. 'Are yer going out with Monica tonight, then, love?'

'Yeah, just to get a bit of fresh air. After calling at Pete's, we're going to the Blackmores'. We haven't seen Betty for a while, she'll think we've fallen out with her.'

'But they only live four doors away, down the back entry, yer'll not get much fresh air.'

'We won't go down the entry, we'll walk to the main road, do a bit of window shopping, then call at the Blackmores'. It's not far, but it's a break.' Kate could see her husband's appetite wasn't up to par. Usually he tucked in with gusto but tonight he seemed to be eating just for the sake of it. 'If yer don't feel well, I won't go out, love. It's not important, I'd just as well stay in.'

'Mam, yer haven't told me dad about the policeman coming,' Nancy said. 'Had yer forgotten about that?'

'No, I hadn't, sunshine, but I was going to wait until after we'd eaten, otherwise I might as well have emptied these plates in the midden. I'll tell him later, I won't bother going out.'

'There's no need to stay in for me, love, you go out with Monica. I've made up me mind to go to bed very early and I'll be fine after a good night's sleep.'

'I'll stay in with yer!' If her beloved husband wasn't feeling well, then Kate wasn't going over the door. 'I've got a bit of darning and sewing to do anyway.'

'There's nothing wrong with me, love, I'm just tired with working in the heat. I'm not the only one, I bet every bloke that works in a factory feels the same but I'll be right as rain in the morning.' John smiled at her. 'I'll see the children to bed, then hit the sack. So you keep yer promise and go out with yer mate.'

'I'll make sure I'm back for nine to see to the kids.' Kate didn't want to upset him by insisting she stayed in, but she certainly wouldn't be away for long. 'Then I might darn a sock before turning in meself. I'll try not to wake yer if ye're asleep, I'll be as quiet as a mouse. And I'll tell yer all about Sergeant Bridgewater tomorrow, when we're having our breakfast.'

Pete's mother was over the moon. She brought her husband to the door to see the photograph. 'By, it's a treat, that is. Never seen nothing like it, except in books they have in the library.'

'I would have got a copy for yer, but they're so dear, I didn't like to ask yer. We only got them done to send to Miss Parkinson, and we sold something to raise the money.'

Elsie Reynolds was as pleased as Punch, and her husband, Vincent, looked as though he'd come up on the pools. 'If the chance does come, and yer see the feller again, we'd like a copy. It would be nice to look back on when we get older. And Pete, of course. The only time he's stopped talking about it is when he's eating his dinner or sucking a bull's eye.'

'If I ever see the photographer again, I will ask, I promise.' Kate began to step back. 'And when I've got the money to have it framed, if ever, I'll let yer see it again. So ta-ra for now, Elsie, you and Vincent go back to listening to the wireless.'

'Yer might not believe it, looking at us now, girl, but me and Vincent were two of the best jazzers in Liverpool. Out every night dancing, we were. And the toes were tapping when you knocked, 'cos Ray Noble and his orchestra are on, with Al Bowlly singing. And I'd swap that for a roast dinner any day.'

'Oh, er, am I missing that?' Monica shook her head from side to side. 'Al Bowlly is me favourite singer. I've told my feller I'd leave him any day if Al Bowlly asked me to.'

'Take no notice, she's got a smashing husband.' Kate took a firm grip on her friend's arm and was about to pull her away when, on impulse, she looked up at Elsie and handed her the envelope. 'Yer can hang on to this until tomorrow so yer can have a good look at it in peace. Pete as well, as long as he washes his hands first. I'll call for it in the morning.'

'Thanks, girl, that's the gear!' Elsie was delighted. 'And yer can rest assured that no harm will come to it.'

Monica waited until they were several houses away before asking, 'What did yer do that for? What if they bend it and spoil the bleeding thing? Anyway, I thought yer wanted to show it to Betty and the family.'

'No, they won't! If the boot was on the other foot, I expect

371

Elsie would do the same. I'll show it to the Blackmores another day, so stop yer fussing.'

They turned into the main road, spent a few minutes gazing into the windows of a block of shops, then set off up the next street for the Blackmores' house. 'I hope Betty doesn't mind us dropping in unannounced, they might be busy doing something. We should really have let them know we were coming.'

'Don't be daft, Betty's not like that! She'll be pleased to see us.'

And Monica was right for Betty's face lit up and she welcomed them with open arms. 'I was beginning to think yer'd fallen out with us. Come on in and tell us what yer've been up to since I last saw yer.'

In the living room, Margaret and Greg were sitting next to each other on the couch, humming along to Ray Noble and his orchestra, while Jack's head could be seen over the *Echo* as he relaxed in his favourite fireside chair. 'Put that wireless off now, Greg,' Betty said, 'we've got company.'

'Don't put it off, lad.' Monica's shoulders were swaying to the strains of a waltz. 'It takes me back to the Grafton on a Saturday night, that does. When I was single and as free as a bird. I had half a dozen partners to choose from, but I was a love 'em and leave 'em, good-time girl until I met my feller.'

Jack folded his newspaper and stuffed it down the side of his chair. 'Lower it a bit, son, and we'll all be happy. Monica can dream away to her heart's content and we'll be able to hear ourselves talk.'

When Greg moved, Margaret got to her feet and waved the visitors to the couch. 'Sit here and me and Greg will sit at the table.'

'Oh, this is dead romantic, this is.' Monica grabbed Kate around the waist and lifted her arm to dance her around the room singing along with Al Bowlly, 'The Very Thought Of You'.

Much to the amusement of the audience, Kate tried to pull away. 'Let go of me, yer daft nit, people will think we're crazy.'

'Listen to me, girl,' Monica said, not flinching when she banged one hip against the table and the other against the sideboard. 'I've known the Blackmores long enough for them to know I am crazy. But if they don't mind, why should I worry?'

'Now, you listen to me, sunshine! I don't care that the Blackmores know ye're crazy, I don't want them to think it's rubbed off on me.'

The music came to an end, and Kate fell on to the couch. 'Do us all a favour, Greg, and put the wireless off altogether. She'll never sit still while she can hear dance music.'

Monica sat down beside her. 'Will yer tell me something, girl, honestly?'

'I don't tell lies, sunshine, unless it's to stop someone from getting hurt, so of course I'll be honest.'

'Right! Well, I was just wondering whether yer were always this miserable? Yer know, did yer cry a lot as a baby?'

Kate joined in with the laughter. 'Me ma used to say the only time I stopped crying was when she stuck a dummy in me mouth.'

Monica nodded her head. 'That explains why yer've got a thick bottom lip then. It happens to babies that always have a dummy in their mouth.'

'I'm going to agree with everything yer say, sunshine, otherwise Betty is never going to hear what we've been doing with ourselves.'

'Yeah, what have yer been doing? Anything exciting?'

'Well, yer know Miss Parkinson moved, don't yer? I think the whole neighbourhood was upset over that, 'cos she was well liked.'

'I was more than upset,' Jack said. 'I was bloody mad! If I could have got me hands on the bloke that broke into her house, I'd have flayed him alive.'

'I'd have helped yer, 'cos I believe she was really old.' Greg looked as though he meant it. 'My grandma is eighty and I'd go mad if that happened to her.'

'Yer'll all be happy to know, then, that the blighter got his comeuppance. The police officer came to tell us today that the thief was sentenced to six years in Walton Jail.' There was complete silence in the room while Kate's words sank in. Then it was as though everyone was rubbing their hands with glee that the burglar had got his just deserts. 'I'm writing to Miss Parkinson tomorrow to tell her.'

Kate looked sideways to where Monica was sitting. 'That's my bit of news, now you can tell them about the photographs. But don't make a meal of it, 'cos yer know I don't want to be out too long with John being off colour.'

While Kate was listening, she told herself her friend had lost her vocation. She should have been an actress. She didn't just tell them about Will, she acted it all out with her hands and dramatic pauses in her speech, eyes wide and rolling. She had them all sitting forward hanging on her every word. Not many people could do that when all they were talking about was a bloke taking a few pictures.

'Why didn't yer bring them with yer?' Betty asked. 'We'd love to see them.'

Before Monica put the blame on her, Kate said, 'I'll bring them down tomorrow. It's been such a hectic day, I don't know if I'm coming or going.'

'If it had been six months later, me and Margaret might have gone after that house,' Greg told them. 'I'll be out of me time then, and could afford it.'

'Ye're all right here for the next year.' Betty sounded adamant. 'We're managing nicely, and I can give Margaret a hand with the baby.'

Betty wasn't telling the whole truth. The reason she wanted her daughter near her was to protect her from the gossips. There was already talk in the street and it would get worse as the girl began to show. Several near neighbours, women she regarded as friends, had been asking questions, and there were sly looks in their eyes when they said, 'Fancy Margaret getting married in such a hurry.' Or, 'I'm surprised Margaret didn't get married in church.' She had answered all of their questions with the same words. The young couple wanted to get married but couldn't afford a big white wedding. And if the gossip-mongers who thrived on other people's misfortunes didn't like or believe what she told them, then it was just their bad luck. She didn't care what they said behind her back, but she did care about her daughter being hurt. That's why she wanted her and Greg to stay where they were until the child was a few months old and Margaret could manage the baby without worrying about unkind taunts.

'Yeah, you stay with yer mam, sunshine,' Kate said. 'Make the most of it and let her spoil yer. Once yer get yer own place yer'll have to manage on yer own, and believe me, it's no picnic with a young baby to look after.'

'I'll help her as much as I can.' Greg smiled across at his young wife. 'I know I'll be at work all day, but I'll be the one getting up in the night if the baby cries so she can have a good night's sleep.'

'Ah, now, there speaks a man in a million.' Monica slapped him on the back and nearly knocked him off the chair. 'I'll be telling my feller about you, and asking where he was when our Dolly used to be screaming for a feed every couple of hours through the night.'

'Talking about husbands, mine didn't look too good tonight.' Kate pushed her chair back, knowing if she didn't make an effort her mate would keep them here for another hour. 'So I'll be making tracks.'

'I think I'll slip me coat on and walk to the bottom with yer,' Betty said. 'Just for a breath of fresh air.'

And as the three women walked down the street, Betty poured

her heart out. She couldn't do it at home because it would upset her daughter, Jack and Greg. But with a sympathetic friend either side of her, she got it all off her chest and felt so much better for it.

'Betty, they're not worth bothering about, sunshine, they're really not.' Kate felt heartily sorry for the woman. 'They have so little happening in their own lives, they have to pick on someone else.'

'Kate's right,' Monica said. 'If they say anything, tell them to sod off and attend to their own business. They should have more to do than stand around being nosy. If I hear anyone say a dickie bird about Margaret, they'll be sorry they opened their mouths. Yer've got enough friends around yer, girl, so don't worry yer head about the no-marks.'

'Yeah, ye're right, both of yer.' Betty took a deep breath, and when she blew out slowly, she felt as though she was blowing all her fears away. 'I feel better after talking to you two. I'm glad yer came. But how's Winnie? I haven't seen her for a while, either.'

'She's fine. She's been with us all day, but me and Monica didn't think about coming to see you until she'd gone home. Otherwise she'd have been with us now.'

'Bring her with yer next time yer come, she's such a good laugh. Margaret and the two men thought she was so funny, they talked about nothing else but her the day after the wedding.'

'She is funny,' Kate agreed. 'But she's more than that, she's a little love.'

Monica nodded. 'I'll second that, girl, she is definitely one little love.'

Chapter Twenty-Six

'This time next week yer'll be sitting in yer classroom.' Kate eyed her children as she put the tea cosy over the pot. 'I suppose yer'll be glad to get back to school after nearly seven weeks with nothing to do. I think the holiday is far too long, they should make it a couple of weeks shorter in the summer, and extra at Christmas.'

'I won't be glad to go back,' said Billy, thinking any kid that liked going to school wanted his brains testing. 'I'll be going in the seniors, and the teachers there are very strict.'

'They'd have to be if all the boys are like you,' Nancy told him. 'I wouldn't have their job for a big clock.'

'Yes, yer'll have to work harder, son.' Kate smiled as she gazed into the face that was so like his father's. He was John all over, only a miniature version. 'Yer need good end of term reports from now on, to help when yer leave school and are looking for a job. Employers are more likely to take yer on if yer have decent reports and a good end of school reference.'

'Blimey, Mam! I've got a couple of years to go yet. I'll be well good by then.'

'Only if yer knuckle down to it and work hard. An hour's homework every night would help. It would do yer more good than kneeling in the gutter playing ollies with yer backside stuck up in the air, yer knees filthy and yer face as black as the hobs of hell.'

Billy gave his mother a sly glance. 'It's not that long ago that you and me dad were telling me to enjoy me childhood 'cos it wouldn't last forever. And now yer've got me going out looking for a job!'

'I'll help yer, Billy,' Nancy said. 'I'll give yer a hand with yer homework every night for about half an hour.'

Her brother grinned and rubbed his hands together. 'Thanks, our kid! You can do me homework for me, and no one will be any the wiser.'

'Only yer brain, soft lad! It's no good me knowing the answers when it's you the teacher will be firing questions at. I said I'll help, I didn't say I'd do the work for yer. What good would it do if yer knew the answer to a sum, but didn't know how yer got it? The teacher would soon twig, and then yer'd be for it.'

'Yeah, I never thought of that.' His face doing contortions, Billy nodded. 'I couldn't very well tell the teacher to run along to your class to ask how I'd done it.'

Then Kate had an inspiration. Appeal to his pride, that was the way to give her son an incentive to try harder at school. It might just do the trick. 'If I were you, sunshine, I'd be ashamed to ask me sister to do me homework for me. My pride wouldn't let me, even if it meant getting me head down every night and slogging away instead of going out to play. Think how good yer'd feel if yer'd done it all by yerself?'

Billy's brow furrowed as he thought about what his mother had said. And she was right! If Pete or anyone in the class knew his sister was the brainy one and did his homework for him, he'd be tagged a cissy for the rest of his life. Of course Nancy was the brainy one, but that was only because she was two years older than him. He could catch up with her if he put his mind to it. 'I'll do me own homework, without any help.'

'Oh, I didn't mean yer shouldn't ask for any help, 'cos we all need help at some time, even Nancy. It would be only natural, if yer got stuck on some subject, to ask her to explain something yer didn't understand. There'd be no harm in that, it wouldn't be as if she was doing the homework for yer. Or yer could always ask me or yer dad.' Kate chuckled. 'Not that I'm very clever, I was nowhere near top of the class like Nancy is. In fact, if yer asked me a question, yer'd have to check the answer with someone else to make sure I was right. But I've got by, sunshine, and so will you if yer put yer mind to it.'

'It won't be long before the dark nights are here and yer won't be able to play out,' Nancy said, having a lot of sympathy for her brother, 'so if yer get homework every day, it'll give yer something to do.'

'I've made up me mind that I'm going to get stuck in so one of these days I'll be better than you are.' He gave her a playful push. 'And when I pass yer, I'll wave to show I'm not too bigheaded to say ye're me sister.'

'Don't get carried away, sunshine, because yer might find it harder than yer think,' Kate warned. 'Get some knowledge into that head of yours before yer start bragging. And I'm talking as one who knows. Yer see, the only thing I can remember from all those years of history lessons is that the Battle of Hastings was in 1066. Not much for nine years of schooling, is it?'

'Oh, go 'way, Mam, to hear yer talk, anyone would think yer were as thick as two short planks.' Nancy didn't like her mother to run herself down. 'And yer know as well as I do that ye're not thick.'

'No, I'm not thick, sunshine, but I'm not clever, either. And if I had me chance over again, I'd listen to the teachers more than I did, and take in what they were teaching me. But I've done three very clever things in me life, for which I give meself a pat on the back.'

Billy's eyes widened. 'What were they, Mam?'

'Was this while yer were at school, Mam?' Nancy asked.

'No, the first happened when I was nineteen. I met yer dad and fell in love with him. We got married when I was twenty-one and he was twenty-three, and we feel just the same about each other now as we did then. So it was clever of me to find yer dad, don't yer think?'

'Yeah, he's lovely, me dad.' Nancy gave a sigh of pleasure.

'I'm not half proud of him 'cos he's very handsome. And he's nice with it.'

'It was lucky for us that yer met me dad,' Billy agreed. 'Otherwise yer might have married someone who was miserable, and beat his children. A lot of the men in the street hit their kids, yer know, Mam, some with a leather strap. I wouldn't like yer to have married someone like that.'

'I wouldn't have done that, sunshine, 'cos I can't abide a violent man. And the next time I was clever, and very lucky, was when you were born, Nancy. Me and yer dad were so happy that day, we thought our hearts were going to burst.'

Billy sat quietly, listening and waiting. He had to come somewhere in this. Surely when he was born his mam and dad would have been just as happy, thinking their hearts were going to burst? They loved him very much, he knew that because they were always telling him. And Nancy of course, they didn't leave her out.

Kate could see how her son's mind was working, and wouldn't leave him in suspense. 'The last time I was clever was when you were born, Billy. You were what we were hoping for to make our family complete. They say a father always wants a son, and a woman wants a daughter, but that wasn't true in this house. We never made fish of one and flesh of the other. We love yer both equally, and always have. And while I said before I wasn't very clever at school, I think I've been very clever in the most important part of my life. That's making a lovely little family who I am very proud of.'

Nancy was moved to tears, Billy was moved to sniffing up. Well, boys didn't cry, did they? But he made a promise to himself that, when he was older, he would give his mother good reason to be proud of him.

'Right, that's it for now, let's clear the table, wash up and tidy the room. Mrs Cartwright and Auntie Monica will be here soon to go to the shops.' Kate began to stack the plates. 'There's two ha'pennies on the sideboard, one each. It's all I can spare, but if yer want to go to the park it's enough to buy lemonade powder with.'

Nancy gave her brother a dig. 'Come on, our Billy, help tidy up so the place looks all right for our mam's friends. Yer've got all day to go out and play, it won't hurt yer to move yerself and give a hand.'

Billy gave her a dig back. 'I was going to help without you asking, so mind yer own business.'

Kate popped her head around the kitchen door. 'Oh, ay, what's happened to my two children? Yer know, the ones I love the bones of? Have they gone out to play and left two strangers in their place?'

Billy looked sheepish. 'I was only acting the goat, Mam, honest! So was our Nancy, we didn't mean nothing, did we, Sis?'

'Not if you say so, our kid. Now take the cloth out to the yard and shake it. And shake yer leg while ye're about it. The sooner we're finished, the sooner me and Dolly can go to the park.'

'I'm surprised we haven't had an answer from Miss Parkinson by now to say she's received the photies.' Winnie shifted the weight of her basket to the crook of her other arm. 'It's not like Audrey, she's usually spot on with everything. She was very efficient, punctual to a minute always.'

'It'll take her a while to settle in, it's only been a couple of weeks,' Kate said. 'Don't forget, everything will be strange to her and it'll take time for her to adjust. But I bet we hear from her by the end of the week.'

'Are we finished shopping?' Monica asked. 'I'm dying for a drink, me mouth feels as though it's full of sawdust.'

'Is that a hint, Monica Parry, that the next stop is my house? It seems the only place yer think of when yer want a cuppa, even though yer have to pass yer own house to get it.' Kate sighed.

'Sometimes I think yer've forgotten yer've got a home of yer own.'

'Oh, stop yer moaning, girl, ye're giving me the willies! To shut yer up, we'll stop at the cake shop and I'll mug you and Winnie to a cream cake. Does that make yer feel any better?'

'I'll buy the cakes, queen.' Winnie had cut down on food in the last few days for just this very purpose. She didn't want to be a hanger-on, a scrounger, taking all the time and giving nothing back. 'You bought them last time so it's my turn now.'

'No, I'm feeling in a generous mood, so I'll do the honours. Cream slices all round, is it, ladies?' Monica licked her lips. 'Me mouth's watering already.'

'If you've got money to throw away, sunshine, who am I to object?' Kate said. 'But I've got to tell yer that I won't be returning the favour 'cos I can't afford it. I'm sticking to the promise I made meself, and putting coppers in each of me Christmas clubs every week.'

Monica kept a straight face. 'Oh, I wouldn't expect yer to, girl! Not when yer've kindly offered to have the party at Christmas. I mean, that will make up for a whole year of cream slices.'

With a quick shake of her head, and a few tuts, Kate began to walk in the direction of home. 'Come on, people are having to walk around us, we're taking up the whole pavement.'

'Now that would be terrible if some poor bugger had to walk around us, wouldn't it? So, to save anyone the inconvenience, we'll make our way to the cake shop. Perhaps the smell of home-made bread will improve my mate's crotchety mood.'

They were leaving the cake shop when young Billy came bounding towards them, his face red with the exertion of running hell for leather. 'Mam,' the boy bent double to get his breath back, 'there's some people moving into Miss Parkinson's house! They're carrying things in off a handcart.'

The three women were taken aback. 'A handcart? Are yer sure, sunshine, that they're going into Miss Parkinson's?'

'Yeah, they've got the door open and they're taking boxes into the house.' Billy felt very grown-up being the bearer of such news. 'It's only a handcart, though, like the rag and bone man has.'

'Are they big tea chests they're carrying in?' Kate asked. 'Yer know what they are, big square ones?'

Billy shook his head. 'No, only small cardboard boxes and orange boxes.'

The three women looked at each other and their thoughts were alike. 'Come on, let's see what's going on.' Monica placed the cake bag on the top of her basket. She was usually very careful with them, in case the cream got all squashed, but the news Billy brought was more important than a few flipping squashed cakes. 'It's a wonder the rent man didn't tell us they'd let the house.'

'Bill did say there were a few people after it, but that was all he could say. It's up to Mr Coburn who gets the tenancy, not Bill. He can recommend, but doesn't have the final say. He should be around for his money soon, anyway, so perhaps he'll be able to tell us more.'

It seemed the arrival of the handcart had caused considerable curiosity in the street, because when the friends turned the corner they could see a lot of women standing at their doors, Maggie Duffy being one of them. When she saw her neighbours, she hurried towards them. 'I don't know what to make of it, but I smell trouble. Look at the state of the cart, and that's in good nick compared to what's being carried in.'

'Have yer spoken to them yet?' Monica asked. 'Just to say hello, like?'

'No fear! And yer'll understand why when yer get a bit nearer. The mouth on the woman is terrible, but the man is worse. God only knows where they've come from.'

Winnie was showing concern. She'd go mad if her friend's little house was let to bad people. 'Have yer seen any children?'

'Oh, yeah,' said Maggie, pulling a face, 'I've seen five so far.'

'Five kids in a two-up-two-down!' Kate's voice was high. 'What is the landlord thinking of? Unless they didn't tell him they had so many children.'

'Let's cross over,' Monica suggested. 'We can see what's going on from our front windows. If they've let that house to a bad lot, I'll have something to say to our Mr Coburn.'

As they walked towards Kate's house, all eyes slid sideways to the open door through which a man's voice could be heard, loud and coarse. It was echoing against the walls of the empty room, and every other word was a swear word or blasphemous. There was disgust on Kate's face as she put the key in the lock. 'Fancy having to live near that!'

Just then three children came running out of the house, having been chased out by the man with the rough voice. There were two girls and a boy, and there didn't seem to be much difference in their ages. Guessing, Kate thought the girls were about four and five years of age, and the boy six. They looked bedraggled and neglected. The clothes were old, frayed and dirty, and the girls' hair was matted as though it hadn't seen water or a comb for months. Kate felt a pang of pity until she heard their shrill voices shouting obscenities which should never be heard from children who, at that age, should know only innocence.

The children who lived in the street had been drawn by curiosity to the handcart, but now their mothers were either calling them in or, shaking their heads in disgust, dragging them in by their ears if they were reluctant to move away from the only excitement going on. Most of the women could use swear words when things got on top of them, like the kids playing them up or worry over money. But their curses were mild compared to what they were hearing now, and without exception the local women feared their new neighbours were trouble-makers and felt they would do well to give them a wide berth.

'Let's get inside,' Kate said. 'And you come in with us,

Maggie, so yer can see what's going on? As for you, Billy, play down at the bottom of the street with Pete. And if those children speak to yer, ignore them.'

While Kate carried her shopping through to the kitchen, her three friends stood in front of the window, anger mixed with sadness as they remembered the love and care that house had known for so many years. 'Has there been any big pieces of furniture taken in, Maggie?' Monica asked. 'You know, wardrobes, beds, tables and chairs?'

'Not that I've seen, love, but they wouldn't get big things like that on a handcart. Maybe there's a removal van bringing the big stuff later. All I've seen is boxes and bags being carried in.'

Winnie stroked her chin. 'Well, it's a mystery to me. If they've ordered a removal van, why would they be bothered dragging that bleeding handcart with bits on? I'm blowed if I'd make a fool of meself by walking through the streets with that, if I didn't have to.'

As she spoke, two older children came out of the house, a boy and a girl, probably nine and eleven. They didn't run out, as the others had, but swaggered, looking really cocky and sure of themselves. They were scruffy, and looked as though they hadn't used a block of soap in a long time, but their appearance didn't seem to worry them.

'They look like gypsies to me,' Monica said. 'I don't know what the landlord was thinking of when he gave them the tenancy to a house that was spotlessly clean and didn't want a thing doing to it. That lot will have it ruined in no time. I'd say we're in for a very rough ride with them. The kids are brazen-faced, yer can see that a mile off. And I wouldn't like to tangle with the mother, have yer seen the arms on her? She's built like a bleeding ox!'

Kate came through carrying a tray. 'Here yer are, ladies, a nice cup of tea. But ye're not getting saucers 'cos I don't want a stack of dishes to wash.' She put the tray on the table and began to hand cups around. 'I've been listening and I've got meself all worked up. Fancy our kids playing in the street and listening to the language of that lot! Just wait until Bill comes for the rent money, he'll get a piece of my mind.'

But when the rent collector called an hour later, the house opposite was closed up, the handcart had gone, along with the man and woman, and the children had disappeared. Winnie was certain there was something fishy going on. 'There was a man and a woman, five kids and a bleeding handcart! Now don't tell me that Monica, Kate and meself have all imagined this 'cos even in me wildest dreams I could never imagine kids of that age using the kind of bad language that even I draw the line at.'

Bill looked bewildered. Several of the women this end of the street had had a go at him about the new tenants, and he'd thought they were exaggerating. But they couldn't all be wrong. 'I was told there were two children, with their father and mother. Mr Coburn wouldn't let a two-bedroomed house to a family with five children.'

'He's been had! Taken for a bleeding ride!' Winnie's face was red at the very thought. 'The crafty buggers must have sent those two eldest children out to look for you, and when they knew yer were near, they all scarpered! They'll be back later when they know the coast is clear.'

'Winnie is right, Bill,' Kate said. 'This is one time yer boss has slipped up, and I'll swear he'll have reason to regret it. The sad thing is, everyone in this street will regret it, too, because we're the ones having to live by them.'

'Go and give them a knock if yer don't believe they've done a bunk to avoid seeing yer.' Monica was livid. 'They should be here to pay yer the rent money.'

'I don't need to call there today, they paid a week in advance. And even if I knocked, and they were in, I couldn't do much because they are legally entitled to be there, having paid their rent. I can only suggest we leave things be for now, and wait until they do something to warrant being evicted. I will have a word with Mr Coburn, though, he needs to be warned.'

With that the ladies had to be content, and went about the business of making a meal for their families.

As Kate was putting the meal out in the kitchen, John was washing his hands at the sink. She was telling him about the unusual day they'd had, and about their new neighbours. 'Winnie was right, too, 'cos they all came back an hour after the rent man had left the street. All seven of them, plus the ruddy handcart with more boxes and bags. I'll swear he's a rag and bone man, he's certainly got the voice for one. And the kids! Well, the carrying on and the language out of them, yer'd have to see and hear it to believe what I'm telling yer.'

She carried two plates through and put them down in front of her children, then she went back for hers and John's. 'There's something radically wrong somewhere.' Kate pulled a chair out and sat down. 'No chairs, beds or tables. Where are they going to sleep tonight, and what are they sitting on?'

'The big lad is not half cheeky,' Billy said. 'Mrs Jones from the bottom of the street told him off for swearing, and yer should have heard what he called her! I can't tell yer, 'cos yer'd give me a clip around the ear.'

'They sound a right crew, but there's nothing yer can do about it, love, except wait and see what happens. The furniture might turn up tomorrow, yer never know!'

'The children are not nice, Dad, they're really hard-faced. Two of them asked to have a go with our skipping rope, and when me and Dolly refused, they started pushing us, trying to pull it out of our hands.' Nancy had never known children like them because none of the other kids in the street would answer a grown-up back, and they weren't as dirty, either. 'They didn't get it, 'cos they're only little and we could easy push them away. But yer should have heard what they called us!'

Joan Jonker

'Keep well away, have nothing to do with them, either of yer.' John could see the day coming when he'd be having words with the father of these children who, by the sound of things, were definitely out of control. 'They're not your sort, steer clear.'

There came a tap on the window, and Kate looked over to see Monica making signs for her to open the front door. 'Ooh, I wonder what she wants? It must be important 'cos they should be sitting down to their dinner at this time.'

Monica, her face radiant, stepped into the hall and put a hand on each of Kate's cheeks. 'It's been a lousy day, hasn't it, girl?'

Kate backed away so she could look her friend in the face. 'If yer thought it was so bad, what have yer got a grin on yer face for?'

'Go into the living room, and all will be revealed.'

'But we're having our dinner! Whatever it is, can't it wait?'

'We were in the middle of our dinner as well, girl, so don't be feeling sorry for yerself. In the living room, so John can hear why I'm feeling on top of the world.'

He was smiling when the two friends walked in. 'Can't you two go for more than an hour without seeing each other?'

'I'd have burst if I'd had to wait any longer,' Monica told him. 'Yer see, I've just had the most marvellous news. Tom has been made up to floorwalker – he'll be a boss!'

'Oh, that is wonderful news, sunshine, I'm really happy for yer.' Kate gave her a hug. 'But don't think that gives yer the right to have airs and graces, and throw yer weight around.'

John laid his knife and fork down. 'I bet Tom's over the moon. Did he have any idea or has it come out of the blue?'

'He knew they were looking for one because the old floorwalker retired last week. But Tom didn't have an inkling the job would be offered to him. He thought they'd bring somebody in from outside. He's still in a state of shock, but nice shock, if yer know what I mean.'

'And have yer left yer dinner on the table, sunshine?'

'I couldn't wait to tell yer, girl. I'd started to eat me dinner when Tom dropped the bombshell, and yer were the first person I thought of. I don't even feel hungry now, I'm too excited.' Then came a throaty chuckle. 'I was eating me dinner, and talking with me mouth full as usual, telling Tom about the goings-on over the road, when he told me he'd been promoted to floorwalker and I nearly bloody choked meself!'

'I'm made up for yer, sunshine, yer lucky blighter.'

John nodded. 'Yeah, tell Tom I send my congratulations.'

'Yer can tell him yerself, 'cos he's taking yer for a pint tonight to celebrate.' Monica had been warned not to repeat all her husband had mentioned so she settled for, 'Don't say yer can't afford to go because it's Tom's treat. And yer never know, lad, a bit of his luck might rub off on you. Stand next to him at the bar, rub shoulders and make a wish.'

Kate could see the children and John had stopped eating. She cupped her mate's elbow. 'Go and finish yer dinner, sunshine, and let us get on with ours. But when the men go out, come and sit with us for an hour to pass the time.'

John hated to go to the pub when he hadn't any money in his pocket to pay for a round, but to refuse to celebrate Tom's good fortune would have looked churlish. So he bit on his pride and sat at one of the small tables in a corner, while his friend went to the bar for two pints of bitter and two glasses of whisky.

'Hey, what's the idea! Yer shouldn't have got me a whisky!'

'Shut up and get it down yer,' Tom said. 'It's only once in a lifetime yer get news like I got today. It means an extra ten bob a week, and that's not to be sneezed at.'

'It certainly isn't, yer've landed on yer feet.' John sipped on the whisky while Tom downed his in two gulps. 'Mind you, yer've been there since yer left school so no one can say yer don't deserve it or don't know the job inside out.'

Tom looked at his neighbour over the rim of his glass, then

after drinking deeply on the beer, put the glass down. 'There'll be a vacancy after I start my new job next Monday. How would yer feel about applying for it?'

John looked surprised. 'They've probably got someone lined up for it, I wouldn't stand a chance!'

'Yer won't if yer don't bloody well try! I can put a word in for yer, recommend yer, that should give yer a start. I get on well with the manager so yer'd be in with a better chance than most. Unless ye're happy where yer are. In that case just forget it.' Tom knew his friend wasn't on good money, and Kate was always having a struggle to make ends meet. 'But it would mean an extra seven and six a week in yer wage packet.'

John's mouth dropped. 'I knew yer were on better pay than me, but I didn't realize it was so much more. That does surprise me.'

'It would surprise Monica, too, if she knew, so silence is golden. I don't keep her short, in fact she does very well. But the more I give her, the more she'll spend. She's not as thrifty with money as Kate is.'

'Kate wouldn't know she was born with an extra seven and six a week, she'd think she was a millionaire.' John swirled his beer round in the glass, and in the golden liquid could see images of his wife's face. She kept the house and family going on the lousy wages he was on, with never a complaint out of her. How he'd love to be able to hand her a decent wage packet every week so she could go out and buy herself and the children new clothes. Then she wouldn't have to strain her eyes nearly every night, darning and patching. 'D'yer think I'd be in with a chance, then, Tom?'

'I can't promise yer'd get the job, but I will say yer stand a better chance than most if I can pull a few strings for yer.' Tom peered at him over the rim of his glass. 'I can put a few feelers out tomorrow, if yer like, and get yer an application form.'

John felt as though his heart was on a trampoline. 'I'd be

really grateful, Tom. But don't mention it to Kate until we know some more. I'd hate her to get her hopes up, and then have them dashed.'

'I'll not say a word, mate! And I'll tell Monica to keep it to herself. She knows I'm asking yer, 'cos it was her what suggested it. As soon as I told her, the first one she thought of was Kate. She was out of the door like a shot. I had to shout after her not to say any more than that I'd been promoted.'

John grinned. 'She won't like keeping quiet about that, yer know what her and Kate are like – as thick as thieves. They couldn't be closer if they were sisters.'

'I'll have a good talk to her, she knows which side her bread's buttered.' Tom, like his wife, had a very throaty chuckle. 'I'm at the head of the bargaining table right now, and in bed tonight she'll try and get round me to say how much of a rise she'll be getting. I can read her like a ruddy book. She'll be as sweet as honey at first, but if I say she's not getting as big a rise as she's expecting, she'll blow the roof off. Then there'll be a little haggling, at the end of which I'll pretend to give in – even though I had every intention of giving her what she wanted anyway. But there'll be conditions attached, and one of those is that she doesn't breathe a word to Kate. So don't worry on that score.'

As the two men walked home from the pub, John felt uplifted. For the first time in years he had something to hope for. 'How are we going to get around to filling in the application form if Kate knows nothing about it?'

'I'll think of something, that's the least of yer worries,' Tom said. 'And if yer get as far as an interview, it will mean yer taking a few hours off work. Would yer be able to manage that?'

'I've never taken time off, Tom, yer know that. But for a better job, and a better way of life for me family, then I'll go sick for a few hours. Plead a stomach ache or something.'

As they neared their houses, they could hear a racket. This

was unusual because after ten o'clock at night there was seldom anyone in the street. 'What the hell is going on?' Tom quickened his step as the noise grew louder. 'It sounds like kids, but what the hell are they doing out this time of night?'

'It'll be the new kids from opposite,' John said. 'Kate said they were holy terrors.'

'I believe so, but holy terrors or not, they shouldn't be allowed to disturb people this time of night. Some folks will be in bed!'

The noise wasn't only coming from the five children. Their mother was sitting on the step and the father leaning against the wall. They were talking and laughing at the top of their voices, with no thought for the noise they were making. The two men were horrified at the language used by both parents and children. Smoke came from the cigarette being smoked by the man, and there was a low glow of tobacco from the clay pipe the woman had in the side of her mouth.

'Sod that for a lark,' Tom said. 'I need a night's sleep if I'm to work tomorrow, so I'm going to tell them to keep quiet.'

'Yer might make things worse, Tom.' John put a restraining hand on his mate's arm. 'Perhaps it would be as well to leave it until yer know what sort of people ye're dealing with.'

But Tom wasn't prepared to leave it. 'Would yer mind making less noise?' he shouted across the street. 'There are people trying to sleep.'

'Ah, go in and mind yer own business, yer stupid bastard.' The man had moved away from the wall and was standing at the edge of the pavement. 'We're outside our own bleedin' house, so we can do as we like.'

'Oh, no, yer can't!' Tom was on his way across the cobbles now, with John behind him. 'Ye're new to this street, so yer may as well be told now that none of yer neighbours like to hear noise like you're making at this time of night. So I'll ask yer again, will yer lower the racket and get inside the house? Those children should be in bed now, anyway.'

Doors began to open now and amongst the neighbours who came out of their houses were Kate and Monica. 'Oh, my God, their first day here and they're causing trouble.' Monica shook her fist. 'What sort of parents are yer, teaching yer children words that only a fishwife would use? Get inside and put them to bed.'

Tom, who was no lightweight, stood in the gutter looking up at their new neighbour. 'Now, are yer going to go in and shut the door, or do I have to make yer?'

The man's head dropped back and he roared with drunken laughter. 'Did yer hear that, Ma? The stupid bastard thinks he can give me sodding orders!'

Kate was getting worried as well as angry. She didn't want John getting involved with these people who would probably just as soon stab you in the back as look at you. 'John, leave it be, they're not worth wasting yer breath on.'

The other man, egged on by his family, began to get cocky. And he wasn't to know that Kate wasn't Tom's wife. 'That's right, love, take your feller in before I knock his bleedin' block off. Put him to bed with a dummy in his mouth.'

That did it. Tom stepped from the gutter on to the pavement, adding six inches to his height. And John, the same height as his mate, stood beside him. 'Repeat what yer've just said,' Tom told the man, who by now wasn't quite so cocky, 'so I know I wasn't hearing things.'

There was quite a crowd gathered by this time, and there were dark mutterings because most people had been getting ready for bed. But with his children shouting to him, 'Go on, Dad, belt the miserable bleeder,' the man didn't want to be seen to lose face. But he couldn't see any other way out. Both the men facing him looked as though they could handle themselves, and he'd rather lose a little pride than a few front teeth. 'Yer've taken it the wrong way, matey! I didn't mean nothing by it! It's all a misunderstanding. Me and the missus and the kids have had a busy day moving house, we were just getting a bit of fresh air before going to bed.'

Tom took hold of the man by his lapels, lifted him off his feet and pulled him forward so their faces were nearly touching. 'So this isn't a nightly occurrence then? It won't be happening tomorrow night, or any night in future? Are yer quite sure about that? If ye're not sure, then speak out now so I can tell yer what me and me friends will do if there's any more messing. Yer see, this is a nice respectable street, and we intend keeping it that way.'

When the man didn't answer, John said, 'What my mate has just said goes for me too. And I'll also add that if any of yer children go near mine, or upset them in any way, then you will be sorry because it won't be yer children I chastise, it'll be you.' He touched Tom's arm. 'Come on, mate, I think we've made our point. If not, there's always another time.'

Kate folded her arms and hugged herself. 'Did yer just hear what John said, sunshine? Oh, I'm so proud of him.'

'Ay, don't yer be leaving my feller out, I thought he was brilliant!' Monica watched the two husbands coming towards them and whispered, 'I've got a feeling it's going to be a good night for Robin Hood.'

Chapter Twenty-Seven

After closing the door behind her, Kate stood between Monica and Winnie and linked their arms. 'Shall we go to the butcher's first? I'm thinking of getting sausage to have with mashed potatoes.'

'D'yer know what I fancy?' Monica asked. 'A pig's knuckle, or a shank. I could put some peas in steep and make a nice thick soup with the shank. I haven't done that for ages, and Tom loves it.'

'Ooh, yeah, that's a good idea!' Winnie nodded in agreement. 'I could get two days out of a pan of pea whack.' Then she changed the subject. 'Ay, that new family have been quiet since Tom and John had a go at them. It's been a week now, and there's not been a peep out of them.' She pursed her lips. 'They're still a bleeding mystery to me, though. Not one stick of furniture has gone in that house, so what the hell do they sit and sleep on?'

'God knows, but as long as they stay out of our lives, sunshine, I don't care if they sleep standing up. I know the names of the man and woman, I've heard them shouting to each other. She calls him Jacko, and she's Rita. I don't know about the kids, except they're around all day and none of them go to school.' Kate kept her eye on the house opposite to make sure her own children stayed clear. 'I'm surprised the School Board hasn't been after them, 'cos yer can get into trouble if yer don't send yer kids to school. I bet any money if I was to keep one of mine off for half a day, they'd be down on me like a ton of bricks.'

'Yer'll probably think I'm being bad-minded,' Winnie said, 'but I think they probably did a flit from where they lived before, and the School Board won't know where they are.'

'I think ye're probably right, girl!' Monica had been of the same mind since the family had turned up with the handcart. 'I said they looked like gypsies the minute I set eyes on them. It will be interesting to see if they pay their rent today.'

'We'll find that out when Bill comes, sunshine. That's if he gets an answer.' Kate's face broke into a wide smile. 'I know I shouldn't say this, but wouldn't it be a scream if they didn't open the door and he couldn't get their rent? Mr Coburn wouldn't like that one little bit, and he'd be sorry he ever set eyes on them. But it would teach him a lesson for the future.'

'Ay, queen, the butcher's is packed. D'yer want to get the rest of the shopping first and come back when we've finished? Bob mightn't be so busy then.'

The three women peered through the window. 'It's packed all right,' Monica said. 'But we may as well wait and get it over with.'

The shop was so crowded the women were squeezed tight against the back wall. And there were a few titters when Monica shouted, 'Busy day, Bob? Yer'll be up till the early hours counting yer takings.' Then she thought of giving the waiting customers a laugh. 'Yer'll be able to buy yer wife a fur coat for the winter, and yer know what they say about women what wear fur coats, don't yer?'

Kate gave her a sharp dig in the ribs. 'That's enough, Monica Parry, don't yer be making an exhibition of yerself. And me into the bargain.'

But Monica had managed to liven things up. Bob, the owner of the shop, let out a loud guffaw. 'Oh, I'll sort that out, Monica! I'll buy her the knickers this Christmas and the fur coat for next.'

Winnie had to keep standing on tip-toe to see the butcher. She liked to see a person's face when she knew they'd have a smile on it. And on one of her hops she noticed a familiar figure standing in front of the counter. 'Ay, there's Margaret at the front, by the counter. She must have packed her job in.'

But Winnie wasn't the only person to spot the young mother-to-be. For standing in front of the three friends, a little to the right, were two women who lived in the same street as the Blackmores. One was a real busybody who thrived on gossip. The other woman was a decent respectable person who was inclined to get on with her life and leave others to get on with theirs. Winnie was known to both women, and she was just about to stretch her arm over to catch their attention when the busybody moved her head closer to the other woman and said, 'There's that Margaret Blackmore in front. She had to get married, yer know, 'cos she got herself in the family way. I believe the lad didn't want to marry her but they forced him into it. I don't know how she's got the nerve to show her face, she should be bloody well ashamed of herself.'

Monica gasped, as did her two friends, and moved forward, mouth open, ready to bring the gossip-monger to task. But Winnie gripped her arm. 'Leave this to me, queen, I know both of those women.'

But Kate feared a scene. 'Don't start an argument, sunshine, 'cos if it gets to Margaret's ears she'll never leave the house again, she'll be so embarrassed.'

'Don't worry, queen, I know what I'm doing.' Pretending she'd only just spotted the busybody, Winnie leaned forward and tapped her on the shoulder. 'Hello, Fanny, I've only just noticed yer! How are yer?'

'Fine, thanks, Winnie, how's yerself?'

'On top of the world, queen, on top of the world. And d'yer know, Fanny, every time I see yer I keep meaning to ask about yer sister's girl, and then it slips me mind. Yer know who I mean, the one what's expecting a baby. Did the bloke ever marry her, or did he leave her swinging to face the music on her own?'

Well, the woman didn't know where to put herself. But her companion did. 'I've decided not to wait, I'll come back later.' She gave Fanny a withering look and pushed her way through

the crowd behind. As she passed Winnie, she shook her head and
tutted. 'Some people have nothing better to do. I'll see you later,
Winnie.'

'Okay, Iris, I'll see yer. Take care now.' Winnie turned back to
the unfortunate Fanny. 'Yer never said what happened to yer
sister's daughter. Did the bloke marry her, and has she had the
baby yet?'

'She hasn't had the baby yet.' Fanny was cursing herself for
not carrying on to the Co-op shop like she'd had a mind to when
she saw the queue at the butcher's. But she was cursing Winnie
even more. 'The lad, Dave, said he might marry her after the
baby's born.'

Kate and Monica bit on their bottom lips to keep the chuckles
at bay, and left it to Winnie to finish the job she'd started. 'Oh,
he's one of them, is he? Waiting to see if the baby looks like him
before he'll commit himself? If he's that sort of feller, yer sister's
girl wouldn't have much of a life with him, he'd be throwing it
up in her face all the time. She'd be better off without him. But
isn't it a pity that he's not a nice lad, a gentleman, who'd do the
right thing by her?'

If looks could kill, Winnie would have been a dead duck.
Fanny was silently calling curses down on the woman who
seemed to be intent on finding out about her sister's girl. The lad
had no intention of marrying her 'cos the girl was a fly turn and
she'd thrown herself at him. Of course after he got what he
wanted he had no respect for her and walked past her in the
street. The stupid cow had gone crying to his parents, but after
telling her she was no angel, they'd closed the door in her face.

At that point Margaret, having been served, made her way
through the crowd and smiled when she saw the three women.
This of course played right into Winnie's hands. She could rub
the salt in a bit more, and then perhaps Fanny would keep her
mouth shut in future.

'Hello, queen, doing yer mam's shopping for her, are yer?'

'We tossed up who'd do the washing and who'd come to the shops. I won, 'cos shopping is easier than washing and mangling.'

Kate and Monica made a fuss of Margaret, and then Winnie topped her performance by saying, 'And yer know Fanny, of course, 'cos she only lives a few doors away from yer?'

Margaret was pleasant with the woman and smiled, but Fanny thought her face would crack when she tried to smile back. That did it for her. 'I don't think I'll wait any longer, me feet are getting tired. I'll go to the Co-op and come back later.' With that she pushed everyone out of her path in her haste to get away from Winnie. Not realizing how warped her thinking was, she got outside the shop and muttered, 'I'll stay clear of that one in future, she's a trouble-maker.'

Although they were laughing inside, and mentally patting Winnie on the back, Kate and Monica didn't mention Fanny's name. They would when Margaret left them, of course, because they thought that although Winnie didn't have a hammer, she'd certainly hit that nail on the head.

'Are yer in a hurry, sunshine?' Kate asked. 'Or would yer like to wait for us and come shopping?'

'That's an idea, girl, it would do yer good to have a bit of company.' Monica stepped back a little way from Kate before adding, 'We all have a cup of tea at Kate's when we've been shopping, so yer might as well join us.'

'Me mam will be waiting for the stew to get the dinner on,' Margaret said. 'She likes to let it simmer for hours on a low light.'

'Well, you take yer shopping home, queen.' Winnie could see Kate's eyes rolling but knew that if her friend made a song and dance about it, it would be through habit, she really didn't mean it. 'Then come to Kate's. And as it's my turn to buy the cream cakes, yer'll get a nice cake with yer cup of tea.'

Margaret was torn. She'd love to go to Kate's and have a

laugh with the women, 'cos she didn't have any friends of her own age now. She used to have three or four when she went dancing, but as soon as she thought she was pregnant, she'd stopped going out through fear and shame and had lost touch with them all. Even though she was married now, she didn't like seeking them out. But after the baby was born she'd vowed to look up one particular friend, Freda Kennedy, whom she'd known since they were in the infants school together. They'd always been good mates and Margaret did miss her.

'I'd love to come but I'll have to see if me mam needs me first. I only packed me job in on Saturday so I don't like leaving her to do all the work while I'm out enjoying meself.'

'Who said anything about enjoying yerself?' Monica grinned. 'We eat our cake, drink our tea, making them last as long as we can, then Kate throws us out. She's got a little card on a piece of string behind the front door with "Cafe" on. And when she's had enough of us, she turns the card around to read "Closed".'

'Take no notice of her, sunshine, we have a damn' good laugh. Usually at someone else's expense, of course, but we don't mean no harm by it. Hurry home now, give yer mam a hand, then bring her with yer. She enjoys a good laugh. And with these two,' Kate jerked her head to where Monica and Winnie were standing, 'she's guaranteed one. If not, then she can ask for her money back.'

'That would be nice. I'll get home sharpish and see yer later.' Margaret was on the pavement outside when she called, 'What time?'

'In an hour or so, sunshine. If yer do get there before us, which I very much doubt, sit on me step and wait for us.'

'While ye're at it, girl, bring a ruddy duster with yer and yer can clean her windows while ye're waiting!' Monica jerked her head, rolled her eyes and tutted. 'Sit on me step indeed! What a flaming cheek she's got!'

Kate was ready for her, while the customers waiting to be

served were all ears. 'Don't you bother with no duster, sunshine, 'cos I cleaned me windows yesterday. That's why I said to sit on me step, 'cos I haven't done that yet, and two bottoms moving around on it should rub the dirt off.'

Margaret was giggling as she walked away, and she called over her shoulder, 'I'll bring the little cork mat with us 'cos this is me best coat.'

After being served in the butcher's, the three friends made good time getting the rest of their shopping in. 'I don't want Betty and Margaret hanging around outside the house. They'd think we were fine ones to invite them round and then leave them standing.'

'We'll be home well before they come,' Monica said. 'Margaret had shopping to do, and she wouldn't get around as quick as us 'cos she's really starting to show now and she'll find she can't walk as fast.'

Kate linked Winnie's arm. 'Now there's no one to hear what we're saying, I think yer did a brilliant job on Fanny Bishop, sunshine. Yer did far better than me or Monica could have done.'

'Yeah, it was a great piece of work, girl, I didn't half enjoy watching her squirm. I was going to have a go at her meself, but yer not only beat me to it, yer made a far better job of it than I could have done. Her face was a picture no artist could paint, she didn't know what to do with herself. But how did yer know about her sister's daughter being pregnant?'

'Well, queen, Fanny is the worst gossip in this neighbourhood. I'll swear she listens at windows when the nights are dark and no one can see her. But gossips have one failing: they forget who they've told tales to. She wouldn't remember telling me about her sister's girl, and how she called her fit to burn. She has no sympathy or understanding for the girl, or for her own sister who must be worried to death. All Fanny wants is a bit of juicy gossip and her day is made. Yer see, she hasn't got any real friends, and

I'm not surprised the way she carries on. She has to rely on the suffering and misfortune of other people to give her something to tell anyone willing to listen to her. She's so thick-skinned, she can't see that most of the women can't stand her and cross the street or make a detour when they see her coming.'

'It tickled me when Iris made a hasty exit,' Monica said. 'She'll run like hell when she sees Fanny coming towards her in future.'

When they neared Monica's house, Kate said, 'Nip in and get two decent cups and saucers, sunshine. I'm afraid my cafe can only cater for four people.'

'Yeah, okay, girl, and I'll put the shank in water to steep and get some of the salt out of it. I'll be ten minutes, that's all.'

Half an hour later the three women were sitting around the table, their minds on the cream cakes on a plate in the pantry. Finally Monica could stand it no more. 'I'll give Betty another fifteen minutes, and if her and Margaret aren't here by then, I'm having me cake whether yer like it or not.'

'My mouth's watering too, queen, but I can hold out until the other two come,' Winnie said. 'It wouldn't look very nice if they were the only two eating cakes, they'd feel like monkeys in a zoo with everyone staring at them.'

'We'll wait until they come,' Kate said with determination. 'Even if yer tongue is hanging out, Monica Parry, yer'll not get near my pantry.' She thought a little conversation might take her mate's mind off the fresh cream slice. 'Did I tell yer that my feller went to work this morning looking like a toff, Winnie? Best shirt and collar, and tie. He didn't half look handsome, I fell for him all over again.'

'What's the occasion, queen, is he going somewhere important?'

'Only to the pub with a couple of the men he works with. One of their wives gave birth to a baby and the proud father wants to wet the baby's head. It'll only be a pint in their dinner break, but John wanted to look respectable.'

Monica fixed her eyes on the window to avoid looking at her friend. She was dying to blurt out the truth of why John had gone out looking respectable this morning, but she'd been warned if she didn't keep it to herself, Tom would think twice about the rise in housekeeping he'd promised. And he was right, of course, because there could be disappointment ahead. She could fill Kate with hope, and then feel like a heel when it didn't come off. And it was only right that John should be the one to tell his wife. Good news or bad.

The knock on the door had Monica's chair being pushed back so quickly, it banged against the sideboard. 'Oh, I'm sorry, girl, I don't know me own strength.'

'I'll have no home left, the way ye're going on,' Kate called after her. 'Yer've put more scratches on me furniture than me kids have.'

Betty came in first, followed by Margaret, and they both looked happy to be there because they knew that this was one place they were amongst friends. 'What's she been doing now, love?' Betty asked. 'Knocking yer furniture about, is she?'

'Blimey! Anyone would think I'd put a bleeding hole in the sideboard!' Monica waved a hand. 'Look, there's no mark or scratch, nothing!'

'Well, I'm not letting yer loose on me sofa with yer cream cake, we'll share one of the dining chairs between us.'

'Two of us won't fit on one of those fiddling chairs!'

'Yes, we will! One cheek each! But before that, let's get Betty and Margaret comfortable, then yer can help me with the tea.'

'I'll see to that, queen.' Winnie made her way to the kitchen. 'You sit and talk to yer guests, it'll not take me long.'

Betty pulled out a chair. 'I was lucky, the rent man called just as we were leaving. I've only ever missed him once, and I swore I'd never do it again. I'd put the money away, yer see, full of good intentions to pay him two weeks next time he came. But it's very tempting to have money in the rent book and none in yer purse. So I was dipping into it each day with no thought to how I was going to make it up. I couldn't tell Jack, he'd have gone mad. So I had to pay a week and a half when the man came, and paid the rest the week after. It taught me a lesson, though, I've never done it since.'

'I couldn't have money in the house without dipping into it,' Kate said. 'The temptation would be too great to ignore. I have a struggle to manage every week, but at least me conscience is clear. And next year I'll be on Easy Street when Nancy starts work.'

Winnie was carrying the tray in from the kitchen when she happened to glance through the window facing her. 'Ay, queen, there's Maggie Duffy standing on her step. She seems a bit agitated. Keeps looking over here.'

Kate and Monica went to the window. 'Yeah, she does seem a bit anxious, as though there's something wrong,' Kate said as she hurried to the front door. 'I'd better make sure she's all right, 'cos she'd be the first to help one of us if we needed it.'

As soon as Maggie saw Kate, she waved her over. And she was more than agitated, she was angry and worried. 'I don't know what to do, girl, I'm at me wit's end. I did some washing early this morning, before I went to the shops, and put two sheets on the line. There was no room for any more, 'cos they were double sheets.' She wiped the back of a hand across her forehead and took a deep breath. 'I've just got back from the shops and the sheets are gone – vanished into thin air.'

Kate frowned. 'How d'yer mean, gone? Two ruddy big sheets can't disappear. Are yer sure yer didn't bring them in before yer went to the shops?'

Maggie shook her head. 'Kate, love, I put the sheets through the mangle and took them out one at a time to peg on the line. I've never been more sure of anything in me life.'

'Pull yer door to, Maggie, and come across to mine. Winnie and Monica are there, and the more heads the better.'

Maggie looked uncertain. Keeping her voice low, she said, 'I think next door have pinched them. One of the kids could easy have got over me wall when they saw me going out. I don't want no trouble with them 'cos they're really tough. And if they see me going over to yours, they might take it out on me for spite.'

'Don't be so daft! If they've pinched yer sheets, yer can't let them get away with it because ye're frightened of them. Come over with me, and we'll see what the gang say.'

Maggie was surprised to see Betty and Margaret there. She knew them by sight, but had never had a conversation with them. 'Why didn't yer tell me yer had company, Kate? I don't want to spoil things for yer.'

'Listen, sunshine, if I was in trouble, I'd come to you for help. I wouldn't worry whether yer had visitors or not. Now don't be daft, tell Monica and Winnie what yer've just told me.'

It was all too much for Maggie. As she told her tale of woe, the tears trickled down her bonny cheeks. 'I'm sorry, but I'm real upset about it. I can't afford to lose two good sheets, it's not as though I'm well off for bedding. And I can't see anyone else climbing over me wall and stealing them, only the new family. It's bad enough living next door to them, but if I'm going to have to stop putting washing out in case they pinch it, well, life won't be worth living. Yer've no idea what they're like. There's noise coming from that house twenty-four hours a day, banging and shouting, with language so foul I feel ashamed for them. And if we knock on the wall, and ask them politely to be quiet, we get the height of abuse from them. Ben's wanted to go and have it out with the husband a few times, but I wouldn't let him. My husband isn't a fighter and I don't want him going up against the likes of them.' She lifted her hands in despair. 'But what can I do? Just put up with it, I suppose.'

'Just put up with it?' Winnie's voice was shrill. 'I'm buggered if I'd put up with it! And if yer don't do nothing about yer sheets going missing, they'll think ye're an easy touch and steal anything they can get their hands on.'

'Winnie's right,' Monica said. 'Yer can't let people like that get the better of yer. Stand up to them! We've never had anything stolen from lines in this street before so the chances are it was them what took yer sheets. Although why they'd want sheets when they've got no bleeding beds is beyond me.'

While this was going on, Kate was explaining to Betty and Margaret about their new neighbours. And she agreed with Winnie and Monica. 'They sound a right shower. But yer must never let bullies think ye're frightened of them. That's the worst thing yer can do. Stick up for yerself, and always remember you have done nothing wrong, they have.'

'Come on, Maggie, if you think they've taken yer bedding, then I'll come with yer to ask for it back.' Winnie was on her feet and raring to go. How dare these people steal from ordinary folk who were pushed each week to make ends meet?

'Hang on, I'll come with yer too.' Monica was in a fighting mood and her sleeves were being rolled up ready for action when there came a knock on the door. 'Ah, this will be the rent man! Just the feller we want to see.'

'I'll open the door, seeing as it's my house,' Kate said. 'And I'll invite Bill in so yer can tell him what's going on, Maggie.'

The rent collector was mildly surprised to be asked in, and very much surprised to see so many of his clients there. And being a friendly bloke, he asked, 'If ye're having a party, can I come?'

'I think yer'd better wipe that smile off yer face, Bill,' Kate told him. 'We're all here to do battle. We hope yer'll listen and be on our side.'

'I can hardly refuse so many of my best tenants, can I? What is it yer want to tell me?'

When four of the women began to speak at once, each trying to outdo the other in volume, the poor man screwed his eyes up tight. 'Ladies, please! I can't make sense of what you're saying with four of you shouting at me. Can I ask if one of you would explain, quietly and calmly, what all the fuss is about?'

The women looked shamefaced. 'I'm sorry, Bill, but we've got ourselves in a right state over something that's happened.' Kate nodded to Maggie. 'You tell him, sunshine.'

With all eyes on her, Maggie was embarrassed, and her first words were stammered. Then, as the injustice of the whole sorry tale sank in, it gave her the strength not only to tell the collector about the sheets going missing, but how she was certain she knew who the culprits were.

He sighed. 'How can you be certain if you didn't see them in the act? You can't accuse anyone unless you have proof or you could end up in trouble.'

'Oh, it was them all right!' Maggie was red in the face with anger. 'And I'll tell yer something else, what I haven't told a living soul 'cos I was afraid. But I'm not afraid any more, I'm bloody mad! I don't care whether yer believe me or not, but I think that if yer went in the house next door, yer'd find they've chopped all the inside doors up, and the banister rail. Every night we can hear them chopping, then we get the smell of burning wood.'

'No, they wouldn't do that!' But even while the rent collector was dismissing Maggie's accusation, he knew in his heart she was telling the truth. For he'd had a lot of complaints about the new family, and all from women like these who had enough intelligence to be sure of what they were saying before they said it. In fact, out of curiosity, he'd mentioned the Hunt family to some of his colleagues who collected in different parts of the city. Several of them not only knew of the family, but had had personal experience of their behaviour. From what they'd told him, the alarm bell was now ringing in Bill's head. But it was more than he dare do to pass on that information to these very irate ladies.

'There's only one way to find out, Bill,' Kate said. 'And that's to see for yerself when yer go to collect their rent.'

He had a sinking feeling in his stomach. 'I don't have to collect the rent, they paid it into the office on Saturday morning.'

'Now I wonder why they'd do that?' Maggie asked, her voice thick with sarcasm. 'And I wonder how anyone can believe them before us?'

'I didn't say I didn't believe you, Mrs Duffy, but you must admit it would be difficult for me to act without discussing it with Mr Coburn first. But I promise I will see that something is done today, without fail. And once Mr Coburn has evidence of them mistreating his property, I can assure you they'll be out on their ear in no time.'

'So ye're not going over now to see if they've got Maggie's sheets?' Monica asked. 'If yer don't, they'll probably have flogged them by the time someone gets around to it.'

'If you ladies will pay me your rent, I will just finish this street off and then go back to the office to have a word with Mr Coburn. He is a good landlord, you must admit, and looks after his tenants. I've got a feeling he'll be here with me within the hour. You see, I don't have a key to any of the properties, and if I knocked at the Hunts', even if they open the door they can refuse to let me in. But when I come back, it will be with my boss and a set of keys.'

Winnie had her rent in her handbag, so while Monica and Maggie nipped home for theirs, Bill marked Winnie's and Kate's books. Throughout the commotion, Betty and her daughter had sat mesmerized by all that was happening. They wouldn't have missed the excitement for the world. Kate heard Betty whispering to her daughter, 'I'm going to slip home to make sure the stew isn't boiling dry, but I'm coming back. I wouldn't miss the next instalment for a big clock. You stay here, I won't be long.'

Margaret was thinking of the husband she adored. 'I won't

half have a lot to tell Greg when he comes in from work. I bet he'll be really surprised.'

Kate grinned and ran a hand over the girl's long hair. 'It adds a bit of spice to life, doesn't it, sunshine? Mind you, I wouldn't want too much of it, me heart wouldn't stand it.'

'Yer don't mind if I run home and come back again, do yer?' Betty asked. 'I wouldn't be able to sleep if I didn't know how it ends.'

'Of course I don't mind! I think I'll make a charge, though. Tuppence for a window seat and a penny for standing at the back.'

The rent man heard and chuckled. It was nice to have a bit of light relief. 'In that case, I think I should charge. If you're going to be the audience, then I should be treated as an actor and paid accordingly.'

'Oh, aye,' Kate said, head tilted. 'And what d'yer think ye're worth?'

'How about sixpence an hour?'

Winnie huffed. 'Sod off, lad! I'd expect James Cagney in person for that.'

Betty chuckled. Ooh, she had to be back in time for the show to begin! The last hour had really bucked her up. 'Excuse me, I know I'm an outsider, but could I ask yer not to raise the curtain for the start of the big picture until I'm seated in me tuppenny window seat?'

'I'll keep a seat for yer, Mam,' Margaret said. 'You go and see to the dinner, but don't take too long because I think this film is going to be a thriller, and if yer miss the beginning it'll take yer ages to figure out what's what and who's who.'

Chapter Twenty-Eight

When a car pulled up outside the house opposite, Kate glanced at the clock. 'Bill kept his promise, it's exactly one hour.'

The sofa had been pushed away from the window to give all six women a decent view of what was going to happen. Now, as they watched, the drama began to unfold. The car door opened and Bill got out on the passenger side, by the pavement, while his boss, Charles Coburn, stepped out on to the cobbles. And what an unusual sight he was in this narrow street. With his fine three-piece beige and brown check suit, heavy gold fob watch stretching across his chest from the pocket of his waistcoat, and his hard brown hat set at a rather jaunty angle, he was what you would call a dapper man, very sure of himself and always in control.

'My God,' Winnie said, 'that outfit he's got on must have cost more than it would take to keep every house in this street in coal for the winter.'

'Don't begrudge the man, sunshine, he's probably worked hard for it.'

'I don't begrudge him, queen, I'm just bleeding jealous.'

Charles Coburn looked up and down the street before stepping on to the pavement. Then he peeled off his soft leather gloves before taking a set of keys from his pocket and handing them to Bill. They exchanged a few words before the rent collector gave several sharp raps on the knocker. It was an ornate brass one which Miss Parkinson used to clean religiously every day. Now it was a dark brown colour as it hadn't had a cloth to it since she left.

'If they're in, they have no intention of answering,' Monica said as the collector gave another few raps, harder this time. 'But Bill's got the keys, why doesn't he just go in? After all, Mr Coburn owns the bleeding house!'

She'd no sooner finished speaking than the landlord gave a nod to tell the collector to use the keys. Then the two men disappeared from sight into the darkness of the house. 'Go over, Maggie,' Monica said, 'find out if yer sheets are in there.'

She shook her head. 'I'm not going over until they come out. And I'll have a bet with anyone they'll both be sick as parrots after they've seen what those villians have done to that house. It breaks my heart to think of the way Miss Parkinson kept it like a little palace. But I will go over when they come out and ask about me sheets. I can't afford to buy new ones, and I'm not getting a Sturla's cheque, either, and be in debt for months to come. All because of those ruffians and thieves the landlord let the house to. And I'll tell Mr Coburn I'd have thought he'd be a better judge of character, with him meeting so many people. He should know a rotter when he sees one.'

It was twenty minutes before the two men came out, and both looked shaken. The women saw Bill nod his head towards Kate's house and begin to lead his boss across the street. 'Oh, my God, they're coming here, and look at the state of the place!' Kate began to panic. 'Quick, push the sofa back into place and take those cups into the kitchen. Mr Coburn will wonder what sort of people live in this street.'

'He'll think yer house is perfect after he's come out of that hell-hole,' Maggie said, walking towards the door. 'I'll let them in.'

'I don't want no bad language out of you, Monica.' Kate was straightening a lace runner on the sideboard that didn't need straightening. 'Let's all act like ladies.'

'It's too late for me to learn how to act, queen,' Winnie said with a hint of mischief in her eyes. 'So they'll have to take me as I am.'

When the two men came into the living room, their hats now in their hands, the first person Charles Coburn noticed was Winnie. 'Well, I'll be blowed if it isn't Winnie Cartwright!' He seemed really surprised and pleased to see the little woman. 'I never expected to see you, Winnie. It's years since I last set eyes on you, and I have to say you haven't changed one little bit.'

'Yes, I have, Charlie. I didn't have a moustache the last time yer saw me!'

Five women and one man were standing with their mouths open. The women couldn't believe what they were hearing. Winnie had never once mentioned that she knew the landlord, let alone well enough to call him Charlie. The rent collector could have kissed the little woman for taking some of the drama out of the situation and putting his boss in a better mood. At least, he was hoping he'd soon be in a better mood.

Mr Coburn nodded his head to each of the women in acknowledgement. He knew their faces but because he seldom collected the rent himself, couldn't remember their names. However he would do his best not to let them know this. After all, they were good tenants and their rent money kept him and his family in luxury. So his eyes were alert when he asked for, 'Mrs Duffy?'

'Yes, Mr Coburn.' Maggie was sitting on one of the dining chairs and lifted her hand. 'I'm sorry if I've discommoded yer, but it can't be helped. Those people yer've put in Miss Parkinson's old house are rogues and thieves. They'll send me to an early grave with their carryings on, and you'll have no house left 'cos they'll destroy it.'

'They already have, Mrs Duffy. When Bill told me you'd said they were chopping doors up to make firewood, I didn't believe him because I thought it was too far-fetched. But you were right! That is precisely what they have done. They have stripped the place bare. I have over a hundred properties in the Liverpool area, and can honestly say I have never seen such wanton destruction in my life. But let me put your mind at rest, Mrs Duffy, and the rest of you ladies – those people will never again set foot in that house. And although I know it's small consolation after the worry you've been put through, your missing sheets are over there. Bill will get them for you before he changes the locks on the property and informs the police.'

Maggie gave a deep sigh of relief when she knew her bedding was safe, even though she'd have to wash it again. But she still had to say what was in her mind. 'The whole street knew that was a bad family from the night they turned up with a handcart, a load of rubbish and mouths that churned out the sort of language yer only ever hear from dockers or fishwives. So if we could see they were no good, why couldn't you?'

'Yes,' Winnie said, 'I'm surprised at you, Charlie, letting them get through the net. Yer must be slipping, lad.'

'I was given no hint that they were anything but a decent respectable family. A man came into the office, in work clothes, and said he was on his way to his job in the rope works in Hawthorne Road. He paid the week's rent in advance and I saw no reason why I shouldn't hand him the keys. How was I to know I'd been taken for a sucker? The man wasn't a member of the Hunt family, he was just someone the husband drank with and asked to do them a favour.' Charles Coburn glanced at Bill. 'You can tell them what we've found out today.'

'Well, with you ladies complaining about the family, and with me never seeing them, I didn't know what to think. So I asked one of the rent collectors who works in a different part of the city if he'd ever heard of them. He said the family were trouble-makers and a bad lot, but more than that he didn't say. However, I mentioned this to Mr Coburn when I got back to the office today, and we went in his car to find the other collector to ask if he knew any more than he'd told me.'

When Bill stopped to take a breath, Kate tried to hurry him up. 'Come on, Bill, don't keep us waiting, what did yer find out?'

'That the father of the family, Jack Hunt, known in most quarters as Jacko, is a rag and bone man, hence the handcart you saw them with. They make a habit of moving into houses for short stays, but from what we've been told they have a broken-down caravan on a field somewhere and live there like gypsies. What they've done to the house opposite is their usual trick. They've fooled many a landlord with it. They chop everything up that they can and sell it around the doors for firewood, and they'll steal anything they can get their hands on. The kids have been taught to steal from the time they are able to walk, don't see anything wrong with it because they don't know any different. What they rob, the man sells when he's out with his handcart. That's how they make a living. If you hadn't cottoned on to them, Mrs Duffy, and me and Mr Coburn hadn't acted so quickly, your sheets would have been on his handcart tomorrow, and sold to some unsuspecting woman.'

'And what about the damage to yer property, Charlie?' Winnie asked. 'Can't yer do nothing about it?'

'Wouldn't be worth trying, Winnie, I'm afraid. They're down and out rotters and haven't the money to pay for the damage, which I can tell you is extensive. Bill will inform the police in case they come back today and try to gain entry. The locks will be changed, but as they don't seem to have any fear of authority, they may break a window to get in. I don't think they will, but best not to take chances. They've hoodwinked me once, they'll not find it so easy to do it again.'

'D'yer know why me and me mates are so upset about it, Mr Coburn?' Kate asked. 'We were all fond of Miss Parkinson who was a good friend and neighbour. She loved that little house and looked after it well. It would break her heart if she knew what a state it was in now. Twenty-five years it was her home, and this lot come along and in three weeks they've ruined it. If I could get me hands around their necks, I'd strangle them.'

'Well, I don't intend to go as far as strangling them,' Charles

Coburn said, 'but I can assure you I won't allow them to get off scot-free. I intend to make it my business to find out where the caravan is stationed and I'll make life very unpleasant for them. I'm not a vindictive man but I strongly believe that men like this Hunt person should not be allowed to go through life without doing an honest day's work, living on the backs of decent, hard-working people.'

'That's a man after me own heart,' Monica said. 'Whatever yer have in mind to do, Mr Coburn, do it twice. Once for yerself and once for us.'

Thinking of the rents he still had to collect after he'd made the house opposite safe, Bill put a hand on Maggie's arm. 'If yer want to come over with me, Mrs Duffy, I'll hand the sheets out to you.'

'Yes, okay, lad, I'll come with yer. I might be able to get them washed again and on the line before the family come home.' She raised her eyes to the ceiling. 'My old ma used to say that a woman's work is never done, and I know only too well what she meant.'

When Maggie had left with the rent collector, Charles Coburn made a move to follow them. But he changed his mind and smiled down at Winnie. 'We had some good laughs when I was collecting the rents, didn't we? I remember you used to make the best pot of tea in Liverpool, and I can also remember the taste of your rhubarb pie. I used to look forward to getting to your house, my mouth would be watering while I waited for you to open the door.'

'Ah, well, that's yer own look out, Charlie! Yer went up in the world, and when yer started to employ men to do the collecting for yer, we only set eyes on yer every blue moon.' Winnie grinned impishly. 'Yer can't have plenty of money, posh clothes *and* my rhubarb pie.'

'But if I called one day, you wouldn't refuse me a cup of tea and a slice of pie, would you?'

'Of course I wouldn't, yer daft nit! But yer'd have to give me advance warning, 'cos I don't bake every day now I'm on me own. I don't forget friends, Charlie, and yer've done me some favours over the years so I'd be delighted to bake a pie especially for you.'

Kate pretended to look shocked. 'Winnie Cartwright, I do believe ye're flirting with the landlord! What would people think if they heard yer?'

'They'd think I was very enter— enter— oh, what's the word I'm looking for, Charlie?'

'I think the word you're looking for is enterprising, Winnie.'

'There yer are, queen, they'd think I was very enterprising.'

Monica chuckled. 'And forward, throwing yerself at him.'

'If yer insist, queen, I'll agree I'm enterprising, forward, and I'm throwing meself at him.'

Charles was enjoying himself, remembering all the laughs he'd had with this woman who was only the size of sixpennyworth of copper. But what she lacked in size, she made up for in honesty, loyalty, compassion and humour. And she had the courage of her convictions. She would never be afraid to tell you to your face what she thought of you, landlord or no landlord. 'If you're going to throw yourself at me, Winnie, can we do it in private, please? Say I call to your house on Friday, around twelve o'clock, so I'm hungry enough to eat a whole pie?'

'That's fine by me, lad, I'll look forward to it.'

Through everything that had been said over the last half-hour, Betty and Margaret had sat like statues. It was like being in the pictures, only this time they were in the best seats. Betty felt really important when as Charles was leaving he said to her, 'I know your face, you live in the next street, don't you?' When she nodded, he added, 'I'm good with faces but hopeless with names.'

He was almost out of the door when Monica said, 'Mr Coburn, we'll be watching out on Friday, and if ye're in Mrs Cartwright's house more than half an hour, we'll be knocking on her door.

After all, it doesn't take more than that to eat a piece of ruddy pie.'

Kate gasped. 'Monica Parry, don't be so rude!'

But Charles's head was thrown back and he roared with laughter. It was a long time since he'd enjoyed himself so much. 'Ah, a piece of pie, yes, I agree. But I intend to eat more than one piece if Winnie's baking is as good as it was when I last called. However, as you will be keeping vigil, I'll make sure I don't indulge myself too much, and there'll be a slice left for each of you.'

When the two women returned to the living room, Winnie was sitting with a look of pure innocence on her face. Kate stood in front of her, hands on hips and head tilted, and said, 'Well, aren't you a ruddy dark horse! Yer never mentioned that yer were on friendly terms with the landlord! In all the years I've known yer, yer've never said a dickie bird.'

Winnie lifted her open hands. 'What was there to tell yer, queen? I've lived in this street a lot longer than you young ones, so I'm bound to know more people than you do. There was a time when Charlie collected the rents himself every week, and we got on well together. I'd ask him in for a cuppa, and he became very partial to my pies.'

'Oh, come off it, girl, there's more to it than that!' Monica forgot herself and sat on the arm of the sofa until she saw the daggers coming her way from Kate, and quickly transferred her bottom to one of the wooden chairs. 'He was dead friendly with yer, and anyone with half an eye could see he was pleased to see yer.'

'And I was pleased to see him, queen, 'cos he's a nice bloke.'

Kate could see the little woman was reluctant to say any more, and she didn't blame her with Betty and Margaret being there. 'Well, I don't know about you ladies, but I'm going to have to get the dinner on the go. I haven't even peeled the spuds yet.'

Betty quickly got to her feet. 'Me and Margaret will have to be going as well. I just hope the stew hasn't burned the backside out of the pan. But I thank yer for inviting me and Margaret, Kate, 'cos it's been a real interesting afternoon.'

Margaret nodded. 'It certainly has, it's been an eye opener.'

'Yer must come again, when it's a bit quieter and we can have a talk.' Kate couldn't wait to get Winnie on her own. She felt there was a lot her friend was keeping to herself. While she might be wary with folk she didn't know very well, she would confide in her and Monica in private. 'One afternoon next week, perhaps?'

'You come to ours for a change. Say next Monday, and the three of yer are welcome.'

'That's nice of yer, Betty,' Monica said. 'We'll bring some cream cakes with us.'

'Yer will not! It will be afternoon tea and cakes, courtesy of Mrs Blackmore and her daughter, Mrs Corbett.'

'We'll look forward to that.' Kate saw them off before dashing back into the living room. 'Now, Mrs Cartwright, what's this about you and our landlord being on such close terms?'

'There was no reason for me to tell yer about him, queen, 'cos I didn't think I should discuss his business behind his back. But as there's only you and Monica, and I know anything I say will not be repeated, I'll tell yer, seeing as ye're so interested. It all happened a long time ago, I'm not telling yer anything new.

'Charles didn't own so much property in those days, and he used to do his own collecting. He'd tell me about his family while we were having a cuppa, just friendly chats. He had a wife and four young children who he idolized. Then something terrible happened. I can't remember how long ago it was, but it was before my Sam died that he lost his wife suddenly. She'd been complaining of headaches and the doctor was giving her pills to ease the pain. Gradually it got so bad, Charles took her straight to the hospital. They found some sort of growth on her brain, I can't remember what they called it, all I know is she died within two weeks and he was devastated, a broken man. Left with four young children and a business to run, he was out of his mind. I offered to go down every day and see the children had their breakfast and got off to school all right. Then I'd go back late afternoon for them coming home from school. I'd make them something to eat and stay with them until Charles got home. I did that until he found a daily help who would do everything, see to the children, do the cooking and the washing and ironing.'

Kate and Monica were both shaking their heads. 'The poor bugger!' Monica said, feeling for the man. While Kate asked, 'Winnie, why have yer never mentioned this to us? The poor man must have been out of his mind.'

'It wasn't my place to tell yer his business, queen. Besides which, I didn't know yer very well at that time. He took it very badly, as I did when Sam died, and that's only natural when yer lose someone yer love. He started to work harder and harder, buying up as many properties as he could lay his hands on. Not because he's a greedy man, but as he told me, to take his mind off what he had lost.'

'How old are the children?' Monica asked.

'They were schoolchildren then, quite young, but they'll all be grown up by now. I wouldn't be surprised if they weren't married. I've only seen Charlie a few times in the last ten years, and I didn't like asking in case it still hurt him to talk about it. He came to see me when Sam died, and offered me any help I wanted, but while I appreciated his offer, I was hurting too much inside to want to bother with anyone.' Winnie's sigh came from the heart. 'It's funny, but when someone yer love dies, yer try to punish yerself because yer feel guilty that you're alive and they're not.'

'Didn't he ever marry again, sunshine?'

'I couldn't tell yer that, queen, 'cos it's not the sort of question yer would ask. I wouldn't anyway.'

419

'Ooh, I think he will have done,' Monica said. 'With his looks and money, he'd have the women running after him. How old was he when his wife died?'

'This is a guess, queen, 'cos I don't really know. I'd say he would have been in his very early forties. He's roughly the same age as meself, give or take a year or two either way. But what I can say with great certainty is that he's one of the nicest men that ever walked the face of this earth. He doesn't deserve what those scoundrels did to the house opposite. I've never known him do anyone a bad turn.' Winnie gave a shiver, as though someone had walked over her grave, then stood up. 'I'm going to leave you to get on with yer dinner now, queen, 'cos you've had a house full of women nearly all day and I bet yer'll be glad to have it to yerself for a bit of peace and quiet.'

'Well, before yer go, girl, let's be serious for one minute,' Monica said. 'No messing about, like, but are yer really going to make a pie on Friday for Mr Coburn?'

Winnie grinned. 'That's for me to know, queen, and you to find out.'

John tried to show interest when his wife was telling him and the children about the busy, exciting day she and the neighbours had had. Any other day his interest would have been genuine, as well as his anger over the damage done to the house opposite. But he had news of his own, good news. He kept telling himself he had all night to tell Kate how his day had gone, but he'd hurried home, eager to see her face when he told her, and right now he felt a little disappointed.

'It's been some day, believe me,' Kate said. 'Me house has been full right up to four o'clock. Not that I minded, they're all me mates and my window was the nearest to the house opposite. But me head is spinning now.'

It was then that John had an inspiration. 'Then why don't we go for a walk after we've finished our dinner, to get some fresh air? I'm all dressed up, and as that doesn't happen very often, I may as well make the most of it.'

Kate's face told of her surprise. 'A walk! But we never go for a walk, you're usually too tired when yer get in from work.'

'Yes, I know, but it's a fine night so why not enjoy it? The cold nights will be on us before we know it. We could go to the park, that would be nice.'

'Oh, yeah, Mam, I could come with yer.' Billy stood his knife and fork up like soldiers on sentry duty. 'We could take some bread and feed the swans on the lake.'

Nancy nodded her head. 'I was just thinking the same thing. Go on, Mam, say we'll go to the park.'

John felt like a heel for putting a damper on their enthusiasm, but he'd make it up to them some other time. 'Wait a minute, kids, I was thinking of me taking yer mam on her own. We never get any time together, so just for once I'd like me wife to meself. Yer don't mind, do yer, just this once? I can't remember the last time I went for a stroll with Mrs Spencer.'

Billy thought that was dead soppy, but Nancy thought it ever so romantic. 'Me and Billy don't mind, we can play out while ye're gone.' She gave her brother a kick under the table. 'Yer don't mind, do yer, kid?'

But Kate was still surprised. 'I don't know what's got into yer! There's nothing I'd like better than a stroll through the park, but aren't yer tired after a day's work?'

John shook his head. 'I'm not too tired to go for a stroll with the one I love. In fact, now I've suggested it, I'm really keen.'

He looked so boyish when he smiled, and so handsome, Kate wouldn't have refused him anything. 'Right, then let's get our dinner over as quick as we can, and the dishes washed. They close the park gates about nine o'clock and I'd hate to get there to be told we've only got a few minutes.'

'I'll do the dishes, Mam,' Nancy said. 'You go and doll yerself up so yer'll look as pretty as me dad looks handsome.'

Kate didn't need telling twice. Her daughter was quite capable of washing the dishes and putting them away, and she'd tidy the room for when they got back. So upstairs Kate went and rooted out the one decent dress she possessed. She brushed her thick mop of dark hair until it shone. She didn't usually bother about her looks, but tonight she wanted to be at her best when she linked arms with the man she was crazy about. She even dug out a tube of lipstick that hadn't been used for goodness knows how long. When she looked in the full-length mirror on the inside door of the wardrobe, she felt quietly confident she looked her best.

Kate was the first to step down on to the pavement. She turned her head to ask, 'Shall we ask Monica and Tom if they want to come?'

John pulled the door shut, shaking his head. 'I want my wife all to meself, love. Just an hour's stroll, holding hands, like we did when we were courting.'

'Sounds good to me, sunshine, I'm all for it.'

It was only a ten-minute walk to the park, and they found they weren't the only ones wanting to catch the fresh air. There were plenty of people their age but very few children as it was the time youngsters would be getting ready for bed. They walked towards the lake. When John saw an empty bench, he led Kate towards it. 'Let's sit down, love, I've got something to tell yer.'

'Yer know, I could sense yer were on edge about something. I hope it's not bad news 'cos I've had a bellyful today.'

'No, love, it's very good news.' For the first time since they were married John was feeling proud of himself. He'd achieved something today which would make a world of difference to the beautiful woman who was looking at him now with a question in her eyes, and to his two children who never complained when they didn't get as much pocket money as their mates. 'I told yer a lie this morning, love. I didn't get dressed up to go for a pint with the blokes from work, I went for a job interview. I didn't want to tell yer in case I didn't get the job and yer'd be disappointed.'

Kate took hold of one of his hands. 'Yer know I'd never be disappointed in anything yer did, sunshine. We manage, and we'll keep on managing whether yer got the job or not.'

'I got the job, Kate, and it's seven and six a week more than I'm getting now.'

Her response brought a lump to his throat. She stared at him, her wide eyes showing every emotion she was going through. There was doubt at first, as though she didn't quite believe him. Then came surprise, happiness, and a surge of love for the man who always belittled himself because he couldn't give her the standard of living he would have liked for her. 'Oh, sunshine, that's marvellous news!' Ignoring the looks and smiles of people walking by, she threw her arms around his neck. 'I am so proud of you, I love yer enough to eat yer. And to think I never stopped gabbing over our meal while you were sitting with this wonderful news and not being given a chance tell it. Yer should have shut me up, sunshine, I wouldn't have minded. In fact, me and the kids would have jumped for joy. But why didn't yer tell the children instead of making an excuse about coming for a walk?' Then she clapped a hand over her mouth for a second. 'See, I'm doing it again! I should be asking yer where the job is, what yer'll be doing, and when do yer start?'

'It's Tom's old job. And yer can thank yer best mate for me getting the chance of an interview. Tom said as soon as he told Monica he was being promoted, she said why didn't he try and get me his old job?'

This was another surprise. 'Yer mean, Monica knew! Well, I've never known her keep a secret from me before.'

'I didn't want her to tell yer. I was afraid I wouldn't get the job and I'd have felt really worthless if I had to disappoint you. But I've got a lot to thank her and Tom for, they've really been the best friends we could ask for.'

'Well, what happens now, d'yer have to give yer notice in?'

'I'll do that tomorrow. I start me new job a week on Monday. I'll be travelling with Tom every morning, and it's a couple of tram stops less than I travel now.'

'Will yer have to work a week in hand?' This would be a worry because they had no money put by. When John nodded, she asked, 'How will we manage?'

'I'll be drawing me week in hand, plus me week's wages when I leave this job.' He'd been dreading having to tell her this, but he wasn't going to lie to her. 'And I've got a confession to make, love.' He took both her hands in his. 'I know I told yer I wouldn't bet on the gee-gees ever again, but I didn't keep me promise because I wanted to win a few bob for you and the kids, save yer struggling from week to week. Anyway, I've had a few bets, the horse lost every time, and I owe one of the blokes four bob.'

Kate's face set. John knew how she hated gambling yet he'd let her down. And, worst of all, he'd gone into debt for it. He averted his eyes so he wouldn't have to see her hurt. 'But we'll manage all right because it's only four bob, two bob a week out of the two weeks' wages. And if we get stuck, Tom said they'll give me a sub for the first week. He said most blokes get one to tide them over when they first start.'

'Well, you're not like most blokes, John Spencer, 'cos yer won't be getting a sub. We'll get by, even if we go hungry. I've never owed a penny in me life, so the first thing yer do is pay yer gambling debts. And don't you ever put another penny on a horse, no matter who says it's a dead cert. I feel really disappointed in yer, John, yer've let me down.'

'I won't need to back horses when I'm in me new job! The extra seven and six a week should make life much easier for yer. That's all I ever wanted, love, to make life easier for you and the children. I never wanted anything for meself.'

Kate knew this was true, and when she heard the anguish in his voice her heart melted. She put a hand under his chin and turned his face so he was staring into her eyes. 'I know yer'd give me and the kids the world if yer could, sunshine, same as I know yer'd go without yerself to give to us. And me and the kids love the bones of yer, yer know that. Now that everything's out in the open, no more secrets, let's celebrate your new job. I think it would be nice if I linked your arm, as I used to all those years ago, and we strolled back home to tell our children that their clever dad has got some good news to tell them.' She pulled him to his feet, lifted her face for a kiss, then linked his arm. 'I think they could have an extra tuppence a week pocket money, don't you?'

'I'll pass me wage packet over to you, love, like I always have. It's up to you what you do with it.'

'Well, I'm sure about the kids getting an extra tuppence a week pocket money, and I think you deserve another packet of Woodbines and a pint when yer feel like one. And then, for my treat, I'll let yer take me to the pictures now and again, as long as we sit on the back row holding hands.'

He squeezed her hand. 'Your wish is my command, Mrs Spencer. The back row it will be, and I'll put me arm around yer shoulders and steal a sly kiss when no one is looking.' He chuckled. 'Not that anyone would notice, they'd be too busy doing the same thing.'

Monica was welcomed with open arms the next morning. 'I don't know how to thank you, sunshine,' Kate said, hugging the life out of her friend. 'Except to say yer must be the best friend anyone could ever have.'

Monica brushed it aside as though it was nothing, even though she'd jumped for joy when Tom came home from work last night and told her John had passed the interview. 'If yer can't help a mate, girl, then yer wouldn't be much of a friend. Anyway, Tom only steered John in the right direction, he didn't get him the job. Yer husband did that himself, girl, because the boss said he passed the interview with flying colours.' She pulled a chair out from the table and plonked herself down. 'I called last night but the kids said yer'd gone for a walk. I thought they were kidding, but no, Nancy said you'd gone for a stroll like yer used to do before yer got married. She didn't seem to know about her dad getting a new job.'

Kate shook her head. 'John wanted to tell me on me own, and as he was all dressed up, he suggested going for a walk. I thought it funny, but never in a million years would I have guessed why. The children know now, of course, we came straight home and told them. Like me, they're over the moon as I said they'd be getting an extra tuppence a week pocket money.'

Kate wrapped her arms around herself, her face alight. 'I won't know I'm born with the extra money coming in. There'll be no scratching and scraping this Christmas. It'll be the full works, with turkey, lots of food, presents and new clothes.'

'Yer've left something out, girl. Yer forgot to include the party on Christmas Day.'

'Oh, I haven't forgotten, sunshine, we'll have a real knees-up.'

Winnie arrived at that moment, and was so pleased for John and Kate anyone would have thought it was she who would be getting an extra seven and six a week. 'Oh, I am happy for yer, queen, that's marvellous news.'

'Ay, there's another bit of news, Winnie, yer'll be glad to know,' Monica told her. 'In that diary yer keep talking about, yer can fill in that yer've been invited as a special guest to the Spencers' house on Christmas Day.'

'Don't push yer luck, sunshine, it's from seven-thirty on Christmas night, not all day.'

'Yer don't have to do this, yer know, queen, because yer've got enough with yer own family to cope with. I'm very grateful and beholden to yer for thinking of me, but I do understand yer've got enough on yer plate.'

'Oh, but I want to have a party, sunshine, I really do! Every other Christmas I've had to scrimp and scrape. This will be the first time I can go a little mad with money. And as ye're one of me best friends, then of course I want yer to come. In fact, if the house was bigger, I'd invite all the people I like. The Blackmores with Margaret and Greg, Mrs Duffy from over the road, but the place wouldn't hold them.'

'No, yer've got enough on yer plate with us, girl, or yer'd be run off yer feet making cakes and sandwiches.' Monica crossed her legs. 'Anyway, Margaret will probably have had the baby by then. According to Betty, it's around the end of November or the first week in December. As she said, yer can't always tell with a first baby.'

'I bet the girl will be glad when it's over,' Kate said, pulling a face. 'I don't envy her the labour part, but when the baby's put in her arms for the first time, she'll find it's the happiest moment of her life. And Greg will walk around as though he's the only man ever to take part in the making of a baby. But I wish them both well, they're a lovely couple and I can't wait for the baby to arrive.'

'I'm knitting her a shawl, yer know, queen, so will yer tell her when yer see her? I'd hate her to go out and buy one.' Winnie looked at the clock. 'Are yer ready for the shops? After we've done our shopping, I'm going to nip down to the market to see if Sarah Jane has got anything that I might like.'

'Yer've been there the last few Saturdays but yer never bring anything home,' Kate said. 'Don't yer look through the clothes while ye're there?'

'I go to help her out, queen, 'cos she gets very busy on a Saturday. I don't really get a chance to look for anything for meself. Besides, I've got enough dresses to keep me going. But with Charlie coming on Friday, I thought I'd treat meself. I don't want to look like Orphan Annie when he's dressed to kill.'

'I'm beginning to think there's more to this than meets the

eye.' Monica's slowly nodding head spoke volumes. 'There's far more to it than one of your rhubarb pies.'

'As I've told yer, queen, it's for me to know and you to find out. But remember, all is pure to the pure.' Winnie turned her head to wink at Kate. 'Shall we make a move? Oh, and remind me to get some decent rhubarb while we're in the greengrocer's.'

'It seems funny without Winnie,' Kate said on the Friday morning as she and Monica did their shopping. 'I miss her!'

'Yeah, me too! She grows on yer, does Winnie. I've gone from thinking she was a real jangler, to finding her nice, then a good friend, and now to loving her like a mother. I'm wondering what's going on in her house right now?'

'She'll tell us when we see her if she wants to, sunshine. I bet her and Mr Coburn are just enjoying a nice cup of tea, a slice of pie, and a friendly chat. I think it was a spur of the moment thing with him, she'll probably never see him again after today. But I'm glad for her, 'cos she doesn't have much in her life.'

They would have been very surprised if they could have looked into their friend's living room for Charles Coburn had taken his hat and coat off and made himself at home. Winnie had insisted he sit in her best chair, the one she'd been given by Miss Parkinson. As she poured the tea into the best teacups she told him how she'd acquired both chair and china. There were no airs and graces about Winnie, what you saw was what you got. That was what Charles found so refreshing.

One bite of her rhubarb pie had him groaning with pleasure. 'It's even better than I remember.' In no time he'd devoured a generous slice.

'Another piece, Charlie? There's plenty left.' Winnie had been living alone for so long, she'd forgotten the satisfaction of seeing a man with a healthy appetite making short work of her baking. 'And I'll fill yer cup while I'm at it.'

'You're going to spoil me, I'll be coming back for more.' He ran the back of his hand across his mouth. 'I've got a woman that comes in and does the cleaning and cooking for me, but she can't hold a candle to you for pastry.'

'How are the children now, Charlie, they must be quite grown up?'

'There's only the youngest one at home, the other three are married. So there's just me and Charlotte rattling around in that big house. And she's courting strong, so it won't be long before I'm on my own.'

'Yer never married again, then, Charlie? I'm surprised someone hasn't snapped yer up.'

'No, I've never been tempted. Well, I won't say never because there was one woman I felt would make me a good partner. We enjoyed the same things, had the same outlook on life and both liked a laugh. But that was years ago now. Nothing came of it because she'd been through a bad experience and I felt it wasn't right. Whenever I think of her, I tell myself I should have tried harder. But that's water under the bridge now.' Charles leaned forward to put his cup on the table. 'What about yourself, Winnie, have you never thought of marrying again since Sam died?'

She shook her head. 'No, I went through a bad patch when I lost him and for years I wasn't interested in life. I'm fine now, though, I've got loads of friends and have such a busy social life I think I'm going to have to buy a diary to keep up with meself. And I've got one woman to thank for the good life I have now, and that's Kate Spencer. Yer know her, it was her house yer were in on Monday.'

'The one with looks like a film star?'

'That's her, Charlie, and she's the only one who doesn't know how beautiful she is. If I had her looks I'd be walking around swanking. But not Kate, she's one of the nicest people yer could ever meet. I don't know what I would have done without her.'

'How do you manage for money, Winnie? Do you have to struggle?'

Her pride came to the fore. 'Certainly not! I'm not loaded, but I manage very well. I certainly don't go short of anything.'

'In that case, can I call on you again, in the hope you've baked a pie?'

'Charlie, ye're always welcome here. And perhaps I'll make an apple pie next time, just for a change, so yer'll know I have more strings to me bow. But yer'll have to give me notice, like I've said.'

'I can slip away any day in my dinner break, so how about Monday?'

'Ay, yer'll have the neighbours talking! They're probably wondering now what ye're doing here. And some of them have terrible minds.'

'And does that worry you?'

Winnie huffed. 'Ay, Charlie, they're the last ones to worry me. It's your reputation I'm thinking of.'

'Have no fear over that, Winnie, I'm a free man and can do as I wish. So I'll call on Monday, same time, to sample your apple pie. And to repay you for your hospitality, you must allow me to take you to lunch one day. Say the Rose Restaurant in Lewis's?'

Winnie chuckled. 'Yer'll be getting me a name like a mad dog, Charlie, but what the hell? Yer only live once.'

Monica nudged Kate's arm as they turned into the street. 'The landlord's car is still outside Winnie's. I think they were more friendly all those years ago than she's letting on.'

Kate tutted. 'Ye're the limit, you are, Monica Parry! Ten minutes ago yer loved her like a mother, now ye're calling her underhanded!'

'I don't mean nothing, girl, it's just that yer know how nosy I am. I won't rest until she tells us everything that went on.' This time Monica's nudge accompanied an increase in pace. 'Ay, girl, the postman's just put a letter through yer letter box. Come on, let's see who it's from.'

Kate could feel herself being propelled forward. 'Just in case yer've forgotten, sunshine, it's my letter box he's put the letter through. So what makes yer think I'm going to tell yer who it's from?'

'Yer won't need to, girl, 'cos I'll be reading it over yer shoulder to save time and your breath.'

When they got in Kate's house, the baskets were dumped on the floor and there was a mad scramble for the letter. Kate had no intention of being beaten in her own house so she elbowed Monica out of the way and reached the letter first. 'Ooh, it must be from Miss Parkinson 'cos it's got an Essex postmark. I was beginning to think she'd forgotten us.' She tore at the envelope and as she pulled out two sheets of paper, some photographs fell out with them. 'Oh, look, sunshine, what she's sent us.'

'You read the letter, girl, while I look at the snaps,' Monica said. 'Then we can swap over.' She picked up a snap of Miss Parkinson sitting in a chair in a beautiful garden, surrounded by flowers and trees. 'Oh, wait until yer see these, girl, yer'll probably cry yer bleeding eyes out. I'm not far from tears meself.'

'I'll read you the letter first. Miss Parkinson says she's very sorry she hasn't written to thank us for the marvellous photographs which she will always cherish, and how kind we were to have thought of it. The reason for her not writing before now is that she wanted to send us some snaps of herself in her new home and had to wait for them to be developed. She says she thinks of us very often and misses us.' Kate passed the letter over. 'Here, read it for yerself before I start bawling. I keep thinking of how gentle and kind she was, and how sad she'd be if she knew what had happened to her little house.'

Monica sniffed all the way through the letter. 'I still miss her, yer know. But just look at where she's living now, she's much better off. And she's not half pleased with those photographs, girl, I'm glad yer had that brain wave.'

'We'll have to show these to Winnie and Maggie, they'll be

made up. And we'll take turns in writing to her. Even though she's with her family, and being well looked after, it would be nice for her to have friends to keep in touch with. So as I wrote the last one, I think Winnie should answer this letter because they were very good friends. And Miss Parkinson has mentioned every one of us by name.'

'Shall we take the letter and photographs to Winnie's now? I'm sure she'd love to know we've had them.' Monica sat back and waited for the outcry. She didn't have to wait long.

'Don't you dare go to Winnie's while Mr Coburn's there! Ye're a nosy article, Monica Parry, but I'll not . . .' Kate broke off when she saw the smile in Monica's eyes. 'I fell for it again, didn't I? When will I ever learn?'

'The day you learn, girl, will be the day we stop laughing. So keep on being naive, for heaven's sake, or life won't be worth living.'

Chapter Twenty-Nine

As the months passed by, and winter set in, Kate was happier than she'd been for a long time. She didn't have to struggle now, wondering what to buy every day that would be cheapest, and an extra bag of coal wasn't considered a luxury. Not that she was well off, mind, not by a long chalk. But she was a damn' sight better off than she had been before John got his new job. Out of the extra seven and six a week in his wage packet, which he always passed over unopened, Kate gave him back an extra one and six for cigarettes and an occasional pint with Tom. The children got their tuppence pocket money, and an extra sixpence a week went on her Christmas clubs in the butcher's, sweet shop, confectioner's and greengrocer's. There'd be no penny pinching this year, and to Kate that was real luxury. Oh, and now and again she went to the pictures with John, but they didn't always sit on the back row. The first time they'd tried it, they found themselves sitting with young couples to either side who hadn't the slightest interest in the film. Their antics were embarrassing to a man and wife who had been married for over sixteen years. They'd had a laugh about it, but had never tried the back row since.

These things were running through Kate's head as she plumped the cushions on the sofa. Life was good now, no doubt about that. It always had been, of course, because health, happiness and love came before money, and her family had those in abundance. But she wouldn't argue that a few bob extra every week was the icing on the cake.

When the knock came on the wall to warn her Monica was on her way, Kate was grinning as she went to open the door. She was very heavy-handed, her mate, and one of these days she'd knock a hole in the wall. Mind you, if you told her that, she'd just shrug her shoulders and say it would save her the bother of closing her front door and having to wait on Kate's step until the slow-coach decided to open hers.

'Morning, girl!' Monica was rubbing her hands together. 'It's a bit nippy out there, yer need yer fleecy-lined on today.'

'I knew yer'd be cold, sunshine, that's why I've got a nice fire going for yer. Sit in my chair and warm the cockles of yer heart.'

'Ye're in a very generous mood today, girl, and very chirpy. Did Robin Hood pay yer a visit last night?' Monica spread her hands in front of the fire. 'If he did, he was very quiet about it. I didn't hear no bedsprings going.'

Kate tutted. 'You and flaming Robin Hood! I don't know how yer dreamed him up. Yer must have a hankering for Errol Flynn.'

Monica pushed a finger under the headscarf she was wearing and scratched her head. 'Nah, I couldn't see my feller being Errol Flynn, me imagination's not that good.'

'Poor Tom! He's a smashing husband, gives yer everything yer want, and yet yer still pull him down. Yer don't know how lucky yer are, sunshine.'

'Oh, but I do, girl, I'm not that daft. I wouldn't swap him for all the tea in China. Not even for Robin Hood. But I'm not going to tell him that or he'll be getting big-headed.'

Kate gave a last glance around the room to make sure everything was in its place and the highly polished sideboard and grate, lit by the dancing flames from the fire, were shining. 'Shall I put the kettle on, sunshine, or shall we wait for Winnie?'

'Let's wait for Winnie, see if she's got any news for us. Mind you, she doesn't half play her cards close to her chest. The whole street is talking about how Mr Coburn calls to her house once a week, sometimes twice, but she never cracks on to anyone. He picks her up in his car every Wednesday afternoon, and although we know she goes for lunch with him to Lewis's Rose Restaurant, or on occasion the Adelphi, none of the other neighbours know where she goes. She waves to them as she's getting in the car but doesn't mention where she's going or where she's been, and none of them like to ask because of him being their landlord. They've got this cockeyed idea that if they rub Winnie up the wrong way, she'll tell Mr Coburn and he'll throw them out of their houses.'

'That's stupid, that is!' Kate sat on the end of the sofa near the fire. 'As though she'd do anything like that! She minds her own business, and I admire her for it. Yer never hear her bragging about being friends with the landlord, do yer? No, he's just a good friend and they get on well together. Two lonely people who are company for each other.'

'D'yer really believe that, girl? I find it hard to swallow a tale like that. I'm not saying any hanky-panky is going on, because Winnie's not like that, but they must like each other a lot to keep seeing each other. And she feeds him up when he comes, it's not just a cup of tea and a piece of pie any more.'

'None of our business, sunshine, Winnie doesn't have to tell us anything. And although I've got to admit to being a bit curious meself, I don't blame her. I'm just glad that she seems happier now she has someone her own age she can look forward to seeing and having a good chat with. They've known each other for donkey's years so they've plenty in common. We've got our husbands to look forward to seeing every night, Winnie hasn't had anyone for a long time. So let's be glad for her, eh?'

'You're too bloody good to be true, you are, girl. If I'd known her as long as you have, I'd have wheedled everything out of her by now.'

'And what good would it have done me?'

'Well, it might not have done you any good, but it would have done me a power of good, wheedling it out of you.'

'I never betray a confidence, sunshine, yer should know that by now. Not a really private thing like Winnie's friendship with

Mr Coburn anyway. Little trivial things that don't matter, yes, I might, but then everybody does.'

'It's definitely the front row for you when yer get to heaven. And I wouldn't be surprised if yer didn't have a halo and harp.' Monica's throaty chuckle ended in a cough. 'I nearly choked meself then. I opened me mouth to speak and got a frog in me throat.'

'I heard that chuckle of yours,' Kate said. 'Ye're the only person I know who has a dirty laugh. So, come on, what were yer going to say before yer decided to choke yerself instead?'

'It was just that I'd never find out if yer get yer halo and harp, 'cos the likelihood of me ever getting to the pearly gates is very remote.'

'Don't be acting the goat! Yer stand as much chance as anyone. Ye're not a bad person who does lots of horrible things, like the family that were in Miss Parkinson's house and ruined it. Your only fault, apart from being nosy, is the bad language yer sometimes use. And if yer put yer mind to it, yer could be back on the path of righteousness in no time.'

'It's no good yer trying to change me, girl, 'cos I'm not going to. Me ma swore like a ruddy trooper, and I take after her.' Monica grinned at her friend. 'Anyway, let's leave the state of my soul and talk about something else. Like how much nicer it is to look over at Miss Parkinson's house and see clean windows and pure white nets. The window sill and step are probably the cleanest in the street now, and they're a nice, friendly family.'

Kate nodded. 'Winnie said Mr Coburn, or Charlie as she calls him, was much more careful over choosing tenants this time. No more rotters will get past him.'

'Yer didn't tell me that Winnie told yer that! Look, girl, if we're supposed to be best mates, yer can't be keeping things from me.'

'That came out without me realizing, so don't start making

STROLLING WITH THE ONE I LOVE

anything out of it. It was just a chance remark she made, nothing more.'

'I know, girl, keep yer hair on! I was here when she said it, I was only pulling yer leg.'

'Seeing as we're on the subject of Winnie, I'm wondering where she's got to. She's usually here by now. I wonder if she's all right, sunshine. Shall we walk down and see?'

'Yeah, we better had, 'cos she's always here before me. Get yer coat on, girl. But if we meet her coming up, we're coming back in here for a cuppa. And she'll get a piece of me mind for keeping us waiting.'

Kate felt in her pocket to make sure she had the key with her, then pulled the door shut. After a glance down the street, she said, 'There's no sign of her coming up, perhaps she's feeling a bit off colour. We'd better make sure she's all right.'

Monica rapped on Winnie's knocker, and the friends waited. When there was no answer, they peeped through the net curtains. 'That's funny, there's no sign of life.'

'Then there's something wrong,' Kate said. 'Because she wouldn't go off to the shops on her own, that's a dead cert.'

'She may be down the yard, girl, so we'll give it a few minutes then knock again. She's probably on a call of nature, it happens to the best of people.'

But five minutes and half a dozen knocks later, there was still no sign of life. Kate said, 'Let's try next door and see if Peggy Hastings knows anything. She may have seen her going out.'

When Peggy opened the door, Kate asked, 'Have yer seen anything of Winnie? She should have been at my house half an hour ago.'

'Oh, Winnie went out at half-past eight. I was up making me beds when I heard this loud knocking and commotion so I came down to see what was going on. It was Betty Blackmore and she was in a terrible state. Apparently the two men left for work at half-seven, and half an hour later her daughter Margaret went into labour. So Betty rushes round to the midwife's to be told she'd been called out on an emergency call. Winnie was the first one Betty thought of. She really was a bundle of nerves, 'cos she'd had to leave her daughter alone in the house when she was having labour pains. Anyway, Winnie dropped everything and went with Betty. As I haven't seen hide nor hair of her since, I can't tell yer what's happening now.'

'Ooh, we'd better get round to Betty's to see if we can help,' Kate said. 'Don't yer agree, Monica?'

'Yeah, definitely! The shopping can wait, Margaret is more important.' Monica touched Peggy's arm. 'Ay, girl, would yer mind if we went through your house to the entry? It would save us going all the way round.'

'Of course yer can, lass, as long as yer keep yer eyes closed. I haven't put a hand to me living room yet, it's like a muck midden.'

'Ay, yer should see the state of mine, girl,' Monica said, to make the woman feel better. 'I haven't even made me beds yet.'

Kate was shaking her head as she followed the two women through the living room and down the yard. To hear her mate talk, anyone would think her house was a mess. And as for coming out and leaving her beds unmade, well, she wouldn't dream of it. Kate knew for certain that her beds had been made at half-eight because she was making hers at the same time and could hear Monica through the dividing wall. Still, that little white lie was told for a good cause and could be a point in her favour when she came face to face with Saint Peter.

'Thank you, sunshine,' Kate said when they stepped into the entry with Betty's door only yards away. 'Yer saved us the walk round.'

'Let's know if there's any news, lass, won't yer?' Peggy had known Margaret since she was a baby in a pram. 'And tell them I hope it's soon over.'

The Blackmores' entry door was only on the latch. The two

friends were soon up the yard and knocking on the kitchen door. It was opened by Betty. Her eyes were red from crying, and she looked very agitated. 'Come in, I'm glad ye're here. I've had to leave Winnie with Margaret while I came down to make us a drink. What a morning it's been! I wouldn't want another one like it. We were eating our breakfast, and Margaret was fine. Then she suddenly clutched her tummy and let out a moan. I've prayed more in the last hour than I've prayed in all me life.'

'What about the midwife, sunshine, is she coming?' Kate asked. 'I know yer booked her months ago to come when Margaret went into labour.'

'Well, it seems my daughter isn't the only one because the midwife was called out in the early hours of the morning. She wasn't expecting to be needed here because Margaret isn't due for another couple of weeks.'

'My ma used to say a first baby will come when it feels like it,' Monica said. 'Two weeks early or two weeks late. Nurse Griffith is bound to come as soon as she can. Yer did leave word with her husband, didn't yer, girl?'

Betty nodded. 'He said as soon as she got home, he'd send her round. Anyway, if yer want to help, would yer make a pot of tea and I'll go back upstairs? Margaret is terrified, and I'm not a ha'porth of good at times like this. But Winnie's been brilliant, trying to keep our minds occupied and even making us laugh. Still, I can't leave her on her own, I'll get back up there. Yer'll find everything yer want in the pantry, a tray as well. Yer may as well have a cup of tea with us, it'll take Margaret's mind off things.'

'Hang on a minute, girl,' Monica took hold of her arm. 'How often is she having contractions?'

'Every eight to ten minutes now. If she keeps this up, the baby should be born by dinner time. God, I hope so, for Margaret's sake. I'd hate her to have a long labour, she's only young and hasn't a clue what she's got to go through.'

'You go up, Betty, and we'll see to the tea.' Kate gave her a gentle push. 'We'll bring a tray up and have a cuppa with yer. As yer say, it will take yer daughter's mind off what's in store for her.'

As Monica was setting the cups and saucers on the tray, she asked, 'Hey, girl, have yer ever been present when a baby's been born?'

'Only when me own two were born, sunshine, and I was only there because I had to be.'

'Well, what would yer do if the midwife doesn't turn up? Would yer stay in the bedroom and help deliver the baby, or would yer turn tail and run?'

'I would like to turn tail and run, sunshine, but it would depend upon the circumstances. Although I'd be scared stiff, I wouldn't leave Betty and Winnie, I'd stay and give what help I could. Even if it was only fetching and carrying, hot water and towels and things.'

'Then I'll stay with yer, girl, I wouldn't let yer down. But if yer see me lips moving, it's because I'll be praying for the midwife to turn up, 'cos I'm not cut out to deliver babies.'

'There's a first time for everything, sunshine, yer'll live through it. But while we're waiting, you carry the tray up and I'll walk behind yer with the teapot.'

They were on the small landing, outside the main bedroom, and Monica was just going to shout to ask one of them to open the door. Before she had time, there came a piercing scream which nearly caused her to drop the tray. 'Oh, my God! I don't think I can go in there, girl, I'd only make Margaret feel worse. I certainly wouldn't be any help. I'll put the tray down here and Betty can get it when things calm down.'

'Don't you dare, Monica Parry, or I'll tell everyone what a coward yer are. Now let me get near the door so I can knock. And don't be thinking of an excuse to get away because I'll tell them ye're a liar as well as a coward.'

Betty opened the door. 'Come on in and put the tray down on the tallboy. The pains are coming more frequently now, about every five minutes. Will you two stay with Winnie while I run to the midwife's again and see if there's any word of her?'

Winnie was sitting on the side of the bed, holding Margaret's hand. She turned to smile at her friends. 'I'm sorry I couldn't let yer know. I was a bit worried about yer sitting waiting for me, but then I told meself yer'd find out somehow where I was.'

Kate sat on the opposite side of the bed, and wagged her head from side to side as she smiled at Margaret. 'Well, yer certainly picked a fine time, sunshine! Yer should have begun an hour earlier and then Greg would have been here to see what we women have to go through. Not that it lasts long, though, and to be quite truthful I forgot all about the pain as soon as the baby arrived. I never told John that, of course, and he waited on me hand and foot for a month.' She turned to Monica. 'Would yer pour half a cup for Margaret, sunshine, and fill it up with milk? She'll be able to drink it before she has another contraction.'

'Shall I pour one for you, Betty?'

'No, girl, I'll wait until later. The midwife might be home by now, and I can bring her back with me.' Betty gazed lovingly at her daughter. 'I won't be long, pet, I'll hurry all the way. You try and drink some tea, yer must be thirsty.'

Margaret's heart was beating like a drum, and she'd never been so afraid in her life. But she managed a tearful, quivering smile. 'If Greg was here, he'd be lying flat out on the floor in a dead faint. He wouldn't be much help, I'm afraid.'

Kate chucked her playfully under the chin. 'Well, if you are a very brave and clever girl, yer might be nursing your new baby by the time he gets home. And wouldn't that be a big surprise for him to come back to?'

Monica leaned across the bed. 'Here yer are, girl, drink this tea. I've put a lot of milk in it so yer can drink it quick.'

Margaret's hand reached out to take the cup, but was quickly pulled back to clutch her stomach as a scream of pain left her lips. Betty, who was just letting herself out of the front door, turned on her heel and ran back up the stairs.

The only calm person in the room was Winnie. 'I think yer'd better lay flat, queen, and let me have a look what's going on. I've got a feeling ye're one of the lucky ones whose baby can't wait to see its mam. So be a good girl and slide yerself down in the bed.' She noticed Margaret's eyes flicker to where the other three were standing, concern on their faces. When she looked back to the girl, she saw that mingled with the pain was embarrassment. 'Would you ladies wait outside for a few minutes, to let the girl have some privacy?'

Kate took a deep breath. 'Winnie, d'yer know what ye're doing? Why not wait until the midwife gets here?'

'There won't be time for that, queen.' Winnie sensed their apprehension and asked, 'D'yer know Sheila Harrison and Ben Simmons?'

'Yeah, of course we do, sunshine, but what's that got to do with the present situation?'

'I brought both of them into the world, queen, and I managed fine.' Winnie would laugh later when it was all over and she could bring to mind the look of surprise on their three faces. 'So out yer go while I see to Margaret. Then I'll tell yer what needs doing. If the midwife comes in the meantime, all well and good. If not, we'll have to get on with it. Yer'll be surprised how easy it is.'

'Shall I stay, Winnie?' Betty asked, thinking that as the mother it was her place to be there, and not leave it all to a kind neighbour. 'Not that I'll be any help, I'd be useless.'

'What you can do, Betty, is find a small, clean towel, to twist into a roll for Margaret to bite on when she gets a pain. But now, out with the lot of yer so I can go about me business.'

The next hour was hectic. Margaret was having contractions every two minutes, and Winnie gave orders for plenty of hot water and sheets. The baby's head was engaged now, and she allowed no one in the room because she thought they would pass their fear on to the girl giving birth. She was gripping the sheets, her cries of pain dulled by the towel she was biting on. And all the time the women outside could hear Winnie's calm voice giving encouragement and praise. 'Come on now, queen, take a nice deep breath and then push as hard as yer can. Yer've being very brave, and I'm proud of yer.'

Then came an agonizing scream that turned Betty's blood cold. She wanted to be there to hold her daughter. But a second later they heard the sweetest sound in the world: the first cry of a newborn baby. The three women wrapped their arms around each other and shed tears of joy and relief.

The midwife was full of apologies when Betty opened the door. 'I'm sorry, Mrs Blackmore, but I was called out early and it was a difficult birth. The baby was breech, and the poor woman was in agony for twelve hours. I couldn't leave her.'

'It's all right, I understand. If it hadn't been for a certain woman yer probably know, I'd have been out of me mind, but Winnie Cartwright delivered the baby and we'll be forever in her debt. Margaret now has a beautiful little baby girl, and mother and daughter are doing well. But I think Winnie would like yer to have a look to make sure. She's upstairs with Margaret who's absolutely thrilled. No one has ever had a baby as beautiful as hers.'

Nurse Griffith smiled at Kate and Monica as she passed the table to go upstairs. 'Busy morning, ladies?'

Monica rolled her eyes. 'Worse than a horror movie, Nurse. My feller won't be allowed in me bedroom tonight, never mind me bed.'

'If Mrs Cartwright was here, there was no need for panic, she's as good as any midwife.' Rose Griffith was middle-aged with a grown-up family of her own. As she stood at the bottom of the stairs she laughed, saying, 'If I ever get pregnant again, I'll send for Winnie.'

'If I ever get pregnant again, I'll throw meself in the Mersey,' Monica said. 'Either that or I'll throw my feller in.'

'Many a true word spoken in jest, sunshine.' Kate lifted the tablecloth. 'Touch wood, just in case.'

Before following the nurse up the stairs, Betty said, 'I'll have to go in case the nurse wants me to get anything for Margaret, and I want to ask her about breast feeding the baby. Would yer put the kettle on so we can enjoy a decent cup of tea? I'll send Winnie down, she deserves a break if anyone does. She is a brick, that woman, takes everything in her stride and never turns a hair. God alone knows what I would have done without her.'

'You'd better get upstairs, sunshine, and listen to what the nurse has to say.' Kate smiled. 'It's a good job over, a big worry off yer mind. And as yer say, Winnie's been a real hero. Margaret, too! She's been very good considering she's so young.'

Betty's breast swelled with pride. 'Yes, she's been a real trooper. Greg is going to get the surprise of his life when he gets home, and my Jack. There'll be no stopping the pair of them. Anyway, I'll send Winnie down, and as soon as the nurse goes, yer can go up and see the baby before Margaret goes to sleep. The poor kid looks worn out.' She got halfway up the stairs and shouted down, 'Don't forget the tea, I'm spitting feathers.'

Left to themselves, the two friends went out to the kitchen. 'You see to the cups, sunshine, and I'll put the kettle on.' After putting a light under the kettle, Kate leaned back against the sink and folded her arms. 'My ma used to say that yer learn something new every day, and I can see what she meant by it. The last few months have been one surprise after another. There was the day I went to see the headmaster about those bully boys, then Miss Parkinson being robbed and moving soon after. That was a big surprise, and not a nice one for us. Then came the Hunt family to disrupt our lives with their rowdy shenanigans. The next one I can think of was a really good surprise, thanks to you, that was my John getting a new job. But I think today tops the lot, don't you?'

'It puts them in the shade, girl, puts them in the bleeding shade. No doubt about that.' Monica nodded to confirm her statement. 'I got the shock of me life when Winnie said she'd delivered Sheila and Ben. She's never mentioned it! And from the way the nurse spoke, they won't be the only two, either.'

'I feel really stupid now for asking her if she knew what she was doing.' Kate moved away from the sink to turn the gas off under the kettle. 'She's done more in her life than I'll ever do in mine.'

'If you feel stupid, girl, how d'yer think I feel? At least yer've always been a friend of hers, and shut me up every time I said she was a jangler. For years that's how I saw her. Which shows that ye're a better judge of character than I am.'

Kate was pouring the boiling water into the teapot when she caught sight of Winnie stepping off the bottom stair. 'Here she is, the star of the show.' The lid was put on the teapot and Kate rushed to hug the little woman. 'Well, yer certainly surprised us, sunshine, and made fools of us into the bargain. Here's me asking yer if yer knew what yer were doing, and ye're an expert at delivering babies! I feel a right nit now. But I wasn't to know, sunshine, was I?'

'Of course yer weren't, queen, so don't be worrying. Just pour us a cup of tea out, 'cos I'm parched.' Winnie made her way to a chair and sat down heavily. 'I've got to admit I feel a bit tired. There's always worry attached to any baby being born, and yer have to keep yer eye out for complications. Still, everything went fine, the nurse has checked and is satisfied that mother and baby are well.' She took the cup Kate handed to her and sipped on the hot liquid. 'The baby is beautiful – Margaret is near to tears with happiness. We can go up and have a peep when the nurse goes. But only for a minute because she's shown Margaret how to breast feed, and when the baby's satisfied, both mother and child will want a rest.'

'Yer leave us standing, yer know that, don't yer, sunshine? Why have yer never told us about the babies yer've delivered?'

'What is there to tell, queen? I've helped out, as anyone would do, and that's nothing to brag about. It's not my business to broadcast something another person might want kept secret.'

Monica chuckled. 'I can see there's going to be a toss-up between you two on who gets a seat on the front row, and whether yer both get halos and harps.'

'Yer've got me stumped there, queen, what are yer on about?'

Kate opened her mouth but Monica got in before her. 'Well, I think my mate is so bleeding good, Saint Peter will give her a front-row seat plus a halo and harp. But you're turning out to be more saintly than she is, so, as I say, it'll be a toss-up.'

Winnie grinned. 'And where have yer got yerself down for, queen? A seat in the circle?'

'Oh, I'll take any hand-out, girl, as long as it's not too far from me mate. And I won't complain if the halo looks a bit tattered, or the harp has a string missing, as long as Kate is not too far away. She's me best mate, yer see.'

Chapter Thirty

Charles knew there was something in the air when Winnie opened the door. She seemed to be brimming over with excitement. He also knew she was a person who could control their feelings until they believed the time to be right. So he removed his hat and coat, which she took from him and hung on the row of hooks in the hall, and sat in the chair he now looked on as his own. 'And how are you, Winnie? You look very well, I must say.'

'I've got lots to tell yer, but have patience until I've made the tea. I don't want to be shouting to yer from the kitchen.'

'I could come out there and then you wouldn't have to shout.'

'Stay where yer are, five minutes is neither here nor there. Yer can wait that long, surely? Or have yer got an appointment?'

'I never make any appointments on the days I see you. The whole day is crossed off in my diary and nothing will make me alter my plans.'

Winnie came bustling in with the tray, all nicely set as it always was for his coming with Miss Parkinson's china arranged attractively on a hand-stitched cloth, and a serviette for Charles to put over his knees to save any crumbs falling on to his suit. He wouldn't care if they did, but as it pleased Winnie, he did as he was told. He really looked forward to the days he was seeing her because they spoke the same sort of language, being near enough the same age. He was a member of two gentlemen's clubs in Liverpool, and once or twice a year ladies were invited. There was ample opportunity then for him to befriend a female relative of one of the other members but they were a little too sophisticated for him with their airs and graces. He also thought some of them didn't have a thought in their head apart from nattering on

447

about their social life. They'd drive him potty in no time.

'Now we're sitting with our tea and slice of pie, are you going to tell me what is bringing that mysterious smile to your face and the brightness to your eyes?'

'Am I that obvious, Charlie?'

'Yes, my dear, to me you are because I know you so well. Not as well as I would like to, but that is another story.'

Winnie put her cup and saucer on the tray so she could wave her hands about as she spoke. 'Yer'll never believe what happened yesterday, Charlie?'

'I will if you tell me, Winnie, I wouldn't disbelieve you for the world.'

'Well, yer know Margaret Blackmore from the next street, the one that I told yer was expecting a baby? She went into labour yesterday morning, and when her mother went for the midwife it was to find she'd been called out on an urgent case. Anyway, to cut a long story short, I ended up delivering the baby.'

Charles, his mouth gaping, put his saucer down carefully at the side of his chair. 'Did my ears deceive me then? I could have sworn you said you'd delivered a baby. But surely that can't be true?'

'Of course it is, yer daft ha'porth, I wouldn't joke about a thing like that. There was no one else, and it was a short labour so there wasn't time to get her to the hospital. Anyway, the girl didn't want to go so there was nothing else for it. It's not the first time, Charlie, I've had quite a bit of experience. By the time the midwife put in an appearance, young Margaret was nursing her newborn baby daughter. I know it wasn't pleasant for a young girl but she had an easy labour compared to some and there were no complications. The nurse was very satisfied, said I'd done everything right.'

'Is there anything you aren't capable of, Winnie? You seem to be able to turn your hand to anything.'

'Ah, but there's nothing so wonderful as helping a child into the world, Charlie, it's a very satisfying experience. I'm calling round there later to see how mother and baby are, and I just wondered if yer'd like to come with me?'

'I'd love to, of course I would! But surely the family won't welcome a stranger at a time like this?'

'Well, as ye're their landlord, they'll feel a bit embarrassed, I suppose. But only if yer let them, Charlie. If yer treat them as a friend, and not as the man who owns the house they live in, then yer'll be very welcome. In fact, I could nip out the back way and ask Betty, see whether they're ready for visitors yet.' Winnie jumped to her feet. 'I'll be back in two shakes of a lamb's tail, it's only across the entry.' In less than five minutes, she returned with a grin on her face. 'Yer'll be more than welcome, Charlie. We'll just have another cup of tea and slice of pie to give Betty a bit of time to sort Margaret and the baby out.'

'It would be nice to take something for them, don't you think, Winnie? I'd feel awful going empty-handed. How about getting some flowers for the mother, and a toy perhaps for the baby?'

'No flowers, Charlie. Years ago Nurse Griffith told me that it wasn't healthy to have flowers in a bedroom as they use up all the oxygen, so they're out. It's usual to put a piece of silver in the hand of a new baby. Half-a-crown, Charlie, no more. Most of the neighbours will be giving sixpence, or a shilling at the most, and I don't want them to think ye're showing off.'

He chuckled. 'Short and to the point, aren't you, Winnie? You don't think twice about putting me in my place.'

'We're friends aren't we, Charlie? We can say what we like to each other. If I couldn't say what's in me mind, then you wouldn't be sitting in that chair now.'

'Then I have something to tell you that I hope you will consider sympathetically. When my wife died, and you came to look after the children, well, they became very fond of you. They didn't want a housekeeper, they wanted Winnie. Their complaints when I hired one lasted a long time. They've never forgotten you because I wasn't much of a father at that time whereas you brought compassion mixed with laughter into their lives. When they heard I'd met up with you again, they were eager for news of you and would very much like to see you. As we will be getting together, all of the family, for Christmas dinner, they've asked if I would invite you to join us. It goes without saying that you would make me a very happy man if you'd accept, but I know the children would get to your heart before me.'

'That's not right, Charlie, I'm very fond of you. In fact, I always have been. There was always that spark between us when you used to collect my rent even though I loved my husband dearly. And I would love to see your children again so I'll accept the invitation if yer promise to have me home by seven o'clock. Yer see, Kate is having a party on Christmas night, not on a grand scale like yours, just a few friends, but there's no way I would tell her I can't go to her party because I'm going to yours.'

'Then can we compromise, my dear? I will promise to have you back by seven o'clock if you would kindly ask Kate if I may be invited to her party, which I am sure will be a lot of fun.'

Winnie left her chair to cross the room and cup his face between her hands. 'I'm sure she will be delighted, Charlie. As I will be to have you there. And now, let's go and see my baby.'

Betty Blackmore wasn't looking forward to her landlord coming. I mean, how was she supposed to act? She couldn't pretend he didn't own the flipping house and could come in any time he liked. But as soon as Charles walked in, a huge smile on his face, he put her at her ease. He shook her hand, saying, 'I bet you're the proudest grandmother in Liverpool. I'm very pleased everything went off well.'

'Thanks to Winnie it did. I honestly don't know what we'd

have done without her. Kate and Monica were here too, and the three of us were useless. In fact, we were chased out of the room because we were making Margaret more frightened than she already was.'

'Can I go up and see them?' Winnie was like a cat on hot bricks. 'And is Margaret all right about Charlie coming up?'

'Pleased as Punch! She'd invite the whole street in if I'd let her, she's so proud. And yer'd have done no good if yer'd been here last night when the men got in from work. I thought Greg was going to faint when I told him. Then, when it sank in, I'll swear his feet never touched those stairs, and nothing would budge him out of that bedroom all night. I even had to take his tea up to him. Wouldn't leave Margaret and the baby to go and tell his parents. I had to send Jack, and they came back with him. They were so happy, it was good to see them. Maude wants to be called Nana, which suits me because I like Grandma. Jack is Granda and Albert is Gramps.'

'I hope I can be called Aunt Winnie, Betty, 'cos I feel I have a stake in this baby.'

Betty waved her to the stairs. 'Up yer go, and Margaret will tell yer what's been decided.'

Margaret had the baby in her arms, and her nerves were in a state when she heard footsteps. But Charles's words on his entrance dispelled her shyness. 'What better sight could anyone ask to see? A very pretty mother and a beautiful baby. How do you feel, my dear?'

'Apart from feeling a bit weak, I'm fine, Mr Coburn.'

'Can I hold the baby, queen? I've been awake most of the night, waiting for this moment.' Winnie was so gentle as she rocked the baby. 'This is yer Auntie Winnie, sweetheart. You and me are going to be very good friends.' She looked to Margaret. 'Have yer decided on a name yet?'

'Me and Greg talked it through last night, and we've decided she'll be called Beth. But her full name will be Elizabeth

451

Winifred Corbett, after my mam and the woman who brought her into the world.'

'Oh, queen, yer don't have to do that.' Winnie was near to tears. 'What about Greg's mother, shouldn't yer think about that?'

'Oh, yes, we talked it over with them. Greg's mam's name is Maude, and even she said she wouldn't want the baby to have that name because she doesn't like it herself. In any case, we were all definite about you, Mrs Cartwright. Greg will be calling to your house tonight to thank you for what yer did.' Now came the words she'd been rehearsing all morning. 'And we'd both like yer to be one of the two godmothers when she gets christened. We'd like two godmothers and two godfathers, and Greg wants to ask Kate and her husband. I'm sure he's got a crush on Kate, he's liked her from the first time he met her.'

'Yer couldn't help but like Kate, queen, because she's as lovely as she looks. And like meself, she'll be tickled pink. I won't say anything to her, I'll let her get a nice surprise when Greg calls. But don't be rushing the christening, give yerself and the baby time to get over all the hard work yer both did yesterday. It'll be a few weeks before yer feel well enough to be up and about, queen, so don't rush it.'

Betty came into the bedroom. 'Would yer like a cup of tea?'

'No, thanks, queen, we had a pot of tea and something to eat before we came.' Winnie held the baby's tiny hand and wondered how God created such perfection. 'Don't forget I'm making the christening shawl, I haven't much to do on it now, so that's one worry less for yer. And I know Kate and Monica are knitting more matinee coats and leggings, so yer'll have enough to take yer through to the summer.'

'I'm really lucky,' Margaret said. 'Mrs Corbett is buying nightdresses, binders and vests. I've got nearly everything I want now.'

Charles put a hand to his mouth and coughed softly. 'I wonder, seeing as Winnie is to be a godmother and she is my closest friend, would you allow me to buy the christening robe? It would make me very happy.'

Winnie's smile spread across her face. 'Oh, did yer hear that, Beth? Uncle Charlie is going to buy yer a beautiful christening robe. Yer'll be the poshest baby in the church.' She glanced from Margaret to Betty. 'Is that all right with both of yer?'

'It's very kind of yer, Mr Coburn, and we'd be very happy.' Margaret smiled at her mother. 'We don't mind her being the poshest baby in the church, do we, Mam?'

'We'll be the talk of the neighbourhood, but who cares? Being christened will be a big day in the baby's life, even though she won't know it.'

Kate was surprised when she opened the door to Greg. 'Well, if it isn't the happy father! And proud, I bet, 'cos the baby is beautiful.' She held the door wide. 'Come in, sunshine, we're letting the cold air in.'

John jumped to his feet and pumped Greg's hand up and down. 'Congratulations, I'm very happy for yer. All I heard of when I got home from work last night was this beautiful baby of yours.'

'I've just called at Mrs Cartwright's to thank her, I'll always be in her debt. Margaret and her mother said they'd have been out of their minds only for her.'

'Yer can say that again, sunshine. Me, Monica and Betty were just shaking like jelly. Not a ha'porth of good to anyone. And Winnie was as cool as yer like, didn't turn a hair. She was absolutely wonderful, and I'm proud to have her for a friend.'

'Yer know what we're calling the baby, do yer?'

'Yeah, Winnie told me it's Beth. That's a lovely name. And she's thrilled to bits that yer've chosen her name as well. She deserves it, sunshine, she really does.'

'We've asked her to be one of the godmothers, too. And I've come to ask if you and yer husband would like to be a godmother and godfather to my daughter?'

Kate saw John's look of pleased surprise, and answered for him. 'We'd both be honoured, sunshine, and thank yer for thinking of us. We'll do the best we can by the baby.'

Greg stroked his chin. 'I didn't have a shave last night, I was too excited and thrilled. But I'll have to have one when I get home or Margaret won't let me near her or Beth. The christening won't be for a few weeks, but we'll see yer before then.'

'Beth certainly will, me and Monica will be calling every day. That baby of yours is one of both our families now, with what we went through when she was being born.' Kate touched his face. 'Come on, lad, I'll let you out to get back to that pretty wife and baby of yours.'

As Greg stepped down on to the pavement, Kate said softly, 'Yer see, yer did the right thing, sunshine, and wasn't it worth it?'

'It was you who made me see sense, and that's something I'll always be grateful to yer for. There isn't a man in Liverpool happier than I am right now.'

Kate watched him walk away. 'Give them my love, ta-ra!'

Back in the living room, John was really chuffed. 'That was nice and thoughtful of them, wasn't it? I rather fancy being a godfather.'

'I bet Winnie knew all about it when she was here this afternoon, and she said nowt. I could tell she was pleased about something, but the little tinker kept it to herself. She told me she'd taken Mr Coburn round to see the baby, but nothing about being a godmother.' Kate did a little jig. 'It is nice, isn't it? I'd better nip next door and tell Monica, before some other bright spark lets it out. She won't mind us being asked about standing as godparents, as long as her and Tom are invited to the christening.'

'I bet Nancy will want to come, she was thrilled when yer were telling us about the baby.'

'I won't leave her out, sunshine. She can sit in the church with Dolly and watch. I don't know about our Billy, though, he'd say it was only for grown-ups. And I can just see the look on his face when he adds, "They'll be cooing and crying over the baby." Still, I'll give him the chance, the rest is up to him.'

John reached for her hand. 'Life's pretty good now, isn't it, love?'

'Not just good, sunshine, it's perfect.'

Four weeks later, the day of the christening arrived. Betty Blackmore couldn't hide her pleasure and surprise at seeing so many of her neighbours sitting in the pews. She realized she had more friends than she'd thought, and not everyone was talking about Margaret behind her back. There were some people from the street where Greg had lived, sitting in the pews behind Maude and Albert Corbett. This day was making up for the seven months of worry Betty had endured. Now everything was going just right. Her daughter and Greg made a handsome couple, and the baby looked like a little princess in the most beautiful gown she'd ever seen, a gift from Mr Coburn, and Winnie's perfect hand-knitted shawl and bonnet.

The priest was late, and Margaret was beginning to show nerves, so Winnie took the baby from her. They were standing by the font, Kate, John, Winnie, Margaret and Greg. The grandparents would join them once the priest arrived. Beth behaved like a dream. She was fast asleep and there hadn't been a peep out of her. If only the priest would come before she decided she was hungry, that would be great.

There were many in the congregation who wondered why there were two godmothers and only one godfather. When the truth came to light, the surprise they'd expressed at seeing their landlord in the church was surpassed by the gasps of surprise when the priest appeared and Charles left the pew to go and stand next to Winnie by the font. He looked so proud, anyone would think it was his granddaughter being christened instead of his goddaughter.

Beth behaved impeccably until the priest touched her head with the cold water, then she made her presence felt. But it didn't last long, and soon she was back in her mother's arms being protected from any more sudden frights while the godparents listened to what the priest had to say, and declared their intention of carrying out the responsibilities attached to being a godparent.

Charles's car stood outside the church. He opened the passenger door while Greg helped Margaret and the baby in. The front passenger seat was reserved for Betty, so she could be home before their guests arrived to drink the baby's health. When Charles said he would come back for the other ladies, Winnie dismissed the idea. 'Charlie, it's no more than a ten-minute walk. You just make sure Margaret and the baby get home quickly, out of the cold. We'll only be a few minutes behind yer.'

'Are you sure, my dear, because it is bitterly cold?'

'And it'll be bitterly cold when I go to the shops tomorrow, Charlie, but it won't worry me. So stop fussing and I'll see yer back at the house.' Winnie looked into his face and relented. 'Five minutes, I promise.'

The tiny living room was overcrowded and noisy. Most of the men were smoking, so after showing her baby off once again, and delighting in the praise being heaped on her, Margaret took her upstairs to her cot. Because Betty was looking tired and flustered, Kate suggested to her friends that when they'd finished their drinks they should leave the Blackmores and the Corbetts to enjoy the very special day on their own. So after much handshaking and back slapping, the three couples said their goodbyes and Greg let them out of the front door. He was still wearing a surprised look, as though he couldn't believe his own life could be so good. 'Thanks for yer presents, and for coming. We will see yer again soon, won't we?'

'It's Christmas in two weeks, lad,' Monica said. 'We'll be knocking with a little present for Beth from Father Christmas.

Don't forget, we three women were here when she was born, yer'll not get rid of us so easy.'

'We'll see yer a few times before then, son,' Kate told him. 'Now you go in and enjoy the rest of the day, 'cos it's a milestone in yer life.'

'What a nice bloke he is.' Tom walked ahead with John. 'I took to him right away.'

John nodded. 'Yeah, yer couldn't fall out with him. He'll be a good husband and father.'

It was as they neared the bottom of the street that the snowflakes began to fall, lightly at first, then the flakes grew bigger and more plentiful. Kate was like a child, lifting her face for the flakes to fall on and laughing when they brushed her nose. 'Don't let's go home, let's go for a walk. I love it when the snow is clean and white like this is.'

'Yer can't go for a walk,' Tom said. 'It'll be coming down heavy in a few minutes.'

'I don't care! I'll go on me own if none of yer want to come.'

'I'll come with yer, queen,' Winnie said. 'I've always liked the first snow of the winter. I'll hate it next week when it turns to sludge and I'm slipping all over the bleeding place, though.'

'Ye're not going anywhere without me.' Monica linked Kate's arm. 'Even though I do think it's crazy.'

'Count me in.' If Winnie was going, then so was Charles. 'It'll be nice and refreshing.'

Kate brought them to a halt. 'It wasn't so long ago that my husband asked me to go for stroll and I thought he'd gone mad. But he said he felt like a stroll with the one he loved. What's wrong with today, sunshine, don't yer love me any more?'

John moved smartly and held out his bent arm. 'I love you whether there's hail, rain or snow. Lead on, love.'

Monica raised her brows and crooked her finger to where Tom was standing with his mouth agape. 'Now this has turned into a test, my darling husband. A test of whether yer love me or not.'

Tom heaved a big sigh, but he was grinning. Enjoying himself, really. After all, if he went home he'd only be reading the *News of the World*. 'Come on, light of my life, let's go strolling.'

'Silly buggers,' Winnie said, until she caught Charles's eye. 'What are you grinning at, Charlie Coburn?'

'Well, this is a test of our feelings for each other, my dear. Do you wish to go home or will you promenade with me?'

'We've lost the run of our bleeding senses!' But Winnie didn't refuse to take his arm. 'I've heard of going for a walk, but never when it's ruddy well snowing.'

'The fact that we are walking, and it is snowing, means you do have some feelings for me. Am I right, my dear?'

Winnie looked at him out of the corner of her eye. 'That's for me to know, Charlie, and for you to find out.'

Charles arrived in his car to pick Winnie up at twelve o'clock on Christmas Day. He didn't care who heard him when she opened the door and he said, 'You look very lovely, my dear. No, I won't come in because the children will be arriving soon. I've got a woman in seeing to the dinner so there's nothing to worry about on that score.'

Winnie settled herself in the passenger seat. 'I'm really looking forward to seeing the children, but I bet I won't know them, they'll be all grown up.'

'I told you three of them are married? Well, the two eldest boys have babies of their own. They won't be here today as both have nannies, but my daughters-in-law will. And Rosemary's husband.'

'Let me get their names right, Charlie. Thomas was the eldest, then Neil, Rosemary and Charlotte. Have I got it right?'

He nodded. 'You passed the test, my dear.' He took one hand

from the steering wheel and patted her knee. 'I can sense you're nervous, which surprises me. There's no need for it. The children loved you when they were very young, and they'll love you now.'

And Charles was right. There was certainly no reason for Winnie to be nervous. When the car drew up in the driveway of the large detached house its door was quickly opened by a man in his mid-thirties. Three faces were looking over his shoulder. 'We are the welcoming committee, Mrs Cartwright, and we're really happy to see you.'

Such a fuss was made of Winnie her mind was in a whirl. But she remembered to speak slowly so she would have time to stop herself from swearing. 'Oh, yer've all grown up on me! Now, let me see if I remember who is who.' She pointed to the eldest who was very like his father in looks. 'You are Thomas, and yer used to pull my leg something rotten. Then there's Neil, who I remember as being the quiet one. Rosemary, you used to help me with the baking, getting more flour on yerself than went in the cakes. And little Charlotte, you used to pinch the cakes when they'd cooled down enough to eat.'

Thomas cupped the elbow of a pretty, very well-dressed young woman standing by his side. 'And this is my wife, Bernice.'

Winnie smiled as she shook hands. 'That's a pretty name, queen.'

She received a smile in return. 'I've heard so much about you, I feel I know you already.'

'Me, too!' A young woman standing next to Neil introduced herself. 'I'm Lorna, Neil's better half. He's done nothing but talk about you all week.'

'That only leaves me and mine,' Rosemary said. 'This is my husband, Edward, who you'll love because he is so lovable no one can resist.'

Charles's youngest daughter, Charlotte, touched Winnie's arm. 'I'm still on the shelf, Mrs Cartwright, but there's a young man reaching up for me. If he succeeds, then you will meet him next time you come.'

'Ooh, that's a lot of names to remember, I'll have to write them down. Charlie, you can write them down some time so I can reel them off by heart.'

He reached for her coat. 'Will you let my friend in now, please? We can't keep her in the hall for the whole day.'

The big square hall had a huge Christmas tree in one corner with colourful lights, baubles and wrapped presents hanging from its branches, and in every room there were coloured fairy lights. 'It looks lovely, Charlie, very warm and cosy.'

He didn't get a look in with Winnie after that. His children were so happy to see her, they wouldn't leave her side. They wanted her to know how they'd cried for weeks when she left, and asked why hadn't she been to see them since? And their spouses were just as eager for her news. They really did make a fuss of her, and it pulled on her heartstrings. How she would have loved to have had children of her own!

'You have monopolized my guest for long enough,' Charles finally said. 'Now give her breathing space when we go in for dinner.'

There were name cards by each plate, and Winnie wasn't surprised to find herself next to Charles. She congratulated herself on not having sworn once. But the congratulations were a little premature because as she was spreading the table napkin over her knees, she knocked one of the knives on to the floor. As she bent to pick it up, she said, 'Trust me, Charlie, I've only gone and dropped me bleeding knife.'

The loudest laugh came from Thomas. 'Now that's the Winnie we remember! I thought you'd gone all straitlaced on us.' He turned to his father to comment on the way she'd always been able to make them laugh, but closed his mouth when he saw the look on Charles's face. So it was this little lady who had brought some happiness into his dad's life. All the children had commented on how he'd changed in the last few months, becoming more easy-going, quick to smile and laugh. What a pity they'd lost contact with each other for so long, so many wasted years. Mind you, he could have it entirely wrong, they could be just good friends. But Thomas hoped not. His dad deserved someone to hug him and comfort him. Someone to be there for him, and make him laugh. And the little woman facing him across the table certainly fitted the bill.

The dinner was delicious and very filling. Afterwards Winnie went along to the kitchen to thank the cook, finding her red in the face with rushing about. 'You make yerself a cup of tea, queen, and I'll get stuck into this washing up,' Winnie told her.

And that's what she was doing when Charles came looking for her. Without making a sound he crept away, back to the drawing room, and beckoned his family to follow him. They were stunned at the sight for a few seconds, then the four women rushed to help. It was something new to them, they all had housekeepers to do the work, but this little woman was so much fun, they'd fallen under her spell. 'You wash, Mrs Cartwright, and we'll dry.'

Mary the cook made to get to her feet, thinking she'd be in trouble, but Charles waved her down. 'You've been on your feet long enough, Mary, have a rest.'

His two sons thought it was hilarious. 'We'll put the dishes away after you've dried them, ladies.'

Winnie, up to her elbows in soapy suds, turned her head. 'I remember your tricks, Tom and Neil, yer used to put dishes away so I wouldn't find them. Well, just make sure yer put them in the right bleeding place this time, or yer'll find ye're not too old to have yer backsides smacked.'

Charles sat on the edge of the huge kitchen table and watched. And all the time he was thinking this was the first time his children had all been together in the kitchen, doing menial tasks they'd normally turn their noses up at, and it was the first time he'd heard genuine laughter ringing to the rafters as Winnie, in her own down-to-earth way, telling jokes and being just herself, had turned his house into a home. He wasn't blaming his children, he was blaming himself. They must have missed their mother very much, but he'd been so eaten up with self-pity he hadn't considered them.

'Hey, Charlie, will yer be an angel?' Winnie was drying her hands now, the dishes were washed, dried, and being carefully put away in the right places. 'Run Mary home, will yer? There's no trams on Christmas Day, and her feet must be giving her gyp.'

'Of course I will, it's only a five-minute run. But will you be all right here, my dear?'

Winnie chuckled. 'Well, I was thinking of running off with the family silver, Charlie. Then I thought, sod it, it's too heavy for me to carry.'

Charles's four children looked at each other. They'd never heard their father being ordered around before and seeming not to mind. Then they grinned and nodded. This little lady was just the tonic he needed, and they'd do their best to encourage the relationship.

Winnie insisted on leaving at half-past six, even though the family begged her to stay. 'Me and yer dad are going to a party in one of me friends' houses. I wouldn't want to let them down. But I'll come and see yer again, I promise.'

Once they'd driven through the gate and the waving was over, Charles said, 'I think you are as popular with my children today as you were all those years ago.'

'It was good to see them, Charlie, and I have enjoyed the day.'

'The children hope there will be more days like today. Thomas thinks you've put a little zest into my life, that I look happier and more content.'

'Well, you've done the same for me, Charlie. It's nice to have someone yer own age to talk to who yer feel comfortable with.

And I've always felt comfortable with you, I think yer know that.' When they turned into her street, she said, 'Go to my house first, I want to have a swill and comb me hair. I'm not one for standing in front of a mirror preening meself, I'll not keep yer waiting long.'

'I think we've kept each other waiting long enough, my dear, don't you?'

'Now's not the time to be getting serious, Charlie, not when we're off to a party. Just let's be happy in each other's company. I won't be long, I promise, and when I'm ready yer can leave the car outside and we'll walk up to Kate's.'

Winnie stood in the kitchen combing her hair and looking at her face in the mirror. All sorts of things were running through her mind. She'd really enjoyed the day, and meeting Charlie's family. Was she being silly and stubborn for stopping him from saying what she knew he wanted to say? She was torn because she was more than fond of Charles, but she needed time to think it over very carefully because whatever she decided was for the rest of her life. She put the comb down, gave a little sigh as she patted her hair, then walked through to the living room. 'I'm ready now, Charlie, let's go.'

When they knocked on Kate's door, they could hear hearty laughter. Winnie said, 'They're a couple of drinks ahead of us, Charlie, we'll have to catch up.'

Kate opened the door looking pretty enough to be the fairy on top of the Christmas tree. 'Merry Christmas, sunshine.' She hugged and kissed Winnie, then turned to Charles and held out her hand. 'Compliments of the season, Mr Coburn.'

'Oh, I think we can dispense with formalities, Kate. The name is Charles.' He kissed her cheek. 'A very merry Christmas to you.'

When they entered the living room the noise increased as they all exchanged seasonal greetings. Kate took their coats and gave them to Nancy to carry upstairs and lay on the bed. 'We've kept the sofa for you, our two guests of honour, so make yerselves comfy and John will get yer a drink.'

'Have yer had a nice day, Winnie?' Monica asked. 'Were the children glad to see yer?'

'I've had a wonderful time. They're not children any more, they're all grown up, head and shoulders over me. But it was good to see them again, and they made me very welcome and fussed over me.'

'And why shouldn't they, my dear? They have very fond memories of you. You were there when they were most in need of someone to help them, love them, listen to them and make them laugh.'

Tom and John had gone halves to buy a small bottle of whisky, in case Charles didn't drink beer. Winnie received her favourite tipple, milk stout. 'Drink up, ye're way behind us,' John told them.

After three milk stouts, Winnie got into her stride. She kept them all in stitches, telling them tales of her childhood and her gem of a mother. 'We didn't have much money 'cos me da only got a few days' work in at the docks, but me ma wouldn't let on to anyone that we were skint. Too proud she was. I remember playing in the street, and me ma standing on the step shouting me in for me tea. "Come along, Winifred, yer bacon and egg is ready." I believed her the first couple of times, and me mouth was watering by the time I got in the house. But there was no sign of bacon and egg, it was dripping butties as usual. Another time she called to me, "Winifred, d'yer want jam on yer toast or marmalade?" But it was dripping on toast, and I never believed what she said after that.'

When Winnie was repeating what her mother had said, she put on a posh voice and the stance her mother used to take, and sounded so funny everyone was laughing. 'That wasn't so bad, but I hated it when she didn't have the rent money and I had to tell the man she'd gone to me grandma's funeral. Three times I had to tell him that, until the bloke asked me if me grandma had a piece of elastic tied round her waist when she got buried, 'cos she kept popping back up.'

Charles's eyes never left Winnie's face as he listened to the roars of laughter. What a talent this woman had for bringing happiness into people's lives. 'You have some happy memories to look back on, my dear.'

'It wasn't all bleeding milk and honey, Charlie, I can tell yer. I mean, I can laugh about it now, and I loved the bones of me ma and da, but I can remember me tummy rumbling with hunger and holes in the soles of me shoes. But we weren't the only family who suffered. Every one of our neighbours was living in poverty. I think the only thing that kept us alive was always finding something to laugh about. Like one day, me ma didn't have any money for the club woman and said when the woman came I had to hide behind the couch with her.' Winnie started to shake with laughter as the scene came back to mind. 'The only thing was, me ma's foot was sticking out of the side, and when the woman looked through the window, she saw it and yelled, "I know ye're in there, I can see yer leg." Well, me ma went mad and nearly choked the woman for making a show of her in front of the neighbours. As she said, "I might not have any bloody money, but I do have me pride." '

Monica had been watching Charles's face for a while now, noting its changing expressions. He was certainly taken with Winnie, no doubt about that. And without thinking, she said, 'When are yer going to make an honest woman of her, Charles? Yer'd never have a dull moment with Winnie around.'

He took it in his stride. He didn't care who knew about his feelings for Winnie, and her friends might even be on his side. 'I'll marry her as soon as she says she'll have me.'

There was a stunned silence. Kate was mortified. Monica had certainly got more than she bargained for. The men sat forward, waiting for a reaction. Only Winnie remained as calm as ever.

'I've been giving that some serious thought, Charlie, and I'd love to marry yer. But there's a lot to think about. Yer see, all me friends are here, and I really couldn't live without them. And now I've got me goddaughter to think about, I don't want to move out of her life. But I can't see you living in my little two-up-two-down, can you?'

'Winnie, my dear, I could run you here every day on my way to the office. So you could still shop with your friends, have your cups of tea and cream slices, and see our goddaughter as often as we both liked. Say you will marry me, make me the happiest man in the world, and I'll remove any obstacle in your path.' Charles looked around at everyone in the room. 'I've loved this woman for twenty years, don't you agree I deserve to win her hand?'

Nancy and Dolly thought it was the most romantic thing they'd ever seen. Even Billy was on Charles's side. And the rest of the crowd were noisy in their backing of this man who'd had the nerve to say what he had in front of an audience. Winnie thought if he had the guts to tell everyone how he felt, then she wasn't going to be a coward. With an impish grin, she said, 'Of course I'll marry yer, Charlie, and ye're right, we have loved each other for twenty years. We aren't in the first flush of youth, but it's not how old yer are, it's how young yer feel. And right now, I feel like an eighteen year old.' She cupped his face and kissed him firmly on the lips. 'That's to let everyone know how I feel. And I want yer to tell me friends that they'll be welcome in our house any time.'

Charles felt like pinching himself to make sure he wasn't dreaming. 'A quiet wedding in four weeks' time, my dear?'

'Yes, Charlie, that suits me. Just my friends and your family. I'd like that.' Winnie could see tears in Kate's eyes and didn't want any crying on this special day. 'Kate and Monica, will yer be my matrons of honour? And Charlie's two sons can be best men.'

Kate ran the back of her hand across her nose. 'I'm sorry, Winnie, but I'm going to cry.'

'What are yer crying for?' Monica shook her head. 'I'm made up!'

'I don't know what she's bleeding crying for, either, she's me best friend!' Winnie protested. 'You predicted this, queen, remember? Yer said someone would come into my life, and along came Charlie.'

'This definitely calls for another drink to toast the forthcoming wedding,' John said. 'And I think yer make a lovely couple. I'm really chuffed for both of yer.'

Glasses were raised as two people in the autumn of their lives held hands like teenagers. And the whole street must have heard the loud rendition of 'For They Are Jolly Good Fellows'.

Dream A Little Dream

Joan Jonker

Bob Dennison and Edie Brady grew up in the same street of two-up two-down houses. Once they were married, Bob worked hard to make a go of his removal business and soon his family were moving up in the world.

But too late he realises his wife and eldest daughter have lost touch with their roots. Edie has changed her name to Edwina and insists that Bob is called Robert. At least Robert's life is enriched by his two youngest children. Together, they seek sanctuary in the kitchen, where their down-to-earth housekeeper and their hilarious cleaner provide the warmth and laughter that are missing from their lives. It is here that they dare to dream a little dream that happiness is waiting just around the corner.

Don't miss Joan Jonker's previous Liverpool sagas:

'A hilarious but touching story' *Woman's Realm*

'Packed with lively, sympathetic characters' *Bolton Evening News*

'Full of laughter and smiles' *Liverpool Echo*

'A book that will reduce you to tears – of sadness, but of happiness too' *Hull Daily Mail*

0 7472 6384 1

headline

After The Dance Is Over

Joan Jonker

There's never a dull moment when best mates Nellie McDonough and Molly Bennett get together. And there's always something to keep them busy in their Liverpool backstreet, like becoming private detectives to help a loved one – the results of which are funny, warm and wonderfully satisfying.

Then Nellie is walking on air when her daughter Lily hints that she will soon be setting a date for her wedding to Archie. But when news comes that will affect both the families, Molly sheds tears of happiness while her mate Nellie lifts her skirts and breaks into an Irish jig . . .

After The Dance Is Over continues the lively adventures of two of the most entertaining families you'll ever meet.

Don't miss Joan Jonker's previous Liverpool sagas:

'Hilarity and pathos in equal measure' *Liverpool Echo*

'Packed with believable, heartwarming characters' *Coventry Evening Telegraph*

'Touching, full of incident and tears and laughter' *Reading Chronicle*

0 7472 6614 X

headline

Many a Tear Has to Fall

Joan Jonker

Things are finally looking up for George and Ann Richardson. After causing years of worry, their younger daughter Tess, who has always been sickly and small, is starting to blossom into a confident, clever girl. She still has a way to go before she catches up with her older sister Maddy, but with the love of her family they know she'll soon be just as strong and quick-witted. And they've scraped together enough money to take them on their first holiday, to Wales, where the fresh air and country life will be just what the doctor ordered.

But heartache is waiting for the Richardsons when they return to Liverpool, and many a tear will have to fall before they find the true happiness they long for . . .

Don't miss Joan Jonker's previous Liverpool sagas:

'A hilarious but touching story' *Woman's Realm*

'Packed with lively, sympathetic characters' *Bolton Evening News*

'Full of laughter and smiles' *Liverpool Echo*

'A book that will reduce you to tears – of sadness, but of happiness too' *Hull Daily Mail*

0 7472 6613 1

headline